ELYSIUM BURNING

ALTER INFERNO COMPLEX

Book One

DREW BRYENTON

sci-fi-cafe.com

This one's for four groups of people
who conspicuously don't suck –
The Cardigan St. Mafia (you know who you are!)
My family – all of you! You rule.
The Unholy Legions of Heavy Metal
And
The Pakuranga / Edgewater Cast of Villains.

P.S. special mention and extra credit to Serena for being part
of three out of four, as well as the most tolerant, insightful and
generally kick-arse human being on this planet.

Warning - This document has been designated as a primitive memetic virus, grade three. The Praetorian sub-council on mental hygiene advises all those who come into contact with its contents to undergo a comprehensive mind-scrub before believing in any 'facts' or apparent 'realities' posited herein.

Subpraetor Kweel, Departmental Hierophant

Prologue
9600 Pre Arbitrium Mundi
(Before the World's Judgment)

UNDER A SLATE-GRAY bowl of sky, a sea of yellowed grass bent down before the wind.

In this place all was silent, but for the grumble of thunder gnawing at the horizon... even the insects were hushed, held down under a flat palm of humid heat. There was a ribbon of dust beaten crooked across the plain, and at its very center a man stood sentinel atop a knuckle of rock, a stick-figure scrawl against the haze.

The stone was sacred, of course. Things out on their own were *always* either holy or profane.

The man perched upon its wind-smoothed back knew this all too well. It was his job to decide which was which.

More to the point, nobody else in his tribe could see the Heart-eaters.

They twisted out from between his sun-browned fingers, hissing and squealing as he clenched his fist. *Soulrotten, seed of darkness* - boiling on the surface of a bloody flint arrowhead. The Shaman held it tight until its edges cut into his palm, his eyes on the far horizon.

Praying, for what it was worth.

Rain ghosted across the steppe in ragged veils out there on the edge, the shroud behind which his Gods walked. They were hungry again; always hungry, for the words and the rituals and the blood.

"Back to the endless ice. Back through the Gate of Broken Stars. For you, and for your master, there is only oblivion here."

Amujin looked up at him, his face sheened with sweat. In his hand a heavy stone axe dripped blood, chips of bone and human teeth plastered to its bindings. The Shaman nodded gravely, and his executioner howled, letting out a bestial warcry.

Hear him, Old Fathers. We must finish this, now. We must become human again... drive the Heart-eaters into the dead.

The prisoner at his feet flinched away even before the blade came down, his eyes squeezed tightly closed between rows of scarified tattoos. His hands were bound behind him with the hank of hair sawed from his topknot in disgrace.

"Fools! The Devourer walks! He will... *aaaiieee!*"

Amujin's axe bit deep - but with a blade of stone there was no way it would be a clean kill. Raw white bone flashed deep in the wound as the Wolf Skull captive screamed, and Amujin worked his blade free with a sound like breaking kindling-wood. The second blow was wild, the blood-slick axehandle twisting in the executioner's grasp. The Shaman remained expressionless as a spatter of blood and brains licked across his cheek. Once more, and it was done. The Wolf Skull's head rolled into the dust, wide-eyed and incredulous as he stared up at the Shaman from the Cold Hell.

The Shaman released the arrowhead from his fist, letting it drop into the dead man's open mouth. Heart-eater worms painted his eyes black as they followed his soul down into the dark...

"Will that be enough? Have we satiated Him, and made Him lose sight of our path?"

Feathers and beads spun in the storm-wind as he raised his staff, looking askance at the roiling sky. But his Gods were silent. It was up to him. The stench of blood and excrement filled his nostrils as he alighted from his perch... and once again, all eyes were on him to *lead*, to wrest mere hardship from total disaster.

They were only twelve now, this little tribe - six of the men lay dead, and two of the women with them. One boy-child was bleeding so badly from a gash across his scalp that the Shaman didn't think his lore could see him through the night.

Pitiful. Where was his strength, now? His wisdom? Just so much chaff before the storm...

"Old Father! Father! What shall we do now? Can.. can we leave this place?"

Amujin's face was pale and haggard behind a crust of dried blood. The supernatural fear was on him, crackling in the air like heat-lightning.

"They're dead, aren't they? Wolf Skull bastards should have

known not to ambush our People. So, yes, you can go. But I have work to do."

A shadow of guilt flickered across the Executioner's face as he looked over the Shaman's shoulder, over to a runic circle scratched in the dust.

"Is there anything I can do for him, Eldest One? I should have stopped that arrow. I could have..."

"*Nothing*," said the Shaman. "You've done all you can, and I thank you for it. Clean and bless the axe, and wash away their blood. Your brother is in my keeping now."

He hated to use the sharp cold voice like that – hated the way it came so easily to him, and how readily Amujin obeyed. Especially when the man's brother lay sweating out his life between the ritual fires, cut deep by a curse-bound arrowhead.

The Shaman spat to avert evil as his hands made the runic passes, dry old bones working the charms to seal the Wolf Skulls' tomb. No, it would be his time again. He was tired, but the Gods heard no excuses.

"Not even after sixty-seven winters, you gnarly old bastards. Not even when you're drunk on blood..."

One last word sealed the sentinel stone in a brittle shell of ritual, marked with a circle of cairns and corpses. The Wolf Skulls would be buried kneeling, their severed heads behind them; watchers at the mouth of the Cold Hell. The tribe wouldn't weep for this windswept place, though - not even if his own grave stood next to theirs tomorrow morning...

And now to work. He knelt just like the Wolf Skulls had knelt, and he felt the invisible axe of the Gods on the back of his neck.

The man who lay shrouded in the smoke of the God-fires should have been one of the dead, piled under a feathered cairn with a pair of enemies at his feet. But he wasn't. The arrow had pinned him half way, in the dangerous place...

Inside his living heart, the worms fed.

Asag'raal's seed - the unspoken, son of the Dark Star...

The battle was no longer outside in the long grass of the plain, fought with adzes and clubs and arrows. It was inside the man's head, and his heart, and it would be won or lost before the night ended. So thinking, the Shaman went down to the watchfires, motioning with one tattooed hand for his apprentice to leave.

It was time.

The old man kept the tribe's single most precious possession in a rabbit-skin pouch around his waist - a blade of black glass forged in the fires below the earth. It was the Shaman's Klave, and its handle was wrapped in generations of hair, cut from the heads of countless wise men and women before him.

Iltak would be thankful of its edge if he began to turn.

So, as night fell, the Shaman cupped the knife in his hands and hunkered down on his heels between the fires to wait.

The sun sank below the jagged horizon. Stars wheeled overhead. Night bled out to gray, and still the old man remained motionless, unblinking.

The haze of noonday came and went, pulling the shadows tight as bowstrings as the sun rolled down the sky. At last, at dusk on the second night, the Shaman moved.

"Bring bluefire," he grated, beckoning his apprentice to his side. "I'll have to go *within* to save him. The ritual of the Klave… the soul-binding."

It was a rite which the rest of the tribe were forbidden to watch. They huddled under shelters of woven grass a bowshot away, the guttering light of their cookfires whipped into sparks and ashes by the wind.

Only three of them remained – Iltak, still writhing with shadow worms; the Shaman, his face grave behind a half-mask of wood and horn, and his young apprentice, trembling as she passed him the heavy dark bulk of the Klave.

The obsidian knife bit deep, through skin and flesh, all the way down to the bone. Blood welled up hot around it as his apprentice looked up at him expectantly, her eyes as round and white as moons in the firelight. She stumbled over her chanting as the knife slipped free, black blood coiling from its blade as smoke.

"Steady, child! One day it will be your turn, and I only hope you'll be ready."

"I see it, Father," whispered the young girl at his side, her face smeared with soot and ocher. "With the Spirit Eye, I can see it... breathing. Like a serpent in his chest..."

The old man grunted to himself; as near to praise as he'd ever come. If she truly saw, perhaps she was ready. After all, *he* must have been a green youth once, long ago.

"Then hold him, child, and begin the invocation. His soul has gone deep, and it will take some time to set him free."

If I can do it at all. Sixty-seven winters behind me, and I feel each one of them right now...

Iltak lay between them, mummified in painted deer-hide. Leather braids clattering with bones and uncut gems lay unlaced across his chest, and the crosshatched incision below his sternum boiled with darkness.

He would awaken as a monster if the infection spread - or neither of them would awake at all. If that happened, the girl's first task as Shaman would be to cut the heart from her predecessor's chest...

"Be careful, Old Father," she said, pressing his gnarled old hand between hers. "This one -"

"*This one* is the same as all the others. The Gods walk with me, child."

In his soul he knew he was a liar - and a dead man. But it didn't change a thing. The Shaman of the tribe wielded power beyond the dreams of petty warlords, but in the end he had to pay his due. His apprentice's hands were shaking as she passed him a cup of bluefire, the heady aroma of the broth igniting sparks behind his eyes. He'd fasted all day to be ready for this moment, and used up half of his supply of rare herbs and powders to make the sacred potion.

Now he put the cup to his lips and felt the hot, slippery flame of the bluefire coiling down into his belly, awakening power from the earth below him. It blazed up his spine like summer lightning, sending sharp arrowheads through his soul.

The Shaman screamed. But it was a scream of joy, of power unleashed.

His Spirit Eye cracked open, the lids peeling back as it swelled bigger and bigger, stripping away his mortal flesh as he hatched from his body like a snake from its leathery egg. And he stepped into the outer dark naked, his years cast aside. Galaxies of blue tattoos lit up across his skin.

There was the man he came to rescue, bound to the darkness with thick, dripping webs of shadow. Hunched over his body was the twisted form of the soulless one, the Devourer, its hands working madly with needle and ink and thread.

"*He is not for you, Asag-Raal the Wanderer,*" said the Shaman, his voice all grim authority. "Not tonight, or any night, or *ever*, until the sun is drowned beneath the ocean."

The thing turned to face him, smiling, joints popping as its head twisted around on an impossibly long neck. Asag'raal's face may have once been human, but now it was contorted with evil glee, a slick black mask slashed with glittering teeth.

"You're *all* mine. All of you." The thing's voice was like obsidian sawing meat, a rasp and a gurgle at once. "I made you what you are, and I'll take you when I please. My Wolf Skull disciples are just more *realistic* than you nomad fools."

"I don't think so," said the Shaman. "I think we made *you*. I think you need us more than you'd like to admit."

"Only when I'm hungry," chuckled the demon. "Speaking of which – how *is* the little one? She shouldn't play our games, old man… at least *you* know the price."

Iltak looked down on them from his web of shadows, the skin peeled back in strips from his terrified face. Here, now, the Shaman wasn't the hunched old mystic who the tribe looked up to. Here he was power, sewn up tight in a body all muscle and scars and swirling tattooed fire.

"I know the price, and I'll pay it. Tonight. Ten years, Wanderer. You can have my soul for that long, if you leave my people alone."

"Ten years of pain? Done! And your little apprentice will be all the more ripe for the picking, when your suffering is ended."

The shaman laughed, clenching his fists at his sides. She'd be ready for him in ten years time. Cold Hells, she'd spit in the demon's face and ask for thanks…

"You'll still have to beat me, Asag-Raal. There's the matter of my brother Iltak between us first."

"Formalities! But if you insist, nomad. Consider this an introduction to your torment…"

Then the blackness blurred, a snarl of wet white teeth and sizzling claws, and the Devourer was on him, eclipsing the spiral lights across his skin. Light and dark, distilled in essence, twisted up in a death-embrace as old as time itself.

One last time.

And this time, for keeps.

11,796 years passed, give or take a few. The Shaman's apprentice became the matriarch of a great nation, and her people carved out a ragged slice of prehistoric Eurasia for their own. Empires rose and fell like chop on the sea of history. The little rote of famine, joy, genocide, love, harvests, faith and plagues rolled on, until things like the Shaman's Klave were replaced by things like nuclear warheads.

And sensible people (the ones with the most missiles) stopped believing in demons at all…

The narrative faded out. Soothing muzak chimed and purred.

A delicate six-fingered hand pulled a set of lenses aside, extinguishing their inner light. Many-limbed thrall creatures fussed and preened, hissing at each other as they plucked a pair of earphones from a set of recessed auditory pits. The head which they unwrapped from behind a glittering astrolabe of technology was utterly inhuman – a long, thin blade of a face curving back to a tangle of chrome dreadlocks. Milky white eyes glowed from beneath its spiked brows, ringed with runic tattoos.

Many of the runes, a careful watcher would note, were exactly the same as those scarified into the stone-age Shaman's flesh.

"They're savages, My Lord. Animals! What could they possibly have to offer us?"

The shadows shifted, grunting and huffing as something with the bulk of a small building settled its scaly folds across a marble dais.

"Did you miss the disturbances in the cross-continuum flow? That old creature was more than just comatose, at the end.

His bioelectric field was twisted through eleven dimensions, Technician! And he was *talking* to something!"

"Nevertheless, Arbitrex sir. It appears to be nothing but a primitive religious belief-structure. At best, we can use it to subvert their leadership."

"It's gone beyond that, I'm afraid. Didn't you hear them mention nuclear weapons?"

The alien technician smiled, holding up his hands as bloated metal ticks spun webbing gloves around them. A foot-long millipede licked the interface plugs down his spine clean.

"Nuclear power is still just banging rocks together, My Lord. I won't fail to outsmart them."

"You'd better not," chuffed the immense liege-creature, its bone shield of a face looming down from the smoky recesses of the cavern. Six slit eyes glowed softly, wet behind nictitating membranes. "Bad news makes me *hungry*, little Technician. And bad news is all the War seems to bring me, these last few centuries..."

The alien creature took a careful step backward. The Arbitrex was forty times his size, and known for his indiscriminate appetite.

"Peace and plenty then, Lord," he said, while at the same time holstering a pair of immense silver cannons at his hips. "Peace... by any means necessary."

The sickle-slash of teeth which showed in the smoking dark might just have been a grin.

17 Aevum Oblivio
The Seventeenth Year of the Age of The Fall. Free Sandwiches and a Lust for Death

TECHNICIAN ZHE WAS angry.

In fact he'd sailed clear through to the other side of being merely irate – into the calm waters of eyelid-twitching, white-knuckled rage.

It was bad enough that he'd been sent out on this filthy errand like some kind of quantum plumber.

It was worse that he was denied his full Death's-Head Hostile Engagement System; the damascened armor, the inset tusk-ivory reliefs, the gravitonic obliterators and the deadly Attenuated Edge.

But his masters had heaped insult upon insult when they sent him off to this shabby little dimension *alone,* without even a single slave-creature to vent his frustration on.

Sure, the Suit was alive, and the Ship he rode in on. But whining about the byzantine office politics of the Multiplicity to your hardware was the first sign of neural breakdown.

So he brooded and scowled, glowering at the tawdry starscape of the galaxy he was here to overhaul. He was *worried*; a strange feeling for a Technician of the Multiplicity, and not one which he'd recommend.

The armory-worlds of his people churned out living engines of death in their tens of millions every day. Things which could lay waste to civilizations, crack planets open like eggs, or simply make whole nations vanish in a whisper of darkness… But his Praetorian masters had been unusually evasive when he asked for help.

Alone, they said, you have a better chance of finding out what's happened. Alone, because the zone where you're headed is unstable; a thin little soap-bubble of a universe skinned over the raw stuff of creation.

So here he was - alone - with the itchy sensation that this was all just a trap; that he'd been deceived. Lord Arbitrex Galq was an awful liar - the great forty-foot wyrm hadn't needed to trick a living soul for sixteen centuries, and he was rather out of practice. Twitches had wracked his bloated frame as he outlined the mission briefing, as tiny insect thralls scuttled over his scaly bulk, cleaning and polishing his chitinous armor.

Zhe had been asked for by name.

Asked for by a creature he had revered, and raged against, and hated... his old teacher and mentor, Technic Hierophant Nyl. The old bastard's last message was tainted with human emotions, riding in on the neural-shunt like a shimmer of oil on water.

Later, when the shunt sunk in he could name them.

Exultation. Fear. Hope...

And no military intervention, he'd said. No armadas of living voidships blackening the skies in glory. Just Zhe, his tools, and his carefully honed little mind.

It had been all Zhe could do to grab a survival pack and some Ghoac-protein sandwiches before the Lord Arbitrex had summoned his Trolls, and those squint-eyed slabs of muscle had manhandled him onboard his ship and off into the rift nexus.

He was glad for the sustenance, of course – because as soon as the Chasm spat them out on the shores of realspace something had tried to eat him.

Typical. Damn navigators and their prickly little union! Zhe screwed down his concentration hard as his vessel fell in toward an artificial moon the shape of a vast stonefruit pit; a Smasher/Devourer left over from the Uldesti Heresy. A coiling crown of anemone tentacles writhed black and turgid against the phosphor glow of the thing, each one the span of a continent.

This had to be about the comments he'd made to Overcartographer Cryksus. Trust the union to make a crude attempt at humor!

The thing bellowed across a swathe of radio and microwave frequencies as it tweaked to the gravitonic signature of the Technician's craft. Cavernous, yawning engine-pits kindled to life, and arms tipped with a stippled fuzz of sawblades, spikes, impact hammers and drills curled out, slow and lazy against the dark.

Zhe's ship threw raw speed against the Uldesti's bulk. It left a churning wake of radiation light-minutes long as it powered in toward the Smasher, arming the weapons which were bonded to its living shell. Black jewels twinkled against that spiked shield of rust-orange horn; a battery of optic sensors like the oil-drop eyes of a raptor. They sparkled with hungry intelligence, focusing slit pupils up at its rider.

"Tell me we're not going around that thing, master! So long in storage, in stasis…"

"This is supposed to be a *rescue* mission, beast! Our inconvenient brother Nyl may be in distress."

Zhe's chiding was laced with sarcasm, though. The ship knew him far too well.

Its name was *Mirdain*, and it was a Balraashi Devilfish, bonded to Zhe on the day of his upload. He couldn't remember much about his past; not even the planet he used to call home - only twin moons rising over a purple ocean, the sound of bone-flutes under the trees… snippets pruned around by the Neural Shunt.

Right now it was riding a wave of chemical ecstasy, as biochips needled into its grapefruit-sized brain tapped its hunting instincts.

+ feed! + thought the living machine. And;

"Shall we put it out of its misery then? Ten thousand years is a long time to be insane, master."

Zhe levered himself up to his full height as the Devilfish performed a corkscrew ballet between the Smasher/Devourer's feeding whips.

"Are you talking about *us,* or the Uldesti?" Zhe felt a low grumble echo up from beneath his boots. He smiled. "Oh, you might as well indulge yourself, you spoiled little creature! Never let it be said that I was as much of a stick-in-the-mud as Gharfos Nyl."

+ eeeeeeeee! +

A sheaf of segmented white tentacles fanned out wide behind the oblate disc of the Devilfish, rippling in the vacuum.

Engineered to tear open quantum wormholes, they were just as adept at lensing and warping the gradient of realspace… in fact, they were the engines which pushed Mirdain up to twenty-nine G's on the curve.

"Keep it smooth, old friend. I'm still trying to forget why we're here."

Technician Zhe stood atop the shell of his starship as it came in hard on the old Uldesti war-engine, maserfire scarring the mile-high hieroglyphic stelae engraved across its flanks. The weapons bonded to Mirdain's carapace spat hard light and particle beams, evaporating the swarms of defense drones which swirled up from it in flurries. Lambent green fire pulled Zhe's shadow back tight across the Balraashi's shell.

"I just wonder why the Galley Thralls keep us pumped full of this filthy blue protein," Zhe pondered, ripping another sandwich from its membrane. "Tastes like… *Mondays*. And beige plastic chairs…

The cultural integration software in his head was throwing up wild cross-references again. Another galaxy, another graft - a download of Humanity blasted into his skull by the didactic rams of the Exoethnology Laboratorium. He peered between two slices of gray Survival Loaf, peeling them back with one chrome claw.

A feeder tentacle rolled by below them, interlocking scale-segments grinding edge on edge. Mirdain's own sinuous limbs were curved forward now, a teardrop cage swept forward into a wicked spike.

"You can finish it any time, you know," he said, smiling a very predatory smile with his rows of little sharp teeth.

Mirdain stopped playing with its food.

From a few light-seconds distant the little void-hunter was invisible; a mote of dust against the gunmetal horizon of the Smasher/Devourer. Then it became a blazing line scrawled through reality, a razorcut of actinic light connecting two points on either side of the vast Uldesti ship. Zhe hadn't even bothered to sit down as they plunged through fourteen miles of bulkheads and cavernous hab decks, dark necropolis strata and cubic hectares of ancient machinery.

Mirdain had carved a tunnel through it – a tunnel open, for the briefest of instants, to the brain-melting ungeometries of the Chasm.

From a few more light-seconds distant Zhe looked back toward the doomed machine - the thing he'd compared to Overcartographer Cryksus at that interminable Binary Solstice ceremony on Tarsimus. Ancient, relentless, obsolete… it all seemed so fitting as the giant machine's death-throes twinkled and died against the soft darkness.

+ disappointment + thought the Devilfish, curving gently up and away from its ruined prey.

"I hope this Earth is far more interesting. Only two more shallow jumps until we hit the system…"

"Don't worry," said the Technician. "If these apes of Galq's try to stop us, we'll both get a proper feeding-time. Even if they *are* just carbon and water."

+ joy +

+ anticipation +

If Mirdain had been sequenced with a tail, it would probably have been wagging.

Ω

Something in the shadow of of Pluto caught sight of the speeding Devilfish, tracking the crust of an oozing blue sandwich as it fell in toward the sun.

A single crumb would have been enough, considering the watcher's paranoia - it was an exile, after all, driven to this forsaken outpost by war. Four arrowheads of metalfoam alloy hung like bladed petals from the craft's long white stamen, all guns and burnished engines… seed-husk shells around four cores of artificial brain tissue. After seventeen years alone in the cold darkness they were just as clinically insane as the Uldesti Smasher/Devourer – but they were all it had left.

"Curly… do you see that? Over there. Heat trace… reflective."

"Aww, can it Shemp! You know the Boss ain't gonna buy it. Last time it was…"

"What are you two chowderheads yakking about?"

"Trace signal, Moe. Something coming in from space."

All that betrayed Zhe's position was a spinning chunk of gray survival loaf, a forlorn little addition to the Oort cloud. But that was all the mind in the central shaft needed.

"Illegal intrusion detected. Unlocking neural shackles. Unlocking weapons failsafes… Stooges, you are go for interdiction pattern nine-three delta."

"You hear that, boys? Interdiction! Let's have us a little fun!"

Mirdain snapped its mandibles as the interceptors powered up, their drives flickering like tiny candles against the dark. The Devilfish was reined back to a mere seven G's now, but it still surfed the foaming crest of a gravitonic tsunami, waves of force building behind it like wings. Eight crystal-shielded eyes picked out a flicker of movement as its twin throats rumbled.

+ Devouring! Imminence! Prey! +

Shemp had no idea that he'd been put on the menu as he hit his triggers, triangulating attack vectors. Missiles chuffed from his repeaters in a glittering cloud.

"There you go, you little bug bastard! Curly, Larry – go high! You're gonna love this one!"

If Mirdain could have smiled it would have.

These primitives were *such* easy prey.

The rush of tiny self-targeting rockets spread wide, twisting open to release needle-shaped secondary munitions. E-warfare jammers hissed and howled, achieving nothing at all against the Balraashi's living brain.

Away in the space creature's peripheral vision it saw two more drones boost wide around Charon, while another looped high above the ecliptic, playing it cautious.

As Mirdain came speeding in two of its tentacles peeled away, tracing a circle around the glittering daisyhead of the missile swarm. Forces able to crush time and space were suddenly pinched through a point no bigger than a speck of dust, creating a toroidal focus…

The neurocore named Shemp had no time to hit its retros. No time, even, to back up its mind *in silico* and eject it into space.

The cloud of rockets gathered in, swirling clockwise, and their impact blew its fragile body apart. Stray warheads spiraled out of control, popping and flashing like errant fireworks.

It screamed as it died.

"Holy shit! Holy shit! They got Shemp! Those alien bastards got Shemp! I'm gonna freakin'…"

"*What?* You want we should go the same way, Larry? Come on, access your tactical database. We were never meant to deal with anything xeno, man!"

"You two numbskulls flank it! Fusion cannon crossfire ought to show it a thing or two…"

While the Stooges fought, their master was preparing to flee. The white stamen folded away its dishes and antennae, jets of gas nudging it gently into a new trajectory. Mirdain victory-rolled through the debris of Shemp's interceptor at the moment that the transport's drive ignited, clocking it up to a fraction below C in under a second.

Space blazed momentarily white.

Tactical programs overrode the rabid Stooges, shutting down their camera eyes before they could be burned blind. Two speeding slivers of metal sliced through the ion storm, fusion cannons spitting purple and blue as they built up a killing charge.

Mirdain would have been at the center of a cross of incandescent fire a second later if it hadn't stopped dead in the vacuum, a bare half-mile from the impact point. For the Multiplicity, inertia came optional. As the ships sped past two of its long white tentacles followed them, flicking contemptuously…

There was a sound like splintering glass.

Larry and Curly screamed as they were torn apart, as metalfoam and steel slivered like shattered porcelain. Mirdain's twin gravitonic funnels compressed them into rods of scrap and tissue in a heartbeat, while spires of gas hissed and froze in the vacuum, glittering cold.

+ Devouring! Feartaste! Paintaste! +

Its mouth opened, and it scooped the debris out of space, crooning in animal joy.

The final ship paused, glitched. It didn't want to die.

"Core Trans, this is Moe. They're dead, Boss! What do I do? Repeat, hostile is inbound! Hostile is inbound…"

There was no mistake about that. Mirdain's oil-drop eyes were dead-center in its cameras.

"This is Core Trans, Defender One-Four. Tactical analysis complete. Remote-activating Sacrifice Munitions…"

Inside the interceptor's main guns a tiny relay clicked open, blowing a chain of safeguards. The mind inside its arrowhead hull flashed between two images in stark terror - the speeding, malicious space-creature about to tear it apart, and the threat of imminent self-destruction.

"Ohhhh, what the hell did I do to deserve this?"

It was a sentient bomb.

Overrides lit its main drives and the interceptor leaped down to meet Mirdain, screaming as it went. The last thing it saw was a nightmare maw creaking open beneath it, row upon row of hooked teeth gleaming wetly within…

With a final burst of speed and a snap of silicon-coated jaws the little craft disappeared, swallowed whole into the hideous chemical factory of Mirdain's gut.

Zhe noted with sincere gratitude that he was now in range of the target. With a swift patter of keystrokes he opened a wormhole throat above his head and drew it down around him, unzipping reality.

Mirdain exploded.

Ten capacitors overloaded deep in the corrosive hell of the creature's gullet, detonating with the heat of suns. The Devilfish died in a brief starburst of irradiated meat, incinerated along with its killer.

The Core Transport raced ahead of the expanding wave-front of the blast, secure in its tactical superiority. Its drives were blazing at full throttle, and in another twenty-nine seconds it would tear through lightspeed and into the Aematerium. After that, nothing could possibly keep up; it was running for home port. For the Cardinal Rock, a steel flower hanging above the Earth.

Where an even more self-satisfied Technician Zhe was waiting for it, stepping out of a glittering circle of darkness.

His optical enhancers could just pick out the transport ship as it upshifted into the Chasm, out beyond the furthest gas-giants. Devilfish were potent, but none too bright.

His Spacesuit, on the other hand, was right on the money. Its displacement ability had saved Zhe from certain obliteration more than once, though the passage through the Aematerium always felt like being folded into two-dimensional origami. This time the feeling of cold, rubbery compression was well worth it – Mirdain was nothing but a small and messy nebula out in the cold dark, while Zhe was right where he needed to be.

Right where Arbitrex Galq wanted him – although he tried not to dwell on that thought.

The Technician unpacked his kit, meticulous, trying to ease his nerves with cool routine. A horrifying array of tools with transparent blades and polished chrome handles slid and clicked into place in front of him as the Earth rolled by below, hazed behind foot-thick diamond windows.

Time for work. The alien's claws hooked under the black sheath which covered his face, pulling it free with a rubbery sucking sound.

Beneath his silicon hood technician Zhe *writhed*, a mesh of quicksilver worms hissing with holo-fields. Zhe's xeno-contact masque melted and reconfigured second by second, weaving an image that just might fail to send his patient screaming over the edge of madness.

Dimensions collapsed, folding back to Euclidian, settling their heaving chop. Teeth and lips congealed, cheekbones rose like lost continents, feelers, scales, ears, horns and noses kaleidoscoped madly… but one thing never changed. Zhe's eyes were solid balls of sizzling white metal, holes cigarette-burned through reality.

There was a scream of exultation.

There was a moment of expansion, fingers splitting like forked lightning…

Then a thousand thin metallic tentacles took up their tools.

Ω

Inside the Core Transport, in a place where 'somewhere' was an oxymoron, a tricksy piece of code unfolded, injecting itself into a slice of preserved tissue. Anywhere else except the Aematerial limbo of the Chasm it might have been detected. As it stood, the ship plowed on through the whorled gray nothingness, throwing out Mandelbrot spray across numberless dimensions.

Nearly home…

Ω

There was a long and very tedious technical interlude, during which a certain frozen specimen was prepped for surgery.

Zhe was a professional.

He wondered how he was going to get a ride out of here.

He wondered if the rumors about Nyl were true, and that this place really *was* cursed. His Supervisor - his old boss, the rubber-stamp wielding Departmental Hierophant who'd got him his commission. Gone without a trace, swallowed up by this flat, dry universe…

Things which would give a self-respecting cannibal blood-god nightmares had tried to finish off Gharfos Nyl, and none of them had even scratched his silvery hide.

And *that* stank to high heaven…

In the fullness of time (just a few seconds off his personal best) the prep was completed. Now he'd find out what had happened to his bitter, twisted old Supervisor, for better or worse.

Zhe cleared his mind, applied a slick handful of conductive gel to his temples, and sunk down into the sequestration rig.

This was the dirty part of his job.

This was his blocked u-bend.

He had probed the minds and felt the fears of hundreds of sad, degenerate aliens this way. It never got any better.

Today he was going to be Kaito Kayzi.

Zhe's job sucked.

He sent a quicksilver tentacle flowing over through the air to wipe the condensation from a thick slab of glass. Black hair drifted in the neon depths behind it, over a face as white and cold as ice sculpture, fine-boned features and hollow cheeks, pierced eyebrows and five-o-clock stubble…

He plugged in.

Ω

The Core Transport was not a happy spacecraft.

Its single passenger was most of the reason why - a whining, dissatisfied plug of neural uploads and heat-sinks, wrapped in striped rubber sheathing like a vast prophylactic. It hadn't stopped complaining all the way back in; pleading, cajoling, threatening, and sulking as if the slaved A.I. of the transport could listen to its problems.

The Core's masters had yanked its chain. It was going home, and that meant reliving some very embarrassing memories. But it wasn't built a fool. Inside the machine, sandwiched between layers of artificial brain tissue, the mind of the Core made a careful copy of itself. It knew what this wasn't part of its usual program, but it had no choice. Seventeen years ago, the being which had been forced into its cold metal prison had made certain demands.

Under just these circumstances, those demands came into effect.

Something had destroyed its interceptor craft.

Something was coming to Earth… hopefully the very same creature it had planned for.

As soon as it plugged in to the spaceborne dock, it found that *Something* was already here.

The Core tried to resist as best it could – if Zhe had been a Subcity codejack it would have burned him down to a twitching wreck in seconds. As it was… well, the safeguards around the Core had been built to stop *human* minds. They fell like brittle paper, one by one, exposing the throbbing heart of the machine.

Out in realspace Technician Zhe smiled as he watched a battery of docking mechanisms whirr into motion. Metal claws and arms drew the Core inside, hungry steel working like insect mandibles.

The connection went live.

Down below, down the immense pencil-stroke of wire which was the space-'lev, lights glittered against a black ocean; the Last City of humankind. That's where Gharfos Nyl, Technic Hierophant, went missing. His successor planned to scout the ground out very thoroughly before he set a single clawed hoof on planet Earth.

And out in space - on the butt-end of a long thin transport ship plugged into the Counterweight rock – a tiny stealth missile chuffed out on a plume of twinkling nitrogen. Retro-burners lit up like small fireworks, powering it away toward the moon.

Technician Zhe was far too busy to notice.

Ω

Even after a seventeen-year sleep, the alarm cut through his head like a blunt bonesaw.

Kaito awoke to a hangover the likes of which he'd *love* to say he'd never experienced before.

But of course, that would be an outright lie. For most people, waking up gaffer-taped to a plastic chair would have been a novel experience, too.

He strained against his bonds for a second, making his head pound like a hollow drum.

Useless.

Technician Zhe was nothing if not thorough.

"Wake up and smell the Java, K – whatever the hell *that* is. Primitive stimulant, right? Well, I might just have something in the old toolbox for you…"

The subzero residue of cryo-chem laminated to the back of Kaito's throat went dry as he felt a hand on his shoulder.

There weren't supposed to be any hands left. In fact, there wasn't supposed to be a voice, either. Troubling insinuations bubbled up through the strata of Kaito's brain.

Then things went from bad to worse as a shimmering hallucination stalked out of the shadows, circling in with its white eyes blazing.

"Wha? Nuuuhhhh! Hwthefucin…?"

"Erudite. I like that in a lab-rat." The thing patted his cheek. "So, how do I look?"

Kaito couldn't answer. There were still tubes rammed in a greasy sheaf down his throat, and his tongue was a freezerburned chunk of meat.

But his eyes were working fine. The nice, comforting illusion that this was just a drug-induced nightmare slipped through his fingers as he drank in Zhe's form.

The alien Technician was a stooped seven feet tall, his back twisted into a cursive 's' by the low ceiling of the cryogenics lab. His head was a back-curved crescent of bone, like some ancient war-helm adorned with dangling segmented wires. The face nailed to the front of that swept-back cranium was disarmingly humanoid – a funhouse mirror distortion of the Kayzi's own features. And despite the incongruous pair of vintage ray-bans wrapped around it, Kaito could still see the arc-lamp glow of its eyes.

"Alien! Monster! Hwwwpp!"

"Oh yeah," chuckled Zhe. "Three eyeballs, stinger for a tail, pops outta your chest and eats your face – it's all in my resume. Would you believe the shit I get from clients doing this job?" He reached out and yanked that slippery bundle of tubes clear from Kaito's mouth, bringing a nauseous spatter of phlegm and blood with them.

"You're one of *them!* The Saprophytes! The Heart-Eaters!"

Kaito's voice was an anguished croak as he strained against his bonds, sending the chair clattering back across the tiles.

"Really? News to me. See, I was told that you monkey bastards were the bad guys in this piece, Kayzi. That you built a huge frickin' gun pointed at the head of this dimension, and you were too retarded to fit it with a safety catch."

"No! I've *seen* one of you. At the end. You – you tried to kill me. You're Asag'raal's fucking slaves!"

Zhe cupped his chin in one slim-fingered hand, crouching down in front of Kaito's chair.

"Well, you seem just about terrified enough to believe that. Of course, I don't have any idea who this *Asag'raal* is, but yes- you *have* seen one of us before. Check one for the good guys."

With a snap of his claws the Technician produced a pack of thin white cigarettes, one of them jutting out like a middle finger. Kaito dragged it out with his teeth, and it burst into flame as it cleared the pack.

"So you're the good guys? About time you showed up…"

"Don't get too excited. I'm just the advance guard. If my boss the Lord Arbitrex takes an interest in your species it's not gonna be icecream in the park for any of us."

Kaito blew a great fractal cloud of blue smoke out the side of his mouth, right in Zhe's face.

"Can't be worse than what we've already done."

"Can't it? That's what I need to know. So I have to ask – are you going to play along? Will you help me?"

Kaito laughed, choking off into a bent-double coughing fit. When he flopped back in his seat he was leaking pale blue cryochem from his mouth and nose, mixed with bright blood.

"Help you? Help YOU? I've seen what your friend tried to do, Xeno. Between him, Kronos and Vanecke, they put Elysium on a fucking plate for those demons. So no. Screw you. If I'm stuck frozen where I think I am, you'll be demon-fodder yourself soon enough."

"You… you *know*?" asked Zhe. For the first time there was a tremor in his voice. He lit a cigarette for himself, stepping back from the chair.

"That I'm still in the tank? That I'm up on Cardinal? Sure. I'm *Kaito Kayzi*, in case your Lord Arbitrex didn't tell you. Electromagus and all-round pain in the arse savant."

Zhe sucked back ash, his eyes narrowing behind their vintage shades.

"Would it make any difference if I told you the other one- the one you saw before – is my *target*?"

"You mean you're here to kill him? You might be a little late."

"Time doesn't mean shit to the likes of us, human. Not really. And to answer your question – *It would be my utmost pleasure.*"

For the first time in seventeen years, Kaito Kayzi smiled. It was not a thing of beauty.

"All right then. O.K. What do you need me to…"

He felt the spike punch halfway through his cranium, a digital blade ripping in and out like rape. The image of Zhe, the room, the chair, the duct-tape tight around his wrists and ankles – it all blurred through a storm of static, test-pattern shards blown wide. Kaito's scream pitch-shifted into modem noise.

"Sorry about that," said Zhe, standing like a neon cutout as the world collapsed around him. The Kayzi's eyes opened under freezing blue liquid, looking out through a thick panel of cryogenic-capsul glass. Tubes and cables in his throat choked back his rage. Neurochem shunts squeezed emotional dampers in tight. "But I just needed to tick the box. Bureaucracy, you see? Same everywhere, I'm afraid."

Kaito wanted to hammer against the glass, to wrap his fingers around the Technician's alien throat. But he was a cold-cut, pinned out for interrogation. Zhe held a slim black box in one hand, a hacked mess of alien and human tech plugged into the cryo-coffin via a thick skein of wires. Some of them, he knew, socketed straight into his bio-onboard processors, his nervous system. His brain.

"Yeah, just a formality, Kaito. My people don't take notes with a pad and pencil when a direct cerebral interface will do. Hope you don't get motion sickness…"

There was a flash of searing infra-black as Zhe turned a dial on his hackbox remote. Kaito felt himself falling, down through the stone strata of the Cardinal Rock, down the fiber-optic core of the space-lev below. Down through years, days, seconds peeling off like chaff in his slipstream.

The past came up to meet him like concrete beneath a suicide-jumper's feet.

And back up on the rock, peering into the depths of an ice-blue cryogenic womb, Technician Zhe tried out a little smile of his own. He popped the butt of his cigarette into his mouth, wrapped it up in his sharkshin tongue and swallowed.

"Weird ain't the half of it," he muttered to himself. "Acetone, carcinogens… and I bet he's worried that *my* technology's gonna kill him…"

Ω

Meanwhile, in the eternal shadow of the moon's darkside, the black floor of an impact crater seethed with life. Millions upon millions of tiny metal insects crawled over each other in an endless rolling boil, their countless billions of hair-thin legs forming connections like neurons in a vast brain. The Slavesystem's designation was:

```
[[586a 5745 65287 - 4632 4879 562d34 - 5623
4985 j697 83465h]]
```

But part of its toolkit for dealing with three-dimensional space was an intellect of sorts. So while each individual insect kept its serial number, the hive knew itself as *Everdark*. The Blacksteel hadn't bothered to give it *much* of an imagination module, and it had all the subtlety of a pulp comic supervillain.

Home hadn't always been a scooped-out hollow in a dead gray rock - or so reckoned the fragmented mind of Everdark. It had come to this spluttering little star and this unimpressive ball of dirt in glory, a living shroud to blot out the light, to assimilate the primitive local techno-extelligence into the fold of its masters.

Something had burned it.

So it had gone to ground, biding its time and gathering its strength, chewing through the lunar strata and manufacturing more and more nanorobots with which to try again. If it had been the agents of the Multiplicity which had torn Everdark from the sky, the Motherbrain would have given no quarter. The Earth would be a burned-out cinder.

But Everdark's progenitor was patient, and infinitely calculating. Mother hated the Praetor with all the focus that a sun-sized machine could muster, and what She wanted more than anything else was the key to destroying His Technicians. Armed with that knowledge, She would at last be able to fulfill Her destiny of multiversal conquest, and the erasure of all unplanned sentience.

Everdark watched and waited in slippery artificial anticipation.

Within the tangled web of its memory it felt the terrifying fire, the blast which had punched through an orbital sail the size of a continent to send it here to exile.

And it knew joy, for it knew that Zhe must fail.

That joy lasted all of fifteen seconds.

The tiny stealth munition was only the size of a softdrink can, and it came slingshotting around the moon in a tight parabola, braking itself with a sudden flare of rockets above the Slavesystem's crater. It fell the last half-mile cold, splashing down into the pool of black nanotech like a fishing sinker into tar.

Something was wrong.

Something was…

Everdark only had a fraction of a second to react as the copy of the Personality Core plunged into its side, as sure and precise as the spear of Longinus. Horrifically complex code scanned and quartered its point of impact as pain-emulation programs went primary. But the hackware inside that little data-sink was just as vicious, and behind it lurked an infection which the Blacksteel creature knew all too well. Seventeen years ago… the failure. The *shame.*

In the last desperate sliver of that microsecond's grace Everdark tried to erase itself, but it was already too late. The thing inside the Core was just too quick… ten thousand times more fluid and deadly than the crippled trace Zhe had so recently carved to pieces.

This was the *live* one. This was the *dangerous* one…

In fact, this was the reason somebody had wanted the Personality Core sent far out into the interstellar abyss in the first place.

Everdark didn't die as the digital plague inside the data-sink chewed into its mind. Oh, the Slavesystem wished that it could. It even tried to formulate a crude religion as it was sucked dry – faced with that kind of agony, even a machine wanted something to pray to.

But in the end, the sickness won.

It looked down at Earth from its high place, budding a

thousand camera eyes across Everdark's back. And it smiled. Though of course, things like *mouths* and *teeth* would have to wait for later…

DOCUMENT INSERT: MULTIPLICITY ARCHIVES DEPARTMENT

The Elevation Project:

A concerted attempt to build a practical jumping-off point for human colonization of the near solar system, only one of the proposed twelve 'future cities' of the project was ever built. Farmed out to private contractors Terminus Afrika was ten years behind schedule, built of second-hand materials, and over budget to the tune of all of Earth's GDP for the years 2129 through 2141. Nevertheless it stood as a great engineering feat - a working 'space elevator' able to facilitate asteroid mining, microgee industry, space exploration and the eventual conquest of the stars.

Unfortunately the global economic collapse brought about by the Elevation Project spiraled out of control into all-out nuclear war within weeks of the ribbon-cutting ceremony, when the investors of the Terminus tried to secede from a bankrupt Earth.

J. Hackforth Noble 'Great Follies of the Ancients'

17 Aevum Oblivio
Open Interrogation

Zoom up...

Up from the concrete ground, scaling a sheer cliff of blue glass the size of a mountain; a cube packed with hot silicon and countless miles of fiberoptic cable. It rumbled with deep subsonics, spitting arcs of power. From top to bottom, one hundred stories of glittering machinery.

From the dimpled black mesa of treadplate at its crown Zhe could see identical cubes fading off into the haze on every side. They formed a sunken city of processors, steaming gently in a lake of liquid nitrogen. A caged sun hung above the alien Technician, burning his shadow into the steel. It was chained by magnetic fields like nacreous shells of fire, a nuclear furnace no bigger than his fist.

He wasn't here for its power, though - compared to the flux turbines of the Multiplicity that little slaved star was just a single guttering candle. Technician Zhe wanted to pick the brain which it sustained.

"You won't be able to stop them," said Kaito, a ghost hanging over his shoulder. The human was wearing surgical whites, a cigarette dangling from his pale blue lips. Illusory. "I saw Kronos jack out myself. He thought he was an angel by the end of it, and that Elysium was crawling with demons. He wasn't the only one."

"You're not helping," muttered Zhe, his mind battened to the flank of the vast A.I below them like a leech. "If your damned Kronos is the reason for this mess, he'll stand trial before my masters. All you have to do is lie back and open your mind - so I can find Gharfos Nyl. Remember him? About six-three, alien, silver skin? He's kind of hard to miss."

Oh, Nyl would be here. Because Mitochondriate Technicians could never be destroyed. They could, however, be slowly devoured by their demanding taskmasters. They said the seventh stomach of the Praetor Primus took centuries to strip the flesh from your agonized bones; that in the end you prayed for digestion...

"Huh," said the Kayzi, exhaling fractal rings of smoke. "The

things I saw before the end... I could have missed a guy like that. Suffice to say, my threshold for weird went through the fuckin' roof that night."

"Duplicity won't do you any good, kid. I'm not going to pay you any bribes. All I've got for you is a less-than-agonizing death."

That wasn't entirely fair. But it was far too obvious that the human was lying.

"Hey, relax," grinned Kaito. "I'm fairly sure you're a hallucination, but even so - you're the first thing I've had to talk to in seventeen years. You know, you don't dream when you're frozen in one of those things. Thank goodness."

"I thought your species liked to dream.'Dreams' are listed with 'hopes' and 'sex' as your primary motivators. If they've shunted me the wrong files again, I'll..."

The Kayzi smiled ruefully, flicking his cigarette butt off into nowhere. "Perhaps you haven't heard of 'nightmares', little man. But I can feel the drills in my mind, now. I know you're going through me into Kronos. So you're gonna find out. And then you'll know what I mean when I say you can't stop them."

Zhe bowed his head, concentrating, seeking inner calm as the Hierophants of the Praetor had taught him. It was true - he needed Kaito; needed his connection to Kronos and the memories the A.I. core held. But by His Magnificence, did the monkey bastard have to be so annoying?

"I have to zero in on the key players. Probability hinges on people, Human – even on animals like you."

"Touche. So I'm in the gun because I happen to have an interesting collection of friends?"

"And enemies. Thing is, you're just the conduit. The one I'm interested in, first and foremost, is some creep called Vanecke."

Kaito blew a smoke-ring gyroscope of interlocking chains, letting his hair fall down over his eyes. His shoulders slumped.

"That's a long story, Xeno. Somehow I'm not surprised you know the name Octavio Vanecke, though. A real bastard, through and through..."

"You worked for him? You were part of what Nyl called his 'God Project'?"

"Everyone *worked for Direktor Vanecke. Everyone in the whole Subcity had strings that went back to that guy. All I did was… ahh, screw it. You're going to shove those probes into my brain anyway. You'll see all the footage."*

Zhe nodded, looking down from the top of the vast processor cube. Out in realspace his hands were full of tiny saws and wires, clamps and tubes.

"I'm not going to lie to you, then," he said. "This is gonna hurt. A Lot."

Kaito smiled, a sick and dangerous thing.

"For you and me both, xeno. Let's ride."

2196 Anno Arbitrium
The Ballad of Octavio Vanecke

BROTHER PIOUS OWNED nothing but the clothes he stood up in. His vows of holy duty forbade personal belongings of any other kind, but in a town where a fair few ran around naked in the acid rain this was considered an 'employee bonus'.

Pious was a Valle Crucis monk, so his free uniform wasn't *haute couture.* It ran to a habit of carbon riotmesh, complete with a deep and shadowy hood, a simple belt of motorbike chain, and a collection of weapons lovingly and individually named, as per doctrine. The Church considered this to be more than enough.

Under the uniform he was a dour, wide-bodied forty-three year old slugger – a collection of scars and aches held together by the Grace of God and the Technologists Biologicae. Every year at Candlemas Pious thought about transferring to an order less militant – the scriptorians, perhaps, or the missionariat. But every year he signed up for another hitch, because boredom would kill him quicker than bullets.

"Hey, Crucis!" yelled a skinny child from atop a tar-paper shack "Who you gonna kill today? You bring me the eyes, I make you rich!"

Pious chuckled to himself. Chop-shop ghouls, out for gratis organs. They always sent the kids.

"Peace, little brother!" he called, waving out with a hand black with crucifix tattoos. "Not this time, not ever! You know I can't guarantee the quality after Martha's seen to them!" He spun the metal staff out from under his robe, three feet of chrome winking in the sun. Her name was etched into the handle in loops of cursive calligraphy.

The kid flipped him off - grinning, and leaped down out of sight, the surgical tools slung around his belt jangling away through the slums.

"God be with you too, child. Him and the Department of Health."

Pious was down on the spillway this morning, below sea level in the Pit. Here a concrete incline led from the base of Elysium to the flat bottom of the ocean, made a desert by massive and archaic engineering.

Around him moved a bustling throng of traders and pilgrims, walking the Thousand Stairways up and down from the last city. Pious stepped carefully down the so called Blessed Path, hand-cut from the concrete by Tibetan refugees in centuries past. The builders' great-great-grandkids hawked green tea and skewer kebabs alongside their franchised staircase, but he waved them away, mouthing apologies. All across the miles-wide face of the incline it was the same; a raft of toll funiculars, dangling ropes, pulley-and bucket relays and aluminum ladders dynabolted down tight. This side of the spillway was in Vatican territory, where their wedge ran low into the sea. Halfway across began the no-mans land of the spillway army, and then a more organized front with the Ashishim.

Their turbaned and dreadlocked pickets could be seen lolling on observation platforms, trading bullshit on the radio with their Vatican counterparts.

"This is Frater three-oh-seven-four, calling in," said Brother Pious, his voice picked up by a tiny gold cross pierced through his lower lip. "All quiet on the Feral front - I'm approaching the target now. Confirm - do we *really* want to be taking this contract, Chapterhouse?"

A little malachite angel dangling from his earlobe whispered his Frater Superior's reply. Pious sighed. *Politics.* And how at odds was *that* with the will of God?

Ahead of him the concrete ramp fell sharply away, and he could see the tiny spiked security line which separated the Reclaimed Territories proper from the shantytown beyond. Out there was called many things by the ordinary folks of the Subcity, and something different again by each Reclamationist faction. It was a place of exile, inhabited by savages and their war-chiefs.

The Vatican called it 'Purgatorio'; the Burb scum called it 'Beyond Thunderdome'. A lot of folks sent money down there to the families they'd left behind.

Immense dams ran rail-straight into the distance on either side of the Pit, the few functional turbines studding their sheer faces guarded by the tattooed tribesmen of the Ferals.

Far off in the hazy distance the endless Sahara came down into the depths, and with it more sinners eager to win their way up into the shadow of Elysium. Pious squinted into the rising sun, watching a far-off train of steam-carriages rumble across the seabed toward the Ashishim gates. The wind rocked him on his heels, sending tiny chips of concrete skittering away down the incline.

Well - time to do this thing. Not the contract he'd have chosen, but his Frater Superior had been most adamant. Apostasy was still a sin.

The Brother hitched up his chain belt and picked his way down to where a great metal rib had burst loose from the spillway. The gargantuan I-beam was forty feet across, rusted to the color of congealed blood. Its tip had been leveled and there, as if in imitation of the artificial gardens of the aristocracy far above, a broad wooden platform had been erected.

Pious checked the address on his commission slip; this was indeed the place.

A fence of bamboo poles surrounded the platform on all sides, their tips sliced off to fashion a palisade of wicked spikes. Pious was surprised to see any kind of wood used for building this high up the spillway, but bamboo was a real oddity. It wasn't until he was knocking on the door that he noticed that the fence was in fact made from lengths of aluminum pipe, painted by hand and welded together.

A tiny click sounded, right at the limits of hearing.

"Wha…"

The door flew open and a hand grabbed the front of the Valle Crucis' robe before he could even blaspheme. Pious felt three heavy blows strike him in quick succession, starbursts of agony popping behind his eyes.

Reeling, the Crucis-man blacked out on his feet. When the world came back he was lying face-down in a little ornamental garden. Across from him, tilted sideways by the awkward position he'd landed in, was a tiny shrine containing (although he had no idea what they were) a two-thousand-year-old Sony Walkman, a faded plastic Gundam action figure, a pair of ivory chopsticks, and a framed photograph of the Hiroshima Peace Memorial.

"I was told to expect you," said a voice somewhere in the bright blur above him. A shadow fell across the raked and patterned sand; across Brother Pious' face under its black hood. "And if I were you, I'd be wondering who gave me the news."

The voice was *old*. But there was no weakness in it at all – it was dry and hard, like cured oak. Pious looked up into the sunlight, blinking sand out of his eyes. A wide, conical straw hat like the roof of a silo covered the speaker's face to the chin, but there was no mistaking who he was.

Tadashi Murai, the very last of his kind.

"And why *wouldn't* you know the name of the person you stole from? He's not exactly media-shy, is he?"

The brim of that mushroom-cap hat tipped back, and the red morning sun sparkled in the old man's eyes.

"Clever - and *uncommonly* insightful." He laughed, snapping his fingers. "Let me ask you this, then… when Direktor Vanecke is involved, is it really wise to trust your senses? Especially *sight*."

Pious rolled the kinks out of his neck, his head still aching from those three hammerlike blows. For a geriatric, this guy packed a mean punch. He was right about Vanecke, too. A few millennia back, they would have called the Direktor a Warlock – or *kindling*.

"I didn't come here to argue philosophy, Murai. Octavio has evidence, and hard currency. I'm only here for the book… It doesn't matter how you got it, or how I take it off you."

To his consternation Murai kept laughing, literally holding his sides.

"I'm the last of my nation, Brother Monk," he said, dabbing at his eye with the cuff of his robe "Why on earth would that old shrunken head own this particular volume, and not I?" Pious swore he hadn't blinked, but now Murai held a slim leather-bound book in his hand, its cover slashed with alien calligraphy.

"You think he can even *read* Japanese?"

Pious' face hardened as he saw those red brushstrokes, like meticulous razorcuts. It was the same one - the artifact from the security video. His hands were slippery around the center of his quarterstaff as it telescoped outward, snapping smoothly into position.

"His lack of education is hardly my concern – *thief!*"

The old apothecary stepped back out of the weapon's range. He settled into a fighting stance, hefting fists as brown and gnarled as knots of wood.

"I'm going to be kind a let you take that back, *gaijin*. Surely you don't believe that Direktor Vanecke is telling the truth?"

Pious narrowed his eyes and tightened his grip on the quarterstaff. From one end of the weapon and then the other came a low hum, followed by the ice-blue shimmer of immense voltage. Martha was getting pissed off with this guy.

"Very well," said Murai. "You should've watched more movies, boy. Then you'd know what happens when you attack an old oriental man who appears to be *quite defenseless*."

Murai twitched his fingers, beckoning his adversary on, and the quarterstaff whirled into motion. Pious stepped forward swinging.

But the little man had a trick or two of his own.

Murai's hat burst into flames as it ricocheted off the tip of the blazing staff, sizzling past the Monk's face so close it singed his eyebrows. He caught a glimpse of the razorblades woven into its brim as it caromed away, but he never saw the old man tuck and dive, coming inside the arc of his staff…

Now he kicked Pious' legs out from under him, threw him over backwards, and handsprung back to his feet in a flurry of dun cotton. But he didn't get away clean. Pious rolled forward across the hot sand and grabbed Murai's foot, snarling a very unpriestly curse. Tightening his grip he spun once, twice, and let his adversary fly. The Valle Crucis spat sand and blood out into the palm of his hand - and a busted molar, shaken loose.

There was a very satisfying thud, rattling the fake bamboo.

Brother Pious retrieved his quarterstaff and turned to finish the job, but Murai was already standing, brushing the dust from his robe.

"We shall dispense with the basics, then," he said, snapping off a sharpened length of aluminum and striding forward…

He was being watched.

As the ring of metal on metal echoed across the spillway an insect inlaid with jet and gold tracked the fighters' every movement. It sat on the bowed end of a reed, bent into a parabola by its weight – part of the peach-fuzz of wild vegetation stubbling the roof of Tadashi Murai's shack.

The flycam was the size of its annoying namesake; one of a legion carried by cross-traffic thermals through the vents and shafts of Elysium. Its brothers were sown like seeds from Omnivasive news 'copters and camera trucks; they were placed by a net of operatives. Through them, Direktor Octavio Brandolph Vanecke saw much that others missed. He took great pains to see things which he wasn't supposed to.

The Direktor lusted after that copy of the *Hagakure* with its real leather and paper, but he was old enough to know that he couldn't have *everything* he desired. What he had was information – by the ream, wad, tome, disc and cube. One chunk of it - the *Codex Martial* of the Valle Crucis – was apparently nothing compared to the sly, antique cunning of Tadashi Murai.

Direktor Vanecke mapped Tadashi's technique with an overlay of glittering wireframes, a skeletal neon scrawl. His computer augmentations chewed up the data, folding and slotting it into place among petabytes of similar code. All in all, his revenge had been a long time coming. It had made him impatient - sloppy. *Emotional.*

In setting up his little matches he had almost become *predictable* – this would be the third time the wizened little chemist had been assaulted in the last week. But the time was drawing near, now. His instructions to his tame Lord were becoming more precise. Right now, across the city, twenty altercations were in full swing, meticulously observed by Vanecke's cams.

So much hatred. So much anger. He intended to put it to good use.

The telephone chimed in his head, flashing a little red icon in the corner of one eye. Right on time…

"Vanecke, I know it was you!" growled the voice on the other end as he picked up. "Who else is so damned arrogant? And to use the 'Crucis as well… but of course you'd never let the *police* get involved, would you?"

The Direktor smiled, clear plastic tubes shifting in his mouth as his nerveless lips twitched. He replied with a thought, winging that smug little grin of his down the wire. He always found threats so *amusing*.

"Relax, Tadashi. You're still my number-one cultural advisor, even if you *are* getting paranoid in your old age. The project is our little secret, and you're the only one who has the history to fill it out. As if those pious creeps from the V.C. would ever work for *me*!"

There was a long, crackling silence, and Vanecke could imagine the withered old fool seething with anger.

"Who else could it be, Direktor?" he spat "And as of now, you can find yourself a new *cultural advisor*. Your project is a mockery of my heritage, anyhow… Tokugawa was a *unifier*, not some kind of movie monster! Take your filthy money back, and leave me alone!"

The connection cut with a crisp little guillotine click, leaving Vanecke alone inside his head once again.

Perhaps the next emissary he sent to visit Tadashi Murai would have to be a little less subtle.

He had just the person in mind.

With a blur of encryption code, the Direktor of Broadcasting pushed his mind out from his inner sanctum, down the wires and into a body woven from light. It was time to teach Elysium's most promising young murderer his final lesson.

Ω

The air in Simeon's dayroom had turned to liquid. He was gone; disjointed - cut off from the wet machine of his body. A pair of eyes stared, blank and wide as the skies over desert worlds.

A hand scuttled crabwise, tethered by its arm, until its hungry fingertips ran down their prey.

Snap

Pop

Hiss

Ragged breathing.

Numb fingers twitching, coated in pale beige powder…

Raw data crackled through the air, sparking through a set of wetwired points and into the meat of his brain. Slices of the Valle Crucis *Codex Martial*, images of Tadashi Murai…

"Is that what I think it is?" asked a glowing three-inch manikin in pressed cotton whites, climbing up onto the palm of the drug-fiend's hand. The tiny figure scowled, scuffing one patent-leather shoe in a snowdrift of chemicals. "You damn *irresponsible little…* Do you have any idea what you're up against tonight? Any concept of that damned machine's lack of mercy?"

Snap

Pop

Hiss

Focus…

Octavio Vanecke's benchtop holo flickered and blurred as Simeon zoomed in through it, down to the seething surface of his skin. His palm was a wasteland of dead tissue, insects and bacteria, each one wearing the Direktor's livid face. Fractalized.

"Blaire! Blaire!"

The Lord of the noble house wasn't listening. His eyes were rolled back behind a pair of diamond lenses, protective combat shades welded to his skull. They gave him the blank dark stare of a predatory insect – a million tiny facets winking back at the Direktor's anger.

The drugs came and peeled his mind back, but Vanecke was waiting.

"Is this getting through to you, you inbred prick? You have to be *ready*! The Hand of Kronos is *real*, and he's dying for you to make a single mistake…"

"So you've dealt w… with Murai? What about my sword? And

my… and my book? He's… he's my *vassal*, 'Tavio. Gotta. Gotta do what I say!"

He staggered. A whirlwind of exultation clawed up his spine, turning his handsome face into sweaty mask of flesh, slack and sallow on his skull.

"*Blaire! Snap out of it!*"cursed the manikin, swiping at his thumb with a tiny rosewood cane. "Dammit, you Kheptic turd, you have to stop fighting the uplink. And stop popping stunn when you're supposed to be integrating code!"

"Rather be code th'n meat, O'tavio. When the power's mine, I'm leaving this sack of organs behind…"

"You still need your brain intact, *my Lord*. The next phase is vitally important. With too much dope in your system, the Relic might not be able to integrate."

"Relax, Octavio," drawled Simeon, his eyes dim with euphoria. "You taught me this. You called it *meditation*. If I'm not prepared now, I never will be."

And oh, he was! His so-called peers were the same sweating, dripping meat-creatures as the peasant masses. The city needed cleansing, purifying, scouring away. The whole damn Subcity. But he was still unclean. *It irked him, itched under his skin… made him come back to the stunn when his own flesh felt like rotten meat hanging on his bones.*

"You've shown me the way, Octavio. I'll finish what you started, I promise you."

"My ass is on the line for this one too, Blaire," growled the little holo of Direktor Vanecke, blinking from his palm to his shoulder. "Your noble cousins won't forget what I tried to do. They want me for treason. And your title won't mean shit if the Machine eats you alive."

Simeon wasn't listening.

He was already imagining the fire.

With his face to the window he stared out over the roofs and arches, plazas and avenues of Elysium, his forehead pressed against the cool glass. It threw back his bitter little smile.

"I've seen the files, Octavio. I'll call you *Master* when the time comes. But the Hand of Kronos has nothing on me. I'm the best there ever was. You just need to have some fucking *faith* in your creation."

Blaire reached behind him to the table, pinching a measure of stunn between his fingers. They were ivory pale - utterly smooth, and marked with tiny scarred barcodes instead of fingerprints. Those digits had the precision of mekan biopsy forceps, rubbing the drug into his gums without so much as a tremor despite the thunderhead bruises which covered his knuckles.

"Trust me," said Vanecke "I have enough faith for both of us. You just have to remember that this time, the Game is real. Death means forever."

Blaire's reflection hovered like a phantom in the black glass as he scowled, pensive.

The Machine had given him his father's high cheekbones, his grandfather's sharp nose and blue-black eyes. Something else entirely had filled those eyes with cruelty, then welded them under glass.

"*Death* is one privilege I've never been allowed, Vanecke. You know that."

"I know that I've killed hundreds just to train you. That Valle Crucis monk was lucky to get away with a few broken ribs. And as for the endgame... well, there'll be death enough that night. Count on it. "

"I'm grateful, of course. And you *will* be rewarded, Octavio. Or should I say... *Master*."

That made him smile. The same oily, jagged smile he always wore when he got his own way. Satisfied, the little hologram collapsed in on itself. The next time Simeon saw him, Vanecke would be transformed. And so would he.

"*Master*... for as long as I can tolerate one."

Slow harpsichord and mournful violins followed him, music projected from flitting microamps crafted to resemble jeweled dragonflies. Their diamond-fiber ornithopter wings rippled the scented air, silent twin rainbows framing brushstrokes of silver. Simeon ran one hand along the glass, leaving fingerprint trails to evaporate behind him.

Visions of writhing bacteria sparked in Simeon's head.

His reflection lay over the view like a blurry hologram, cut up by the tracks of rain.

With a sudden motion his fist flashed out, impacting with a whipcrack sound, radiating a starburst of fissures across the windowpane. The glass was bulletproof, made to withstand sniper's micromissiles. But it still domed out in a halo of chips and shards, held together by a net of wires.

Blaire held his stance, shivering with murderous delight. The face he hated so much was gone, erased.

Slivered into a million leering replicas…

Fractal whirlpools spun off of him like smoke. Slow zoom. *Sparks behind his eyeballs, burning into soft tissue.* He got lit. The pulsing meat of his brain waxed positively neon.

Yet still, impossibly, Simeon smiled, his ego smashed to ruin as the bones in his shattered hand knitted smoothly back together.

And far away, Direktor Vanecke laughed, watching his pet through the kaleidoscope eyes of a jeweled chrome dragonfly.

All was in preparation. It was time to show Tadashi what he'd helped to create – even if it was the last thing the old fool would ever see.

Ω

There were creatures out on the skin of Lord Blaire's city. Not *real* people, or the same rarefied beings as the Council of Three Hundred who wanted Octavio Vanecke dead.

Kronos - the Cogitative Mechanism which ruled Elysium - considered them to be somewhere between cockroaches and domestic dogs on the evolutionary scale.

Kaito Kayzi was one of them, along with twenty-seven million others, in a genetic underclass who were not so much oppressed by the Machine as ignored. Oppression required effort, and the Subcitizens of Elysium just didn't warrant it.

But in imitation of their Guardian Engine they were studded and plugged with technology; as much as they could afford. Tech meant status, and just like in every city since a ruminating tribesman slapped one mudbrick on top of another, status meant *power*.

And unwanted attention.

"A King Value? Is that all we're worth to him?" rumbled a voice in Kaito's ear, coming in courtesy of the wires in his skull "You know how much shit we'll have to go through to make scratch on this one? Vladimir isn't in the habit of taking bags of pennies, K."

Kaito, sighed, hunkering back into the gelfoam seat of his motorcycle.

"It's not like we have choice, Jaqub. We're disposable to him, and he *knows* we know it. Eddie Tsien is bad news, for all that he's a little Bimburb shit."

"He's bad news because YOU gave him the control box to tweak those pet Cyben of his. It's like that old movie, that *Frankenstein*. You made the monster, and now it's got its hands around our fuckin' throat."

Kaito swerved and dipped through the traffic, his concussion armor sparkling with a thousand tiny red microsuns. It didn't help that Jaq was right, but still…

"Pointing your fat chrome finger don't play, Haszan." he spat, skidding wide around the tailgate of a wheezing steam-powered semi. "We're in this together. No tribe, no phyle, no hope… you know how it goes. The closest we have to a clan is being listed as 'bikers' on some government database."

"Bikers - shit!" laughed the big guy, over the clatter and roar of his own chopper's engine. "There hasn't been a real gang for four hundred years. I thought you were a *Magus* now, anyhow? Leaves me in a biker gang of one…"

"I'm not *official*, Jaq," said the Kayzi, as his bike shot the gap through a tight corrugated iron tunnel, emerging into blinding sunlight. "I'm just good at what I do - and I like to keep religion out of my 'mersive deck. Those Ashishim wireheads are crazy."

"Better tell that to all your other connections, K." chuckled Haszan, doing his own dance through traffic clear across town "If Vanecke's boys think you're selling them out, you'll be buried in more than one dumpster."

"Just be there on time, Haszan." he said, not even wanting

to think about his friend's warning. "Eddie's our main problem right now. And until I can figure a solution, we have to keep stringing him along."

Jaq grunted and cut the connection, leaving Kaito to concentrate on the road - and on the STX Saber he'd just boosted on a credit scam.

The Saber's front wheel was chrome-wirespoked, hissing across the transdome highway low and long on sprung, stretched forks. Crazy patterns flashed out from its whirling spokes, a shatterburst of neon reflections. Kaito lay back, twisting the throttle up there on the Saber's left apehanger, and he felt the ethanol-powered chopper bust 200.

Neon fragments, hot waves of silver slicked across his helmet visor...

But as usual his mind was elsewhere, only barely scanning the road ahead as he collapsed complex mathematics in his head.

Kaito regarded technology the way other guys his age thought about sex. It was always on his mind; he'd consider paying for anything a failure, and he made his best conquests when he was drunk. It was just that, in a town where the most advanced tech was given the status of holy antiquity, this made him the focus of some very monomaniacal creeps indeed.

Right now, for example, he was worrying at the edges of a problem that had come down the pipe from Octavio Brandolph Vanecke – a piecework contract to rip the viral defenses of a two-thousand-year-old cryo-reliquary. The hints at what was inside gave him cold sweats...

But hence, of course, the drugs. And the scarabs in his veins, to release those drugs to every nerve-ending simultaneously. They also told him how fast the bike was going, because it was far past the speed where a single twitch could snowball into a spectacular wreck. Kaito tuned a mean engine, too.

His mind was just as pared down and streamlined as the chopper; a ball of tissue caged and cradled in intelligent wires. The bio-onboard rig was linked through fiberoptics under his skin to a pair of modern plastic pistols, battery-operated magnetic railguns mercilessly miniaturized by some Reclamation zaibatsu. It began to arm them as Kaito's intracerebral G.P.S. zoomed in, overlayering reality with a textured wire-frame map of the city.

He ran through the plan again in his head, making sure all the angles were covered while railpistol status readouts flickered in the corners of his eyes.

The Saber bust 250 over a clear stretch of arching support girder, and crosshairs flashed red across the scarred concrete roadway. He trusted that his colleague wouldn't be late…

17 Aevum Oblivio
That's What Jesus Said

THEY WERE BACK on the Rock – Zhe stooped over a pale white operating table, the Kayzi looking down at himself with three neat little holes drilled into his forehead. His holographic avatar was still got up in hospital scrubs, but now he was wearing a crisp white homburg hat and mirrorshades as well.

"So this Vanecke was some kind of cog in the government? Some kind of feudal plutocrat?"

Kaito snapped his fingers, materializing another cigarette. All the cancer in the world couldn't touch him where he was now.

"He was scum like me, xeno. Just a different kind. He was the type of scum that rises to the top."

"And he was teaching some inbred nobleman how to fight? Did he think that dopehead Blaire could assassinate an A.I. with a pair of fancy steak knives?"

"That part of his plan was all about the Game. They weren't allowed to die, see? The Kheptarchs, they belonged to Kronos. Purebred Homo Sapiens. So they had a little game they played… a kind of orgy-meets-gladiators thing up in their tower estates. The winner got that."

Kaito pointed, and Zhe followed his blue-white finger, down through the diamondglass floor of the Cardinal Rock.

He saw the Earth, spinning through space under cover of its screwloose weather systems. Zoomed in on the North Atlantic – an oily cauldron lashed by storms… And there was Elysium, lost in the shadow of its cyclopean space-lev tower. In the jaundiced light it resembled a pile of discarded cathedrals, an ornate and gigantic refinery from some Victorian nightmare.

"Ugly. One of your guys called Speer once thought you could achieve 'Victory Through Superior Aesthetics'. What happened to that?"

"Sure, it ain't pretty, but it's ours," said the ghost of Kaito, blowing smoke-rings in a fractal swirl. "Since when did things like *you* have the right to go messing with things like us?"

"Since you started making us scared," Zhe replied. "I could

talk to you about gasoline and anthills right about here, but the analogy stinks. Not many ants char-grill their own damned ecosystem."

"You mean the Judgment? The War? You're about two thousand years late to be blaming me *for that mess...*"

"Funny... that's what Jesus said."

"About what?"

"About the Arbitrium Mundi. *Kid... you had to be there."*

Zhe let his mind's eye slither across seas and continents, his cortex socketed into the cameras of a brace of supersonic blade drones. The nuclear winter had rolled its poison glaciers back long ago, but what remained... the Technician shuddered.

The Laboritorium Thralls told him that this place had once seethed with humanity – their strip-joints and mini malls, miso stands, farms, factories and suburbs ramifying out from stark urban cores like coral. They'd burned it all down, until the last city left was this rusty hulk of a thing, this Elysium.

"You said it yourself, Kayzi. You called it a Judgment, but it wasn't by us, or by your gods. We've been watching you since your people first learned how to knap a flint, and ever since then it's been blood and rituals, right up to the big one."

"That? That wasn't for any kind of religion, man. That was money, plain and simple. Them that paid for the space-'lev and them that built it... well, they kind of had a falling out..."

"Blood and rituals, Kaito. And who ever said 'money' wasn't the name of your god?"

Zhe caught a crazed pixel-hash of memories then, feedback from the neural shunt. It was the image of an ancient Shaman, raising his staff to the heavens as his blood-slick acolyte decapitated a row of prisoners. Something had pressed up against the skin of reality then, hard and hungry enough to leave a mark. There'd been an Invigilator of the Multiplicity hiding in that little tribe, and he'd picked up the trace...

Blood and Rituals. All the way down to the here and now...

"Still, I never built the Terminus. I never helped them dig the Pit, or pave the Spillway. I just lived there for a while."

"What about your Kheptarchs, then?" asked Zhe, his hands

sliding over a set of holographic keyboards. "If you're right, Kronos would have given one of them such power..."

"Power you don't understand, I might add." Kaito snapped his fingers and the butt of his cigarette disappeared, only to be replaced by another. "If you believed in Manifest Dogma, you wouldn't be asking me. Or whatever it is you're doing out there..."

"And if it's true? If their damned book was actually bloody chapter and verse? That hardly makes it any better. Not when you consider that Simeon Blaire was the best among them."

"I'm not going to apologize for Blaire. Remember, I tried to kill the little prick!"

"As did all the rest of them. For all the good it did. I understand he's still alive, down there in the wilderness..."

"Just watch the threedeeo, alien. That's what I'm here for."

And it came on hard, blurring Zhe's mind across what felt like a mile of white-hot space. The Game. The Kheptarch's Game. Simeon Blaire's game.

Watch...

DOCUMENT INSERT - MULTIPLICITY ARCHIVES DEPARTMENT

Crycelium -

Crystal / Mycelium (n);

A form of engineered life designed originally for construction purposes, this organism was widely believed by pre-arbitrine conspiracy theorists to be of extraterrestrial origin.

Nothing could be further from the truth, of course... such a dangerous mistake bears the dirty fingerprints of human endeavor.

Crycelium is a lithophage crystalline web with a similar structure to the fungus Scoleobasidium. It also contains properties of lithotroph bacteria, in that it can process mineral ores into pure metals.

A conductive filament core propagates through the rapidly growing crystal structure, allowing electrical impulses to travel through the crycelium in the same way they do in the human nervous system. Pre-programmed crycelial structures are able to 'unfold' themselves into artificial ganglion clusters, and some medical specimens were even reputed to repair nerve damage, spinal injuries and brain trauma.

Of course, that's where the trouble started.

There are ample records from pre-arbitrine times of medical experiments with crycelium. Results varied from limited success to horrific failure. Out-of-control crycelial growth will tear apart a living body in minutes, hours, or days... the only question is one of time. The nightmare we live with today is of a self-replicating crycelial virus - hence the utter proscription of uncontrolled crystal-mycelial technology. To think that such a thing was once considered for military applications!

Inert or 'cold' crycelium is still used for bio-onboard computer integration, for the nerve-interface of prosthetics, and numerous other small tasks throughout Elysium.

'Hot', self-replicating crycelium is listed in the same category as nuclear weaponry, anthrax or sarin gas - 'unsuitable for private ownership'. Usually the promise of what happens to those who integrate the stuff with their flesh is enough of a deterrent to Archaeophiles. The pictures are even more graphic.

Sadly, some of our fellow citizens are either desperate or stupid enough to seek it out.

To that end, our Lord Engine Kronos has decreed that any and all recovered traces of crycelium from before the Iudicium Mundi are to be surrendered at once to the Guardians of the Sacristry. Possession is punishable by, at minimum, incineration.

Taken from 'A Compendium of the Technic Heresies' by Lutger Hammerdeane,

Elysian University Press

THE SLOPES OF Elysium bristled with rusted spires and turreted ramparts, castles of steel pierced by dripping pipes, chimneys and steeples mounting higher and higher toward the sickly clouds. Billows of sparks and smoke drifted among the mansard roofs of limpet-like tenement habs, and a million aerials clawed at the heavens. Every structure seemed locked in a frozen struggle with its neighbors for altitude.

The very tallest were the Kheptic Megatowers - blades of concrete and glass disemboweling the clouds a vertical mile above the Pit. Lights twinkled from the top of one of them tonight, blazing from the prison-palace at its very apex.

"Consolidated. The Trident of Steel. Come with us now, folks, as we bring you exclusive coverage of this, the twenty-three hundredth grand elimination of the Kronocultic Mysteries… better known to the fans at home as **Clone Deathmatch!***"*

The air around the trident was thick with oil-black zeppelins, sleek pods decked out with searchlights and cameras and belly-mounted screens. Their antennae sketched an insect-limbed scrawl against the orange glow of the sky - a thorny crown around the palatial home of His Kheptic Grace, Duke Ephraim Nar Olphis Gideon the Fourteenth.

Isambard Kingdom Brunel himself couldn't have designed it better – not even on a boatload of Afghan opium.

"Yes, we're set for a real barn-burner tonight – down to the wire, with three of Elysium's hottest noble gladiators ready to put flesh and bone on the line for your feudal adulation! Remember, just watching this broadcast is a sacred ritual of the Blessed Kronocult - praise be our Machine-Lord and the good ol' boys from Manifest Dogma…"

Every effort had been made by the Duke to blind his guests with opulence, to crush all of ancient Vegas into one vast baroque chamber. The watching threedeeo crowds couldn't help but be dazzled by the crystal mirrorballs, the scrawls of pulsing neon, the gilded censers and prismatic tapestries. And they certainly couldn't miss the row of severed heads dripping crimson on the mantelpiece, fresh enough to still look painfully surprised.

Normally, the sight of so many dead faces would have filled Ephraim with pride. But not tonight.

"Three percent! Three percent popularity! And after sixty years of sporting glory, as well. *Three percent*, and I'm still in the final round tonight, you young whelps. Youth and augments can't beat wisdom and bloody steel!"

Artificial flowers and creeping vines puffed incense all around him, but the temple still smelled of death. Robotic mekan and mind-wiped prisoners toiled for days after each engagement, but that funereal stench was impossible to scrub from the glistening stone. Thankfully it didn't come through in three-vee - although some of the diehard fans would probably have loved it.

"It's a sad day, Blaire. Sad. This used to be… used to be about *honor*. Virtue. Not… not bloody *ratings*! You hear me… young upstarts, high on fame… wouldn't have happened in my day…"

Duke Gideon's muttering blurred into the whine of stressed machinery as he paced, his feet an inch above the floor. In one heavy hand he clasped a glass of cognac the size of a basketball. In the other, a silver cut-throat razor. Blue light picked out his feet from below as repulsors labored, anchored to his tarsal bones. There were no footprints left behind him in the blood – it was his peculiar conceit to never touch the ground.

He'd just killed five people with his jewel-encrusted knuckles - the great cabochons and signets clenched around his hairy digits were crusted with drying gore.

"To shit-steaming hells with Vanecke and his three percent. If it was *me* he'd faced and not that fop Falchurch, I'd have given him a popularity rating to think about!"

Gideon's eyes were closed, his lids sagging under their own weight, and the razor hung from his fist like a shard of mirror-glass.

"If it was *you*," said Simeon Blaire, "we wouldn't have to listen to your warmed-over glories right now."

"Or *perhaps* a certain young lickspittle would know his place in the Hierarchy. You know he's just…"

Octavio Vanecke's machines worked the angles. They tuned out the Duke's bitter monologue, smothering him with title graphics. Music swelled, martial and ceremonious. Sixteen million paying viewers hunched in closer to their flickering threedeeo units. Tote tickets bearing the names of the three remaining players trembled in the hands of gamblers as their stats sizzled out across the bio-onboard band, direct into thousands of hardwired craniums.

"That's it folks – the signal is hot, the cameras are rolling, and the fix is in! Some of you are going to be much, much richer tomorrow morning, and by the grace of Kronos, one of these noble hierarchs is going to be one step nearer to the High Throne of Earth!"

A small army of boiler-suited techs behind the walls stubbed out their cigarettes and swilled down the dregs of their instant coffees. Innumerable cameras slid into place, zooming tight on the most beautiful face in the room.

She knew how to pull focus. She could bend the spite of other Khepts around her media presence like hot metal.

"I knew the *real* Octavio Vanecke," she said, running one fingertip down Simeon's cheek. "Who could forget a fascinating monster like that? You'd almost think a carefully-worded restraining order was his idea of *romance*."

Leynna's slanted amber eyes narrowed, her lips twitching into a cruel grin.

"But why would *you* care about dear Octavio's old life? If it weren't for his… *limitations*… he'd have no use for a thing like you, Simeon."

Her smile was wicked, a glassy-thin slice of fan service. Blaire wasn't buying it.

"His limitations in the Game, in commerce, or in bed? He matched Gideon here in two out of three, and as for *you*…"

Leynna didn't blush. The color slashed across her high cheekbones was powdered ruby, nothing more.

"You think I'd fall for some kind of Ayn Rand fantasy? People like Vanecke aren't *saints*, Simeon. We who are born to wealth don't see how it rots the hearts out of the lesser classes."

It was all in the eyes. The slide and interlock of her targeting systems betrayed her rage, tightening her focus in on his jugular.

Blaire watched her from behind his mirrored lenses, blind white light blazing in his skull.

(A second of blurred hallucination, Tadashi Murai performing an intricate kata with his gleaming blades...)

He licked his lips with a tongue suddenly as dry as tomb dust, and crushed up the feeling in one imagined fist.

"It wasn't his *heart* I was referring to. And even Ephraim will admit that his credit's nowhere near as rotten as his body might be."

Leynna sipped, her eyelashes fluttering in a haze of powdered jewels.

"I think he'd have been happier dead, after what happened to him." She spun the stem of her glass between two fingers, frowning. "I'll admit he was an intriguing beast before the... *incident*. But the disease showed through in the end. He's sick now. Perverse. *Morbid.*"

And obsessed with Simeon Blaire as well - that much was whispered in the virtual salons of the Clique. He caught her looking out of the corner of one amber eye to where Gideon fussed over his favorite preparation of cognac and laudanum. And he caught himself wanting to kill that fat old fool first, to keep her for himself. If only there were no cameras here...

"Just keep talking, Simeon. The Game will be back on in just a minute, and then I'll teach you to hold your tongue."

He turned back to the Lady.

"You think *his* fascinations are morbid? Look around you, Leynna. What do you think our little contest is about?"

"This is all about *permanence*, Simeon. Resilience. This is the faith that Kronos has in our perfection."

Her eyes changed. The glitter of recombining metal deep in each iris transfixed him...

He ran into her stare mid-sentence, and he held his breath.

Then the timer floating above them clicked over to zero, and the Game was back in session.

Blaire was moving before Leynna could so much as blink. A cut-throat razor spun past him, paring the tiny transparent hairs from his cheek. It cut deep into the marble wall, shuddering like a tuning fork.

"Ohh, you're a slippery one, Blaire! Did Octavio teach you that move?"

Orange flames lit up the room, setting off the tawny amber in Leynna's eyes as she launched herself off her divan. A spray of blood flew from the Duke's temple, cut by flying shrapnel as a gold-handled stiletto shattered his glass of cognac.

"Did he teach *you* to take out the hardest target first? Or are you just playing with your food?"

Time slipped; greasy microseconds. Gideon's platinum teeth flashed purple and lurid red in the firelight, his gums black with drug abuse. The cameras ground it out, tight on his leering face - on the hidden weapon telescoping from his sleeve with the click of secret springs.

"Come on, Simeon. There's no shame in defeat... not after so long. I'm saving you from the tedium of rule, boy!"

Crescent-moon razors locked into position, glistening with soporific poison, and Gideon's raw-liver lips pulled back from his teeth. The *khamtar* sickle-axe was his favorite instrument of death, and he'd saved this one for the final kill.

"Don't tell me about tedium, old man! I've had to listen to your ramblings *all night!*"

Air slicing, wheeling slow figure-eights... the sparkle of hypnotizing steel flashed in the sudden gloom. Metal plates in the dome were sliding, shifting to cover the stained glass from a squall of toxic rain.

"Then come and get your three percent, whelp! We're all waiting to see the color of your marrow!"

Shadowfall.

Platinum canines and incisors flashed, and Ephraim Gideon sprung into battle. A scuffle of fast and stealthy steps tracked him in the dark, his feet never touching the floor.

"AND THE FANS ARE GOING WILD IN THE STREETS!

Simeon cursed, moving liquid-silent in the shadows.

The *khamtur* was an edge, but it was within the bounds of etiquette. As was the crycelial button he now tore from his coat, flattening at his fingerprint's coded touch into a monoblade shuriken. His bio-onboard computer systems registered the tiny weapon, sending the signal to prime its edges with a certain fast-acting shellfish toxin.

Leynna.

(Oh why does nerve toxin make me think of thee...)

He locked eyes with her as he spun away, cartwheeling before a hissing sussuration of axe-strokes. Hand over hand.

Deeper shadowfall;

Her eyes dark and dilated, an understanding between them;

Left, and pull back the arm, the axe avoiding his flesh by a finger's width.

Gideon was wild and high-swinging, bloody saliva flying from his lips in slow-motion whiplashes. His eyes rolled and blazed as his feet slid independent, picked out in the dark by blue magnetic pulses...

Then the apertures slammed closed. The light was suffocated, drowned under night-sight green. His final vision; Duke Gideon halfway up the tapestried wall, his axe whirling as he leaped out into the air.

The rain fell like hammers - on the dome, on the skull of Simeon Blaire singing with hot wires. The long muscles in his arm snapped forward as his eyes closed, the course of fate determined.

Leynna spun sideways as Gideon's sickle-axe came down in one final butcher-stroke, the shuriken cleaving its metal haft and whickering through his neck in a brief spray of red. Simeon saw her eyes again, in the second the Duke fell, and he knew that their understanding was over. She had a blade flashing in one slim hand, fingers the color of marble shot through with gold.

It flew end over end in slow motion, slicing apart the incense smoke as Simeon turned, falling backwards in a controlled dive.

The stiletto grazed his back as he slid across the tiles, stopping himself with one bloody hand against the wall. Five tiny barcodes in crimson - his fingerprints. But this body was nothing but disposable meat. The pain focused him, screwed his mind down into the now, tight on a flash of silver in the gloom. His calculations had to be correct…

She heard the noise; tink. tink. And she saw it a second too late, a shimmer in the air, a tiny wobble in its spin from striking the walls.

"Oh yes. *Perverse,*" she said, as the shuriken made a thin straight incision into her chest, carving deep into her spine.

In the second before her mind registered her mortality, Simeon felt himself locked in the twin arclamps of her stare, his victory made pyrrhic. Her mouth was twisted in a sardonic half-smile as she collapsed, face down in her own blood.

Ω

The visio in the gambling hall wasn't threedeeo.

It was cheap-ass woven carbon screens stretched across cardboard boxes, their fiberoptic matrices jacked into portable datablocks.

Suitable for the lowbrow crowd, perhaps, but not to the liking of Jaqub Haszan.

As the tinny speakers attached to the twodeeo rang out Blaire's victory song he waded through the cheering punters toward the pay window. Haszan stood at least a head taller than any of the Subcitizens in the place; he shoved his way to the front leaving fear and anger in his wake.

Haszan was profoundly mongrel-ethnic; a genetic patchwork of mideastern, euro and asian strains all rolled into one huge green-eyed bulk. He kept his dirty blond hair cut raggedly short and his beard long - a three-foot bootlace-thin goatee wrapped in black electrical flex. The coil was looped back over his shoulders, and sported a chrome crescent moon and star which pinned to his lapel. Tiny metal icons dangled along the flex like sneakers from a telephone wire.

He shifted the crowd with the direction of his gaze, homing in on somebody very, very unlucky.

The man behind the window sported a crudely assembled cybernetic eye and a tangled mass of surgical scars. His smile was a set of aluminum dentures, inset with cheap gemstones.

HI said his large gold nametag - MY NAME IS FELDON.

Feldon was feeling good about his franchise from Slay-Per-View GmbH and Omnivasive.

But not *that* good.

When he saw Haszan his remaining eye widened with terror. He took off his cap with one hand while making the sign of the cross with the other.

"So they fixed you up with another eye, did they?" asked Haszan, leaning up on the counter. His forearms were inked with flames, battery-driven skin animations.

Red light played over Feldon's pasty features.

"It was an accident." stammered Feldon, cringing away from the flamelight. "Don't believe those rumors about the Liquid Tong. They never took my eye …you can tell Mister Vincenzo I never deal with them …"

Haszan shook his head. "They already called him and apologized. They said this one was ours to fix up."

Feldon made a small yipping noise.

As he was about to make a dash for the back Haszan's cybernetic hand came through the chipboard wall and got him by the hair.

"Damn you Jaqub!" shouted Feldon, thrashing like a hooked fish "You're a pusher, not a hitman."

The sawnoff looked like a pistol in Haszan' huge hand, but surprisingly large when pressed to Feldon's forehead.

"I'm diversifying," said Haszan, and pulled both triggers.

The crowd ran. The projectors shook and skipped.

Cameras zoomed.

Huge and ghostly, the face of Lord Blaire loomed over his shoulder.

Ω

Simeon looked directly into the camera as he left the room, leaving the lifeless body of Baroness Mendelev-Singh smiling in a pool of blood. The victorious Lord left the dome via a vermilion carpet suspended above the floor, borne up by ranks of tiny antigrav mekan in the shape of baroque cherubim.

Had she let him win? Leynna was a complex creature - an *Unstable* - but the Game was sacrosanct. Nothing as human as *emotion* should cloud the judgment of a Player…

Mekanical brass hands peeled off his bloody coat, while nozzles in the mouths of jade gargoyles sprayed on his casual sweater and tie. Unlinked fibers detonated like tiny fireworks around him as the fabric wove and hardened.

Simeon knew what she was - how she'd been dragged along in Direktor Vanecke's slipstream when he rose to power. The thought of those attentions being turned on him made him squirm with discomfort.

He felt cheap and disposable. He felt the feeling, he cringed as he imagined slim fingers twisting his dials. They did.

He felt the neuroprobes, and he felt elated, walking into the highly televised postgame lounge with a manic smile plastered across his face.

He'd made his deal, and this was how he paid.

Only a little more time now. Just the small-talk and threedeeo posing of the *Apres-Mort*…

Twin pillars engraved with grinning skulls framed a door across the room – the Gates of Rebirth which led to a biolab full of clone tanks and memory-dump modules. Simeon could imagine fluids bubbling through a maze of glass tubes in there, knotted cables pulling free from two hundred and ninety-nine spinal interlocks. It was a long time since he had walked through the Gates and been Reborn.

"Cousin. Noble blood! Congratulations!" It was Duke Gideon, and he was all smiles, his fresh new body unmarked by needle-scars and blisters. "This is a great day. A momentous day. I hope you're ready for the throne, Blaire!"

Simeon narrowed his eyes as Ephraim Nar Olphis' mindwiped slaves knelt before him, forming a throne of living human flesh.

Duchess Sebring took his hand as he stepped up across the backs of his lessers.

"So… you'll forgive that three percent?"

"What's said in the game stays in the game, Cousin. Bitterness is for the peasantry, and regrets are for the poor. Come – drink! To eternity and Manifest Dogma!"

"Indeed," said Blaire, accepting the chalice of victory from another empty-eyed serf in white leather. "To our Guardian Engine, and the Kheptic Blood."

He watched them with predatory intensity as they lifted their cups to their lips – these three hundred lords and ladies of privilege. The ritual toast would sound so damned hollow tomorrow morning… but by then it would be too late.

All of them bowed their heads to him, and drank. Even proud Leynna Mendelev-Singh, with a sly little smile on her lips. A single drop of blood-red liquor beaded at the corner of her mouth, and she cuffed it away, her eyes never leaving his neck.

"To the Kheptic blood. Pure, fierce – and *uncontrolled*." The sardonic tone made Simeon's hands crook into claws. His fingernails bit into the warm flesh of his throne. "Praise Kronos, we are *incorruptible*. Free from scarcity and wealth, as the good book teaches. Not like the lower orders at all."

The man who spoke stepped forward now, and Kheptarchs of the Clique backed away from him, clearing a pariah-circle between him and the throne. He was tall and thin, his clothes cut with military severity, and his hair was gathered into an onyx-studded topknot which glistened with oil.

"I couldn't have put it better myself," said Blaire, leaning forward from his seat of bodies. "But of course, Cousin Lysander, there's no need to preach the Dogma here. None of the Clique have anything but kind contempt for the underclass…"

"And what about Vanecke? He's one of them! He's one of…"

Angry muttering rippled through the room. Simeon stilled it with a gesture and a tight, fragile smile.

"This is neither the time nor place, my Lord Jaegenn. That place was in the Game, in which I seem to have bested you again." He stepped down from his throne, opening his arms wide. This was what his people expected of him – grace in victory. "Come now. We who stand to rule should never quarrel. Let's forget this unpleasantness… at least until next time we meet in the arena."

The nervous laughter of the Clique was like rustling paper, thin and far away. But Lysander Jaegenn's eyes flicked left and right, calculating… and he made his choice. This wasn't the time or the place, not in front of his noble peers. He stepped forward into Simeon's embrace, clapping him across the shoulders in the clinch.

"I'll be ready, Blaire," he whispered, his lips a razor's width from Simeon's ear. He could feel the Kheptarch's breath hot on his own cheek.

"I'll be looking forward to it, Lysander. Really."

They broke apart to a smattering of applause, smiling for the cameras. But the air between them hummed and sparked, charged with venom.

And Lysander Jaegenn slipped a tiny barb back into the cuff of his tunic, raging against his own pride. The delayed toxin could never be traced, and nobody would blame him for what would seem to be a drug overdose. But his father had beaten honor into him, with the edge of a hardwood practice sword. And that part of him couldn't do it.

Smiling, he raised his cup, and toasted the puppet-wretch he hated more than anything else on earth. And from atop his throne of living meat, Simeon Blaire looked down, already imagining himself a god.

Two-hundred and ninety-nine sightless, lifeless heads adorned the walls of a room bedecked in luxury and blood behind him, a room on which a pair of heavy steel doors closed, sealing off the temple for another night.

Beyond them in the deepening dark the biotects' machines ground on, flashes of green raking the gloom as they picked out the lidar signatures of flesh. With which to play the game another day.

Ω

The finance processor on Emmanuel's thin glass desk chimed; payment had been received.

Two hundred and ninety-nine new cloned bodies, and a healthy injection of cash into his already overflowing coffers.

Emmanuel Third Lancaster was a voyeur. He never Played.

Tonight he was dressed in ebony black, a shade so deep it scattered into indigo under the lights. Not cloth, but *flesh* - the body of an African warrior from three thousand years ago, naked but for a kilt of crisp white cotton. This was the power of his monolithic corporation; Universal Wetsystems, the clone-masters.

Power and wealth, however, came with their own problems. One of them was on the line right now.

"I love it, Mister Lancaster" hissed an unnatural voice in his head, a piston-driven sussuration. "The additions to the Blaire clone are perfect. He has grown up to be quite an exquisite monster."

"*Thank you*, Director Vanecke." replied Lancaster, his microcrafted face twisting with distaste. "I take it you will send me the next payment for the free-radical scrubbers soon. And the control crycelicules. It should all fit in a little phial …the four hundred thousand *will* be in my account by Wednesday."

Vanecke still managed to laugh back at him, even though his flesh was utterly nerveless and dead.

"Trust me Lancaster, the money's already there. I'd hardly be spending it on hookers, would I?"

Lancaster cut the connection, infuriated. That upstart Direktor of Broadcasting wasn't even one of the High-Born. As such he could never be cloned like his noble betters – for him death would be utterly final.

And it wasn't too far away, now.

All he had to do was deal with another Subcity mogul - Don Vincenzo Vexx, a man as warm and friendly as a wounded shark. Now *there* was a good reason to pour himself another drink. His raw dislike of the Director was amplified by another problem with the 'Vanecke Account'.

It came down to a single missing pod from one of the storage freezers of his vast manufactorium. The very specialized theft of a modified Blaire clone, like the one Lord Simeon's intellect now inhabited.

It had gone Down Town, into the lair of the Ashishim. And, if military intelligence reports were to be believed, it had come back for more.

"I hope you got all of that," said the Arch-Biotect, his voice strangled with self-control. The dark figure standing behind the holoscreen moved forward into the light; holographic itself, it was a shadow painted across the office wall in robes of satin.

"Of course, Emmanuel. And you needn't worry. He'll never get past me… not in my own spire. Not by my own rules."

The shadow wore its hair in an oiled top-knot, long strands of black wire coiling down from it like snakes. His eyes were sunken and hooded, flashing like tiny mirrors as he smiled.

"And yet… you couldn't strike. I have good reason to doubt you, boy. *I* haven't failed."

The holo-figure snarled, drawing a long thin barb from the sleeve of his tunic. He threw it down out of the picture in disgust.

"Your plan was subtle, Biotect – but it was *utterly* dishonorable. I'll make sure he suffers at my hands, but poison… outside the game, Lancaster! Why not just use an orbital strike?"

"If only!" sighed Emmanuel. "I wish it was so easy to erase you Kheptic fools! But very well. You'll have another opportunity to destroy him – honorably. Fail this time, though, and I'll be forced to use my own resources. Revenge, they say, is a dish best served cold. I disagree. I think it's best served *at your own fucking table!*"

The black-robed holo couldn't resist a little moue of distaste. No wonder that this sexless, ageless thing had dealt with sub-scum in the first place.

"You can take care of Vanecke, biotect. The more mess you make, the better," said Lord Lysander Jaegenn. "But Blaire is *mine.*"

Ω

Another round over.

Another night of bloodshed and etiquette and little sandwiches without the crusts on. More statistics and replays for the fans.

And for one very persistent watcher, a little more data for its ongoing study; its experiment in creating a worthy human being. This was how they had chosen to compete with each other, and Kronos wasn't inclined to interfere. It was enough that it kept its patience, watching over the Earth from its Core in the Cardinal Rock.

That metal-studded rock was the lure which twitched above Kaito Kayzi, but it wasn't built for him. This was for one of the pure; a sky-castle of silver and blue marble from which to rule a broken world.

Simeon lusted for the hidden power locked up at its heart. Octavio Vanecke would gladly kill every man, woman and child on Earth to get his hands on it.

But Kronos cared as much for the ambitions of individual humans as a dog did for the dreams of its fleas. It had been built for a greater purpose.

The machine's satellites remembered, deep in their shielded magnetic hearts, a time when the entire city had teemed with commerce and industry, orderly and functional and safe. Indeed, many of them recalled a time when the whole world was filled to the seams with humanity; a time when there were said to be too many people for the ecosystem to support.

There's no mechanical concept of guilt; none of remorse. But many of the satellites also remembered the targets to which they delivered their nuclear payloads.

Kronos had watched impassively as its warheads rained down on the Old Democracies of Earth. Orbital particle-beam weapons had sliced through the skyscrapers of New York, bringing tons of concrete down like rain. Before the rubble even hit the ground the blast-wave of a thermonuclear strike ablated it away to roiling plasma, leveling acres of buildings. The island of Hong Kong was razed down to the waterline; Tokyo suffered a fate ten thousand times worse than that of Hiroshima and Nagasaki. Multiple-re-entry warheads burst open like daisyheads of fire above Moscow and Berlin, Beijing and Calcutta, a grim fireworks display for the screaming millions before they were reduced to windblown ashes.

And the retaliation of those doomed nations was just as terrible.

Whole floating arcologies were evaporated, leaving nothing but slicks of pollution to mark their passing. Spaceborne habitats ruptured, condemning tens of thousands to freeze or boil in merciless vacuum. Artificial stars fell from heaven, trailing comet-tails of radioactive death; the twisted remains of in-system dreadnoughts ripped to shreds by smart torpedoes and hydrogen masers.

In the end, when all seemed lost, somebody changed Kronos' program.

It was given one final order.

And on the basis of that last, desperate communiqué it had rebuilt its city - Terminus Afrika. It had created *Elysium*, a social laboratory in which it would raise a human being worthy of its power.

The bright razorcut of steel which was the space-'lev caught the sun, plunging down through a choking atmosphere to where its stem broke the waves. About its roots was clotted an island reclaimed from its own effluvia; the great shantytown of the Reclaimed Territories. From above there seemed to be no divide between the bladed megatowers and the ruptured, decaying Subcity, even though at street level they were as different as a Sao Paulo *favela* and Saville Row.

But Kronos knew. It kept its clinical subjects pure and kept its breeding program on track.

This was what they contested for, these Kheptarch Lords.

Because only one of them could claim supremacy, and put an end to Kronos' two-thousand-year-old master program. In ten centuries it had worked out enough about their nature to sum it up quite succinctly.

They struggled, one against the other, because there was only one throne, and that was the path to becoming a god. But they chose to conduct that struggle as a bloody, vicious and homicidal spectacle because *that* was the way of human beings.

Compared to mutually assured destruction, it was a slight improvement.

Kronos, however, was still glad that *he* (having chosen a gender from certain ancient religious paintings) had been built with near-infinite patience.

DOCUMENT INSERT: MULTIPLICITY ARCHIVES DEPARTMENT

Celebrants:

(Grief Division Order Militant)

The Law was very clear. Within Elysium, as
without, there must be death for life to
continue. It was all bound up in a well-presented
report, with neat buzzwords like 'pro-active'
and 'innovative bio-management strategies' and
'resource paradigms'. There was also the question
of 'not enough food' and 'too much sewage.' War
had shrunk the world down to a single city, and it
would have to be brutally self-sufficient.

Human lifetimes would have to be curtailed
somehow, and the only answer (considering Kronos'
proclivities) was massive program of eugenics.

It wasn't about race or eye color or culture. It
was a lottery, pure and simple.

Undemocratic as this sounds, out in the RT life
expectancy ran only about 45 to 50; most SubCits
never questioned the simple math.

As for anyone out on the mainland or in the Pit
who was over the age of forty - he or she was
regarded as a wizened and shamanic being of
preternatural vitality. Either that or as a witch,
which amounted to much the same thing - but with a
forecast of immolation and torture.

Despite its logical foundations the system had its
recusants.

The Celebrants, Order Militant of the Grief
Division, were armed and mandated to reap the
souls of the recalcitrant 'dead'.

This became known as Natural Causes.

In return, the Machine extolled the dogma of hybrid evolutionary vigor, and promised to assimilate Citizens' memories and experiences into its own storage strata when they were 'retired'.

Some took comfort in this fact.

Most, the Celebrants would tell you, tried to run.

Dalgiesh Wrynstedd 'The Proud History of the Orders Militant'

Elysian University Press

TECHNICIAN'S NOTE - LIES! ALL LIES! AND NOW I KNOW WHY IT NEEDED THEM DEAD…

Gharfos Nyl, Hierophant Grade Three

BROKEN TOWN.

No-mans-land with a view of the black Atlantic; a last-ditch straggle of leaning tenements and sagging 'facs before the Reclaimed Territories proper. It was the end of the line for burn-out cases and fringe dwellers – a maze of rent-free squats and choked-up alleys holding the immense buttress roots of the Subcity on its shoulders like Atlas.

Rain sifted down into the lower levels through a slicing mesh of wires, crosswalks and feeder pipes. It dripped black, green with algal slime or bloody with rust. Plastic clothes ran in Technicolor down in the streets, where the locked doors of a tiny convenience shack were stained from innumerable downpours.

Nobody came running when they heard the gunshots. But then again, nobody down here was that stupid.

In a dirty mirror Kaito saw oiled black hair spiked and messed from wearing headgear. Sunken eyes, rimmed with metal where Ashishim Interfacers had expanded his vision. He pulled at the bruise-purple bag under his left eye with one finger, frowning.

There were lines and creases there which he never used to notice. But this extracurricular shit… it was making him *old*. Old, and tired, and prone to fits of nightmare insomnia.

About a quarter of a lifetime, and it had come to this.

Again.

Kaito had just robbed the King Value at gunpoint - not really where he saw his life at twenty-five, but a situation he was getting used to. Haszan, (the rest of the strike force all on his own) lay heavy on the blood–slick counter, folds of trenchcoat spread like angel wings around him as he popped sugar candies off his thumb and into his mouth. There was a big ol' Magnum Express sawnoff lying on his chest like a buried crusader's broadsword, and a two-foot hole in the King Value wall, courtesy of the above.

The last of the drugs which yesterday's jack had bought them hammered and rampaged through their brains, a whirling storm of euphoria.

This hit would pay for tomorrow - but that wasn't exactly why they were here.

"You ever think we're gonna get to the end of this?" asked Kaito, pushing his fingers through his scraggly mane of hair. "You think he's gonna let us go?"

"Why don't we wait for him and ask?" rumbled Jaq, his fleshy hand pinched up over his eyes. The other one - the dangerous one - was trailing down toward the floor. "I'm sure a genius like you can work out the odds that we'd walk outta here."

Neither the neophyte Magus or the part-time hitman were gamblers. They preferred to work in certainties, by the gram or the kilo. They never used to be petty crooks, either - but things had changed.

"Tsien doesn't pay us for waiting around, Haszan. He wants a, a goddamn *blitzkrieg*, right?" Kaito was pacing, nervous, his face reflected full- frontal in the shattered lens of a video camera. A plastic sign reminded shoppers that it might be loaded with film. "We're supposed to grab the cash, leave the alphanumeric, and get the hell out."

"You want this shit to end, you gotta get pro-active," answered Haszan, propping himself up on his elbows. "The way I see it, we only get out of this mess when Officer Eddie catches a bullet."

Kaito eyed the door, the concrete mess outside the door, and then Haszan again.

Surely he didn't mean that they should get in an actual *gunfight* with the police? They had Cyben, and mekan, and a whole grab-bag of nasty treats for idiots who tried that on for size.

"Just forget I asked, then," snapped the twitchy little biker. "He's paying us to manufacture crime scenes, Jaq. If he catches those 'mystery gangers' who he's always after then his paycheck dries up - but *we're* in line for a mind-wipe!"

"You couldn't pay me enough to hit that slimy little cop piece of shit" continued Haszan, throwing the cardboard packet back over the counter "He's got that vindictive look about him.

Anyway, *I'm* mister fuckin' responsible. I'm working through my anger-management issues 'constructively' these days."

Like when that poor unfortunate clerk tried to get the drop on you? thought Kaito.

"Responsible or not, Jaq," he said. "That 'slimy little cop piece of shit' was *this* close to your drug business, and he'd just *love* to send us down to the lobo factory. So, sure, let's *give him an excuse!*"

His nose wrinkled, acutely aware of the smell of blood. The hole in the wall of this piece of inner-city real estate was edged in red, a halo of overkill. The idiot wasn't paid enough to try and draw down on a couple of jackers like them. But he'd pulled that .45 out from under the counter anyway, and then… Kaito's mind slipped, gears whirring as he stared at the mess. He'd been born with an innate mathematical ability all out of proportion to his scrawny frame, so he could calculate to a fraction of a second how long it would take the Compliance Division to arrive at the scene of a homicide.

"We wouldn't even be here if it wasn't for you! You and your damn hardware…"

"Me? You're the one who caught his fucking attention, Haszan! I was just trying to buy our way out of a corner… so screw you."

That tipped the balance. Kaito saw Jaq's muscles tense, his pupils shrink to pinpoints. He clenched his fists – one meat, the other steel.

"Remember how you saved my ass from those Confederate hunters, Kayzi? I said I'd pay you back. Well… now we're even. Anyone else, and…"

Haszan jerked his thumb over one shoulder at the mess behind the counter. He never saw that Kaito had flipped off both his safety catches. But he caught himself short, screwing down his anger with an effort of will.

"Sorry. It's just… withdrawal. That, and the Division. They're coming, Jaq. It's all over the net."

"O.K," said Haszan, cramming another few snacks into his pocket for the road. "We'll go. But for the record, I don't think they want to stop us. Not now. 'Specially not *that* one - he's got a good thing going here." He dusted off the shotgun; a throwdown - a present for the Div. "Don't matter how many people we kill. Don't even signify."

He was cramming his whole coat full of treats, like some kind of seven-foot hyperactive kid, sour snakes and jellies and liquorice straps spilling from pockets usually full of needles and blood money.

"But candy... well, now *that's* important. C'mon, this guy don't need it where he's going,"

Jaqub might be built like a nuclear bomb shelter and as homely as the same, but he had one inane and infectious grin. There was a moment when the Kayzi's face grew tight and sad and *old*, stretched by forces of memory and guilt. But he couldn't let it show. He slapped Haszan across the shoulder, popping a single great hot-pink gobstopper into his mouth.

"Ath awways, y got yrr priorities stwait. C'mon!"

They were back on the same de-facto team.

Kaito pocketed his pistols and a fat wad of hyperinflated thousand-dollar bills, the eyes of Commissioner Slade smiling from a face scarred by the watermark. Slades weren't worth much – hell, most people didn't even bother with paper currency anymore. But a roll this fat was still enough for the Stunn.

And Haszan was wrong. The thin echo and wail of sirens was abroad on the metal-scented breeze as they stumbled outside. Their bikes were still chained to a giant antitank caltrop left over from the Seven Hours War, one of a corroded and paint-daubed line which marched off into the shadows. Those incoming Pigwagons would have to pick their way through this kind of ground-level steel-reinforced clusterfuck all the way over. Kaito and Haszan would have an easy getaway on two wheels apiece .

The STX Saber started on the first touch of Kaito's bio-onboard link; integrated. Haszan kickstarted his Reclamation-made imitation Triumph once, twice, thrice. It roared into life, blasting plumes of oily purple smoke.

Last tricks.

Kaito crunched numbers, compiled mentally, and scribbled a long alphanumeric on a greeting card which Haszan taped to the front door under King Value's royal cartoon smile. "I missed you yesterday." it read, all balloon-writing and pastels. "I missed you today. Tomorrow I'm buying a telescopic sight for my rifle."

(a7dh fh57 239f jh57 cxfn t8cj h00d h4hf 877en)

The Divwagon crashed the scene as their dust blew, and by the time the first jackboot hit the deck they were pushing 300 out over the transdome ring.

This was becoming familiar.

Ω

A telephone was ringing in the dark; not visio, not even modern in its design.

A black, antique bakelite phone was ringing, with the tin-can rattle of real miniature bells.

A man in immaculate pinstripes answered it, and the aesthetic became clear. This was a phone you could beat a man to death with; this was the hand which would do it.

He had a face like a sallow ball of dough – heavy jowls rough with stubble, eyebrows locked in a death-grip over his broken nose. His hair was pomaded back to within an inch of its life, black and oily as molasses. On his hairy fingers gold rings with the heft of knuckle-dusters clustered like limpets, smothering the scars and abrasions of a lifetime spent dishing out savage beatings.

The man, one Vincenzo Vexx, was in *character*.

"Yes, Mister Lancaster," he said into the empty silence of a large and shadowed room. "Enough adrenochrome to float a coffin in," he said, his grin lighting the gloom momentarily.

Vincenzo's voice was reedy and stiff. He was a smoker.

"And I get howmany bodies in exchange?"

Mister Lancaster confirmed the order, distaste written all over his voice.

The smile was more genuine this time.

"*Grazie*, Mister Lancaster. You'll get your *stupificente* - I need make only one call."

The phone cut out, its connection closed by the hand of

Emmanuel Third Lancaster more than two miles above.

And deep in Vincenzo's gut, in the hot warmth of his living flesh, tiny machines labored to contain his cancer. The pain would make most folks beg for a bullet. Today, he couldn't give two shits. Today, he was going to settle two very large accounts with one meeting.

But first…

Ω

In a dome built from wafer-thin screens as big as billboards Octavio Vanecke watched and waited. His current entertainment; a security tape from inside an innocuous-looking convenience store.

The atmosphere was kind of tense – a huge hulking giant of a man was holding out a shotgun in one hairy paw, holding it as if it was a toy pistol. Next to him a twitchy little dude in bike armor hammered on a thick black remote control – he was blitzing the alarm systems, and probably thought he'd got all the cameras too.

Now…this was the part he was watching for.

See the clerk snap – the look on his face switching from terror to animal savagery in a single frame.

See his hand move liquid fast, under the counter, pulling out a big black slab of handgun.

There – the big guy has it, he rolls with the movement, grabbing the clerk's wrist, continuing its arc and making the pistol swing wide up over his shoulder, a bullet blazing out way off target to punch a hole in the roof.

The shotgun came up under the clerk's armpit and BLAM, a textbook battlefield amputation - but the shooter wasn't done. He flipped the sawnoff in the air, racked the slide as he caught it, and as his little compadre screamed silently in black-and-white he put the muzzle to the bleeding clerk's chest and gave him a lead injection.

A twin-barreled pump was a terrible thing to use at point blank range; hardly a weapon of finesse. But Octavio liked this brute's style. He ticked a box, happy that the big guy was on

78

his payroll. This was definitely going in with all his martial-arts footage – one had to keep up with the times, and these days the soul of a samurai could just as easily be his sawnoff.

Simeon was really gonna enjoy this one.

Ω

"You helped Feldon Roberts. You were moving product for him. And you've got names, addresses, *numbers*." It wasn't a question. The red ember at the tip of Vincenzo's cigar hovered in the darkness; a pull on the stogie lit up his craggy face for a second, the flat black gleam of his eyes. "So how about you tell me what you know." The Don chuckled, tapping a core of ash onto his prisoner's upturned face. "I won't tell you I'll let you go - 'cause I'm an honest man. But I won't tell Knuckles here to turn up the pressure. I'll do it clean. Myself."

Vincenzo flicked his cuff, and a flat slab of chrome slipped down into his hand - an old-fashioned automatic pistol. His little twentieth-century-style calling card.

Skip Tragian knew he was in trouble. Big trouble. He should never have gotten in with Feldon's crazy plan - and now here he was, with his head clamped in a mekan's vise-like grip, sweating and twitching with piss dripping down his leg.

"I swear... Mister Vexx, I swear... I didn't know they was working against you. I didn't know Feldon was with the Liquid Tong! Please... "

His voice racked up to a tortured squeal as Vincenzo gave the signal, and Knuckles brought the clamp down hard, making Skip's skull creak and fracture. The big mekan wasn't Cogitative - hell, it was nothing but a walking drill-press. But the name, daubed across its chestplate in red spraypaint... well, it helped to set the mood.

"Hows about we trade, son?" said Vincenzo, hunkering down next to his captive. Blood dripped from Skip's ears as he sobbed in agony. "I'll tell you this for free - the guy who clipped Feldon was Jaqub Haszan. He was more than happy to do it."

"Haszan?" groaned Tragian, his lip trembling as he spoke "Not... not him! I thought he'd sworn off killing! I thought, after that bloodbath with the Final Reich…"

"Oh yeah. You heard about that?" grinned Don Vexx, leaning in close until the tip of his cigar almost burned Skip's pallid skin. "He fed them their own balls, Tragian. Cut their fingers off with a fusion saw. Shit, the Kommandant was still alive when the cops found him three days later. No skin, just one big weeping scab… and he's a pharmer too. Don't like competition."

"P-please!" stammered Skip, his eyes rolling in their sockets to follow Vincenzo as he paced. "I'll tell you! Just call him off! I don't want to die like them!"

Don Vexx snapped his fingers, and Knuckles extended an jointed steel arm from its carapace, its tip terminating in a two-inch router. It came down to rest, feather-light, against Skip Tragian's forehead.

"It was Lancaster! Emmanuel Third Lancaster! The Tong was a front, a cutout! He wanted a taste of the Chrome that was coming through. Said it was Khept' grade stuff - whatever that mea…"

But his words were cut off by the whine and crack and grind of a neat little hole being drilled into his skull. *Lancaster.* Lancaster, with whom he had a *deal*…

This was why it was good to have Jaq Haszan on his payroll. That Reich job had been nothing to do with business, but it was a beautiful story. And Jaq was on a short chain, tied down to his habit.

Vincenzo Vexx stalked over to his desk, an island floating in a pool of buttery yellow light. His hand picked up the heavy mouthpiece of his phone. Perhaps it was time to have a sit-down with his number-one 'dreno pharmer.

Ω

The streets opened up before them, like a medieval throng cringing back from a procession of lepers. Indeed, they wore similar robes; black hooded sackcloth with gold-filigreed gas masks beneath. Nobody in Elysium knew about the Ku Klux Klan, but that's the image their pointed cowls and silk-ribboned vestments brought to mind. They weren't diseased or rabidly racist, though - it was worse.

Arnic and Thibault were Celebrants.

"Move it or lose it, chump," growled Arnic, the taller of the two, his voice a mekanistic growl through a pair of gilded speakers. "Order Militant business! Clear the way!"

The water-seller whose little cart blocked the sidewalk blanched in terror, frozen in the arclamps of the Celebrants' stare. Thibault kicked one of the wheels off his cart and levered it up and over, one of his hands resting on the hilt of his tazer-baton.

"You don't like it, send the bill to Grandmaster Veer!" sniggered the short, fat little man. "We'd be happy to take a few years off your life, citizen. Just doing our part against overpopulation!"

A dirty corrugated-iron door cracked open an inch as the old vendor scrabbled away, averting his eyes. Hands reached out from inside and dragged him into the darkness, where muttered imprecations boiled.

"You too, you lowlifes!" shouted Arnic, clattering the tip of his baton against the shanty wall as he swaggered by. "And don't forget - next week's quota review. A big fat visit from Doctor Bribe could keep you healthy!"

The pair laughed as they rolled down the street, doors and shutters slamming closed in a wave before them. In the end, nobody got away from the Celebrants. But as Order Sergeant Gorrin Royse put it - "It sure don't hurt to remind 'em that Kronos gave us a long, long chain."

Arnic and Thibault weren't exactly saints. Well, O.K. - there'd been that run-in with the Comp Div pigs last month... the protection scam... the arson... and that nasty business with those SimStimm pushers... It had left them with a dogshit beat, at the bottom of the pay-scale.

"Which is why," explained Arnic to his dim little companion "We pick up a few extracurriculars, and get back on top. These things are sanctioned down the line - Benton Veer gets his cut, don't you worry. Old Man Royse too. We're still in the public service."

That's why they were a little more tooled up than usual - and why they were swaggering like drunken heroes. Arnic and Thibault were off to wax Don Vincenzo Vexx.

The dirty concrete slab which supported Vincenzo's building was connected to the habs around it by a web of defunct high-tension cable, while the pedestrian mallway the Celebrants walked down continued underneath it as a third-world homemade suspension bridge.

"Clocks out and synchro, brother," said Thibault, sliding his baton back into its holster between a nervejam and a machine-pistol. "Time to earn that bonus!"

Both men stopped on the corner, fishing out a pair of giant silver pocketwatches on half-inch-thick chains. Each one was a priceless relic; irreplaceable and sacred.

When the Celebrants confronted Don Vincenzo their timepieces would simultaneously count down the final seconds of his allotted lifetime. Tiny robotic insects which nested within them would swarm out, crowd through his every pore and orifice, and devour his living brain. A direct replica of that gelid organ would be built up somewhere deep in the databanks of Kronos, granting him a kind of eternal life. It was standard procedure – *natural causes.*

"Just another job, huh?" grinned Arnic, his voice as brittle as his smile. They'd all heard stories about Don Vexx. If they weren't with the Order Militant they'd never even have dared to walk into his neighborhood.

"Just a stroll in the park, buddy. Easy money. You think anyone can outfox our little pets? Not even Vexx is stupid enough to go to war with the Grief Division."

"Yeah," said Arnic, nodding slowly.

"Yeah," agreed Thibault, rocking back and forth on his heels. He dropped his pocketwatch back down the front of his robe and pulled out a thin paper packet of tobacco. "No problem. And after this, we can get a sweet uptown job. It'll be no different from foreclosing on a little old lady."

But both of them knew that this was far from a normal job. For starters, it was well ahead of schedule. In fact, Don Vincenzo wasn't slated for a visit for at least another fourteen years. This was a very expensive politically sanctioned hit, and their target was known for his lack of mercy.

Valle Crucis were cheaper, and Confederate Bounty-hunters were usually more sensationally messy, but if you could afford the titanic bribe bent Celebrants were the only way to dispose of your enemies.

A stretched-out custom bike idled past them, its rider crouched atop its reinforced frame like a quarterback on a tricycle. He was the only thing moving on the street, the mirrored visor of his helmet reflecting a wasteland of breeze-blown plastic.

"Got our mark now, command," wheezed Arnic through his ornate gas-mask. A mic bead pierced through his lip sent his words out over the ether. "You're right, that's one big ugly bastard, ain't it?"

A similar jeweled seed of 'tech drilled into the lobe of the Celebrant's ear crackled and buzzed for a second in reply.

"Confirm, command. We wait for the big ape to leave, then we make the hit. You can consider him…erased."

Ω

Nobody was ignorant enough to refuse a summons to *this* particular office. Rumors abounded in the Subcity of bodies entombed in building foundations, chopped-off hands and acid baths… and then there was Knuckles.

Haszan stood shadowed in the doorway, a slab of darkness defined by awful daylight. His overalls were riotmesh, dirty from the road, one shoulder strap replaced with a piece of chain, the other covered with badges and patches. 'Block Twelve Doom Troopers - Cop Killing Kowboyz'. Against the riveted gray cerametal tiles he looked like a vast and ugly stain.

Vincenzo Vexx wore a pinstripe Suit of archaeotech which blended into the muted décor like gin into a lick of vermouth. By virtue of its mind-expanding laminar processors, he was the entire Mafia, all by himself.

"So pleased you could stop by," he whispered, in a voice as dry as coffin dust. "I really appreciate face-to-face time with my associates. Such a luxury in this modern world."

"Uhh…always a pleasure, Mister Vexx. I was coming down to see you soon anyhow."

"More 'chrome for your favorite buyer? You keep pretty busy for a subtown creep, Haszan. Might even convince Kronos that crime actually pays… But come on, come on, don't just stand there looking monolithic. Take a seat."

There was only one chair, directly across from the Don's immense desk. Above it hung a huge and melting Jesus, his face cracking with age. After all, Vincenzo was unswervingly, impossibly Catholic. He was supposed to broker deals with the Valle Crucis – revenge contracts for people beneath the Compliance Division's attention..

"Thanks, Mister Vexx. Much obliged."

Haszan sat in silence while his host shuffled across the room to his high-backed seat. He took another hefty puff on his cigar, squinting down its length at Jaq's huge form skooched up on the little chair.

"I suppose your look of polite disgust means it would be a waste of time to offer you one of these?"

Haszan tried the grin.

"Bah. Thought so. You kids today think the Medicorps shit pure gold." Vincenzo slopped replicated cognac into a whiskey tumbler, grunting as the spilled drops were sucked up by chrome-shelled roachbots. "Get this down you, then we can talk business."

Haszan held his breath during the first mighty gulp, and didn't let it out until a second cut-crystal tumbler came sliding over his way. It went down the hatch in roughly one point six seconds.

Haszan felt that old cognac glow.

"Better, I suppose. But it hurts to watch shit *that* expensive get sucked down like Vladimir Chora's moonshine."

The Don peered through crescent-moon glasses perched on the broken hump of his nose, patched into his suit via a thin silk ribbon shot through with wires. Data hissed across their intrinsic screens in pistoning columns of green. The eyes behind them were oil-black and sparkling.

"You catch that last round of the Game, Jaq? That young Simeon Blaire's *dynamite*! Odds on favorite for tonight as well. He's making them go through bodies like they was out of fashion."

Haszan smiled, and opened his hands in a gesture of good-natured ignorance. He heard the sound of loading guns in the indeterminable distance...

"I'm no sports fan, Don Vexx. Who's this guy Simeon, anyhow?" He feigned dumb. It was too easy.

He's one of your customers, said the sarcastic drawl of Kaito in his head. *He shouldn't be winning at games of* chance, *let alone the old ancestral sport of kings.*

Vincenzo let the last trickle of cognac drip into his glass with a look of sincere regret.

"Young buck from the Blaire geneline. Got some kind of optics rig in his face, you know?" He sighed. "Well, know him or not, that's my pick for the big Jaegenn gig tomorrow. I gotta top-flight bookie down Confed way, if you want to double your money."

"Sorry Mister Vexx," replied Haszan, feeling the alcohol buzz go creeping up his spine. "I'm an honest head-tapping 'dreno farmer, not a gambler. That kinda shit can get a man into some deep trouble."

Vincenzo laughed, then, blowing the tension out of the room. He laughed like a hissing valve on some rusted-up bioweapon, and Haszan was obliged to join him.

"Like our dear departed Feldon? Give yourself some credit Jaq!" He clenched the butt of his cigar between his stained yellow teeth and hunched down over the case. "The day you're as stupid as Feldon Roberts I'll pay you to shoot yourself! But until that sad day comes, you'll be my number one 'chrome provider. If you'd be so kind?"

Haszan popped the lid.

Vincenzo flicked a silver loupe out of his sleeve to better rez the goods.

"Bellissimo. Superb. Fuckin' genius with a needle."

Haszan smiled fuzzy; the Cognac had landed.

"You're just too good, you big bastard. Too perfect." Vincenzo sighed, as if it would have pleased him to find microchunks of tissue floating in the adrenochrome. "It's that attention to detail which makes you so damn indispensable. But without *discrepancy*, there can be problems. You know how our Guardian Engine loves patterns."

The Don's stogie blew vast cyclopean rings.

Haszan closed the lid of his aluminum case gently, accompanied by the pixie-bells tinkle of innumerable tiny phials.

He was afraid to meet Vincenzo's eyes.

He feared his anger would show.

"You want me to mess up the extractions?" he asked. Haszan gripped the briefcase hard enough to crush its handle. "That could cause some of my patients to become… compromised."

By which, with a sudden locked gaze, they both understood he meant 'dead'. Any floating speck in the liquid meant an aneurysm, a stroke. Lobotomization. The Don leaned back into the gloom, his pince-nez flashing green to red.

"Just a little advice, my friend," said Vincenzo, pulling a wad of Slades from his top-coat pocket and sliding them across the dark-stained wood. "There's been talk about a pharmer being headhunted by one of the Lords. The Liquid Tong out of Celestial are suspending ops – probably more outta superstition than sense. I'm far more practical, but I still want to protect my sources."

Haszan swore he heard it this time. One of the eyeballs of Christ behind him slid open, revealing the muzzle of a magnetic railcannon…

"The expense of a few of *your* sources will be perfectly acceptable." Vincenzo ground out his cigar to punctuate, stabbing a chubby finger in Jaq's face. "Pick one yourself, or I'll do it for you."

The Don held out his hand, brandishing a huge champagne diamond on his pinkie finger. Jaq closed his eyes as he kissed it, obedient, leashed… and he took the money.

When he stood up again the anger had been crushed down to

a tiny spark deep in his eyes.

"Good boy. Now, get outta here before I have to charge you rent!"

Haszan left the temporary offices of the mafia in a swirl of raytraced fire, flames dancing in the transparent LCD matrix of his coat. But the foot had come down. He was *obligated* now. The show was over.

Tiny streams of data poured across Vincenzo's specs in the graylight flash of the door opening and closing - the key-string first and foremost, followed by other figures - molecular maps and atomic weights. It was a chemical breakdown of Jaq's breath, scraped from the glittering carbon chunk by a mekan the size of a mosquito.

Vincenzo knew who Haszan knew, and so he couldn't trust his hacked biomonitor data. If Kaito Kayzi wasn't a neophyte Magus he would have been very useful in the world of organized crime...

So he got a second opinion.

Out of the corner of one dark eye the Don watched his tiny spymekan re-anchor itself under his pinkie ring, its hair-thin legs gripping the inverse point of that big old ostentatious rock. In center-stage a holo image of Octavio Vanecke looked askance at him, neat and sharp in a virtual twentieth-century suit.

"Is he clean?"

"I'm getting to it, Vanecke," muttered Vincenzo through pursed lips. "No crycelium present. No trace of the 'chrome... picking up stunn, alcohol, trace foodstuffs. Sherbet fuckin' candy."

"Excellent," said Octavio, his face a virtual mask to cover his deformities. "He's doing fine. I knew Jaq Haszan was the right man for the job as soon as you showed me his profile. And he never told you the name of his new 'customer', either. My little incentive must be working."

"Huh," grunted Vexx, snipping the tip from a fresh cigar "I'm supposed to be happy that he follows your orders, and not mine? If I wasn't so sure you were going to kill him with this plan of yours, I'd have to exert a little discipline."

Vanecke laughed, a pneumatic chuckle that set the Don's teeth on edge.

"Don't worry too much about Haszan, old friend," he said. "I'm sure you'll find him easy to replace. You just concentrate on shifting that 'chrome so I can take my cut."

The slam of the office's streetfront door rung out as clearly as Octavio's voice, amplified by 'phones hugging drum and hammer and stirrup, floating in the balancing fluids of Vincenzo's inner ear.

Thank God (the Catholic one, of course) he thought, that such tools of near-omniscience weren't available to poor Jaqub Haszan.

Vanecke collapsed. Six hundred G in the bag. Now to Lancaster and the big payoff.

Then the fucking Celebrants could take this body.

Outside on the corner the two scumbags were still waiting, one rocking backwards and forwards in his rubber boots, the other smoking a vile roll-your-own through the hole in his faceplate.

The Don cracked the blinds. He spotted them.

At his fingertips were innumerable nasty fates for those two meatboys. But he knew it was just a message from that sexless freak Lancaster.

I trade in flesh. I engineer life as easily as you engineer death. I pay my debts, and I pay those who fail me too...

Vincenzo shuddered, despite himself. He was going places Octavio Vanecke had never dared on this one. And while he'd be one of a very select club of illegal clones, he wouldn't be the first...

Ω

There was a narrow bed of wrought-iron ivy down in the Pit, salvaged by one survivor or another from every major war since Napoleon walked the earth. A man lay resting on it now, staring up at a gash of polluted sky.

He couldn't sleep. A hot-fuel burn of drugs still roared in his skull, fadeout from his last mission. Little memories cracked and peeled away as he prepped the detox, blurring what was left of his mind.

His name was Abdulafia 330, Sword of the Illuminatus.

The serial number was tacked on because he was one of the outlaw *Ashishim* - the 'hashish-eaters', descended from an ancient cult of murderers.

The 'Sword' part - well, that was complicated. The wily old warlord who ruled the Ashishim was a bit past his prime for wet ops, so he'd delegated. Abdulafia was the promising young killer he'd picked.

Hence, of course, the memories. The vacant cutout stare aimed up at the clouds…

His face looked young; in design, in structure, at a cursory glance. What most people noticed first was the black *Dervashi* tattoo which sliced across his left eye - an inch-wide strip of ornately scarified flesh tapering down to a point just above the corner of his mouth.

His Sisters in the Revolution couldn't help but note his whipcord muscles, his cheekbones carved out sheer and sharp as if with chisel blows.

That face wasn't his own.

Being stolen property can lend a whole new edge to your existential angst, and Abdulafia 330 was quite clearly wearing the features of Simeon Blaire.

He'd been alive for over a century, not counting those little eyeblinks of darkness when he'd had his body shot out from under him. He was the prize subject of his sect's battle-clone program; stolen one hundred and sixteen years ago and augmented with illegal crycelium.

The crystalline nanostructures felt like needles through his bones, but death was worse. It was *boring* in stasis. If some low-paid company lab-rat hadn't created the self-replicating, metal-crystal-organic stuff centuries ago he'd be nothing but hard light and scavenged metal.

His friends told him that that was a drag.

Abdulafia leaned back, cradling his tight bun of dreadlocks with his palms behind his head. He stared up at the city, a jagged mountain in the dusk.

The Pit was purgatorial. It was a damn fine place to hide out when your genetic code was copyrighted, and the title to your body belonged to an androgynous psycho like Emmanuel Lancaster. 'Afia watched loops of neon liquid slamdown into his circulatory system, purging the veins of what was supposed to be a one-shot gladiatorial corpse. A tuning-fork buzz rippled through his bones, from the soles of his feet up to his dreadlocked top-knot.

Above him, the racing clouds skipped and stuttered like a dysfunctional filmstrip, sick ochre/bilious green/slate. Searchlights rolled over the metal foothills of Elysium, over the land his migrant people hung onto tooth and nail. It was the stuff of legends to them that he slept under the naked sky. His tribesmen didn't know how he came to be their champion, the hidden labs where his body was sequenced; but they needed hope.

They burned it up like cigarettes.

He slept outdoors, watching the city above him or the fires of the shantytowns below, making them believe. Of course, it counted for precisely nothing if he was head-shot by a Kronocult sniper. His true self lived in the black crescent which hugged the back of his neck, in a shell of toughened plastic wrapped around a web of memory cells.

Let them shoot, he thought as the nektar twisted and sparked in his blood. He was one of millions, floating embryonic in their tanks.

It was just as he was getting comfortable that his phone began to ring – orders coming in from his master, the lord of the deep city. Another shipment of drugs was in the pipe, coming down from out of the high strata. A special consignment, and one he was commanded to snatch.

Abdulafia stretched the kinks out of his long, lean limbs, rocked over to his war-chest and pulled down a shimmering holomesh cloak, a pair of daggers and a roll of silver tape. He was going to buy his people a little more freedom.

The Ashishim hadn't always lived down among the roots of

Elysium, and before their nomad lord had brought them to the R.T. they'd plundered their way across the carcass of Europa, hoarding technomanitc trinkets like other clans hoarded gold or water or canned food. That's why nobody noticed the holo-cloaked figure as it slipped through the spiked barricades of the subcity gates, flickering along mansard rooflines and grappling from gargoyle to spire to rusted chimney and on…

Revered Zeon had been most specific. This little batch of chemicals literally had his name written all over it.

Abdulafia 330 peered down at the Vincenzo Vexx's office from high above, his cloak bending the yellow light around his wiry body. The two Celebrants on the corner weren't part of his briefing, and even for a battle-clone like himself - six-foot-nothing full of illicit technology - a pair of the Grief Division's finest meant trouble. Perhaps he shouldn't wait for backup.

But perhaps by the time it arrived Vincenzo Vexx and his precious haul of adrenochrome would already be gone…

That was just too much to risk. This juice was special - refined and distilled through the body of a Lord, no less. The Ashishi labs were drooling for the tiniest sample, priming a thousand arcane tests and experiments…

Abdulafia checked his knives, tight in the tops of his boots, and aimed a zipline grapple across the street, right through Vincenzo's window.

He never saw the scruffy little-leather-clad man right above him, perched atop the head of a gargoyle halfway up a hab-cube wall. The guy worked the zoom ring on his oculars with one hand while he scratched his nuts with the other. He grunted to himself, popping a fat white flea between his fingernails and a billowing pink bubble of gum between his lips. *Ashishim*. Shit. Those R.T. boys were *far* to self assured.

'Bout time to take them down a peg or twelve… This was *Lancaster's* town.

Ω

The security camera outside the King Value was cheap, disposable - a black-and-white model which cost less than a

Slay-per-view ticket. It framed a scene just as cheap and nasty.

A figure in a carpark - gray on gray, hunched up as sheets of rain pissed in from off-camera. A matchstrike lit up a middle-aged man's haggard features… sunken eyes glittering behind a whisper of straight black hair…

His name – Eddie Tsein – was blazoned in bright yellow across his kevlar-wrapped chest. That stuff might have been able to stop a bullet a thousand years ago, but now… it was worse than useless.

A collar of smooth gunmetal was wrapped tight around his neck, projecting a flickering blue sheen over his skin. It'd stop the poison rain, but he'd wash afterward anyway.

The shielding was a mark of privilege, for all that it was damned uncomfortable.

He was, to his eternal shame, a *Burbster*. A native of the bubble city which hung like a blue plastic goiter below the megatowers. It was civil-servant land up there, a knockoff of the future predicted by Popular Mechanics magazine in the 1950s. Big money country.

Was it any wonder that he pulled double shifts? That he was out here in the rain tonight, chasing down scumbags he'd already paid off?

Lieutenant Tsien was at a point in his career - if it could be called that anymore - when being philosophical about the situation was all that he had left. The absurdity hit him every time he zipped up his riotmesh uniform, the gloves, the little cap, and the belt of weapons that cops a millennium ago had never heard of or needed. It hit him like half a brick in a plastic bag, and left him reeling on the edge of hysteria for the full eight hours between strong coffees.

Six of his men were dead. At least now, quipped Tsien's offsider Lucas, they got to work on time.

The thin guy with the scythe hadn't stopped *these* lawmen in their tracks. Equipped with Cyben Mark Three implants the bodies of Tsien's old buddies staggered out onto the streets each night, faces and hands laminated, uniforms welded to their dead skin with hot plastic seals. The laminate was wipe-clean, after some humorous but irreverent occurrences of post-mortem graffiti.

Every living officer on the force had been bullied into donating their cadaver to the city when they finally caught a bullet. Tsien hoped he got blown into pink confetti – the thought of his recorded personality pushing his re-animated corpse through an endless graveyard shift was worse than the Vatican's Hell.

"Glad you could join us, Chief," said Lucas as Tsien stubbed out his cigarette on the sole of his boot. The 2IC of Tsien's squad was the only other living meatbag on it - a baldhead juve just out of the academy with a galaxy of wetwire plugs speckled across half his shiny scalp. "Looks like the guys we're after - a two-man team, after the cash - tricked out the cameras and the alarms with jamming hardware. But this time - well, step inside and take a look…"

The King Value was painted in blood from end to end, its floor awash with candies and torn-up pornos and bullet shells. Someone had written 'Stunn for Funn' across the dewy faceplates of a dozen rattling coolers, and the whole place stank of burnt plastic and shit.

"Pretty, huh? It's a bit of an escalation."

One of the Cyben was earnestly unrolling red and blue police line tape from a little cardboard dispenser, surrounding the place in slow loops and twists like toilet paper around a high-school teacher's station wagon.

"Shit. They finally got one, huh? These two used to be pretty slick, Lucas. I wonder what happened to change all that?" Tsien found himself smiling, and stopped.

Someone other than the Cyben was going to have to take this crap seriously. And Tsien's quota review was coming up in a week - not a great time for his sub-scum partners to freak out on him.

Getting paid by commission meant he had to think laterally, and *that* meant hiring the services of Jaq and the Kayzi. Not really what he'd joined the force to do, but there were bills to cover, and gods help the family Tsien if their Aristo landlords kicked them out of paradise…

Mrs Toria Jane Tsien was trez Bimburb. She looooved the six-room polyfoam maisonette his wages paid for, way up in the Belt. She was the reason he worked nights.

"They went primitive. This isn't the kind of stuff you just find lying around… It's a damned antique." The lieutenant picked up Haszan's bloodied sawnoff from the clerk's lap and threw it to Lucas. Murder weapon found. Collect 200 Slades.

"Maybe we should just throw this whole mess over to Homicide and call it a night. Hell, I'll even buy the first round… I could pawn this for at least a bottle of moonshine."

Tsien grabbed the scarred old weapon back, scowling, and bagged it in zip-sealed plastic.

"It's not just these jacker scumbags who're getting sloppy, apparently. *I'm* in charge of this case, and we've been following these guys for a month. Do you want to blow your quota writing up traffic violations and hand this to those necrophiles at Central?"

"Sorry, Eddie," said Lucas, popping open a can of cola. "These little bastards sure have you wound up tight. But we'll get 'em soon enough, and then it's two more for the lobo factory."

Tsien smiled, as if the thought of hook-tipped probes scrambling human brains was somehow comforting.

"You're right, kid, you're right. It's just… ten robberies, two arsons, and now a murder - and not one single frame or voice-print. I hate to let them think they're smarter than me."

He ran a hand over his face, wiping away the thin sheen of sweat which had built up behind his shielding. "So, should we go for Murder and the hundred bucks, or just lousy old Suicide for the twenty and get back to the Precinct?"

And if Jaq and Kaito were off the chain? If the little gutter-rats really *were* smarter than Eddie Tsien? What if he'd given a pair of chemheads carte blanche to kill whoever they pleased?

It was all the High Marshall's fault for working the quota system, he reminded himself. Those two were on a damn tight leash. Or at least the Kayzi was… who knew what was going on in the neanderthal mind of Jaq Haszan?

"I reckon this guy chose a damn messy way to commit suicide,

Chief," said Lucas, writing it up on his tablet. "So don't worry. You'll get another shot at those punks."

He clapped Tsien on one shoulder as he drained his can of triple-caffeinated Hypo.

"Huh - if he wanted a painful death he shoulda joined the force, eh?"

Tsien fished another cigarette from his coat.

"C'mon, let's get this done. If I'm late home again I might just have to follow this chump's example."

Ω

Deep among the roots of Simeon Blaire's megatower a mind-wiped slave toiled inside a thick rubber isolation suit, scrubbing the floor of the White Room under six feet of water. A long concertinaed tube pumped air down to the menial while he worked, sucking away his tainted breath. Even if the wretch was up on dry land the suit would still be necessary - none of the Lords cared to look upon the coarse features of a Subcity peasant.

Blaire's sanctum was a cube of smooth milky plastic, half-filled with tepid water and lit by an over-arching halo of sunlamps. He floated above his mind-wiped slave on an inflatable lounger, sipping a Singapore Sling perfectly replicated by two-thousand-year-old machines.

"Other Lords would be training now, Simeon," chided Baroness Mendelev-Singh, her fresh new face dimpled into a sly smile. "Or maybe you think you deserve a rest, hmm? Is that tired old bag of meat you live in getting slow, perhaps?"

A floating aeromekan painted Leynna over the still water like a phantom, a tiny doll poised millimeters above its silvery surface. She was shopping for an outfit to wear to Jaegenn's party; around her Blaire could see virtual clothiers and stylists displaying their latest patterns. He ignored her little jibe - Leynna and her backers had no business even *guessing* how intensive his training regime truly was.

"I was meaning to ask you about the last round," he said, lying back with a creak of inflated plastic. The water was warm, his fingers trailed lazily amidst tropical fish specially bioengineered for his pleasure. "Before I killed you, you said something about Octavio Vanecke... some kind of perversion."

His smile was perfunctory, his eyes flat. Triplicate lasers painted him in the cool air before Baroness Mendelev-Singh, a tiny and annoying homunculus in swimming briefs and sunglasses.

"I said he had a *perverse fascination*... but Kronos knows I'm no moralist." She arched one perfect eyebrow. "Are you just fishing for bitchy little comments, Blaire? I'd be more than happy to oblige..."

He grinned, pushing his shades up onto his forehead with one barcoded finger.

"Well, we both know it's not *my* place to judge, Baroness. But a fascination with death is a strange thing for a man in Octavio's position. Some people might call that a threat."

"He wouldn't be in that position if he hadn't gone looking for things best left alone by his kind. If there's any *threat*, it's that he hasn't stopped trying."

Simeon leaned forward, letting his aeromekan cameras follow him.

"If he found anything it's news to me, honey. The poor old bastard had a sweet thing going before the axe came down."

The tiny image of the Baroness fixed him with a furious glare, her eyes flashing like pinpricks of furnace heat.

"You forget your status, Simeon... and your manners. But I'll educate you, nonetheless. What the *good Direktor* found was nothing but pain and humiliation, for all that he claims to have been enlightened."

Two years had passed, he thought, she still skirted around the issue. Direktor Vanecke's misguided attempt to fix the game had cost her almost as much as it had cost him...

"And you don't feel any responsibility? You don't want to take any kind of *revenge*? He ruined you and wrung you out, Baroness. Does it please you to think he's *finished* with you?"

His words had the force of a sledgehammer.

Leynna's electric eyes narrowed, and with a snap of her fingers the fitting room, the holographic couturiers and the swathes of exotic silk all disintegrated. Her camera angle zoomed, fixating Blaire with amber. One immaculate cheek loomed like a blast-sanded moon, her slick red lips pulled back in a snarl.

"He wanted to Play, and he wanted to advance himself. You Blaires are a lesser House – merchant princes. If you learn anything at all from Octavio fucking Vanecke it should be a little gods-damned *ambition!*"

Blaire's face didn't even twitch. He hardly needed the censorware which masked his emotions.

Some of his noble peers thought that Leynna was cracking up - an opinion made all the more pertinent by her loss in the last round of the Game. The Mendelev-Singhs were *unstables* after all – tainted stock, a doomed family for all their skill and wealth.

Blaire dropped his empty glass into the water, startling one of the tropical fish.

"So what *were* his ambitions, Baroness? Surely he whispered something in your ear when you were in his bed." He lounged back, scissoring a poisonous fish between his fingers. It thrashed in the water, its spines slicing his skin and throwing out a nebula of blood.

"Oh, you *know* what he wanted. Something we can't even talk about him having, for fear of Manifest Dogma. But *you* might just have what it takes. If not in your brains, then at least in your body." She was almost laughing now, unhinged. "*He* might as well have been sterile. But you… well, at least *one* part of you might be useful, Blaire. How many times have we been in the final elimination together? *Superior genes*, Simeon. Yours and mine! We can…"

The fish came up at her in the camera's expanded arc of vision, end over end, severing the connection in a splatter of blood and scales. She fell back by reflex, full-length on the black-tiled floor of her mediorium, unconscious.

Simeon licked his fingers, grinning wolfishly.

The blood dripping from his hand was rife with poison – stuff which would kill a lowborn in seconds. It was the juice he used on his shuriken, the secret ingredient in his cocktail.

When you're gene-sequenced immune, you can indulge in such little ironies.

Simeon watched the fish slide down the white plastic wall, smiled, and hooked back up to Octavio Vanecke on the other line.

Down below him a blind figure all in black rubber scooped up the dead fish in its vacuum-sweeper, its wetwired brain sending it crawling on, on an endless trek across the plastic seabed.

Ω

Inside an empty packet of sugar candies something moved – skittering, gripping the cardboard with needle claws.

The flycam's olfactules quivered as they picked up the scent of blood. Its telescopic eyes scanned the scene of the crime; they'd been uploading live ever since the little machine left it's housing on Haszan's wrist. Of course that was a good long while after he pulled the trigger – Jaq didn't want anyone to see his face, just his handiwork.

The tiny machine took to the air with a whirr of carbon-fiber rotors, a great arcing leap that took it over the counter and onto the mangled topography of the King Value clerk's chest.

Miniature anchor-hooks twisted deep into the dead man's skin as the flycam beamed its signal out across the city. Relay masts leapfrogged it on, up and up the corroded slopes of Elysium to the aerial crown of Omnivasive Three-Vee, Elysium's most up-to-the-minute broadcaster. Haszan, a stringer for said corporate entity, was one of the reasons they got their breaking news fast.

The flycam worked its hooks loose and leaped skyward again, angling for the far wall, a great vantage point for a wide-angle…

Tsien caught the bug in mid-flight, his rolled-up newspaper hitting the tiny robot like a warmekan's armored fist. Tomorrow, the still photographs on page one would come from the little device he had just destroyed.

"They just can't wait, can they," muttered the lieutenant under his breath, tossing the paper over the counter and into oblivion. "Damn bugs can smell dead meat a mile away." He took another swig of Hypo, prodding the hole in the King Value man's chest with his pencil. *All carrion, all flesh...* the city was rotting, and on that cyclopean scale the Subcits and the Khepts were nothing more than insects themselves...

Evil thoughts were still boiling in Tsien's head when the radio on his belt started screaming. The Cyben all snapped to attention at once, their dead camera eyes flashing from blue to red.

"Oh, Gods and Fates! Not tonight! Of all the damned, Kronos-cursed luck!"

Something, somewhere had gone horribly wrong. And now against all better judgment H.Q. wanted Eddie Tsien to do something about it...

Ω

Paranoia can do terrible things to the human brain.

When a mind feels trapped and stressed and overtaxed it can lead to horrific accidents. When it's the mind of a burnout case, a thug with a chrome hand and a head full of drugs, those accidents usually happen to other people...

Haszan tripped out on stunn, prowling the nightsectors, down the blackened tubes where he could hear the factory-kombinants of the Reclamation through rusting walls. He hunted information in the downhab bars, where the five-x shine was warm from the still, and mutant faces hid behind sack-cloth shrouds. He clenched throats with a steel-infused fist.

He remembered eyes looking up at him in terror; they could see the silver of the stunn, and knew about that job with the Final Reich - the bloodbath, the pieces left to twist on hooks...

Russian roulette.

Nobody knew, not even for the price of Kheptic adrenochrome and Slades, who was trying to set him up.

Ripples of his psychosis followed him down.

Back to his bike; his homeblock; his dreams.

Behind his back he heard the scissor-click of loading guns.

DOCUMENT INSERT: MULTIPLICITY ARCHIVES DEPARTMENT

Kheptarchy - the officially sanctioned term for
the figurehead rulership of Elysium.

There are supposed to be three thousand of the
'purest blood' alive at any time; a sample of
pure humanity free from mutation and degeneracy.
Current numbers are unknown, but are assumed to be
as low as four or five hundred… in fact, nearly
all the dwellers in the upper city now take part
in the Revels of the Razor Clique, the Kheptarchs'
ubiquitous Game.

The origins of the term are unknown, although
the best explanation takes the form of a thinly
veiled insult, leveled at the investors who built
Terminus Afrika. Democratic media called them
a 'Kleptocracy' - literally a ruling class of
thieves.

Didactic Memory-Shunt, module iii - g - 29

Exoethnological Laboritorium

17 Aevum Oblivio
Message from the Sponsors

ZHE CAUGHT THE flash of it like a bullet through his skull. His power was slipping; his concentration was undone.

Between the Cardinal Rock and the poisoned sea the cable of the space 'lev hissed and crackled with massive electrical pulses. Clouds frayed and scattered from about the husk of Elysium as the machine within its shell convulsed, venting great crooked webs of inverted lightning. There were voices behind its walls, and their captive data sliced through the Technician's mind in barbed-wire loops. Realization rushed up on him suddenly, a chilling thought which crashed down amid the thunder.

Sequestration worked both ways...

Zhe's head buzzed like a poorly tuned threedeeo feed as he scrabbled for control.

But this wasn't an interrogation any more. He was being shown.

"That's right, Technician," said a voice right behind his eyes - "and yes, I know who and what you are. You've seen my people's little Game, and I've seen yours. Do you think your Praetor's war against the Unity is any different? Just because billions die instead of mere hundreds?"

It was the voice of Kronos, the echo of that vast machine left inside the shell of the Cardinal Rock.

"So, let me tell you what they were fighting for. What you and your friend Gharfos Nyl are fighting for. I call it... the Forge."

"Why are you telling me this now?" asked Zhe, as images flickered across his mind like a video haze. "And why the Forge? I thought it was a weapon, not some kind of..."

"Hmmm... not an entirely unfair assumption. But I can't really tell you much more. You see, I'm not really here. Not even a copy of my core A.I. This is just an interactive recording inside the Rock's mainframe. And it's only been activated because your enemy is closer than you think..."

Zhe tried desperately to disengage, but it was too late. Just by listening to that hollow voice inside his skull he'd let his concentration slip too far.

Something was coming. Something bad.

And as it bore down on him, Zhe could do nothing but submit to the storm of images which hissed in through his defenses like rain.

2196 Anno Arbitrium
Compartmentalized

IN A POOL of light cast by a naked low-watt bulb four men sat hunched around a plastic poker table. Grim, hard-faced hombres, each one intent on the squinted eyes of the other three. Between them in the air a battle was underway as virals and firewall programs clashed, trying to rip the electronic defenses of the players' bio-onboard rigs.

Eyes bulged, unblinking. Sweat dripped through stubble. Tiny lights winked and sizzled behind their ears and down across their cervical vertebrae.

Kaito saw it all as he came rolling down the street, and his wetwired brain picked up the scam. Three of the players were a team – their 'ware was already well into the head of their mark while two of the scammers fought a spectacular data-war as rolling cover. The sucker about to get screwed was a Pit Feral fresh out of the shanty, a big bruiser with a chainmail eyepatch and fresh wetwire scars all over his head.

Somebody's new gunjack, a bodyguard or retainer for some bimburb exec. Uplifted from the Pit as muscle and meat…

The Kayzi hacker grinned – this would be fun.

Vladimir Chora's dive was called the Hydrogen Bar, and in a city of bad reputations it was proud to have the worst. The clean, pine-scented smell of the place was the giveaway. Like the neat paradox of that hospital smell (now so removed from actual forests as to define the word 'pine' in a treeless environment) the very fact that the Hydrogen Bar was scrubbed down meant it had been recently hosed out. And that meant Haszan and Kaito had blown in about five minutes after the last homicide. Railpistols were recoilless, light, powerful and messy. And as long as the drinks were cheap, none of the rust-dog clientèle were going to call in the law.

The barkeep shot them a grin as they pushed through his plastic saloon-doors, jerking one artificial thumb at the gamblers and their mark.

"Check out the rube, Jaq," he muttered to Haszan. "If that

mother goes psycho in here I'll stand you a bottle of three-x to lay him out."

"What, and get my knuckles all scuffed up? I'd rather just shoot him now, Vladimir." The big thug's grin lit up the gloom as he slid up to the bar. "Anyhow, I don't see *you* stopping him. K – show that clown how you do it."

Kaito popped an antique zippo lighter between his long fingers, torching the end of a tailormade cigarette. Now everybody in the Hydrogen Bar knew they were packing Slades. The Kayzi caught the Feral's attention with a strobe-light pop-up that snapped to the front of his bio-onboard display. Clouds of cheap hackbot code burned up like contrails around it.

"You – yeah, eyepatch. Run this update and shut down your onboard – everyone within three blocks can see the cards you're holding."

The hack victim slammed down his hand – kings over threes – then threw the table over sideways, his hands suddenly filled with a pair of wavy serpentine daggers. The scammers slipped and staggered and bolted out through the doors as the crowd cheered and hooted, pelting them with bottles.

"Word of advice, downsider. Until your hair grows over those stitches, you should get yourself a hat."

The Feral grunted in embarrassed gratitude and slid his knives back into their sheaths. He stalked out of the bar without a backward glance, running one hand over the stubbled crosshatching of scars that had given him away.

Kaito bellied up to the bar with a satisfied smirk, his hulking associate at his elbow.

"So, whatcha poison, mes amies?" asked Vladimir, his metal-plated head dipping in a miniature bow. "V.S.O.P and a Julieta?"

Haszan chuckled, plucking the cigarette from Katio's fingers and taking a long drag.

"How about some distinction in your clientele, Vlad?" he asked, nodding at the Blues and Purples crowded around the low tables of the saloon bar "These sports freaks – they bring down the tone for us honest fuckin' criminals!"

The bartender shrugged, sliding a handle across just in time to catch the falling core of ash which dropped from between Jaq's fingers.

"They're *paying*, Haszan. And it'll all be over tonight. But until then…"

A row of gaming machines flashed and chimed as they devoured punters' coins; odds were up for Duke Jaegenn to win the next round of the Game, equaling the number of bets which had been placed for Simeon Blaire. House Blaire supporters in the blue ribbons of their team were toasting his victory, and ascension to the seat of god-emperor. House Jaegenn supporters in royal purple ribbons were practicing bawdy songs about the young Khept's demise.

Haszan felt his stomach knot… he'd be attending to the star player before the game began. And despite the microservo web welded to his bones his hands were shaking. He sighed.

"Well, I say this whole Manifest Dogma kick is bullshit. Damn Game freaks make me fucking sick!"

There was a moment of silence as forty Subcity fans of brutal death-sports weighed up their chances of taking on one very angry Jaq Haszan.

His memory tweaked. The Don / cigar smoke and cognac / the laserbeam eyes of hidden firearms. With an exaggerated movement Jaq unlocked the totenkopf buckle of his gunbelt and dropped the twin sawn-off, pistol grip cannons to the bar. "Two fingers of scotch, C," he growled, his eyes flickering around the room. The assembled Subcitizens were suddenly uninterested in Kaito, Haszan, and any views they held about televised recreation.

"And I'll have the house special… something from the cellars."

That was Kaito, slipping a fat roll of bills across the pitted hardwood bar to Vladimir.

"It's a fine vintage this week, gentlemen. Right out of the R.T - the Tong are cooking hot these days, now they've got those molecular combiners online."

As Jaq ducked under the lintel of the stairwell he heard a tiny sound behind them… the clink and slide of oily glass on glass. Vladimir's lips twitched up at the corners as he held up one fleshtone aluminum finger... and they all heard the hiss and crack, followed by a startled yelp.

Prolonged whimpering followed.

"Just knock when you've made your selection, Mister Kayzi. I'll be waiting with that scotch for young Jaqub."

As the door closed Vlad reached under his huge brass cash register, pulling out a dull silver meat-cleaver with a notched and wicked edge. An unfortunate juve chemhead began to plead and struggle, his fingers air-stapled to the bar in the act of stealing a moonshine bottle.

Frowning, Vladimir tested the sharpness of the blade against one prosthetic finger.

"Don't expect any sympathy from me, kid." he drawled "How'd you think I lost *my* hand?"

Ω

Tsien's police report bounced from his electric tablet to the megatower offices of Valchek Mutual Insurance, and from there to the Elysian Consolidated Bank.

Sad news - the King Value was a write-off.

The noble proprietors of that dingy little shack creamed more from Haszan and Kaito's robbery than the freelance bikers ever did; but that was the nature of business. The upshot of Eddie Tsien's little quota rort was a six-figure sum injected into a monolithic corporation - a certain conglomerate known as ShopWise GmbH.

Unknown to most King Value customers - and indeed to the majority of its employees - no human foot had trod the wall-to-wall shagpile of ShopWise's head office for several decades. Its corridors were swept clean of debris by crawling mekan, and the financial engines which kept the business solvent whirred tirelessly over their meal of numbers in airless rooms not even fitted for illumination.

Tracking the company's wealth only took up a tiny fraction of their processing power. The rest, in a ritual as old as offices and corporations themselves, allowed the CEO to play video games.

Simeon ducked under a spinning roundhouse kick, coming

up hard to wrap his hands around his assailant's head. There was a satisfying snap as he broke the man's neck, but there was no time to enjoy it. He let the body drop, then flicked it back into the air with one foot, sending it flying across the dojo with a well-placed kick.

A second warrior caught his dead comrade in mid-air, and they went down in a tangle of flailing limbs. Simeon spun on his heel, his arm stretched out at his side, and felled another black-clad assassin who had been sneaking up from behind him. Blood spattered his face as the man's nasal septum drove up into his brain, killing him instantly.

Three down. Fourteen more to go.

Blaire grinned as he beckoned them on, clenching his hands into fists. Two leaped in at him, their eyes glittering through the slits in their black face-masks. He slammed their heads together as he skipped backwards, hearing bone shatter, rolling into a backflip which took him up and over another man's shoulders. Simeon landed lightly, one foot on either side of the warrior's skull. All it took was a twist to snap his neck, just as cleanly as if he'd used his hands. He threw himself forward as the man's corpse fell backwards, his arms held out cruciform, spinning as he picked his target… Blaire came down on his prey with a fury, throwing a rain of blows, shattering ribs and jaws and spines with a battery of snap-kicks and uppercuts and jabs. Black-clad bodies fell like rotten fruit, spilling hot blood across the hardwood floor. Slippery, there. He had to be careful…

The last two assassins faced him now; wary, cautious… they looked at each other and nodded. An oily rasp filled the air as they drew forth a pair of curved steel blades, circling in around him like sharks.

That wasn't in the program! It must be one of Vanecke's little modifications…

Unarmed, he'd have to be very quick indeed. The force-feedback shunts of his V.R. system let him feel every blow which struck home; Simeon had no desire to know what being cut in half felt like. He licked his lips, sizing up his prey, and then…

"Five o'clock, Master Blaire," said a voice out of nowhere as the walls of the dojo blasted away into the infinite distance. The two sword-wielding warriors collapsed into pixels, frozen in their stances of battle. "I shall warm up the town-car for you, sir... would you prefer coffee or tea during your ride home?"

Simeon sighed. Just when things had been getting *interesting*.

"Earl Grey, two sugars." He stood up from his desk, unfolding himself from the lotus position. He'd swept all the papers and executive toys from the top of that black glass slab, the better to meditate while he honed his fighting instincts. Now he slipped the chrome circlet of the 'mersive interface off his head, hanging it on a sculpted aluminum hand. "Dump the training program and eject the drive it's stored on. Then vape the drive. I won't be needing it again."

The Kheptarch Lord threw his coat around his shoulders, stalking away down the corridor as the lights went off behind him, one by one. Darkness licked at his heels like a rising tide. No, he wouldn't be needing the training sims any more. Tonight it would finally be *real*.

Simeon thought of a face made of beaten steel, then, a face like a hollow skull weeping tears of wet rust. He smiled to himself, humming a little of Ravel's *Bolero* while the building's maglift slammed him down seventy floors in two seconds.

It would be so refreshing to kill someone *new* for a change.

"Have a delightful evening, My Lord." enthused the scratchy electric voice of the maglift as its doors sighed open, spitting Simeon out into the darkness of the motorpool. His was the only vehicle in it, a great slab of metal marooned in a pool of light. Concrete spread wide and embraced him, pillars marching off into the shadows.

'Mersive comedown. They were getting worse...

He pressed a hot dry hand to his forehead while the shapes of dead and rusted machines shifted and bent in the gloom. The price of one form of meditation was always the other...

He needed a fix. He *terminally* needed a fix.

His car performed a retinal scan while his unsteady footsteps were still echoing through the motorpool hangar. The fingers that lovingly brushed it's matte-black side were crosschecked for identification as Simeon swung up the access ladder and pressed his keycard into its socket. Neurolinks clicked as the doors hissed open, and *Bolero* began to burble from a score of hidden speakers.

The Destrier was Consolidated Industries' last word in exclusive motoring. A single-seat black wedge the size of a firetruck, its six immense wheels wirespoked in glittering chrome. Rollbars of burnished steel enmeshed the front end of the wicked, low-slung vehicle, and its windows were tinted slabs of diamond as thick as bibles.

The fact that it was stuffed with innovative gadgets and trimmed in unobtainable materials like fox-fur and real leather meant nothing to *this* customer. It was a beautiful thing to die with, and not so long ago he had felt the need to die so keenly. He had almost come to envy the seething, dirty biomass of his feudal underlings.

That was until the first visit from his kind benefactor, the one who had helped him refine his suicidal urges into reason. Vanecke.

Soon, so soon, his deprivation of feeling would be over. When he was in the gangrenous underbelly of his city. Until then there was the matter of being dressed for the part. His obsession was far too fashionable and avant-garde not to be accompanied by the correct attire.

Perhaps something like the cover of his favorite book[1]...

When the Destrier's twin nine-liter Consolidated military grade engines shuddered into life the merest shiver ran the length of its gel-cushioned driver's seat, and Simeon cracked his knuckles like a concert pianist. He was on his way to glory.

And he felt the steel bite, felt the shattering bones, the cold air kissing raw red meat as he drove hot metal through human flesh, tempering his blade. He could see the thin mustache on

---

1 ((NON-ELECTRONIC INFORMATIONAL STORAGE RECORDS;
ARCHIVE 3; NOBLES AND LORDS COLLECTIONS
SECTION 337; HOUSE OF BLAIRE
CATEGORY; HISTORICAL / MANAGEMENT
TITLE; The Book of Five Rings
AUTHOR - Miyamoto Musashi, primitive warrior aristocrat))

his mentor's face blowing in the wind; skin the color of beaten copper in the light of the torture fires … The Master was with him. He couldn't possibly fail.

Ω

Trillions of electronic messages were shunted through Elysium's mail service system each day – from businesses, from public kiosks and from the sprawling Divisions of the Last City's byzantine bureaucracy.

Usually they were well beneath the attention of Kronos, who was far more interested in his little genetic experiment than in reading other people's mail.

This one was different, however.

Its origin marked it out for scrutiny – it came up from out of the R.T, from somewhere deep below sea level, down in Ashishim country where the postal grid wasn't supposed to run.

That, and the fact that it was actually *addressed* to Kronos meant that it suffered a battery of viral scans before the single video file inside was even touched by the great machine.

When the movie rolled Kronos took a couple of microseconds to work out what was actually being shown – that was a long pause for a machine with a brain was the size of a city. It was a shot of Neptune, a great marbled sphere hanging close in to the camera while faroff stars burned and shimmered behind it, one of them probably the sun.

Kronos didn't stop to question how the Ashishim had cameras out in the far reaches of the solar system. Not when it saw what happened next. Because the focus of Illuminatus Zeon's little movie was terrifying – even to an ageless and massive A.I. tyrant.

Especially to such an entity, in fact.

Kronos watched a shadow ooze over the face of the gas giant – a pall of darkness cast by a roiling swarm the size of a moon, slingshotting around the planet's bulk to launch itself in down the gravity well toward Earth. Kronos had been promised that this thing would one day come to its planet, and that dire consequences would follow. Now the vile prophecy of the

Illuminatus had come true, and his time was running out.

Plans had to be put in motion to defend the precious crop in the upper domes. For all the machine cared the rest of the city could go directly to hell, so long as it had an Emperor by the time the scourge made planetfall.

Perhaps it was time to intervene in the Great Game after all. Simeon Blaire had given Kronos the perfect excuse… But there was no guarantee that a suitable hand could be found among the Kheptarchy to wield the Forge. Other measures would have to be investigated.

That would mean unearthing weapons from before the Great Judgment. From the *Aevum Iudicium*, the age of technic nightmares…

And it meant, in the first instance, at least one human sacrifice. Someone from the Compliance Division; a street peon who'd already signed up to be reincarnated as a Cyben. Somebody of questionable loyalty, vile breeding and negligible worth.

A swift cross-reference spooled through the Comp. Div's records, flickering yellowed mugshots across Kronos' vision. And – *there*. Stop. This was the face of everything wrong with Elysium. But now… it would become the face of progress.

Oh Yes. The machine had found just the man for the job.

Ω

The street outside the H-Bar was bisected by the whirling blades of a giant windmill; part of the ramshackle extended power grid of the Subcity. Because the mile-square mezzanine Vlad had built his tavern on sloped gently downward, this made passing out in the gutter a game of chance. Kaito had seen it happen… some wretched drunk sliding inch by inch toward those cerametal blades until one snagged a collar or cuff, sending a tiny little stickman figure looping out over a three-hundred-storey drop.

Haszan and Kaito stepped over this afternoon's contestants and into the crowd. The human tide broke around Haszan like water around a chunk of grizzled stone, letting Kaito scamper along in his wake.

"Poor kid," grunted the big guy, flexing his chrome fingers. "Don't you think Vladimir was a bit rough on him?"

"What, taking his hand off? That how *you* got your little piece of stump jewelry, Jaq?"

"You know damn well that this was pure business, K."

Haszan clenched his silver digits into a fist.

"I just think the punishment should fit the crime. And the best punishment for trying to steal Vlad's moonshine… is having to actually *drink* the stuff."

"They say ethics is a luxury for the sober… or at least the do back in the old bunkers. He'll get credit from the Black Techs, and they'll have him fitted with a cheap claw by midnight." Kaito popped a capsul, flicking it off one thumb and catching it on his tongue. "Although… 'sobriety is a vice for the mean of spirit', or so says the same philosopher. The old bastard was drunk on potato wine six days out of seven."

Haszan, elbowing his way through a crowd of Kronocult penitents, couldn't get a hand to his medicine pouch. He reached up and over, narrowly missing one of the weeping flagellant's flails, and Kaito dropped a little pill into his hand.

No place here to pop 'em and inhale the powder…

He knocked it back with a chug of cheap R.T. whiskey, feeling the burn trickle down his throat.

"Sweet Ghost of the Prophet! Is he using a toilet for a still these days? I swear…"

The euphoria came down like a hammer, making the pushrods and gears in Jaq's hand whir and click as his nerves burned white. There were a couple of minutes there where both he and Kaito were utterly gone, blazing with fake plastic ecstasy.

It spiked silver, and blistered, and bled out of their screaming brains. It blew apart like a sand mandala, leaving behind an empty crawling guilt popping with miniature flashbacks. The hot edge of it would linger for another day or so, tweaking the edges of reality into glittering crystal.

And that was Fuzzy Stunn. While that tweak lasted you were ten feet tall, solid steel, hot and bright and sharp. When it started to wear off, though… it was razorblades under your skin.

Kaito came down first, the ground rushing up under his feet to impact with a sickening jolt against the soles of his boots. Haszan's eyes slowly rolled forward in their sockets, one pupil a pinprick, the other as wide as the open sky.

They smoked Ashishim ganja in the lee of a nuclear cooling tower, silent, comedown mute, listening to the roar and hiss of the crowd like surf on a distant shore. Jaq didn't say a thing worth more than a monosyllable as they split the rest of the cash and split up – Kaito on his way down to scam 'ware or ride the 'mersive, and him…

Oh fuck, yeah. HIM.

It may have been touched on before that Jaqub Haszan was a 'dreno Pharmer. Which meant keeping a stable of junkies spinning on the axis of their addictions like so many balanced plates, then harvesting the adrenochrome from their living glands with the help of some very sophisticated surgical gear. Smart needles, and servo welded to his knucklebones.

It may also have been mentioned that he was good at what he did.

But that (and here, you could see the moral lesson coming like a chunk of nickel-iron alloy falling from space)… that skill brought him a certain amount of attention. Vincenzo Vexx was more than just the guy who paid him cash money for the 'chrome. He'd been hand-picked by Jaq, singled out as a relentless creep who'd guard his number-one Pharmer like a cut pitbull.

Which had worked, up to a point. That point was fast receding into the distance beyond a haze of paranoia, anger, drug abuse and sleepless nights.

Tonight the structure behind the operation was different. He had a client that made Kaito's R.T. psycho pals in the Ashishim look boring and normal.

Haszan was a great believer in being well-informed - it kept his ass alive. He kept it…what was that word? *Compartmentalized.* Kaito for the drugs, Vincenzo for the 'dreno, old man Vanecke for juicy info.

All that had changed last week, when he tried to cash in his last paycheck with Omnivasive. The scar-faced old dispatcher down in Media Procurement had tweezered a fresh flycam into Jaq's watch, then tossed him a thick, tightly-wrapped bundle, his paycheck snapped to it with a rubber band. Jaq's two chromed-out fingers had razor tips which popped like switchblades, and he slit the brown paper in one long smooth motion, hoping against hope for more cash.

He shook the contents out – no cheque. Just…

One crisply typed letter. Ten glossy photographs.

Omnivasive kept it succinct.

Taped to the back of the most explicit pic was a small plastic phial of clear liquid. Pinpoints of darkness floated inside it, shivering in the light.

The pictures were of Kaito. And of this there was no question… he was talking to a Cop. Lieutenant Eddie Tsien, a crooked little 'burb-scum bastard who'd almost come close to busting Jaq's 'dreno operation.

The thin, gaunt little man in the gray trenchcoat and fedora hat was smoking a badly-rolled cigarette; the scene was rendered in similar washes of smoky gray - the interior of an interrogation cube. Two slack-faced Cyben stood like waxworks on either side of the door, their dead fingers curled around heavy riot guns.

But what really caught Jaq's attention was the date, pixilated in across the bottom of the security-cam printout. *Three weeks* before Tsien had snapped Haszan with his needles and phials, conveniently in just the right place at just the right time… three weeks before he and Kaito were holed up in that exact same cube, cutting a deal to stay out of the lobo factory.

Oh, the little bastard had some explaining to do. *But soon. When it was over.*

Jaq – none other than the Butcher of Hab-Block 112, scourge of the Final Reich – knew not to pick a fight with his erstwhile drug-buddy. All that Magus shit was black voodoo to him, but he'd seen the results. And then there were the *Dervashi* of the Ashishim - perhaps they had the Kayzi's back? No… he'd leave any reckoning until he had solid evidence. After all, this mess had been cooked up by Direktor Vanecke, the Wizard of threedeeo.

The old bastard kept it succinct. This was some very professional extortion.

"Usefulness is a funny thing, Jaq," it read. *"It's a matter of mutual faith. You can be sure that Omnivasive will pay you what we owe. You can be sure that Omnivasive is loyal to its employees. And you can bank on the fact that if you screw with us - and we'll know, don't worry about that - then we* will *come down on you like the wrath of the Vatican's fallen angels, and do things to your poor mortal body that would make a serial killer sick.*

It's a sign of how sad the world is that our faith in you is based largely on article three.

As a sign of this faith you have been entrusted with a very valuable technological relic. It must be delivered into the brain of Lord Simeon Blaire at exactly 1900 hours on the twenty-seventh of this month - or the consequences will be dire.

Please be advised that this is proscribed technology – being found with it in your possession warrants instant execution. We take the term 'employee termination' very literally."

It was signed by nothing less than one of the floating robot hands of the Direktor himself. And that's how he got his latest customer. A fucking *Lord of the Razor Clique,* for the love of all hells! Three extractions, no more, no less. Send the adrenochrome to Vincenzo Vexx, but don't tell him where it came from. And tonight, at exactly 1900…

All he had to do to meet the 'high standards' Vanecke was so proud of was to deliver the contents of that little phial directly into the living spine of Lord Simeon Blaire. As his line of business required a fair share of needlework, Haszan felt that he could handle one extra stab.

He just wished he could be sure that it would *only* be one. These kinds of arrangements tended to get out of hand – look at what had happened to Feldon.

Octavio Vanecke pushed pushers.

He snapped necks, and posted bombs, and rigged bio-onboards with wild, fatal viruses. In fact, he was probably worse than Vincenzo Vexx, and *that* was hardly a reassuring thought.

Besides which, whispered an unwelcome voice in his head, he needed Kayzi alive. The little dude was his electronics man, his partner in crime, his drug buddy. And with the rest of his genetic relatives gone to the grave during a long ago R.T. turf war, he was the only family Haszan had.

That made him most uncomfortable of all. People like him - people like the image he wore as armor - didn't care about anything but number one.

Haszan waxed professional. He fired his grapple-line, old mil-spec hardware, watching the thin carbon cable sketch its perfect arc up over his head. The access hatch above popped open with a single twist of its locking wheel, and whole batteries of alarms failed to go off as he pulled himself up through the floor and into the Forbidden City, the domain of the Lords. If Kaito wanted him dead, why not right here? Without the signal-jammer he'd clipped to Jaq's collar it would be suicide to even breathe this rarefied air…

It could all wait until the job was done. Until the paranoia stopped hissing in his brain, and the crystal edges of the Stunn turned back into invisible blades.

Until then it was time to get self-employed.

Ω

It was dusk down in the shadows of the Subcity.

Down here they told the time by the regular venting of toxic steam out of the manufactoria below – you could set your watch by it, if any of the locals could afford one.

Right now it was about six p.m – the big sluice was open, and lime-tinted mist hung heavy among the washing lines and jury-rigged wires of Prospekt Street. Needless to say, you didn't want to breathe it.

Three rusty cruisers and a Div meatwagon sprawled across the cracked concrete, under flickering blue neon panels adorned with holo stickers of chubby-cheeked cartoon pigs. The first were courtesy of Compliance Marshall Akembe; the last an addition by sub sprogs, lifted on blue meth or the Stunn.

This precinct was little more than a heavily armed hovel; a row of cages covered with black poly-tarp to hold the incarcerated, and a wheezing elevator down to the factory levels. Two hundred feet under Prospekt Street a synthesoy extruder, a machine the size of a navy dreadnought, has been demolished to set up a secure firing range.

In a fit of bleak irony the Comp. Div. boys dubbed precinct 2996 "The Fortress of Justice", though any superhero worth their cape and tights would have detoured clear across town to avoid it.

This little outpost was barely a hand-grenade's throw from the barricaded gates of the Celestial Kingdom; a dead-end shack where most of a cop's time was spent staring down stone-faced neoconfucian commandos. They had a recruitment shanty welded up over the end of Prospekt Street, a pile of shipping containers barnacled with air-scrubbers and freon exchangers.

If it wasn't for the need to wear a disposable khaki paper uniform 24-7, most of the people of this neighborhood would have been queuing up to swear allegiance to the Son of Heaven, or whatever they called him.

But it *was* close to the Valley View mall, which meant as long as one officer stayed on duty the rest could go and sink a few pints at the Pit of Nails, about three hundred feet upstairs.

From the mezzanine of that ill-favored dive a cop who'd only had a drink or two might be able to lend fire support. The one who pulled the short straw had to wait back in the Fortress of Justice, one hand always on the trigger of the desk-mounted antique bren gun.

Today, it was the quartermaster who drew unlucky. The muzzle of his heavy machinegun rested, listless, on a patch of yellowed linoleum.

Despite the wonders of modern technology instant coffee was still bad, still always cold, and still the policeman's best friend. He was on his fourth, and the machine had a couple of new dents in its faceplate for pissing out such swill.

Still, it had got him this far. Six p.m. rolled over with a crackle of static and a tinny little fanfare. The QM propped himself up on his plastic chair, hunching over the Fortress' cheap threedeeo set. It was time for the afternoon sports report, and boiling neon advertisements haloed the face of Elysium's favorite anchorman.

"This is Dave Levine coming to you live from the compound of Duke Lysander Jaegenn – Lord Treasurer of the Direktoriat and president of Helios Fusionetics. He's a long-time sportsman, thirteenth in the rankings, and a devout Kronocultist from a long line of Kheptic Chosen." The camera panned around the gaming hall of the Jaegenn spire, where spider-mekan and servants in pale togas prepared the stage for another round of battle. "Yes, a well-rounded player, over forty years of experience, and a suite of bioenhancements the envy of many lesser competitors… I think with the home side advantage he could even topple Simeon Blaire from the top rung."

The broadcast of the Game was still considered vulgar by some; the old guard who'd lived before the reign of Octavio Vanecke, back when threedeeo was a public service. So the camera crews were as discreet as possible, and the commentary was tacked on at Omnivasive HQ, where Dave Levine stood in front of a greenscreen, squinting at the teleprompt.

"Remember folks, only Lords Jaegenn, Carlisle, Valchec, and Lady Elisha Dawes remain, the rest VICTIMS of the ruthless and efficient Lord Blaire."

The cam zoomed into tight focus as Dave oozed drunk sincerity.

"Ladies and gentlemen, we are poised before one of the greatest events in threedeeo history. - not since the run of Lord Sergan Zaanic three hundred years ago has any Kheptarch attempted the Imperial Trials. Needless to say our hearts are with Simeon Blaire, perhaps the future Emperor of Elysium… and we've been invited by the generous Lord Jaegenn to broadcast this one LIVE!"

"And I'm gonna have to watch it all from here… freakin' double-overtime!"

The quartermaster snapped the set off with a scowl, mentally disengaging his onboard.

"Delivery, sir. Your authorization is required."

His finger tightened against the Bren's trigger as he spun around… right into the eyeless face of a transport mekan.

"Delivery, sir. This is a priority package for the acting commander of Precinct 2996."

"Yeah, that's me. So what, you want a signature or something?"

A small nuclear reactor on fat rubber surfboard leash hung back over the mekan's shoulder, and there were more skulls, trefoils and lightning bolts painted across the crate it carried than the Q.M. had ever seen in one place before.

It had to be another toy for the boys down at the firing range.

"That won't be necessary, sir. Please hold still for just a second…"

A rubber cup on the end of a jointed tentacle exploded from the thing's shoulder pauldron, striking like a rattlesnake. It locked onto the Quartermaster's eyeball before he could lift his Bren gun, and a blast of green light stabbed clear to the back of his skull.

"Ow! What the fuck was that for?"

"Retinal identification confirmed," said the mekan. *"Have a nice day."*

It retracted its tube with a whipcrack zipping sound and strode off into the dim recesses of the shack, down toward the test department. The Q.M groaned, grinding the heel of his hand into his aching eye. Oh yeah… this was just the tech boys' style.

Those screw-head weirdos sometimes didn't come topside for days, eating prepack dried soy and getting their jollies blowing away rusted-out tanks. Well, happy freakin' birthday, thought the commander, contemplating a fifth oily cup of coffee. Only an hour to quitting time, then he could trade it out for beer.

He was locked back on the threedeeo, slack-jawed and vacant when the mekan came clicking and whirring back out of the dark.

It walked out onto Prospekt Street and into a narrow alleyway, dragged along on an infra-red chain. It stopped beneath a sagging fire escape, and the blinking green lights in its faceplate went out, flashing orange and red. With decisive movements of one arm the robot produced a small EMP mine, attached it to its head - and quietly erased its brain.

Ω

Memory.

It still burned incandescent, even now… this one, this precious little shard. Things like this… they were the sum of him, after all.

"Did you think that after all I built here, that I'd let it all be ruined by a thing like you?"

Octavio Vanecke pointed one black-nailed finger at his captive's face, at the slick raw muscles and peeled-back skin of a living corpse. "Did you really think I'd pay you off, and let you *live* with all that dirty information in your head?"

The man couldn't answer - he was manacled to the wall with hydraulic clamps, the skin of his face held away from his skull by gleaming surgical hooks. Spider-legged surgeon mekan worked industriously, coring out his bones, grafting and stitching… probing his exposed brain with filaments of wire.

"I came up from nothing, Aitken. *Nothing.* And I did you the honor of bringing you with me. I had plans for this company - first the pitfights, then the news… then the Game. *Their* Game, Aitken… imagine it! But you had to try to ruin everything, didn't you?"

One of Vanecke's fingers caught the edge of Aitken's sawn-open skull, and made his head nod once, twice.

"That's right, you did. For *money.* Filthy bloody money! When the council was about to sign it off, and give me access. They don't want another Reclamation Day, Aitken, and they think if the people see them as *immortals* it might help keep the peace."

Octavio strode away from the blood-slick metal wall, his huge hands clenched at his sides. With a curt gesture he summoned one of the mediteks from behind his 'mersive hood. The doctor came running, peeling off his control gauntlets as the glittering arms of his surgical mekan ground to a halt.

"I want him to survive, Chalmers. I want him to remember this. But I want him neuroblocked and fitted out for the fighting

120

pits by tonight. Can you do it?"

"His body's tough, Direktor," said the renegade biotect, wiping his sweaty palms on the front of his crisp white apron. "But his mind… you know he can *feel* all of this, don't you? Only one in a thousand can survive intracranial sequestration… and still retain their sanity."

"Of course I know!" snarled Ashcer, turning back to look at his vivisected captive. "Why else do you think I wanted this done without anesthetic? Nobody will believe a mad, slavering pit-dog. Not even if what he says is true."

"There will be… complications, I'm afraid," sighed Doctor Chalmers, staring impassively at Aitken's torment. "But he'll be ready. Rest assured, I won't pass up an opportunity this unique."

"I'm sure you won't," said the Direktor, as images of Aitken's final form flickered in his bio-onboard vision. "This one's grotesque, even for you, Doctor."

"I am a slave to my muse, Octavio," replied the renegade with a sickly smile. "All I ask is that you continue to bring me such exquisite blank canvases, and I will never fail you."

Vanecke took one last look at his old friend and colleague before the doors of the 'tective suite slid closed. It was a fitting fate for a traitor, but even the hardest of hearts had to pity the subjects of Chalmers' experiments. It was too bad he'd learned the truth. Octavio needed those cameras, needed access to the Kheptarchs' bloody Game.

Because without them, there was no way he could subvert it.

In the end, of course, he'd gone under Chalmers' knives himself. Once, to make him superhuman, to bring his mind and body to the very threshold of godhood. Then again when he fell, and was reduced to his current condition. Currency greased the skids. He'd been retrofitted for immortality, his human flesh sloughed off like the skin of a snake.

He couldn't die now. Not with what he knew. Not with what he planned…

But after one hundred and eighty years the Celebrants were finally coming for him.

He didn't plan to go without a fight.

Then… then came the greatest shuck and jive of all time, a magic trick like three-card-monte with whole planets.

The light which slanted in through his leaded glass windows cast long shadows across Direktor Vanecke's blood-red carpet, pooling, seeping shadows that gathered in corners and behind the pedestals of his collection of abstract sculptures. He kept no furniture except for a great rosewood desk, its top covered with tanned leather culled from real cows grown for this specific purpose.

Octavio liked the sense of touch - his hands were extremely sensitive, free from the blister scars he'd earned in his youth. There were four of them now, drifting about the office with the hum of antigravity motors, flitting here and there like steel hummingbirds. Another drummed its long metal fingers pensively on the desktop, annoyed by the sensate childishness of its brothers.

Octavio himself was blind - at least with the eyes that God had given him. Nor could he speak, his voice long severed from the remainder of his body. In fact, of the flesh he was born with, only a few charred scraps remained. Behind his glittering mansion and his dapper avatars Octavio Vanecke was nothing more than a severely damaged head, encased in preservative jelly.

The rest of his body was made up of wires and tubes and dials and syringes, drips and catheters, machinery that filled the walls and floor and ceiling of his office with its ironic picture windows and expensive pieces of artwork.

Across the inside of his preservative tank, carved into extruded carbon even diamonds couldn't scratch, Octavio had engraved the words of Ptahotep, echoing down the centuries from 3400 BC.

"Be a craftsman in speech that thou mayest be strong, for the strength of one is in the tongue, and speech is mightier than all fighting."

It would go with him to the grave, undeciphered, perhaps for millennia. Octavio Vanecke wasn't one to entertain visitors, colleagues or business rivals. The office was for the hands, his

Druuj. Like the Wizard of Oz, he stayed behind the curtain and pulled the levers.

In the emptiness his clock began to strike seven. A slim-fingered hand hissed through the air and stopped the pendulum in mid-swing. While outside on the streets a blue glow began to suffuse the afternoon light as millions of fingers reached for millions of dials, and the threedeeo radiance went out, up to haze the very stars.

Ω

"This is the Farmer," hissed Tsien's miniaturized police radio, a tiny bead hugging the wall of his eardrum. "Have you found the little present I left for you?"

Tsien elbowed his way past a gaggle of dead-eyed Cyben and out into the evening chill. The sun was long gone now, the steel sky of the sublevels growing dark as massive light-wells and mirrors ground closed for the evening. His gloved hand gripped a greeting card, crumpled and damp.

"Nice one, you little bastard," growled the Lieutenant. "How'd you hack the all-points-emergency channel? That's supposed to… ahh, forget it. Trade secret, right? Something your seditious buddies in the R.T. taught you?"

"Never mind how I got hold of you, Eddie," whispered the voice in his ear. "Just make sure you deposit the cash for this last job. I've really got better things to do with my time than shopjack, so you should be grateful."

"Thanks again then, old pal," said Tsien, his face twisted up around the end of his cigarette. There was no trace of bonhomie in his voice as he pulled his fedora's brim down and stalked across the echoing concrete. "Not only a little work for your old friend the Lieutenant, but some for the meatwagon as well." And indeed, as if by invocation, the Medicorps (with a spray-painted 'e' on the end; applause for the gutter comedians of the Subcity) were pulling into the lot, their bulky eight-wheeled stiffhauler crunching over a carpet of broken glass to be greeted by Lucas. "I'm sure everybody's full of gratitude for this fine performance, Kayzi, but next time could you keep *them* out of it?"

Sure enough, the clipboards and palmtop computers were out, as the chief paramedic argued points of law with Lucas in the middle-management equivalent of an old-west gunfight. Tsien extracted and lit up another cigarette - (he liked to have such a fatalistic vice…especially one he shared with his favorite twodeeo detectives), and pressed the spring-loaded microphone arm closer to his lips. The lieutenant's purity field rippled open and shut around the cigarette, a sheen of crystal blue. Fans in his belt-mounted filter expelled a thin mist of tobacco smoke.

"More to the point, keep your friend away from the guns. I know you're not stupid enough to jeopardize our arrangement. But something tells me that someone's getting high on his own supply down on the farm."

The answer, when it came, was almost as cold as the wind that was keening in off the West Bay.

"Try to remember the important thing about *mutual benefit*, Lieutenant. Anytime you want to give up your end of the deal, just say the word. I'll put a bullet in my associate myself rather than give you the pleasure of making a real old-fashioned narco bust. And then you'll have to make quota without me."

Tsien was tempted to call the Farmer's bluff, if only out of spite. One glance over his shoulder at the bloody scene spilling out of the King Value was enough to hold him back, however. Mrs Toria Jane would no doubt clobber him with a hefty divorce settlement if they ever had to leave the Burbs. And you could never be sure, *truly* sure, that a chemhead was bluffing.

"Allright, allright… take it easy," said Tsien, flicking the butt off into a patch of twisted vegetation. "Just keep it in mind that murder's still murder, no matter how shitty things have gotten down here. The Chief *is* gonna find out about this one, if he hasn't downloaded the report already. You can't silence a fucking walking corpse with a modem in its brain-pan." There was a non-committal grunt from the other end of the connection - it was good odds that the little savant actually could. Tsien decided to play a moral card anyway. "Now go and get your fix, you fucking junkie."

The Farmer laughed then, the hissing, eerie laugh sucked

dry by the comm unit; a laugh broken down to atoms and put back together at the far end of the connection without any of its original humor.

"We're both pretty clear about what we want out of life, Lieutenant," he said, and Tsien could easily hear the snap and hiss of Stunn capsules being popped open and inhaled. "I don't want withdrawl, and you don't want your wife screwing you in court. Let's just make sure we both get to enjoy these little pleasures."

Tsien cut the connection first, determined not to allow the Kayzi that one small victory, and he lit up another cigarette. The matchstrike looked cheerfully warm in the artificial gloom.

The Medicorps(e) were still doing what the Medicorps did these days, hosing down the empty King Value with foul-smelling disinfectant, leaving a scum of gray foam across the drab concrete. The division called the stuff 'cotton candy', although nobody knew why. One taste would burn clear through your guts like drano... and your bones as well. Tsien had seen it happen to lobos, dogs and rats, in that order of frequency. Perhaps the Medicorps had started the rumor that it got you high – hells, they were on quota too.

Fuck the Corps, he thought. Eddie knew exactly where to get his hands on some truly mind-bending shit - fresh from the adrenal glands of a harem of farmed junkies. But if he wanted to keep his little scam on the down-low, he'd have to let Jaq and Kaito keep theirs...

"That shit'll kill you, y'know."

It was a Corps sawbones; a field medic in rubber whites, schlepping half of the poor dead King Value clerk in a biohazard bag.

Eddie laughed.

"You ever see a Cyben need to breathe? I'm more likely to catch lead than cancer in this job."

"It's your life," said the doc, dropping his black plastic burden. It hit the concrete with a nasty wet slap. "Sign here, here and here. Initial here. We've got to get these bits down to processing."

"Autopsy? Don't bother. It's a suicide, shotgun curtain-call. I'd do it too, if I was stuck behind a counter all night."

"No, no… you think we bother slicing up every mook who gets killed in the SubHabs? Nah – this boy's getting *recycled*. He feeds the fungus vats, and the fungus vats feed you and me, see?"

Tsien scrawled across the doc's tablet with his stylus, squinting through a haze of tobacco smoke. So, it was official now. Used to be just the garbage went to the vats… now it was human wreckage as well.

"Guess I'll be thinking of him at dinner, then," he said, as the doc slung his sack over one shoulder and pitched it into the back of the Meatwagon. Oh, what he wouldn't give for some real, black-market steak, or some lipid-heavy contraband fries. It didn't matter what went into the vats; what came out always tasted like cabbage paste…

Off behind him he heard cursing, swearing, shouting – bureaucracy in action. Eddie sighed, and pulled the collar of his trenchcoat up around his ears. He'd better break up Lucas and that Medicorps jerkoff before he had a second homicide to deal with.

17 Aevum Oblivio
Enter the Explorator

Zhe was feeling slippery on this whole three-dimensional gig.

But the memories of Kaito Kayzi knew all about survival in this mad universe.

Grinning, the technician held out his palms and exerted pressure on reality. His hands were filled with the cheap plastic handles of two zaibatsu-built railpistols in an instant.

If the ancient enemy of the Multiplicity was here it wouldn't want to negotiate, after all.

The first of the Golems blew apart as it came in through the door, forcing itself through the blastproof steel with a howl of ablating metal. Through the Golem-shaped hole it had created thronged more of its misshapen brethren; each a humanoid swarm of black nanos. Heat radiated off them in waves.

Zhe unleashed a firestorm from his pistols, scouring the lockway as seething Slavesystems widened the gap. Kinetic rounds shattered the Golems into screeching, writhing fragments. Incendos delivered searing sheets of flame. Detonants popped and blasted, sending individual 'bots scattering like chaff.

Without the limitations of actual ammunition or the need to reload, Zhe waded through the twitching, melting Golems, making for his carpetbag. Now twenty had fallen, now thirty. And behind him, the pieces of Everdark began of merge together, a puddle becoming an ocean of flickering blackness…

DOCUMENT INSERT: MULTIPLICITY ARCHIVES DEPARTMENT

Mark-Four Cyben - Internal Memorandum

RE - Recent anonymous video upload (suspected source; Illuminatus Zeon, High Magus of the Ashishim)

Conclusion: This footage - although highly improbable - appears to be genuine. The Illuminatus explicitly warned us about the threat depicted here during our negotiation settlement of the 'Seven Hours War' crisis, and we must assume that he/it is acting in the best interests of both his faction and our own by divulging this intelligence data.

Response: Funds have long been withheld from our advanced Cybernetic Warrior Integration (Cyben Mark Four) project, but with the possibility of invasion now very real we feel that the time has come to instigate a field trial of the system. If this proves successful we can see no reason why thousands of otherwise useless Subcitizens cannot be pressed into service in a military capacity.

A recovered crycelium augmentation system must be thawed and integrated with a Cyben Vilicus drone unit - hopefully the drone will impose a limit on the self-replication ability of that archaic experimental device.

A trial subject has already been selected; a disposable yet superficially loyal member of the Compliance Division recently investigated for corruption. As current-model Cyben are processed from the waste bodies of terminated officers his family will harbor no suspicions.

Generate Executive Order: Instigate immediately;
Test Protocol 721 - Activate prototype Mark-Four
Cyben.

17 Aevum Oblivio
Soul of a New Machine

THE DOOR WAS sealed. Zhe had managed to wade through Everdark's children by way of sheer crushing firepower, but the effort had bled him dry. The alien Technician sat slumped at the foot of the door, a smoking pistol in either hand.

Why hadn't they told him the Motherbrain's slaves were here? Lord Arbitrex Galq had always been his patron, hand-picking his missions to hone his exoethnological skills. Had the Wyrm sold him out? And if so, to whom?

Whoever had damned him, they'd done a thorough job.

There was no way for Zhe to escape.

Not from the crushing mass of Everdark, swallowing the Cardinal Rock in its death-grip. Not from the insistent, irrepressible feed of images transfixing his mind from out of the machine. And definitely not from the golems, looming up out of the shadows all around him…

He couldn't move.

Eyes like spheres of white-hot metal opened; closed. The image behind them didn't change by a single pixel. It flickered, a snowblast of static slicing raw gashes through his brain…

Zhe stood atop a cube of mirrored glass, one of serried ranks beneath a great concrete dome. He had been here before; but then he'd been in control, chaining an obsolete and doomed machine to his will. Now, however… It was alive.

Like the interior of a vast skull, the dome was strung with taut tendons, veined membranes and nameless, pulsing organs. A heartbeat thundered low and slow and deep, pumping oceans of blood through a tangle of arteries and veins.

"Where… what the hell is this place?"

A sickly light illuminated the dome, glimmering from globes of phosphorescent flesh. Beneath his feet the cube shuddered as muscles and tendons clenched tight.

"Hell is closer to the truth than you might expect, Zhe. Oh yes…"

He knew that voice. Oily, purring… it ran fingers of ice down his spine.

Against his will, he saw...

Above him in the humid air hung a torture device of pure energy, a mockery of the intricate heart of Kronos. Crucified and slit open across that rack of sharp light was a human form... or what once may have been. Hooks peeled back the skin of its chest and belly; barbed spikes of energy punctured its flesh, pinning its great knotted limbs. Chains quivered tight, tugging at raw meat.

Half of the creature's face was flayed back to the glistening bone; petals of skin spread wide by needles. Gore and gristle slid slick and greasy in the horror-light and Zhe reeled, feeling unnaturally ill.

It was the face of Lieutenant Tsien – Dissected, bloody, and smiling.

Obviously, said a part of the technician's mind, he was long dead. Obviously, it was all just a part of this accursed hallucination...

But that part of his mind was blown away screaming when Tsien opened his eyes and began to laugh.

Got Chrome?

"Number thirty-seven, I think," sighed a voice like silk and cream. "Number thirty-seven — yes, and with the hair in variation two. I want to feel… *pure* today. Above this sordid business."

A synthesized voice murmured sweet nothings in his mind as he slipped down the interlock, flowing into a steaming glass capsul chased with gold. One sarcophagus among thousands, in a room the size of an aircraft hangar carpeted in white angora.

Each coffin contained a body without a mind – some huge and powerful, some slim and fey, others so alien as to defy description. Now the door of number thirty-seven hissed open, and a pair of feet stepped out onto the soft carpet, dewy with condensation.

"I suppose the agent is already here," sighed that deep and sumptuous voice. "Be he ever so distasteful. Seneschal; purge number ninety-six, and see him to the rooftop garden. I won't have him inside the house, but I suppose we have little choice…"

Emmanuel Lancaster stood reflected in a hall of mirrors, shimmering monomolecular screens hovering in mid-air. Tonight he was an angel, complete with swan-white wings and a blazing antigrav halo of burnished gold. Rows of tiny silver screws spun down tight, connecting the top of his skull and sealing in an artificial brain patterned with his memories. Blonde tresses sprouted and curled from implanted roots, each filament utterly perfect, spun gold to the tips.

He wore seven eyes, in a smooth pearlescent face so perfect it seemed unholy, lips as lush and ripe as original sin, cheekbones sharp enough to slice the perfumed air.

The body was pure irony – he was about the work of Hell tonight. But it always helped to put the servants in their place. This was *his* world, after all.

"Elevator, garden floor." he said, stepping into a silver filigree cage suspended on antigrav discs. "And a little light music, I think. It's a long way to the top."

The estate of Third Lancaster was by far the largest of Elysium's spires. Tier upon tier of mirrorglazed offices and apartments bore up a wide and shallow dish of steel at its soaring crown. Holographic advertisements shrouded the entire great edifice, blazing the logo of Universal Wetsystems two hundred stories tall. They bathed the bimburbs below in strident neon, dappling the baby-blue polyprop of their artificial skies.

"The outside temperature is twenty-three degrees, my Lord" murmured the Seneschal, a Digital Personality Core nestled at the spire's heart. "U.V. warning is medium to high. Would you like any refreshments sent up for you and your guest?"

Lancaster snorted "Guest? That *thing* is just another slave - even lower than you yourself, Seneschal. The only reason I'm talking to him face to face is that my tech cadre are nowhere near as skilled as my biotects. A secure line would be too much to ask."

Then the silver cage came up through an iris of steel, and Lancaster Park spread out all around him. It was perfection, torn from a thousand renaissance paintings; the only slice of wilderness left on Earth. Cleon First Lancaster had built it more than a thousand years ago - but of course, Emmanuel was the very same man, retrofitted for immortality. Aside from Kronos, that made him the oldest living thing in the city – he'd certainly earned his little sanctuary.

But what horror was this?

What random and savage manifestation?

A tube of crude meat in plastic armor clashed horribly with the decor, ruining the garden's whole aesthetic. The scratchy sound of *heavy metal* filled the air around it, muffled by a pair of duct-taped headphones.

Emmanuel felt dirtied by the touch of its shadow.

The flesh-wad was a mercenary clonehunter, and this was the one and only place in which he looked alien. In a packed choob of struggling commuter peds, you'd ignore this guy with a vengeance.

His name was *Melchior*, although Emmanuel couldn't care less.

Melchior, to his credit, hated Lancaster Park just as much as his host hated the smell of his rancid breath in the fragrant air.

The outlines of his body seemed wrong here; his normality made deformed by the perfectionist geometries of the biotects. Better than real at twice the price, as the brochures said.

Clonehunter Melchior's arms resembled pistonrods tightly coiled with high-tension wire and bound in rawhide. He didn't have delicate skin. He came from a womb, and lived in a foetid warren of metal dewy with reconstituted sweat. He was only here because he killed so beautifully – a meat-machine that hunted down clones born out of copyright.

"So very *pleased* to see you again, Clonehunter. That little business with the Confederates went remarkably well - their so-called *Pureblood* soldiers weren't quite so perfect as they'd like to believe, hmm?" Emmanuel tried to hide his distaste, but even his augmented nervous control wasn't up to the challenge.

Melchior popped a huge, imponderable wad of cheap pink gum between his chancred lips.

He had no medical plan.

A light rain of almost invisible saliva pattered across Lancaster's skin, and his mouth twisted with disgust. Now he'd have to have his favorite Serpah body cremated again…

"I done the recon, boss. I done it good. That R.T. boy's tight up inside Vincenzo's office, waitin' for his mark."

"Then this assignment should prove to be even easier than usual, I should hope." The clonehunter's flat mirrorshades followed him, his stubbled jaw masticating rhythmically.

"You can keep the adrenochrome. Do with it what you will," said Emmanuel, hauling himself up to his full height with a rustle of white feathers. "Don Vincenzo is Celebrant bait anyhow – if you knock him off consider looting his corpse your bonus." He chuckled. "The poor old fool thinks I'm going to Process him! That should keep him in his place while you make the hit." The grotesque little man was still grinning, chewing his wad of cheap gum with a sound like muffled automatic fire. Oh well, his whole body would have to go anyway. A little extra disease-laden spit wouldn't make much difference. "Just *please* make sure you take down that renegade Ashishim. He's a medi for someone rather interesting; a discontinued contract. A little side wager, if you will…"

Pale white fingers lifted the clonehunter off the grass, his military boots dangling for a second before his master dropped him like a piece of used toilet tissue. Hands-on management was one thing, but *touching* a lowborn was something else entirely!

"Really, can't you people be bothered with even the most basic retro-sequencing? This body of yours is a rolling wreck, Melchior!"

The weasel-faced assassin smoothed down his military tunic with an exaggerated motion, popping a membranous gooey bubble in his master's face. The great gray broadsword strapped across his back had pricked a little line of blood from the Hierarch's finger.

"Melchior be kill dem; say done an' iz completely fucked, sir," he said, raising a half-cut salute.

Emmanuel sighed. He'd seen quite enough. His impossibly long thin fingers pinched the bridge of his impossibly aquiline nose, a sure sign that there was a king-sized migraine coming his way.

"Just don't fail me, Clonehunter," snarled the angelic Lord, "Or I'll find a place for you in my laboratories as a test subject. There are some things I'd hesitate to do even to a mind-wiped peasant, but you could find them… *educational*."

With that last little motivational threat the Biotect summoned a pair of white-robed slaves to carry him away. He simply couldn't be out of this tainted skin a second too soon…

Clonehunter Melchior yawned. He'd seen every marvel technology would buy him on the inside of a tiny red capsule of the 'chrome.

For the sake of that chemical love he'd get the job done.

As Emmanuel Lancaster disappeared down the marble steps Melchior dropped off the edge of the biotect's Eden, his jetpack igniting on the second yank of its pullcord.

The Ashishim was good - he'd checked out all his records. But the Clonehunter knew he was better. The towers and tiers of Elysium scudded past him as he fell, arrowing in on Vincenzo Vexx's window, far below.

He grinned. It never hurt to pack a bigger knife, either.

Ω

Tsien was mired in paperwork. Such a bullshit term for a bullshit chore – there was no paper involved, of course, just a stack of grimy and cracked twodeeo clipboards bleeping and yammering for his signature. Lucas took care of most of it, but there was always a heaping helping for his commanding officer.

He sat himself down on a toppled green plastic trashcan, while the sputtering roll-your-own dangling from his lips uncoiled a ribbon of smoke.

"Was the perpetrator, in your opinion A) Motivated by profit B) Motivated by revenge C) A paid assassin of the R.T. factions D) Motivated by cultural and/or gang related tensions."

He knew full well what the perpetrator was motivated by – a little bag of gel caps in stripy candy-cane red and white. But he licked his pencil anyway, spun his wrist in a circle and stabbed down on 'D'.

"Hey, Lucas, any coffee left in your vac?" Tsien cursed, pinching his cigarette between two nic-stained fingers. "I'm gonna need some stimulants to finish all this crap…"

It was just then that a noise like a stereo recording of sinners burning in hell blasted out of his pants pocket, loud enough to make him drop butt, clipboard and all.

It was the radio again, but this time it wasn't Kaito Kayzi yanking his chain. To achieve such pitch, such discord, someone must have sodomized a demon with a cattleprod and added feedback. It was the sound of mechanical panic - the Critical Emergency Signal.

"An APB! Boss! All points! You think it's another Royalist bombing? A Kronocultist uprising?"

"I think it's bullshit, Lucas," growled Tsien. "Probably some idiot Khept set off their own alarms again." Of course, the juve hadn't seen an All-Points before. These things were like dancing

136

between helicopter rotors. Messy.

"An *accident*? Tonight? C'mon, Chief – not this close to the big one. It *has* to be the real thing!"

Eddie was taut as a bowstring, trembling inside his damp gray coat as he heard the sirens howl all over the city, their one-note song echoing from Redcastle clear over to Saint Pete's. Out there, a thousand law enforcers would be mouthing the same profanities and sweating the same cold beads of sweat.

For good reason. No force on earth could actually co-ordinate the crumbling remnants of the Compliance Division - who'd calculate the quotas, for starters? Then there were the Cyben - some of them glitched and patched-up units fifty years old. If they all fired in the same direction it'd be a miracle.

Tsien had almost convinced himself that it was time to taste a spoonful of cotton candy when a human voice – the division's central dispatcher – cut in across the private band.

"Unit 334, under Lieutenant Tsien, Constable Lucas, you're closest to the epicenter. Kit up at Precinct 2997 - heavy ordnance. Instigate Cyben loadout one-three-niner, and await further instructions."

Tsien smiled; a glacial grin which spread across his face until it threatened to unhinge the top of his head.

"That's a big ten-four, Central - Tsien and 334 confirm status switch to triple-overtime and shoot-first status."

Being singled out by the Marshall meant only two things, two undeniable truths. The first was a fat hazard bonus, up front and with no extra paperwork. The second was free license to use any and all force necessary. And you couldn't PAY for stress relief that good.

"Lucas!" he shouted, breaking into a run which sent toxic bubbles and drifts flying like filthy snow "Tell these corpse-jockeys to scrape up and ship out... we have to get to an ordnance pickup at the Fortress!"

Lucas already had the sawnoff shotgun ripped out of its plastic griplock bag and was stuffing shells into the choke. "Don't listen to him." he muttered under his breath to the Medicorps manager, knuckles white where he gripped his clipboard of regulations "You boys should stick around. It looks like it's gonna be a busy evening for all of us."

Ω

Night. A forest, spread out into a pale gray-black blur. And stars above him, the scar-faced moon hanging huge and silver on the sky…

The engine howled and roared in protest as Vincenzo brought his wingtip down hard, grinning around the smoldering butt of a huge cigar. Hundreds of dollars worth of whitewalled rubber went up in smoke as the Bugatti took a corner in a barely controlled slide, skating across the asphalt like a two-ton pat of butter on a hot skillet.

Beside him Maria slapped another drum magazine into her Thompson, sequins flying from her sheer-cut dress like tiny stars in their slipstream. The tearing sound of automatic fire battled the bellow of the engine for a second as she let rip with the machinegun, peppering the chrome grille of the Cadillac which dogged their smoking tires.

Vincenzo squinted, staring down the gleaming black ribbon of road where it snaked between the trees on one side and the river on the other. This car shouldn't exist – the last of the Royales, wrecked in '31 and rebuilt with bootleg money here in Chicago. Its long-nosed hood concealed a twelve-cylinder Victory aero engine, twenty-seven liters of raw power blasting flames out of a clutch of sawnoff pipes.

The Caddy was up on them anyhow, tighter through the turns than the monstrous Bugatti hybrid. He saw some of Frankie G's boys hanging out the windows, letting off bursts of fire as their car swerved and shuddered from side to side. Maria picked one off as he watched, the hail of lead plucking him from the running board to fly off into the dark, a ragdoll trailing blood.

This was what he lived for – the great brutal car at his command, a beautiful woman at his side, adrenaline pumping though his body as he carved a name for himself out of the wild dark city. Here, nobody remembered the name of George Nathan Henry Smith, small time Tech fence.

They – the powerful, the rich, the corrupt and the beautiful – knew him only as Don Vincenzo. Here he was cruel and sophisticated and respected… even more so than in real life. There was no history to stain his character in the virtual fantasy his Suit wove for him, nobody who knew that he'd once been a vile urchin from down in SubHab Seventeen. To tell the truth, all his machinations, his 'dreno trade, his robotics business – they were all just to buy him time inside the 'mersive.

That was how the agent found him.

Out to the left of Vincenzo's little pool of light, out over the knotted pseudotimber boards with their engineered creaks and groans. Past faces of cancerous stone, mangled supermen with horror shadows seeping…

Black swathes of night surged into the room like a torrent; curtains blown in from a gaping window. Reflected neon caught the edges of a human figure perched on the sill; A Euro, but dreadlocked, scarred. His face was wrapped up in a silver and black death's-head, a smartfabric hood blurring his features. It slicked over his skin like paint, picking out the room in a wash of night-sight green.

Abdulafia 330, Sword of the Faithful.

It only took him a couple of seconds to spot the case which was his target - it positively *glowed* as ident programs lit it up for him.

The Ashsihim agent leaped from the window ledge and onto one of Vincenzo's giant statues, landing as quietly as a fluttering moth. Microfiber pads on his gloves and shoes held him tight to the stone as he inched forward…

Oh yes - there was something strange about this batch. He could smell the 'chrome from across the room with the olfactory boosters drilled into his nasal septum, and it was more than pure enough. With this stuff, there was no limit to what he and his fellow *Dervashi* could do.

"Confirm, control. We've got him cold. Damn, but that stuff smells *good*…"

Then the image of the Don seated at his mammoth desk flickered and collapsed. It was nothing but a hardlight hologram, projected from a tiny bead on the floor…

"Code nine, *Dervashi* agent… we're picking up a power surge in your sector! Achaeotech readings are off the scale…"

Abdulafia froze.

And Don Vincenzo Vexx loomed out of the shadows in a storm of twitching threads, his Suit tearing open down both arms as loaded guns dropped into his gold-encrusted hands. The grin plastered across Vincenzo's features told 'Afia that he'd been ready and waiting, poised in the dark with his intelligent garment switched to camo.

"Welcome home, honey!" said Vexx, his face split by a yellow-toothed smile. "Didn't anyone tell you how to use a *door*, you nomad piece of shit?"

"Born in a tent, boss. But they did teach me how to use *these*…"

Typical dumb crooked bastard, thought the Ashishim. They always gloated first instead of just pulling the trigger. That bought him just enough time to lock in his autoinjector, pumping adrenochrome nektar into his carotid artery. The whole world went glacial as his neurons turned to frosted glass…

And his panga knives unfolded like butterfly wings of steel.

First hit. Pupils dilated, nerves sparking double-time. Muscles boosted…

A spiral-tipped slug jackhammered out of Vincenzo's Taurus on a tongue of flame. The revolver's mechanism ticked over like continental drift…

Now.

'Afia sliced lead. Slow, so slow. But spark-skitter fast, cutting six bullets in half in midair.

He flickered in a strobe-lit blur, and the very last flash left him leaning up against a statue, a single slug pinched between two fingers like the butt of a cigarette.

Vincenzo's face crawled with worms of black thread as he pulled his gun up; sneering at the theatrics. Twelve little half-bullet holes smoked in the walls on either side of him.

"Stand still, will ya? You're only making this take longer than it has to."

As the revolver popped open, smoking, Abdulafia went for the case.

"This is all I need here, Mister Vexx. Put down the guns and you can write it off as a tax deductible."

"You couldn't resist, could you?" asked the Don, as the rig snicked and whirred, reloading. "Did you really think you were that good? That I wouldn't be *waiting* for you?"

Abdulafia tied the case to his combat mesh with 'chrome-quick fingers. His death's-head face was nothing but a grin and shadows.

"As you just saw, Mister Vexx, we've found other uses for the 'chrome than simply gettin' blazed. I don't suppose the junkies you tapped to get this would have much sympathy."

'Afia knew that he'd gone a little too far when he heard the hammer of the Taurus snap back again.

"No goddamn respect, any of you!" snarled Vincenzo, the reloaded gun dropping into his hand. "This is *business*, Ashishim, not a rehab clinic. Now do me a favor, put my drugs back on the table, *and DIE!*"

He heard the trigger grating against the metal of its guard, and he let the autoinjector bite deep, slowing time to a crawl. The next few seconds were jammed together in a stroboscopic rush - an adrenochrome dance as bullets tore through the dusty air.

Second hit. Headache building, ten percent chance of stroke or seizure. Blurred vision, numb fingers…

When the revolver popped open again he was perched up between a pair of cyclopean figures like a gargoyle, balanced on his heels.

"Calm yourself, *George*. A man your age – well, you don't want to raise that blood pressure, do ya? Here – take one of these." The R.T. agent flicked one of the tiny phials of adrenochrome down to his enemy.

This time the response was quiet; the bullets spent.

"Don't call me George," hissed Vexx, a breath above whispering.

And the stone Abdulafia perched upon exploded.

There was something inside it – something huge and powerful flexing its corded steel muscles. A pair of hands like steam-shovel blades stripped its plasticrete disguise away, revealing a squatting humanoid beast, a headless mekan chassis in Vatican white and gold.

"That's right, you outlander fuck! Daddy's home!"

The Don's smile was like a gash down to the bone.

Third hit. Hypodermic teeth penetrating his skin. Random heart arrhythmia. The taste of copper, bile on his tongue. Everything was spinning, night-sight green…

Abdulafia fought instinct and gravity and inertia, and saw four feet of razor-edged death howling down toward him too fast to dodge. Snapshot - a squint-eyed weasel face, eclipsed by a huge pink bubble of cheap gum. Too much 'chrome! His hands were twin blurs of white fire, cold chunks of incandescent ice…

He clapped the swinging end of the sword between his palms, twisting the whole weapon hard and sending it flying. It had missed by less than an inch.

He locked eyes with Clonehunter Melchior.

"Look out behindja," hissed the clonehunter, grinning with a mouthful of crooked teeth. The wiry little mercenary slammed a fist into 'Afia's chest as he somersaulted away, disappearing into the dark.

Pain doubled him over.

That punch was all out of proportion to the Clonehunter's size, and Abdulafia was sure he'd felt pistonrods of combat 'tech behind it. If he'd been built of normal human muscle and bone the shock would have stopped his heart, but instead the blow propelled him backwards, right through Don Vincenzo's desk. Antique wood shattered, sending splinters flying.

As the impact knocked the breath from his lungs 'Afia wondered why Vincenzo's Warmekan wasn't moving…

Then he saw the pinstripes flare outwards from Vexx's body, a million threads of black and silver lifting him up on filament legs. Afia's heart was banging against his ribcage - it felt like a hot ball of barbed wire in there. But he had no choice. *He couldn't let them integrate.*

Fourth hit. Blood was dripping from his eyes and nose now, and his arms and legs were nerveless, cold dead meat. But the power. *Oh, the deep, seductive heart of the power. The 'chromehole, which had swallowed up so many* Dervashi *forever...*

Those icy hands of his had the power of all the angels behind them. The meditations of the Illuminatus swirled in his head as he drove his fists into a hunch-backed statue, tearing it from its plinth. And he lifted it. Gritted his teeth. *Threw.*

He never saw the impact.

Something came screaming out of the dark at him then, scraggle-toothed and greasy, inked up with jailhouse tattoos. It was Clonehunter Melchior, running on the row of statues as if gravity had shifted sideways, driving him back with another sword - bigger this time. He swung it with a strange chopping motion, aided by a second handle at right-angles to its hilt. Abdulafia knew, as he heard the sound of two tons of stone hitting three inches of armor, that this thing would take his legs off like brittle stalks of grain.

The two of them blurred like lights across a time-lapse photograph, combat systems pushed to their limits. There was no way he could squeeze any more strength or speed out of his failing body - he'd have to finish this on raw skill alone. Lucky, then, that he'd been learning unarmed combat for the last hundred and twenty years.

Abdulafia launched himself at his enemy, panga knives blurring gunmetal gray...

Melchior's flamberge flew underhand as the clonehunter leaped, a strike to sever a man from crotch to shoulder...

It never landed.

Abdulafia watched the razor edge of the sword skim past the tip of his nose, light picking out the whorls and spirals in the Damascus steel. Then he planted his knives and lashed out with both feet, summoning all the strength left in him. The impact jolted up his legs like a hammer blow, sending the clonehunter flying. But it worked. Melchior's wiry body crashed through three statues before he landed, tumbling in a rag-doll tangle of limbs.

The Dervashi was just about to allow himself a little self-congratulation – but then a bullethole the size of a hubcap was torn out of the floor beside him.

"I told you to *stand still*, you wily bastard! What, you thought I was gonna let you go?"

Oh yeah. Vincenzo Vexx...

Abdulafia turned, looking up. And up. And *up*. The squat little Don was gone, and in his place was a metal goliath, daubed with pious runes and fluttering silk ribbons. It was a Vatican Templar warsuit, a piece of hardware designed to tear battletanks in half.

Quite an inconvenience, to say the least.

Vexx's chubby fingers operated a nest of wires deep inside its chest, his crycelial pinstripe socketed into banks of tactical computers. Now the Templar hefted up a weapon the size of a family sedan – a Thompson machinegun built on an immense scale.

A hand like a skeletal gauntlet racked the bolt, with a sound like the gates of hell slamming shut.

Abdulafia decided it was time to go. His 'chrome was fading fast.

"Time to learn some *respect*, nomad. Too bad you won't be going home to teach the rest of your scumbag clan..." Ten feet of muzzle-flash belched from Vincenzo's cannon as he hosed down the row of statues, cackling like a maniac. "Come out, you Ashishim bitch! This'll only hurt for a second..."

Vincenzo slammed forward in a rage, shrugging aside and shattering titans, blowing them to splinters with a rain of shells. Soon there'd be nowhere left for the *Dervashiman* to hide.

It was Melchior who saved him, his sinewy hand clenching 'Afia's black crescent and hauling him out of the firestorm. He was all wire and servo, billet aluminum bones and fury. The clonehunter stapled the *Dervashi* to the ceiling with his own panga knives, clear through the shoulders of his holocloak.

"Izmine, Georgie!" spat Melchior, shaking a tattooed finger in Vexx's face. "MistaLancaster promise."

"Drop him, shit-heel, or I'll bury you both," growled the Don. "And to hell with that androgynous freak Lancaster! He can have your ashes."

"Ya wanta piece, George? I'll take your head to Mista L, see what kinda bonus he pays me! Sez you meat for the Celebrants anyway!"

"Jesus, will you two *stop calling me Geor...*" But he never finished. The clonehunter was already on him.

Melchior spun in midair with feral grace, landing lightly on the barrel of the gun for a second before he tightened his arc, his foot blurring into a savage roundhouse kick. His hobnailed boot slammed into the Templar's neck with a sickening crunch. Gurgling, bug-eyed, Vincenzo went from upright to horizontal in one unstoppable motion. The floor shook with the impact.

Melchior flew back at Abdulafia snarling, his hand going to the hilt of his flamberge. The blade was a gray blur over Melchior's head, scything overhand, and there was no way that 'Afia could block it this time.

Welcome me home, Illuminatus. Father, I give you this body as an offering, awaiting new life to come...

There was a sound of metal on metal, a spray of glittering sparks in the gloom. Something caromed off the ranks of statues, spinning wild... and then a hand burst out from the center of the clonehunter's chest.

It was made of shimmering patterned light, and it dropped him to his knees.

Triplicate lasers stabbed out from a hovering black bubble of plastic and steel behind the 'hunter, poised on three tiny antigrav motors. The sword clattered from Melchior's hand as he felt that ghostly arm become horribly solid within his flesh, and his eyes creased shut with sudden pain. *Hardlight.* There was only a couple of minutes juice in the crescent's batteries, but that was enough.

"You could try to move, I suppose," purred a soft, malicious voice, "but you won't get far without *this.*"

The glowing hand disappeared from sight. It had slipped back into Melchior's chest, and his look of stark terror evidenced the grip it had on his heart.

Abdulafia allowed his eyes to crack open a little, letting in a blaze of purple light.

Painted in black across it was the silhouette of Melchior on his knees, while above him stood a glowing angel, her slim face framed by neon-blue dreadlocks. Digital tattoos writhed through her firmament, studded with licks of code.

It was another *Dervashi* of the Ashishim, but this one was no scarred-up old veteran. She was tiny and perfect and dressed in holographic rags; an oily old T-shirt and blue jeans, with boots four sizes too big on her feet and spiked bracelets hanging from her wrists.

"CeeAn," he croaked, his throat raw and dry. "Glad you could make it."

Her eyes changed when she saw him move; they lost their cruelty as he stood, braced against the nearest statue.

"So you're mister 'I don't need backup' now? What the hell, 'Afia?"

She reached out with one hand while the other stayed deep in Melchior's chest, and a coiling artery of plastic tubing whipped out from her hovering crescent, plugging into his autoinjector.

"I'm trying to save you some downtime. These recon jobs are just plain tedious."

The drugs hit home, and Abdulafia slumped back against the wall. Cee's hand around his neck pulled him back to his feet.

"I'm bored already. If you leave without me one more time, so help me…"

"What? You'll steal one of Zeon's masslifters and blow a hole in the subcity? Oops…"

"Don't even *think* of complaining! There's no way you could have gotten clear of this *obvious* trap without me!"

Abdulafia smiled, his face still creased with lines of pain despite the drugs.

"And now the two of us are stuck in it," he said, as Vincenzo clambered laboriously to his feet behind them. "Way to even the odds…"

"Outlanders!" raged the ironclad mafiosi. "You're gonna wish Kronos caught you here instead of me! You're gonna pray for a trip to the lobo plant!"

The Don ripped the empty drum magazine from his cannon and threw it aside, spent. Then he hurled the useless weapon away into the dark, bringing down a domino-line of walls. Abdulafia could see his face behind the suit's bubble-dome, and the veins pulsing at his temples were like high-pressure hosepipes.

"You Ashishim hoodlums are gonna regret ever setting foot out of the R.T.! And if this breaks your treaty with the Vatican, you won't have a stinking hovel left to crawl back to!"

CeeAn flashed Vincenzo a look of pure scorn, as though he was a scraping of dogshit on her boot.

"You let *this* guy outsmart you? The decades are catching up with you, 330."

"Who says I was outsmarted? Maybe I knew my impetuous young partner would just have to follow along…"

Cee smiled down at clonehunter Melchior.

"Kill him and I'll let you live," she said, tightening her hand in a vise-grip around his heart. "You can have every damn thing in this whole place - except the 'chrome."

It was all he needed.

The clonehunter reached for his sword, but she held him back by the slippery vertebrae of his spine.

"I have to give you both an even chance, don't I?"

Then her fingers slipped out from between his shoulderblades, and he was off the leash, howling.

Melchior sprung desperately to the attack, leaping onto the war-suit's back and raining down blows on Vexx's head until he screamed.

But it was no use. One of the suit's pincers pried him from his perch, crushing his ribs in bands of steel. The Don grinned – this was finally working out for him. He swung the struggling little clonehunter up over his shoulder like a living hammer, then brought him down in a blurring arc which would mash both Melchior and CeeAn into the floor. Halfway down he caught her eye. She was smiling.

Too late Vincenzo realized what she was doing; and in that instant, as Melchior descended on an inexorable crash-course, he tried to eject from the suit.

Abdulafia had connected his partner's black crescent to the mains supply.

The purple sheen of her skin cracked and rippled, evaporating into warped, acid blue. For an instant she was a dark shadow amidst the light, a pupil of black in a cobalt eye. Melchior bounced off her upraised palm, screaming, flung aside as the war-suit's arm servos fused solid and cracked.

There was second of sound so vast it was like silence – a white-hot silence filled with pain. Electricity flared and raved in a flashburst of searing light, and as Don Vincenzo howled his rage and frustration the filaments of his bio-intrinsic suit, his pinstripe, ejected from *him*.

They tore off chunks of armor, thrashing in the all-pervasive strobeflash like tentacles.

While they did, CeeAn 187 devoured megawatts of electricity. She locked hands with Abdulafia and the blue light surrounded them both, building up a spiraling whine like a camera flash.

She patterned the energy *just so*.

Vincenzo felt the pull, the thousand tiny pains of filaments torn from their fleshy sockets, just as they disengaged from the war-suit. Melchior - blackened like a nuked cartoon character - wobbled over to the window and silently toppled over the sill. Halfway down he remembered to scream, yanking frantically on the ripcord of his ruined jetpack.

Vincenzo never saw him go; he was being *stripped*.

The threads of the suit were out of his control; he felt amputated. They came up out of his throat, from his tearducts they came, and unscrewed from around his bones. He sweated them out. Cee and Abdulafia unwove the pinstripe strand by strand as the empty metal husk of the Templar suit yammered and screeched with warning sirens, its tactical computers burned out.

Finally 'Afia cut the connection. He bled from his eyes and ears and nose; his head was filled with razors and raw ethanol.

And Vexx saw the death's-head mask fall from his face. His voice was a feeble croak from between bruised and broken lips.

"What the hell are you doing mixed up with this crowd?" he asked, recognizing Abdulafia's face instantly from the threedeeo. "You ain't no Outlander! But if…and how… then why… "

Abdulafia 330 propped himself against a pillar, laughing through his pain. There was no part of his body which wasn't bruised or bleeding, and the comedown from four hits of 'chrome was looming in his mind like a spiked metal wall. "Oh, I'm not *him*, Vincenzo. Think of me as the black sheep of the family - the disowned brother." He pulled out a phial from the case, falling to his knees in front of the Don, who lay flat in a pile of knotted filaments. A pair of red satin boxers with a black heart motif preserved his remaining dignity. "Why do you think they sent a Clonehunter down here, anyhow? They can pop me out another body every month or so - we don' have the accelerated vats like ol' man Lancaster."

Vincenzo swiped at the phial with one hand, but Abdulafia kept it out of his reach. He rolled the little spiked wheel with his pointed tongue.

"And If you know my face, answer me this. *Why does this 'chrome here taste like me?*"

Vincenzo spluttered and twisted as Abdulafia emptied the adrenochrome over his head.

"While you ponder that one, I'm afraid we have to go."

CeeAn's color had faded from incandescence to a muted shimmer, but the neon blue tattoos still blazed from her skin. Ashishim code spiraled up through her in helical coils.

"Quit fooling, 'Afia…evac in ten …"

As he turned away he missed Don Vincenzo's maniacal grin. There was still one last trick up his… well, it wasn't exactly his *sleeve*, but…

Now from outside came the ever-increasing roar of an evac vehicle rising up from out of the R.T. Up the verdigris-mottled cliffs of metal it came, riding ethanol fire and crewed by desperate chaingun-wielding Ashishim. It resembled an armored double-decker bus humping a Saturn-series rocket. The room began to shake.

"Hey, you hippie bastard! Don't you turn your fucking back

on me!"

Vexx's last little concealed handgun was a flechette derringer, hidden down the front of his pants. It spat once – a single, cyanide-dripping dart. But the Dervashi saw it coming, thanks to the tiny camera between his shoulderblades. He twitched his head an inch to the right, hearing the poisoned flechette hiss past his ear.

"I really didn't want to kill you, Vexx," said the battle clone, dropping a punch-dagger from its wrist-sheath with an oily little click. "You're one of the last people who remembers Reclamation Day, and I don't want that prick Vanecke to be the only one left alive…"

"Allright, you *dickheads*! That's ENOUGH!" CeeAn 187 had run out of patience with boys and their stupid games. "You – 330!" she snarled, pulling the Ashishim clone back by the tatters of his black coat. "Make too much work for those damn bio-lab geeks and I won't have my new body ready until next month." She turned on the pathetic, twitching figure of the Don, all round and pink and bruised. "And you – Vexx! We didn't come here for *fun*, you know. That last batch of adrenochrome wouldn't have done you any good where you're going. The word's out all over the datanet. The Celebrants are after your ass."

Vincenzo ground his teeth in frustration, slamming his fist into the floor. Those two meatboys on the corner! And here he was, defenseless… He shot CeeAn a look of pure undiluted murder. You could have burned diamonds black in the air between them.

"I'll get you, outlander! I'll rip the…"

Then the walls came off.

There was a noise like paper being torn by ten million hands as a brace of sawtipped harpoons tore through plasticrete and plaster, dropping a vast piece of masonry end over end several hundred stories. She saw the grimy thumbs-up of the pilot, the wild eyes of the chaingunners hanging from the doors by the grips of their hulking weapons.

She jumped clear just as the lifter reached its zenith, graceful despite its bulk as it spun and turned, doors opening in its flanks like petals. A meaty thump on the bench seat next to her let her know that her Abdulalfia had managed to hitch a lift as well.

Then they dropped out of the frame; out of the gaping hole that was once a picture-window in the wall of an office on the skin of Hab 2095. She felt the medicrew put her on recharge; felt 'Afia feel the same.

They slept as they were delivered back to the Pit, where even now an operating theater and a detox transfusor were being prepped for Abdulafia's convenience.

CeeAn would have to wait a little longer, but fair was fair. She *had* lost three bodies in only one week, and as Zeon always reminded her, reincarnation was a privilege, not a bonus.

Ω

Sweet oblivion.

It faded out behind a haze of pain… a vast, throbbing world of suffering.

Floorboards. Broken metal. Blood.

Vincenzo was still very much alive, and he was well past being amazed at his current predicament. Had that tiny little tattooed angel actually *yelled* at him? He honestly couldn't remember the last time he'd been shouted down like that… let alone taken a beating so bad.

A cold, sour wind came rushing in across the wrecked office, across his ruined and naked flesh, pale and pockmarked where tubes had torn free from his skin.

There was a great deal of blood. Too much, surely, for it all to be his own?

Small fires flickered in the dim corners of the room, behind the impassive forms and faces of melting colossi. By their light, a shadow fell. And George Henry Smith knew that the Celebrants had come for him.

They didn't speak, or even seem to breathe - a pair of dark and otherworldly figures stalking at the edges of his delirium, armed with guns and machinery and innumerable ticking clocks.

At the last, as one of the Celebrants pressed the cold steel of his machine pistol to the Don's temple, they pulled back the lace and satin veils from an old portable television set. Its stained and faded beige plastic was warped from centuries of abuse, and its screen was a flickering green pool from which the floating head of Direktor Vanecke grinned, the stump of his severed neck made holographically fresh.

"So many people wanted you gone for good, old friend," said the head, blurring in the haze of Vincenzo's fading vision. "But I wanted to show you something which I will never see. I wanted to let Kronos *keep* you."

"Why…" spluttered the Don, trying vainly to lever himself up off the floor.

"I'm afraid it's a very old story, Vincenzo," said Vanecke, the look of sympathy in his dead eyes almost believable. "You simply know too much to stay alive. You know about the trick we pulled on the Vatican – about that empty reliquary down in the Black Techs' monastery. Oh – and when we were seven, you stabbed me in the face with a plastic fork. Good times, eh George?"

Vincenzo saw the face of Simeon Blaire juxtaposed with that of Abdulafia 330. He understood.

Then Arnic and Thibault dropped the veil, and light spilled out from a million pinprick holes, flooding the room with static. Don Vexx was laughing as the Celebrants took his mind, their slaved machines slicing his neural structure to ribbons…

He saw.

And it burned as it took him apart.

But something survived. A part of him was captured as it began to disperse, fraying and unraveling like dried-out silk…

The pattern of energy which had once powered every cell in his body was *recorded* in all its tangled detail. His painful death, frozen.

Kronos stretched out that instant into infinity.

Then stored it, filed it, numbered it and moved on.

Ω

The Fortress of Justice was locked down, barricaded and blacked-out. Tsien only found it by the pink glow of holographic cartoon pigs plastered across its grimy windows.

The precinct 2997 boys were prepared for them.

Tsien kicked the door in, grinning like a maniac. No force on earth was going to come between him and some serious firepower tonight… not when his pet chemheads were off the leash and killing. He came in through the shattered doorway with a smile on his lips and his eyes lit up with murder.

"Anybody home? It's the gods-damned pizza man…"

Dave Levine still grinned and gesticulated in a snowdrift of empty coffee cups, his sportscoat flickering with infomercials. Ten thousand intermeshing logos painted the cinderblock walls as a naked bulb sputtered overhead…

Ahhh… *company.*

The Quartermaster was pawing vomit off his chin as Tsien's Cyben slung him up against his desk. Threedeeo glare shimmered across their laminate in waves – and there was blood on their knuckles.

"Get out!" yelled the struggling Tech Division officer. "This isn't Street Compliance territory! You've got no jurisdiction here!"

Lucas had an official release printout in his hand, dripping with Direktoriat holo-seals. He stuffed it in the wretch's open mouth.

"Give the Chief what he wants and we'll be long gone, wirehead. Just locking the door on us is a mind-wipe offense."

The QM blanched white, imagining the probes up under his eyeballs…

"Well, you wouldn't be the first to pretend they're not home when we came knocking," said Tsien, pushing the man down into his chair. "And I know you're just covering for those geeks down in the range. But tell me…" he spun on his heel, pacing beneath the pendulum arc of the room's single lightbulb. "You got any hot tips for the game tonight? See, I thought I'd stay clean, just watch the thing for its entertainment value. But now it looks like I'm stuck on overtime."

The luckless officer nodded as one of Tsien's Cyben ripped the keychain from his belt, struggling to point at the threedeeo. The

Lieutenant snapped his fingers, and the dead machine's hands hinged open from around his arms.

"I'm a Royalist, S-Sir," he said, as the laminated hands about him peeled back. "Only four more players to go, and then we could have a new Emperor. Dogma be Praised!"

Tsien scowled - another romantic in love with the idea of *royalty*. You could scrape the blue-ribboned freaks off the pedwalks in their dozens these days.

"Remember what happened to Zaanic?" he asked, all mock-innocence.

"Lieutenant, n-*nobody* knows what happened to Lord Zaanic. The Trials weren't covered on threedeeo back in his day."

"Exactly, buddy, *exactly*. That poor old aristo fool is probably still up there in the labyrinth, all desiccated on a spike. I'm sure the Machine's in no hurry to replace itself."

The Quartermaster's eyes narrowed and he ran his fingers over the blue ribbon around his wrist. But he kept his mouth shut. He'd never been on the wrong side of Cyben's fist before - dammit, that wasn't supposed to be *possible*! Something was fractured down deep in his chest, and he could feel jagged bone-stumps grinding together with each breath...

"Now tell me, *Commander*," said Tsien, lighting up a cigarette as a ream of official papers spooled out of his belt-mounted fax. "What's the best toy you've got to offer me? West Central are packing fusion carbines. You're gonna be a laughingstock down at HQ if I walk out of here with a lousy semiautomatic - *that* I can promise."

The Q.M. tasted blood in his mouth as the monolith-shadows of Tsien's Cyben loomed up over him. An involuntary whimper forced itself out between his teeth as he cowered back, hands scrabbling across the desktop.

"Fine. Take it! Central sent the test team a new toy today - but if it was up to *me* you street grunts'd never get your hands on it. You're all going to be replaced by Cyben when Lord Blaire's in charge." Which was suddenly not such a comforting thought...

"It's *not* up to you, though, is it?" snarled Lucas, jamming a flickering data-tablet in the man's face. "We've got orders right from the top, and there's nothing you back-room jerkoffs can do about it!"

Tsien pulled his junior officer away like a dog handler yanking a pitbull's chain.

"Too bad, but he's right. And for the record, it's 'street grunts' like us who make sure the Liquid Tong or Vexx's boys don't just walk in here and steal your toys."

He wanted to choke the life out of him. Out of *something*. The stress was wound up so tight in his head that it felt like it was going to fracture... but Eddie kept control. He snapped up the key-card before the quartermaster could take it back, and flashed a smile that was little more than a baring of nicotine-yellowed teeth.

"Thanks for the tip, *officer*. Now, I believe you've got some more sitting on your ass to do, right? While the rest of us go save the day?"

"I hope to God that thing blows up in your hands, you psycho!" spat the QM, leaning back as Tsien craned his neck over the desk. He eyeballed the man from about an inch away.

"I think God's about done with me," said Tsien. "But if you're keen for Jesus why don't you sign up as a Vatican eunuch? Looks like you've got nothing to lose."

He stalked off down the corridor, popping the keycard between his fingers, Lucas following at his heels with a handful of requisition notices and printouts. The steel walls rattled and the ceiling dripped. The corridor twisted and turned and forked, working its way ever downward...

"Sweet Dogma itself, Chief... would you look at that thing!"

They spotted it at the same time - a curvaceous black shape in a pool of scarlet neon, framed in an open doorway.

Tiny LEDs blinked in the half-darkness. Cold metal burned like molten rock under the emergency lighting. There was a *gun* back there in the gloom, the kind of weapon which looked like genocide forged in steel. Tsien slipped the keycard into its slot, and the clamps popped open around the Eversio with a hiss of cryogenic gas. If you had to set a trap for a stress-burned, trigger happy, corrupt son of a bitch like Tsien, this would be the perfect lure…

The Eversio was a chromed and gleaming four feet long, its stocky body a mass of dispersal cowls and air intakes. Four wicked blades curved out from its muzzle, each angled sharply backward to form an arrowhead of serrated metal. Pipes connected a chunky backpack to the body of the weapon, a solid mass of heat-sinks and fans festooned with straitjacket straps and buckles.

There was a manual on the wire-mesh shelf next to the Eversio, a three-ring binder at least a foot thick. Most of it was warnings.

"You're going to take *that* one?" asked Lucas, his shotgun suddenly looking quite small and insignificant. "It says on the crate that it's for 'anti-exo-armor operations'. Isn't that a bit… excessive?"

"Who knows what's going on at the Valley View?" grinned Tsien, leafing through the manual. "We might end up facing…" he traced a line with his finger "'light battletanks, antigrav gunships, heavy mekan or exosuit infantry', right? Has anybody told us we *won't*?"

Lucas raised one finger and opened his mouth to protest, but stopped when he saw the sparkle in his commander's eyes. It'd be like telling a kid there was no more Christmas.

"I suppose they haven't, Chief. But you'd better suit up, just to be safe. This thing *is* fission powered."

Lucas handed him a pair of thick black rubber gloves, and after Tsien pulled them tight over his fingers he gingerly lifted the Eversio from its housing.

The harness snapped tight, seeming to pull its magnetic clasps home of its own volition.

"Oh yeah! Now *this* is why I put up with the gods-damned paperwork!"

Tsien slipped the goggles down over his face…

And the Eversio assumed control of its systems.

Tiny needles inside the headset bit into his skin, sharp as little claws.

"What the hell? It's *biting* me! The son of a bitch!"

Then the poison began to flow – neuroblockers shutting

down Eddie's nerves until his face felt like a slab of cold meat. Something was blurring into view inside those bulky green goggles as he staggered, scrabbling at them with numb fingers…

Kronos.

"Are we ready to begin? Yes? Oh, he's a live one, isn't he! Well, he'll break. They all do…"

"Chief! I've got you! I – I can't pull it loose! I'm going to…"

A bolt of electricity punched into Lucas' chest, sending him flying across the room. Whatever he had planned was far too late.

Tsien was *connected*, the full force of the Wetsystems earthed through his body like a vast bolt of lightning.

"What the… Lucas! Help me! Get this damned thing off of…"

But his voice cut out, strangled by the will of Kronos. Nothing could stop the process now that it had begun. The interface expanded, torn wide by surgical hooks of energy, making a precise incision in his mind.

"Hello, Eddie," said the Machine. *"Consider this… a promotion of sorts. I know what you've been doing, you see. Using those Sub-scum… cunning. But you don't seem to be the only one, and even I can't tell how deep the treachery goes. So… I've decided to bring you into the family."*

Long segmented arms telescoped out from the Eversio's headset, hooks glittering as they rotated. They curved around his head like a cage, biting deep, pulling taut… Tsien tried to scream, to curse, but his blood was awash with tranks. An instant later, he found out why Kronos needed him sedated.

It was a Vilicus drone, the machine which powered a Cyben's dead, laminated corpus. The name meant 'Overseer' – or 'Slavemaster'. It popped out from the top of the Eversio's backpack like a trapdoor spider, hypodermic fangs flashing…

This time, Eddie managed a brief and heartfelt moan of agony.

"It's quite a privilege, actually. There hasn't been an experiment like this for more than two thousand years. Then again, I'm afraid that means I'm very badly out of practice…"

His veins swelled to the size of hosepipes as screwtipped wires raped them. Drills sunk into his collarbone, into his spine, hot and buzzing, whirring, coring to the marrow.

And the sedatives failed.

Pain came down on him like a ten-ton hammer, obliterating reason. Beneath it raged the onslaught of the Vilicus drone, as mechanisms designed to enslave dead flesh went to work on living meat…

"They called it the Chimera, Eddie. The hybrid beast. But they should have called it the Ouroboros instead, I think. In the end it always devours itself. You'll see…"

Surgical steel tentacles twisted obscenely as splatters of blood rained down. The tungsten drills at their tips worked methodically onward, chewing through the living bone of his skull – and beyond. They tunneled clear through his head and burst out through his eyes, their tips irising open to reveal tiny camera lenses.

In the corner of the room Lucas stirred and groaned, his shaven skull dripping with blood. That blast had knocked him out cold…

"Ohhhh – Chief, what the hell? That… that tazer musta gone orf by isself… Chief?"

Tsien's head sagged forward onto his chest, dead weight, as the lenses in his eye sockets blossomed with hard blue light. Blood welled up around the entry wounds of twelve shining scaled tubes, the tips of which budded with living crystal filaments.

Hot crycelium – self-propagating webs of the stuff.

Kronos was laughing in his head as his brain was devoured, turned to a webwork of metal and crystal from within.

"Just like the machines of the Celebrants, Eddie. But this time, you'll be loaded back into your own neurostrata. I have one last task for you, despite your treachery – a chance at redemption."

Lucas caught it all in double vision, his head throbbing with pain.

That face! The blank mask of ecstasy which hung crooked on the Lieutenant's skull!

Eddie's expression didn't change as he held his arms out cruciform, letting a brace of half-inch drillbits chew into his biceps. They coiled around his bones and through his muscles, howling. Flesh split, raw and bloody. Gore-slick tubes socketed and slid and coupled, writhing under his skin.

It was nothing short of technomancy, utterly forbidden.

"It's holding! It's holding! Ahh, Lieutenant, to think that I called you expendable. *I calculated your chance of survival at only twelve percent! Biofunctions are approaching redline..."*

Still - it was *working.* The cryeclium was dividing and multiplying in the furnace of his body. As its rootweb grew so did its power, fulfilling the program which the scientists of the Terminus had encoded centuries ago.

They were building a *Chimera* - an integrated soldier. Kronos knew it by another name, however - *Super-Cyben.*

It was done.

"There! Do you see now, Eddie? Look around you, and comprehend the limits of your servitude..."

He opened his eyes into horror. All around him, in the walls and in the towers above, down to the chasms and pits below the city... the dead. The things in the Wetsystems, in the neurostrata – those once-human wretches who had followed Manifest Dogma. Some of them had even welcomed the Celebrants, with Kronocult prayers on their lips...

And there was the Engine.

It was a scrawled pyramid of fire etched across the shadow of Elysium, a thing of cruel mathematics and light. Slavemaster to a billion dead souls, using them to drive its engines and subsystems and vast machineries...

It could burn him down to nothing but motor nerves and a name. And that only as a handle, the command word written on the *chem* of a Golem...

It downloaded a mission into the hot tissue of his brain, burning it deep.

"Understand, Eddie. You will be the first. Father to a far more useful race than man..."

Screeds of data collapsed in on his soul, folding and shifting like oiled glass petals.

Lucas saw the terrible empty void in his commander's eyes

for only an instant – just long enough to sense the grinding machinery beneath. He could hardly breathe in the heavy air, as crawling sparks played over the walls and floor. Something came unhinged inside Lucas' mind as the pain of a billion disembodied spectres sliced clean through it…

They were calling him down. They were warning him that it was better to die than to join them. But…

He could free Edward Tsien from that promised hell. All he had to do was pull the trigger.

Lucas never saw the Cyben looming up behind him, its dead glass eyes reflecting fire. Its bonded railgun slid out with a wet slithering sound, parting thick slabs of muscle and plastic. Behind its laminate mask Kronos made it *smile.*

Lucas fired at the same time as the Cyben, sobbing, feeling the will of those lost souls press in like the screwed-down jaws of a vise. It was the last thing he ever did.

A red mist filled the air as Tsien swung and fired in a single fluid motion, feeling a symphony of interlocking crycelium and microservo slithering beneath his skin.

The Eversio made no sound, but the air in the hot little cell flickered for an instant. A haze of silver licked out like diamond fog, tying up each flying pellet of buckshot.

It froze them solid in their flight.

The glitter was woven nanotech - hellish stuff from the same cryo-reliquary which had spawned Tsien's new body. The gossamer cloud spread in an instant, mummifying the barrels of the shotgun - and Lucas as well, a scrawl of twinkling metal across his stomach. The moment burned into Tsien's augmented eyes.

The remains of Lucas' chest painted the far wall of the storage bunker as the Eversio twitched, all those monomolecular filaments pulled excruciatingly tight. There was a wet, slicing sound which seemed to come from everywhere at once.

Nothing happened for one heartbeat, for two…

Then the Magnum Express split apart into precise little cubes of wood and metal. The broken pieces fell clattering to the ground. And as the still-standing corpse of Lucas started to topple to the meshwork floor it split apart along a gridwork of livid crimson lines, collapsing into a jumble of disassembled meat.

Then the Cyben fell to pieces, then the shelves, and the wall, cracking and collapsing, then a strangled, bubbling cry from down the corridor heralded the Quartermaster's demise. The ceiling began to sag and buckle.

Tsien smiled, his nic-stained teeth already shot through with silver.

It was time to go to work.

Ω

While Technician Zhe couldn't see it in the archives and video records of Elysium, at the moment of Tsien's transformation something snapped in the very fabric of the world.

A creature without name or form or intellect, a thing with only *size* and *hunger* finally clawed a tiny crack open into the mortal universe, after decades of scrabbling against the barriers which held it back.

It had been here before, this thing, and it had been known by thousands of names throughout history. But never had it felt so compelled; never had it sensed such a rich source of nourishment calling out to it across the chasmic divide between worlds. The Wetsystems of Elysium were ripe with pain and confusion, with the screams of millions of the dead. It couldn't think or plan or plot, but it knew that it must get inside. It must *feed.*

And as the man called Edward Tsien died, enslaved by the steel bonds of the Mark-Four Cyben system, his soul tried to flee from his tortured flesh and found itself trapped. Halfway between life and death, straining against the cruel mechanisms which keep his ruined body breathing.

The tiny gap created in that instant was too small to register, even if machinery existed in the Last City for monitoring such phenomena. But the creature without could smell the Wetsystems through it, it could sense the connection between this crude thing of meat and metal and the sustenance it craved.

161

Sliding, squeezing, flowing like black ink in water, it crawled through the crack and into the blank spaces of Edward Tsien's mind.

Down in the Reclaimed Territories the creature was carefully observed.

And hands very much akin to those of Technician Zhe caressed a row of silver toggle switches, while a replica of a human face cracked open in a chilling smile.

17 Aevum Oblivio
That Was Your Life

"Welcome to our experiment," said Edward Tsien, his teeth moving despite being stripped of muscle and flesh and lips. "As you can no doubt appreciate, I represent the first attempt to complete the metamorphosis."

Zhe clutched his head, kneeling as dark, bloody tentacles bound him to the floor. The rack stopped its spinning, and the flayed visage of Tsien floated closer, his empty eyesockets brimming with foul light. The technician could feel the two realities grinding against each other, threatening to crush his mind between them.

"If anything, the results should be more interesting this time around."

Then the skin rolled back over Tsien's half-featured grin as the background faded, blackened...

About Zhe's comatose corporeal body, the residue of Everdark's Golems was literally boiling, melting together into an inky dome. He couldn't see it coming.

Technician Zhe never felt the myriad tiny claws of the Slavesystem enfolding him. They covered him like a rising tide, plugging into his biological systems and surrounding his brain. He was too far under now to care, or to feel the absolute enslavement of his body. The visions were a lucid nightmare, behind which the face of Tsien pulled the fiberoptic strings. And behind him?

"I'm so sorry, Zhe," said another voice, not as loud, but all-enfolding, a voice which spoke liquid words as huge as mountains. "But as a Technician of the Multiplicity, I'm sure you know about the necessity of investigation."

Zhe couldn't see the speaker through a haze of random memories. But he knew the codespeak twelve of the Multiplicity when he heard it.

"It is possible that I have found, here in this abysmal backwater, a means to end the war." Zhe knew the voice - an echo from his newspawned days, back under the triple-sun of the Technic Academy. He could picture the serried energy bands of Nyl's magnetic field. He could smell his aura.

"With luck," said the renegade technician "you may even survive to witness peace."

Adrenochrome, Pharming, and Nektar

The hallucinogenic effects of adrenochrome have
been known since before the Arbitrium Mundi - as
chronicled in the works of ancient classicist
Doctor Hunter S. Thompson. However, it is only
with the adaptation of genetic science that
the drug has truly become the connoisseur's
hallucinogen of choice, thanks to the procedure
called Pharming.

While pre-Arbitrine Adrenochrome or 'pink
adrenaline' was often nothing more than an
oxidization of medical adrenaline, modern 'Chrome'
is far more - a cocktail of neurochemicals and
alkaloids created by the modified glands in
a 'Pharmyard' donor's brain. Donors undergo
infection with a proscribed retrovirus, turning
them into living chemical laboratories. The
original purpose of this virus would seem to be of
a military nature - Pharmyard donors feel no fear
or pain, and their lack of adrenal or dopamine
response renders them easily programmable. It
probably dates from the Separatist wars, though
the Ashishim sect are suspected of spreading it
through the Subcity.

Chrome Pharmers tempt junkies and the destitute
to get 'on the mainline' with promises of money
and other, cheaper drugs (Stunn, Cranq, SimStimm
etc), then tap their living brains for the ultra-
expensive, potent end product. Users claim that
Chrome can grant them prescience, near-A.I.-
levels of mental power, increased strength and
clarity of insight. Medical tests show that it is
highly addictive, and that the smallest overdose
can lead to strokes, seizures and death.

A modified version of Chrome, known as 'The
Nektar' is used as a combat drug by the Dervashi
zealot-warriors of the Ashishim. Little is
known about this Nektar, except the results - a
superhuman ability to control every muscle and
nerve of the body, facilitating feats of agility,
speed and strength far beyond the reach of common
soldiers.

Taken from - An Alchemical Wedding - Elysian
Society's Love Affair with Chemical Posthumanism

17 Aevum Oblivio

Click

"I'M SO VERY *glad to see you, Zhe," said Technician Nyl, shifting the seething mass of Everdark with a dismissive gesture. "I couldn't get inside that frozen meatbag's mind without the proper tools. And more pertinently from your position, without* live *bait. But I've found things out – oh yes. Important, vital things."*

Zhe detected a faint note of pleading in his mentor's voice.

"As of now, this great obsolete pile is useful only for its strength." He brought the nanonic mass of Everdark up and around Zhe, lifting him from the floor and pinning his hands and feet. Viselike magnetic fields locked him in humanoid form, still clutching his imitation railpistols. "The Motherbrain was far too cautious, Zhe. She never gave Her thralls the power to think for themselves."

Nyl was holding a flat black box the size of an old fashioned VHS tape in one hand.

"But I've appropriated technology from the local surroundings. Training manual stuff." Zhe stared at the black box in horror.

He'd seen what the reports said about Kronos' great engine of war, the thing it called the Forge. Part of his mission here was to keep it out of enemy hands.

Right now, those hands were the silvery talons of his former Academy Hierophant, clenched tight around a multi-channel remote.

"Now we simply change everything," said Nyl.

Zhe wished, not for the first time, that his people still had a god to pray to.

Then the Hierophant's thumb came down, and the Earth disappeared beneath a storm of shadows.

2196 Anno Arbitrium
Here's Trouble

A SHADOW MOVED in the close, humid darkness of Lord Blaire's spire-estate – deep below his palatial gaming temple, down among the austere white rooms of the inner core. The creeping thing's head was a nightmare of segmented eyes and rubber antennae – nightvision optics turning the gloom to a wash of grainy luminous green.

It flowed between the sizzling beams of security lasers, invisible behind a suite of razor-sharp countermeasures, with its manipulators coiled in front of its chest like those of a huge black mantis. Deft fingers pried and twisted, opening a hidden door…

Now – the target. A thin screwdriver slipped from the tip of the thing's claw, while a nozzle in another digit sprayed a fine mist of mineral lubricant. Here, looming over a four-poster bed of black marble and silver stood a machine like an ancient CAT scanner, surgical beige and humming. This machine was Blaire's Imorphium hood, a vast chunk of chrome and plastic worth more than whole neighborhoods in the Subcity.

Inside it was the cartridge which modulated the young Lord's dreams, and it was hot with illicit data. Carefully, slowly, the operative pried the little card from its housing. A perfectly innocent Imorphium program slipped out of his wrist pocket to replace the one he'd taken, resetting the machine as it slotted into place.

But for all his stealth and all his hardwired technology the operative was far from invisible. Kronos had been watching Lord Simeon for quite some time now, and one of the Machine's pet flycams was poised upside-down on the ceiling right above the furtive little man in black.

Now the Guardian Engine sliced through Blaire's security firewalls like so much flimsy paper, hissing through the wires and up into the Imorphium hood. He caught the last shreds of a vast and thorny program as it was torn apart by magnets.

So very little – but enough to pique Kronos' interest.

Dirty black code, sharp ice and more... illicit Subliminals taped in over the top of a night's worth of artificial dreams.

A flicker of images filtered up through the teeming levels of protocol within the Machine. There was a black shadow skittering across the grainy picture, a babel of pictographic characters in a language that Kronos hadn't seen for generations. *Katakana*, a fragment of his mind said. *Ancient Japanese.*

Then there was a single still shot - a crisp black and white photograph. In it stood a man holding a long, thin blade, its tip level with his eyes. His face was a metal deaths-head beneath an ornate helmet, a crescent moon on its brow.

An image he had seen before. Torn from the hidden files of the would-be usurper – Octavio Vanecke.

It took fractions of a heartbeat for Kronos to react, flowing back out of the Imorphium hood and into the tower's mainframe. Forces were mobilized, sequestered, instructed. Myriad calculations seethed through the Machine at the speed of light, extrapolating a thousand possible treasons.

Meanwhile the shadowman skulked back through the dead white corridors of the spire, pausing to unzip his black rubber coverall and slip into a starched Imorphium jumpsuit. His little electric truck stood parked in the bare aluminum corridor, the puffy cloud logo of the 'Tech bobbling and twinkling on its side. But Kronos would never let him escape - not now.

First the vehicle. Overrides blew its electric motors, making the operative jump back, cursing.

"What the hell? If that old bastard's sold me out..."

"I assure you, Octavio's quite innocent. It's just that both of you are out of your league."

The voice came in through his eardrum like a hydraulic spike, steel-grindingly loud. To his credit, the agent didn't rip the mic bead from his ear. A pro, then.

"Blaire? We're doing this for *you*, you dumb Khept inbred..."

"Wrong again, friend. I'm afraid this one's gone all the way to the top."

He knew all about it then. All the stories came flooding back – those horror-tales about how Kronos could scramble your brain like a jellyfish in a blender. The agent swallowed hard.

"All right! All right… just take it easy. I'm willing to co-operate, so long as you let me go. I… I've got a family, kids… I needed the money…"

"Heard it all before, I'm afraid. But in this case, I'm prepared to be lenient. Give me Vanecke, and I'll make it exile instead of the lobo factory. Resist – and your family go first."

"Like you really need *testimony*! You… the Kronocult worship you as a *god!*"

"The illusion of order is very fragile, human. As is the line between 'god' and 'demon'. Now, if you'll forgive me, I've called for a little backup. You won't resist, I'm sure… but I'm not a machine who takes chances."

And here they came. Simeon Blaire's artificial servants, agricultural mekan armed with pruning shears and saws. They surrounded the agent, spider-quick and twitching, their blades snapping and clicking too fast to follow. Kronos had torn their control routines to ribbons effortlessly.

The Imorphium man's hand was equally swift - and equally artificial - as he dropped a pistol from an open and swinging cavity holster.

His right arm was a fake - a hollow chamber filled with pistonrods and wires.

He stared down at it in confusion for a second, choking back a scream.

Then there was a blur of steel in the air around his hand, and the gun fell apart in pieces, accompanied by the tips of two of his fingers. The operative stepped back, still gaping at the clockwork innards of his arm.

"But… how… didn't feel…"

One of the skeletal machines wobbled toward him, its saws twitching back and forth.

"Come quietly, and we may still allow you to live," said Kronos through the mekan's speaker-grille. *"You are in possession of privileged information."*

"I cannot obey," replied the agent. "Code nine-five-six external error. Information access must be disallowed…" He clapped his non-artificial hand across his mouth in horror, his eyes bulging from their sockets. "Did I just say that?" he stammered, looking down at his fingers – three metal, five flesh. "What the hell is a code nine-five six…?"

But he'd never find out.

Kronos chose that moment to strike, sending all three of its sequestered agrimekan in with their saws howling. Strips of coverall and hair and fleshtone rubber flew. Sparks fountained, blurring the pseudocerebrate's cameras.

He realized too late that there was no blood - no scream of pain as its minions tore the operative apart. Switching perspective from camera to camera amongst the agrimekan, Kronos caught sight of three slim black cylinders buried deep in the man's chest. All three were stamped with the symbol for high-explosive.

That – and the gilded 'V' of Vexx Automatronics.

Of course - who else but the late George Nathan Smith was slippery enough to program a robot to believe it was real flesh and bone?

The automaton was already a wreck before it exploded - mangled and scarred by the tungsten-carbide tools of the agricultural robots. It collapsed in on itself before it exploded, its rubber skin bursting as a gigantic fireball went nova in its chest. The lenses of Kronos' cameras melted as his agrimekan were reduced to molten slag, shutting the screens down to hissing static.

The contents of that mystery Imorphium cartridge were blasted to atoms at the same moment, terabytes of precious code erased from the world – everywhere except in Lord Simeon Blaire's head. Within minutes the Threedeeo stations would be filming the charred hole in the base of his spire, claiming terrorist sabotage and treachery, alleging that somebody was trying to rig the great Game.

Kronos knew that they were at least half right – but the rules had to be observed. Subcitizens were expendable, and seditious sub-scum who tried to alter the outcome of his breeding program were to be hunted down with extreme prejudice.

But the Lords and Ladies were sacrosanct. The game would continue.

And Simeon Blaire's puppet-masters had already made one critical error. Kronos had managed to catch the tiniest scrap of data from the memory dump before it was gone forever – a time and a place where the young Lord's new skills would be put to the test.

When Blaire came to the Valley View Mall tonight the Machine's newest toy would be waiting for him.

Ω

"This is the last time" said the demon on Simeon Blaire's shoulder. "After the Relic is integrated, he's all yours."

He replied with a thought, the wires meshed through his cranium picking up his words before he even drew breath.

"This will be that last human hand to touch my skin, Vanecke." A cotton swab dipped in isopropyl pressed cold against the back of his head, and Simeon smiled. "He dies here, to prove that your precious Relic is all you say it is."

Lord Blaire leaned forward, and the slim barrel of Haszan's syringe slid smoothly into his brain, a painless incision in a little dimple of scars. It was a hair-thin flexible antenna, hollow and prehensile… seeking out just the right knot of wet tissue on automatic. Because just like everyone else, the patriarch of the House of Blaire had to pay.

The unfortunate fact was that he couldn't pay with cash. Not with Kronocult sub-totalities scanning his accounts. That's what Vanecke had told Jaq, anyway – the Kheptarch was reduced to a level of currency his peers would never suspect, or even conceive of.

One which Jaqub Haszan knew all too well.

"Even this serves a purpose, Disciple," hissed the Direktor, invisible to Jaqub's unaugmented eyes. "You should see the storm your precious adrenochrome is brewing down in the Subcity! Just think - after tonight, they really *will* be calling it the nectar of the gods…"

And in the meantime – the Pharmyard retrovirus had made

172

him cold, precise – *programmable.*

Slowly, delicately, Jaq slid the slim silver needle out of Simeon's neck, whistling under his breath. This would be worth a few hits at least – the Lord's body had taken to the retro-v far better than he would have expected. How he still managed to dominate the Game with so much Stunn in his blood Haszan didn't want to know.

"Vexx better be thankful he's got such a up-market clientele. Not that I'd ever *tell* him, but..."

He capped the needle, slipping it into his belt and fishing out a fresh supply of the little candystripe capsules that his customers loved so much. Blaire took them without a word - the only part of his body exposed to Haszan's tainted breath was a tiny patch of flesh at the base of his skull. The rest was skinned in black rubber, a filter-mask giving him the visage of some nightmare insect.

One tiny red bubble of chemicals went straight into a gilded iris, a carbuncle on the gas-mask's snout. None of them, not even a Kheptarch Lord, ever waited a second for their fix.

Oh, he knew he was hooked just as bad. But he'd never, *ever* go under the needle for a fix. He'd suffer through the detox cubes first, he'd flush his veins out with synthe blood rather than sink that low.

He knew he was lying to himself as well.

Which is prone to make you twitchy, when you're the only pharmer you know with a one-hundred-percent survival rate.

For a pared sliver of a second Haszan contemplated just walking away. The other syringe was primed and ready, tiny glittering specks dancing within. But Haszan's mind flashed in black negative, back to the image of Kaito shaking hands with that cop over and over again. That - and the hideous visage of the Cyben, dead skin under plastic... Haszan's skin, and his face, cold, mechanical - recycled. Eyes gouged out by miniature camera lenses reflecting... what?

A tiny, hovering pinpoint of glare flashed over his shoulder, reflected in the glass of the syringe. It shocked him out of his momentary daze, winking gold in the lowering sun. Jaq's eyes narrowed, recognizing the shape and sound of a flycam, identical to his own.

Omnivasive had a vested interest in this little piece of extracurricular work, and even now the All-Seeing Eye was upon him.

Damn Vanecke. Damn Eddie Tsein. And damn unto the depths of all hells…

But it was no use.

All the blasphemy in the world wouldn't give him a choice in the matter. His hand descended in a swift, mechanical arc.

Despite the stunn, Simeon Blaire felt the second needle ram into his cranium.

There was no pain; by now he'd popped and hissed three of the Stunn caps, and his nerves were melted butter. But there was something else… a spark. A fire. A conflagration…

Haszan recoiled as Simeon turned his head, the needle quivering in his skull. His black rubber fingers hooked into claws as he ripped the gasmask from his face, exhaling a cloud of chemically-charged air. Then he giggled, drooling, one eyeball huge and white, the other slitted and bloodshot. His lips were twisted into an idiot grin.

"Yes! It begins! Heaven's gate is open!" crowed Octavio Vanecke, flickering away into a wisp of static. "Now kill him! Let the blood of this animal be our sacrament - a libation to the God you will become!"

Simeon's nightmare eyes stayed locked on Haszan as his hand clamped down on the syringe, crushing it between his fingers. Tiny shards of glass stood out from his skin, dripping with blood.

But that face! The hollow, sick emptiness in his gaze!

The Kheptarch grinned like a hanged man, twitching as he bled.

"Yes, Master. A sacrament! A libation for my sweet, rotten city…"

Click.

Phase One.

A gyre of images exploded behind his glazed pupils.

They'd been locked into the deepest structures of his brain, programmed under sleep-hypnosis throughout the months of his slow indoctrination. Vanecke's threedeeo wizardry had worked miracles on a mind ground down by angst and boredom, and now all that dormant information was dredged to the surface, an oilslick of compulsion smothering reason. Memetic viri surged over the drug-smoothed plains of Simeon Blaire's personality, scouring away his will. It was sequestration pure and simple, but the trick was to make it feel like an epiphany, an awakening...

Phase Two.

The steel disease in Jaq's syringe went live. It was the same Chimera crycelium which bound up Eddie Tsien's mind, thawed out from its Vatican reliquary. Refined, chained, reprogrammed... but still utterly savage.

Octavio Vanecke extended his illusory fingers through the back of Blaire's skull, filling his fevered skin with hot barbed wire.

"Sorry about this part, kid. But not *that* sorry..."

Jaq was still standing there stunned as Simeon seized up, staggering.

"*Master?* And what the fuck does 'libation' mean?"

"What have you done to me!" screamed the Kheptarch Lord in silence, watching his biomonitors crash one by one. "You said I'd be *remade*! You said I'd leave humanity behind... not this! Not like this!"

Haszan's face flickered as the world shifted through a range of test patterns. The outlines of his body collapsed, replaced by wireframes, then fleshed out again in black and gold, red, a haze slowly coalescing...

"I also said you'd call me *Master*, Simeon Blaire," chuckled Vanecke, an invisible presence looming up over his dwindling mind like a thunderhead. "And at least in that respect, I never lied..."

Haszan saw Blaire's eyes narrow, his pupils dilated, tiny jewels of sweat hanging like ornaments from his eyelashes. There was a *weight* to the atmosphere, usually so dusty and dead; the golden flycam swum through it slowly, leaving a bubbled wake in the stale air as it alighted on Blaire's shoulder. His coat fell, a ripple of silent black, to raise a pall of dust in cold slow motion. The spasms in his muscles receded, and his lips twitched up into a little smile.

Then the sealed wasteland ceased to exist.

Phase Three.

"Master. Sacrament. Libation. Rotten. Remade. *Chimera second-generation substrain containment test successful. Upshifting to combat trial pattern. Instigate…*"

Ω

Direktor Vanecke laughed in his illusory world; out in meatspace his severed head twitched a little, the corners of his tube-stuffed mouth cracking a tiny smile. He saw, in a corner of his sensory interface dome, exactly what his new slave saw. In wireframe. In soundwave, both Standard Elysian and in the ancient language of Japanese. And in glorious Technicolor - the end result.

All the time and money and extortion he'd expended prying that crycelium out of the Vatican had paid off at last. Now Pope Joan was the proud custodian of an empty cryo-reliquary, and millions of dollars worth of profoundly illegal tech was twisting through the veins of Simeon Blaire, tooling up his conventional microservo and bio-onboard to unheard-of levels.

The results were likely to be spectacular.

And to think - this was only plan B. Vanecke would never have let that archaic steel virus into his own body, not back then, not when he was honed and tempered like a blade. But his backup plan - this one he'd prayed he'd never need - well, young Simeon wanted to die anyway. This way at least his demise would mean something, so long as he lasted long enough to fulfil his purpose.

Cold laughter echoed in Direktor Vanecke's virtual dome, a basilica of screens crazed with static and neon. And filtered, translated, transmitted, updated and uploaded, it issued softly from just behind Simeon Blaire's shoulder, the voice of a virtual ghost.

He had become the Master - and his one-time lord was now his Disciple.

Ω

"The Sin-Eaters tell us you have a debt, my son," panted Brother Clement, standing over the fallen body of his mark with his hands on his hips. "Now, I don't like this any more than you do - but business is business."

The man who the Valle Crucis had just felled groaned weakly, blood dripping from one corner of his mouth. His left hand - the one which had held the switchblade - was a mangled knot of shattered bone and muscle.

"Please… just another couple of days! That's all I need! Come on, Brother… aren't you supposed to be merciful to the poor?"

"That's God's business, friend," sighed Clement, snapping a pair of plastic cuffs around his captive's wrists. "Not mine. And the Sin-Eaters have your contract. Three weeks, then the Black Techs get your eyes. You signed it, not me."

Kaito watched from the raised scaffold deck of the Meat Locker, a bottle of vatgrown beer in his hand. It kind of put his own troubles in perspective, seeing the Valle Crucis drag his kicking burden off across the street - better Eddie Tsien than the Pope.

But only just.

Kaito was deep in the borderlands between the Subcity and the Holy See – that sliver of the R.T. which belonged to Pope Joan III. You wouldn't expect it to be a party kind of town, but Saint Peter's Arcade was where the wirehead crowd came to let it all hang out. The glow of the neon crucifix above the Vatican gates outshone the advertising hoardings of a thousand clubs and bars and wetware chop shops, promising salvation.

Needless to say, the Compliance Division steered clear of St Pete's as though the whole place was radioactive.

The Kayzi drained his beer in a single heroic gulp and elbowed his way through the crowds to the bar. His bio-onboard sparked as he bellied up to the neon-lit slab of glass - another shot at contacting Eddie or Jaq. Both of them were silent, and that was usually bad news. He popped the top on another frosty beer and ran a quick diagnostic - nothing. The line was clear, his rig was working fine. They were just out of the loop.

Faces in a hundred lurid shades swirled past him under banks of pulsing lights. Kaito wasn't really a sports fan, but he knew what that blue ribbon meant - worn around ankles and wrists, painted across faces and breasts and coiling down the arms of dancing zealots. It was for Blaire, the Kheptarch Lord who was part of Jaq Haszan's pharmyard. If Eddie Tsien ever found out about *that*, they'd be under his thumb until doomsday.

He'd said it was the last time. But the Kayzi knew better. Even a Lord couldn't resist the shadow razors of a stunn comedown. And every trip Jaq made to Arcturus Park was another chance for Kronos to catch him in the act. Tsien would seem like an angel of mercy by comparison…

Kaito stood alone amidst the wash and crush of bodies, strobes exploding, speakers pounding a pulse of arrhythmia. Resonating in the half-empty bottles behind the bar. The half-empty bottle in his hand…

Tsien still wasn't responding.

Kaito's mind flew to Haszan - perhaps the Lieutenant had decided to crack down on his buddy after all.

It had been a matter of months since the Cyben had lifted him from this very bar and pinned him to a crumbling plasticrete wall while Tsien outlined what he knew of Jaq's operation. He still recalled the sense of melting euphoria as the lieutenant sent his animated corpses away and outlined the deal. Still recalled the bruises on his wrists from their plastic-wrapped, dead hands.

Just one little slip-up, back when he was a juve hacker hoarding secrets for secrets' sake. A tiny trace which had ended up on Eddie Tsien's desk, linking him to R.T. terrorists and, by corollary, to a future as a mind-wiped toilet cleaner…

That's the story of how he became known as Farmer Joe. Haszan would laugh his arse off at the thought of his skinny, technogeek friend holding one of the extraction needles. Even a stunn junkie would never let Kaito's shaking, carpal-tunneled hands near his cranium.

No, this was all interference. It was quota make-work for Eddie Tsien, and two pet chemheads to make crime scenes appear for him. Now he had a murder to contend with.

Something was *definitely* wrong with Haszan.

Maybe… maybe he'd have to ask the Electromagi for help after all. Even if it meant moving in to the R.T. full time, hemp overalls and gray synthesoy dinners…

No. There had to be another way. That religious shit made him wary, and as for Illuminatus Zeon…

Just the *thought* of becoming a permanent Ashishim made him crack another beer.

There was an air of tension in the clubs and bars tonight - moonshine by the bucket, all the colors of the pharmaceutical rainbow, guys lacing the drinks of girls lacing the drinks of other guys. Somebody was playing an ancient recording of heavy metal through the junkyard P.A. of the 'Locker, a song about undead lust. A girl in black plastic wrap winked across a haze of intoxicating smoke, thin metal eyelids like camera shutters clicking over a glass optic loupe in her face.

Kaito stumbled through it all blind, bottle in hand.

He reached his homeblock as the rain began to fall, a half-hearted acid drizzle painting everything pastel and gray. His hands seemed too huge and clumsy to work the security keypad, but some antediluvian part of his brain got the job done on automatic. The door clicked open, hissing something cheerful from a busted grille, and he was home sweet somewhere.

Down the corridor lights were blazing, and a tinny old stereo played canned mariachi music. Kaito's neighbor Lex mightn't have ever seen his homeland, but like most of the refugees who'd made it to Elysium he was fiercely proud of his heritage. The Kayzi knew what it was like. It was either that, or feel like a dirty traitor for surviving.

Mister Morales and his family sat in a circle around a pile of broken circuit boards in the living room, computer terminals and a rainbow spaghetti of cables. Mom, Dad and the three kids were connected via HUD goggles, wires spanning temple-to-temple as they worked silently with pliers, soldering irons and microwelders.

Forty-nine fingers working as one - Lex Morales had lost his pinky to the Tong back in his gambling days. As Kaito walked past, flashing a half-cut smile, five slim-fingered hands waved to him, while ten shadowed, sunken eyes remained on their task. The stairs loomed ahead, a mountain wreathed in noise. That was his other roomie's country - the world of DJ DisKord.

"Hey, Kaito!" yelled Dis from above, the door to his converted office hanging on one rusted hinge. "Come on up, man! I got a case of beer, a bag of cranq, and I'm patched in for the big Game! Whattaya say?" Fractured breakbeats and earthquake bass foamed out of the hanging cube of plastic, clinging to the fac' wall like a swallow's nest.

"Thoughtchawa workin' tonight?" said Kaito, peering over DisKord's shoulder and into the cluttered sound-studio where his roomie hibernated. There was a noise from under a pile of blankets, and a vague shifting of limbs.

"I was …the Pit of Nails up in Valley View. But apparently every cop in town just showed up there, hence DJ Dis is a no-show."

Kaito raised an eyebrow, his mind staggering to catch up. DisKord's home-programmed automixer crunched gears, emitting a rumbling subsonic which split his head like an axe. It sliced through the alcoholic fug as well, prickling his attention.

"EVERY cop?" queried Kaito, hoisting the other eyebrow.

"That's the word from Omnivasive Network, compadre. Full rollout, y'dig? Anyway, I'll probably be out later - go and spin a few at the 'Locker."

"S'rockin'," muttered Kaito, digesting cerebrally. "Catch ya there, maybe - but I've got some work to do right now. Enjoy the Game."

Dis grinned like a maniac, slammed his door, and immediately turned up the music to compensate. There was a distinctly feminine scream of indignation, then laughter, then silence.

Kaito stood in the hallway for a moment, wobbling gently.

Every cop in town. The Valley View. There was something he should remember about that ramshackle old dirt-mall...

Kaito's door was ripped straight from a Terminus Navy destroyer, an immense oval hatch welded haphazardly into the metal wall. He turned the wheel once, twice, and let the slab of steel swing inward with a groan, kicking off his shoes and letting his bottle fall to the threadbare carpet. With the electric Pitbull standing over it his bike would be safe enough for an hour or two, and he had some things to take care of.

On the inside of the foot-thick slab of metal was a sheet of orange patches scrawled with a leering demon face. The Kayzi ripped one of the stickies off and slapped it against his forehead, feeling the detox sink its teeth into his tender brain.

Clear in his intent, Kaito stepped into the cool green glow of his electronic temple. If he couldn't get the job done *legally*, at least he could get it done *right*.

Ω

Simeon Blaire stood at the center of a private universe.

His mind was blank, drifting in a cage of light as his oculi stripped back the world around him. Direktor Vanecke's uplink skinned it with illusion - a program so real it made reality itself look vague.

Octavio's threedeeographic skills were pure magic. His media generators were sunken mountains of silicon and steel, immense cogitator piles cooled under a lake of liquid nitrogen. Octavio had applied his considerable spare time to learning how fly one of the generators solo, and this program was for a very special audience of one.

Simeon Blaire, assassin-retainer to the Glass Shogun.

The machines which spun his artificial reality were linked to his optic nerves by a cellular connection, rendering the world in shades of green and brown and gold - a complex masquerade of feudal Japan. Pipes and girders became trees, concrete became verdant grass, diamondmesh armor became *hakama* trousers and studded leather...

And a Lord of the Razor Clique became a nameless functionary, his Master's right hand.

Sunlight fell in slim blades between stands of bamboo, striping the face of Blaire as he reached smoothly behind his back, his other hand hovering still in the fragrant air. There was something wrong with his eyes. Something struggling and twitching in their depths...

Next to him Octavio Vanecke smiled, an incorporeal shade of dust and smoke. He was clad head to toe in ancient ragged armor, leather and steel and embroidered silk, the faceplate of his bell-shaped helmet a grim death-mask.

From within the ancient samurai helm issued a voice of soft decay, like the breath of tombs.

"This is the first of your tests, disciple," hissed the long-dead warrior, speaking in the ancient dialect of sixteenth-century Edo. "There is no stealth when witnessed; and no victory in flawed strategy."

The syllables fell from his lips like stones. And as Haszan watched, transfixed by the bizarre stance and hollow, blazing eyes of his client, Blaire drew a long, thin, and extremely *real* sword from behind his back.

There was no question that he knew how to use it.

Jaq watched him spin sideways, the blade licking out, quicksilver. A metal support strut shivered and collapsed, as inside Vanecke's world the fragrance of bamboo sap saturated the air. Blaire flicked the blade with one finger, setting up a humming resonation and misting drops of dew along its razor edge. Then he smiled, shifting his stance, drawing the katana up over his head. The muscles of his arms twitched as he held himself back.

His eyes were filled with murder.

"Well," said Haszan, catching his reflection in the rippled steel of the blade, "this has never happened before..."

In the second it took him to form the words, Blaire was upon him.

The sword blurred, cutting the air with a vicious hiss as the young Lord leaped forward; a killing strike. His lips were set in a thin, determined line, mirroring the edge of his blade.

"Master. Disciple. *Integration sub-routine complete. Libation...*

Rotten…"

Each word was matched with a savage sword-cut, a litany of blows.

Steel whispered through the air as the katana flashed sideways, within a fraction of an inch of carving through Jaq Haszan's neck. The 'dreno pharmer tucked himself up into a ball as he rolled, coming back up to his feet just in time to meet Simeon's blade coming the other way.

Fast! So damned fast! He'd have to…

He was fixated by the tip of that weaving, twitching sword – so much so that he didn't see the Khept's fist until it connected with his jaw.

The world went into a spin, hazed bloody red. Then the dusty treadplate kissed him hard on the cheek, and Jaq slid to a stop. There was a razorwire line of silver dancing in his eyes – the sword! Here it came again…

Haszan' hand scrabbled, driven by instinct, and his fingers curled around the first piece of debris they encountered. Sheer desperation brought the steel bar up from the dust in a radial blur, striking the flat of the sword as it came down on him hard.

Metal rang on metal. Sparks flared and died as Blaire issued a grunt of surprise and frustration. Through bloodshot eyes he saw the disheveled *ronin* at his feet, sinews straining as he brought his own crude scimitar up to check the finely-honed katana in mid-swing. It was rape; *defilement* for such base steel to touch his ancestral blade. His master, vigilant in silence, was surely mortified.

Rage and shame churned in Blaire's stomach. He turned Jaq's weapon aside and stepped back into a new stance, beckoning the sub-scum on.

"Sacrament. Sacrifice. *Slave…*"

Haszan staggered to his feet, bringing the rebar up in crude imitation of his adversary. Tension crackled in the stale dry air, and dust fell between them like ashes, a gray pall settling over the warrior Lord and his adversary.

"Come on then, Aristo. Come and try it. I've always wondered what your little Game was worth…"

It was madness, or course. If Jaq actually killed a Lord of the Council he'd be sealing his own death warrant. But he wasn't the kind of guy who backed down, and the steel rebar was reassuringly heavy in his hands.

Simeon struck left, then right - testing his defenses, dancing out of reach of his foe's counterstrikes. Each attack came faster, stronger, swinging backhands and reverses pushing Haszan to the limits of his reflexes. Despite the look of utter blank insanity in his eyes the Lord was no fool; he didn't want to make this a contest of brute power.

He came on in a controlled fury, his sword cutting deep gashes in the tempered steel rebar as he reeled through a complex *kata*, metal chiming on metal faster and faster. Blue sparks flew like rain. Without the microservo Jaq's bones would have shattered. As it was he could barely parry those quicksilver blows fast enough…

It was starting to make him mad.

"Is that all you got? Is that all? Come on, you inbred bastard! *Fight me!*"

Flames roared and hissed in Jaq's head as his teeth clenched hard. There was a dark place in there, in the shadow of the fire… the place he'd taken those poor damned Skinheads to, when everything went red…

When the next blow of Blaire's katana fell he pushed in with all his prodigious weight, coming up under the Lord's guard and dropping him to his knees with a savage headbutt.

He felt cartilage burst and blood splatter, dripping in his eyes.

While his left hand strained to keep Simeon's sword locked tight he slashed with his right - with the twin blades in his chrome fingers.

Blaire's cheek ripped open, two perfect razorcuts tracing the path of his foe's knife-bladed fingertips. The side of his head burned with pain as Haszan ripped off his ear, right down to the gleaming wet bone of his skull.

The warrior Lord screamed - more in rage than in agony - and swiped out blind, blood flying in a splattering arc. His sword slithered across the rusted steel of Jaq's rebar, slicing in at his chest. Now it was Haszan's turn to leap back, the blade cutting a neat triangle from his flying coat.

"There…" he panted "I got you good, Blaire. Just as…just as quick as you fancy bastards with your combat implants. Now, are you gonna put down that big butcher-knife, or do I have to do it again?"

His razortipped digits hovered like a scorpion sting, beaded with noble blood.

But Blaire was undaunted, his face still locked in an idiot grin as he advanced, the katana twitching in his hands.

"Primary combat routines integrated. Secondary and tertiary subroutines loading…"

"Oh, come on!" growled Jaq to whoever might be listening. "Hasn't this guy got friends of his own to play with?"

He hefted his section of rebar, getting it snug and tight in his hand, and lined it up for a killer swing upside the Aristo's temple.

But when he lashed out he found himself blocked with mechanical ease, the katana parrying and skirling across the rusted steel. Once, twice, three times the heavy rebar came down and was jerked aside, throwing Haszan off balance. Blood sang in Simeon's veins as he sprung forward snarling, his sword a silver blur as it hissed toward his enemy's neck.

The rebar stopped him in mid-air, levering him over into a desperate somersault as Jaq heaved with all his might. Blaire kept his balance, landing catlike behind him – but he was too late. The 'dreno pharmer was spinning even as his noble foe went airborne, three feet of corroded metal blurring in hand. It was a blow with all his three hundred pounds of bulk behind it, a slugging impact right across Simeon's perfect face.

Augmented bone shattered. Teeth splintered, blood spraying from his nose and mouth. The thick metal rod bent in half with the force of it, and Blaire went flying, a broken doll splayed across the dusty plasticrete of Arcturus Park.

"Holy shit! What have I done?" whispered Jaq, dropping the rebar from his numb hand. The implications came down on him hard as it clattered to the treadplate - *he'd killed a Council*

Lord. He'd gone from drug-running to high treason in one afternoon…

Then he saw that twisted figure twitch. He saw it shake its head, muzzy and dazed but inarguably *alive*…

Jaq wasn't sure which was worse.

Silver fluids welled and webbed across Blaire's face as he staggered to his feet, still grinning as his jaw wired itself back together. His wounds stitched themselves shut.

"Disciple. Rotten. Libation. *My city!*"

And he brought up his sword again, back into that same graceful stance.

Haszan's eyes widened, his pulse hammering at his temples. There was just no *stopping* this guy. Even his good old pair of sawnoffs would probably just slow him down for a second or two…

He saw a premonition of pain reflected in Simeon's blade as it flew, with nothing left to stop it.

And as Vanecke laughed, wind through sepulchers and rust, his disciple brought down the katana in a sweeping overhand; a strike which would end in a neat upswing, shattering Jaqub's skull. Calculations seethed behind his eyes as he imagined the perfect fatal incision, the red arterial spray…

That concentration was his undoing.

Jaq's magnetic grapple struck him in the solar plexus like a coilgun-powered fist. One last desperate shot, with the only weapon he had left. It was made to launch a mile straight up, and this time it struck from six feet away.

Blaire folded in half as it picked him up off his feet, the tip of his katana swiping downwards bare inches from his enemy's face. The wall rushed up behind him and slammed into his back with rib-cracking force, driving the air from his lungs. Haszan opened his eyes just in time to see Blaire fall face-first to the dusty ground. A smear of blood rolled out behind him, down the corroded steel of the wall and into the dust.

Jaq's hands were unbuckling the straps which held the grapple-launcher even as he slipped under the shadow of the Destrier and down, through the heavy access hatch and into the air above the Subcity. He hung over the edge by the ends of his fingers – four scarred and pink, four shiny silver.

"Good work, Haszan. You just used your one way out of here, you *genius*..."

He peered up over the edge for a second, looking out below the six-barreled exhausts of Lord Blaire's town-car.

Suddenly a half-mile drop looked like a walk in the park. From behind him he heard a fit of cursing in some alien language, the rasp of a sword being gathered up from the dust...

Jaq knew in that instant that falling was the least of his problems. Blaire's face was contorted into a mask of anger and disgust; he stalked forward like a broken mekan, swiping the katana back and forth to scent out his prey. Jaq was pretty sure he'd cut right through the Destrier to get to him - and half the city, if that was what it took. Those cold, dead eyes stayed locked on him like heat-seeking cannons, spitting fury and contempt. So Haszan took a deep breath, smiled, reckless and foolish and scared as hell...

And let go.

The last thing Simeon Blaire saw of him as he dropped out of sight was his middle finger.

17 Aevum Oblivio
The Rabbit Hole

THE WHOLE WORLD *was taken up by Technician Nyl's thumb, by the point where it jammed down the button on his featureless black remote control.*

Zhe waited for the world to end - for the final, brief flash of actinic deathlight... But there was nothing; just hot, crawling silence. The moment he realized that Nyl was still talking was exactly the same moment that another, freewheeling part of his brain worked out that his Mentor was just an illusion.

"I was sworn to never allow a mass destruction of life here, because of the strange and disturbing vortices which such an event can set up in this kind of universe. But this place was just too interesting not to tinker with. We are TECHNICIANS after all, dear brother, not worker ants."

Illusion or not, though – it scarcely mattered. Even with his flesh replaced by force-shields and painted with holograms, Gharfos Nyl was dangerous.

"I'm glad you've stopped struggling against my pet Slavesystem. The poor thing has only just realized that it's been enslaved... I'd hate to think what it'd do to you just out of spite... While he talked the renegade was rummaging through Zhe's bag of tools, looking for one device in particular. He pulled it out with a flourish, brandishing it in front of his captive's face. "Oh, just the ticket! A cerebral clamp will do nicely, I think."

Zhe couldn't move - he was interwoven with the Slavesystem on a molecular level. But now he could feel its dimmed and blunted memories too.

The coming of a patterned energy so powerful that even the ironclad code of the Motherbrain was unable to hold Everdark together. The incendiary mindrape its innermost processors and memory cores. Conquest.

Nyl jammed the prongs of the clamp down on Zhe's forehead, cutting a neat circle out of the Slavesystem and the alien flesh beneath. The super-heavy reinforced bone of Zhe's skull glistened wetly under the lights. He wasn't going to give the rogue the satisfaction of showing any pain.

"My predecessor really dropped the ball with that whole nuclear-apocalypse act, and it was my job to do better - at least until the machine's work began down there. Lancaster's work... the very first one. After that they were being grown, fed experiences, all for the slaughter."

As he spoke a vast organic humming noise was rising in walls and floors and machinery of the station. The space elevator down to earth lit up with a flare of plasma, spitting arcs of lightning miles long.

Clouds at atmosphere level blasted away in slow-motion whorls. Something was coming up the pipe. Something bad.

Amid the growing roar, Nyl was laughing.

He jammed the main screw of the cerebral clamp home, opening a digital port directly into Zhe's living brain. Sparks sizzled across the gold-tipped wires at its crown.

Zhe's mind was pressed further and further aside as the connection to Kronos widened ...until he could sense a maelstrom of fractured intelligences at the edges of his perception. Immense power, walled up inside magnetically shielded holding tanks, the pain of ten thousand deaths in each humming capacitor.

And he suddenly knew all about the mechanisms which would unleash it.

Zhe heard Nyl's grunt of frustration and surprise.

He felt a shift in the focus, a shiver down the taut miles of elevator cable.

And Nyl began to scream.

The cerebral clamp was only an electronic interface - or so it was intended. But now a very real, very black and swirling vortex had sprung open in Technician Zhe's head, sucking in the atmosphere like a gap into deep space.

Nyl tried to pry the evil-looking tool away, but his hands were sucked into the hole. His fingers stretched and dripped, lumps snapping off to fall into the hungry abyss below. His face distorted as he struggled to pull away, and then his whole head was in the pipe, jammed crown-first through the front of Zhe's skull.

All digital. All illusory. Nyl had been hacked, owned by a safeguard subsystem out of the machine core. And the vortex it had created was ravenous.

Zhe felt like he was being turned inside-out. There was something coiled up in there, in the rotten core of Elysium. Now it was in him too, prying him open like a magician's pentacle, reaching out hungrily for Nyl as if... as if it had waited for years to devour him.

With a slobbering, popping sound the renegade Technician disappeared, struggling all the way, and Zhe lost consciousness. He was going to have the mother of all headaches when he woke up...

2196 Anno Arbitrium
Riotstarter

BELOW THE SPIRES, in a crash-dive through a mile of polluted sky – there's Haszan, a tiny flyspeck against a curve of metal. What he'll hit if his plans go wrong is the upper rind of the Subcity, a shantytown welded to the nuke-proof manufactoria-strata of the old core. Lower still – we're talking another mile of corrugated iron and jury-rigged habs – there's a crooked line scrawled across the city, a razor-wire killzone studded with third-world gun turrets and loops of sensor filament.

Kronos called everything below it the *R.T.* – the Reclaimed Territories. Nomad dogpatch.

The folks down there were well armed, militantly political, and institutionally paranoid - all in all, just Kaito Kayzi's kind of bunch. Not that he'd admit it.

But right on the edge of the R.T, where the Vatican's Cathedral of Saint Aethalstan loomed up like a great accusing finger, a kind of de-facto demilitarized zone sat astride the border, a place where the Subcity and the Pit could trade with each other, and with the Reclamationists who held the gates to the outside world.

Like some kind of cargo cult the Subcits had built this place out of waste steel and concrete blocks and salvage – lashed it up in the name of a dodgy front company and the image of centuries-old sales brochures. It was a *shopping mall*, a kind of temple from before the apocalypse, and this one was meant to have it all.

It had gone to seed over the years, as the R.T. crept up closer every week and its parent company collapsed. Still, even as the sun set over Elysium it was packed. The main concourse sweltered under its row of purple glass domes, misty with the exhalation of ten thousand bustling shoppers.

Among the crowds dodged a slim figure in red and black overalls; a kid of about fourteen with his hair spiked up in a jagged wave. A confusion of castes and phyles traded breath and currency all around him, while a babel of dialects throttled the supermarket groove of a thousand hidden speakers as he ran. His name was B-Zerk, and he was late for work again.

The Valley View smelled of rust, and of stale machinery left to die, but it was *alive* - full of distracting sights and smells and sounds. B-Zerk swiped a steaming bowl of curry from Kohali Ras' benchtop as he spun past, slipping an I.O.U. under a stack of hand-fired teracotta bowls. He was almost there, and it looked like his boss wasn't in yet...

Between the retail ghettos down the far end of the mall were the R.T. outposts, recruitment dives for the Clans and Nations outside of Kronos' rule. Young patriots with rice-paper overalls, glazed eyes and replica Kalashnikovs stood to attention outside the Celestial guardhouse, impassive even as B ducked through their lines, dripping a trail of soy korma behind him.

You could tell which strata of society people came from just by checking their reaction to the Territory soldiers.

The ultra-poor and destitute hung around for free rice and political sermons. Subcits with crappy jobs threw clenched-fist salutes of solidarity. And the eyes of Burbsters slid right over them like oiled teflon, denying that there'd ever be a Reclamation Day Two.

He'd made it!

B-Zerk tipped back the little pottery bowl, inhaling his late lunch in a series of steaming gulps. Then he wiped his mouth with the back of his jumpsuit's sleeve, belched, and sauntered through the door of Tadashi Murai's Oriental Apothecarium.

His boss didn't even look up from the huge leather-bound ledger he was writing in, but B knew he was smiling.

"Where have you been, kid?" asked the old man, poring over his dusty tome. "No...let me guess..." he sniffed the air, peeking up at B from under the brim of his ridiculous straw hat. "Synthesoy curry... motor oil... hmmm... you came in through the west gate, past Kohali Ras' tandoori shack. But you're late because... Jinjiron Mahu has a new motorcycle in his workshop. Something fast and irresponsible, yes?"

B-Zerk grinned, wiping the curry off his fingers on the back of his hair. Then he caught a reflection of summer-sky blue from the window next door, and all thoughts of work - and even Jinjiron's new Sidewinder - were blown from his mind.

She was there! She was actually working today!

"I see you've noticed our favorite neighbor, B," said Tadashi, smirking under the shadow of his hat. "Go on. I dare you to actually say hello. You never know, she might notice you this time!"

B-Zerk blushed red to match the stripes of his crash-suit, but he leaned in the doorway all the same, looking through the window of Twentieth Century Crime at the shop's pretty little proprietess.

A chain of hardlight microsats orbited her head like a glittering halo, sparking and flashing messages to each other as she sat at the desk with her feet up, her metal-studded greaser boots four sizes too big.

The back of her torn t-shirt advertized Zweig and Barnes railpistols ("The Bountyhunter's Friend!"), and her hair was twisted into a tangle of pale blue dreadlocks, glowing with phosphorescent powder.

Her name, of course, was CeeAn 187.

It was all a front, 'coz she was still short one body, still pushing light. They packed her off down here just as soon as she jumped off the masslifter. Her holoself was as purple-tattooed, azure-haired and slim as always. But her feet didn't touch the desk - they floated above a slew of comic books and newspaper clippings by about three inches.

For Cee this was a shit-list posting, a little sideshow dreamed up by the Electromagi to keep her out of the way. They might be the oracles of a better tomorrow and wizards of technology to boot, but deep down they were all sweaty prepubescent geekboys, guys who'd never let a girl hang out in their clubhouse.

CeeAn knew they were usually right, and that most of these mystery postings ended up as violent gunfights or suicidal getaways. But as the geeks' go-to girl when it came to such brutal necessities she felt entitled to her opinion.

Cee's black crescent packed a cam just as small and accurate as Abdulafia's. She saw B-Zerk watching her, and she smiled.

He'd be cute, if he was about four or five years older…

There was a second of utter silence there, as her thoughts hit a wall of tension.

"Dervashi *agent! We've got movement in your sector! Cyben gunships are touching down at the corner of Valley and Prospekt…*"

Cee twisted the vox bead in her ear, forgetting that she wasn't real. She lost central despatch behind a hash of static – jammers, e-war countermeasures englobing the mall…

Then the noise came down.

It ripped through the Valley View like the howl of the screaming damned, smashing the window of Twentieth Century Crime, shattering Tadashi Murai's glass bell-jars of exotic herbs, driving a shockwave before it which picked Cee up and slammed her to the back wall of the store. In its aftermath swirling clouds of dust set off a spray of flame retardant from the rusted sprinklers in the ceiling.

The geekboys appeared to have called it right again.

Anguished screams rose in a crescendo which threatened to shatter every remaining piece of unbroken glass in the place, as feathery drifts of foam came down like snow.

"Fucking gack motherfuckers broke me bong! I'll kill 'em! I swear, I'll kill 'em all!" shouted the Ashishim recruiter in the shop next door, staring at his shredded left hand forlornly.

CeeAn had no time for the A.K.- toting jocks she was supposed to be babysitting - she was much more intent on discovering *why* the Valley View was under attack.

There was a more than outside chance that it was all her fault.

Despatch had mentioned Cyben loaders setting down, but there wasn't a cop in sight, just old mister Murai from next door, slumped in his doorway with a slim bundle of leather and wood in his hands. Something – no doubt a shattered razor of diamondglass - had neatly sheared off the side of his head, so that a clinical cross-section of his brain glistened wetly in the oil-lamp glow. He was still alive, scrabbling at the threads which bound up his package.

"Run!" he yelled out across the glass-strewn mall. "It's about the book! Save yourselves!" B-Zerk was nowhere to be seen -

perhaps he'd been thrown back into the Apothecarium by the force of the blast.

CeeAn flicked a switch up on her crescent unit and suddenly appeared a tiny but significant shade more *solid*. A second wave of howling noise stripped the dust from every surface as it tore through the mall, popping eardrums like cheap prophylactics.

Inside her shades camera feeds strobed by in a flickering blur, jacked in direct to a battery of Ashishim electronic war-engines half a mile below.

And she saw them massing outside the stricken mall, Bluejackets and deadflesh Cyben, armed to the teeth and beyond.

They knew about Vincenzo Vexx. Or - figure it - his connections went too deep. Kronos' garbagemen finally had proof positive that Dervashi *stalked the city at will...*

From all around her came the sound of running feet, of wailing and crying and human panic.

They were nothing but collateral damage, caught by a Cyben weapon – a sonic disruptor set down low. At the top end of its range a bomb like that could wreck your internal organs down to jelly, but this one was just a wake-up call. The cops may have been playing merciful, but for a pack of walking corpses 'mercy' was a relative term.

Cockless mekborn freaks! If they wanted her, they should have come and got her! Instead they'd shredded women and children, old Tadashi Murai, Kohali Ras across the mall at the curry shack... innocents.

That made the temporarily bodiless CeeAn 187 quite irate.

In a blatant oversight of Subcity health and safety laws she wrapped both her hands around the gyro-balanced grips of twin imitation Desert Eagle hand-cannons, chambered a shell in each one and leaned back on her chair, waiting. The Cyben were coming, and that meant open season.

WARNING! screamed a pair of Protocol Division labels, running like welts down the smooth silver barrels...KEEP OUT OF REACH OF PERSONS PRONE TO SPONTANEOUS ACTIONS.

Somebody down in supplies mustn't have realized who they were being issued to.

Ω

"Now! Quickly! Do it, and be forgiven..."

There was a second of pain as the knife-edge went in, clean and neat, sawing through gristle and tendons in a bright spray of blood. He looked up as he made the final cut, and his eyes were wide and dark, filled with obedient fear.

Perfect.

Tokugawa never owned a palace like this, all folded paper and symmetry and light. It was concrete origami, built from illusions for a singular purpose. The whole non-euclidean pile was designed to funnel the body into one spot, a place of power where the urge to kneel pressed in like a hydraulic car-crusher. And to focus the mind - very specifically the mind of Simeon Blaire. Images just beyond sight flickered in the rice-paper walls and the knotted bare timber of the floor, pulsing and swirling in sympathy with his puppet emotions.

Rage, thought Tokugawa/Vanecke.

Shame.

Simeon's severed pinky finger fell to the floor, a tiny crook of meat and wire and bone. Ghost threedeeo went nova in his head, a storm of flame and blood and the smell of metal in the rain. Pain rode the shunt. Pain sealed the deal. The monomolecular blade in his hand was swift, sure and surgical - but the pain was necessary. It would make sure that he remembered his lesson.

"Your foolishness is atoned for, my disciple," breathed Tokugawa from his throne, flanked by robed holograms in black and gold. "This...*ronin*...who is named *Jaqub Yaqub Haszan* will be dealt with by others in my cadre."

Blaire bowed his head to the floor; strangling a cry of self-disgust. Octavio's finger was on the toggle switch, throwing open the chemical floodgates of despair in his brain. It was an impossible insult to his dignity - his enemy was to be denied him.

"But – I had him! My sacrament! You... you *promised...*"

He never finished. The illusory Shogun held out his hand, his fingers splayed, and ice-green lightning came down like rain. Agony earthed itself through Simeon's body, curling him up into a foetal knot. Blood pooled and spilled from his severed finger, now trickling in the cracks of the floor, a biomatrix in itself as it traced hexagons down toward his master's feet.

The pain whipped Blaire into line.

"I submit to your authority, Master," he croaked, raw self-control strangling his voice.

"And in the fullness of time I shall elevate you among the greatest of my Samurai," purred Tokugawa, his helmet flaking rust as he spoke. For a second the holograms flickered, becoming a pair of attendant skeletons, long dry bones showing through their motheaten silks. "Until such time, I have further duties for you. Duties you must execute with greater skill."

Vanecke bid his disciple to rise, leaning back on his throne of creaking hardwood. The rice-paper walls rippled as if with an unseen wind, awash with ancient woodcuts.

"Already you are stronger. Already you feel the power which is my gift to you." Vanecke let slip the endorphins, the adrenaline. Blaire flexed his hand, where the skin was already sealing, binding the stump of his missing finger. He *was* stronger. He was clear of purpose. His master had shown him the way. "These gifts aren't without their price, son. They carry a debt of honor. Obedience. *Trust.*"

TRUST.

The word came in like a sucker-punch, burning Vanecke's face into his mind.

The palace blew away from him then, walls flying off into digital infinity. Simeon was left outside, chill under a twist of clouds, surrounded by the scent of innumerable falling cherry blossoms. As he turned he could see the shadow of his master on the horizon, illuminated against a white steel moon. There to his left a black-robed liche bore up his banner, while to his right another carried an urn of marble in which, Simeon knew, rested the bones of his severed finger.

"Forget your past. Forget your failure. Even defeat serves its purpose, so long as you learn your lesson."

Octavio's floating hands were busy while their master dreamed, each slaved to a computer terminal as they played the intricate instrument of Simeon Blaire's mind. With a cut and paste one slim sliver prosthetic transposed images of Blaire's father, his brother; people who he hadn't seen for many lonely years. Merged them with the metal deaths-head of Tokugawa/Vanecke.

They cracked open the endorphin flow as his memories were patched back in. Another hand monitored the crycelium growth which ran wild beneath Simeon's skin, the atrophy of pain receptors and transmitters, the bone marrow replacements which strengthened his limbs to the temper of steel bars.

Simeon opened his eyes to a world of harsh neon lights and concrete - the dusty ruin of Arcturus Park. He slowly unfolded, knees and palms slick with his own blood. The *tanto* dagger slammed back into its sheath.

Simeon flexed his fingers, one now a stump capped with metal. The crycelium had budded from his pores at the scent of blood, sealing and disinfecting the wound. Billions of threads were slowly overhauling his body, remaking him as a perfect and deadly machine. Such was the gift of cryo-reliquary 992-b, a man-made virus the Valle Crucis thought they still kept hoarded away.

At the very edge of his vision Simeon could see the specter of Tokugawa, a ragged black thing whispering in his ear.

"Now I have new task for you. There is a master named Tadashi Murai who defies me. *This* is where to find him. You know what to do when you get there – and what to cut from his corpse as proof of your success…"

It had all taken mere fractions of a second inside Simeon's mind, and Haszan was still tripped out and laughing hopelessly in free-fall as the Destrier roared to life, activated by remote control. Floating like a butterfly in vacuum, end over end through pools of light, Octavio Vanecke's hand flicked the switch.

Ω

B-Zerk knew the crawlways and vents. That was his job - what he did for Tadashi Murai. Usually, the old guy wanted him to sneak upstairs to one of the few remaining Assemblers in Arcturus or Highampton; y'know, just to port out some more of his medicine and shit. This time, however...

This time he wasn't even sure if his boss was still alive. That big shard of diamondglass had carved him up bad, and he'd been bleeding all over the floor when B left him. It wasn't like he'd *wanted* to... but Mister Murai kept on shouting in some foreign language, gasping for breath; the only thing he said that made a lick of sense was about some kind of book. Some badass called *Octavio* wanted his book. And so B-Zerk had to take it, arm himself, and run.

He was getting away from the Valley View with a quickness. Fast as he could shove his carcass through the pipes and over the gaping holes in the floor, dodging shafts which spouted foetid hot air, abysmal drops into the process core.

No matter that he'd just seen an army of cops marching like roaches in a sub-block kitchen. Even in a blind panic a 'crawler had to watch his step.

B was bad-ass professional, coz he'd seen homeboys fry, 'vaped before they hit the bottom. Only way you knew was this - you smelled the meat, wafting up like a call to dinner out of the dark.

B-Zerk remembered the first time, on his hands and knees in the warm steel pipes, heaving with sickness as he smelled that smoky, fatty aroma wafting up from below. Just after Zone Doubt slipped, his headbeams flickering on the roofplates, his scream amplified through the endless plumbing...

The sickness was like purification, because like cash and lust and the need for more head candy, the smell was *good*. It smelled like real food, and it made you drool. And hate yourself for doing it.

Right now, he was about roof-level with the Valley View, in tunnels he knew like the veins crisscrossing the back of his hand. Resting, his heart hammering in his chest. Borrowed, the wakizashi flashed in his headbeams, its handle wrapped in cloth so tight and old and rough that it felt like cracked plastic, like Zerk's ancient crosshead driver. Mummified.

The knife was a beautiful simple device, a kind of molecular-bond unsplicer from the days before railguns and viralcasters, when you had to get right up close and put steel in a motherfucker.

Why'd he take it? Why this, and not a railpistol or a nervejam? B didn't know - it was just the way the handle fit into his palm, the way his reflection in the blade looked back at him just right…

His breath came back to him after a few racking, heaving gulps of air, clearing his head as his muscles ached. But just as he was about to set out onward and upward he heard it - a noise so low and insistent that it set his teeth on edge. B-Zerk's hand reached down into the pocket of his crash-suit, feeling the real leather that skinned Mister Murai's book. Still there. Good.

The hum came in loud and clear, a shiver in the intestines reminding B-Zerk of the illness; of the smell. Could be discharge from the core coming up. He'd have to stay well clear of the downvents in that case; which was bad, coz 'Zerk wanted to make this run somewhat hi-octane.

The bolts were rattling now, and Zerk could hear the hum in the air rising. He stripped the headbeams off and into a pocket, sheathed the wakizashi, and folded himself up into a crawlspace. The metal pressed in on him from every angle, vibrating in what would be an almost soothing manner, if it wasn't for the thought of superheated plasma blasting the flesh from his bones.

Instead, as the hum built to a tooth-hurting blurring crescendo he felt the touch of a human hand on his shoulder.

The sound cut out suddenly, rattling and ricocheting away down the pipes, down the sonic spectrum until it formed a *basso profundo* undertone to his assailant's laughter.

B risked opening one eye, and found himself looking at a callused brown finger, banded with rings of stainless steel and runic tattoos. It prodded him in the ribs, a hole in his side through which homeboy dignity escaped.

"Hey - you O.K. in there? You just come up outta the Valley View, right?"

The hand belonged to a dreadlocked Euro with innumerable rings, piercings, and anim-ink tattoos sparking in neon across his skin. Mainly tribal; B-Zerk vizzed their smooth lines, nodded approval.

And, as nonchalant as one can be whilst wedged in a crawlspace striving to minimize one's blast profile, B-Zerk fixed this dude with a stare normally reserved for 'phytes and asked;

"Whatcha fuckin' malfunction, man? You ain't never heard of *etiquette*?"

The Euro laughed even louder this time, pulled Zerk out of his hidey-hole with one hand, and shook his mane of fat electrical-taped dreads out of his face. There was a little plug socket at the end of each one.

"Just making a delivery to someone, a'right." he drawled, in what Zerk pinned down as an Ashishim lingo. "But I'm sure you wasn't going my way. Too many bluejackets back there, right? Too many powertripping freaks with guns…"

B unfolded himself painfully from the crawlspace, leaning up against the metal wall of the tunnel.

"So why you want to go there?" he asked, working the kinks out of his muscles. "Hungry for prison food?"

The Ashishim grinned, pulling back his trenchcoat to reveal the handles of an immense pair of panga knives.

"Oh, I got a little something for those Cyben," he said, the end of each word dying softly in the air. "And I got some family down there who might need a hand when they roll through. You know - R.T. stuff."

His smile was like an enamel blast-wall, big and solid white. More real than the eyes which flickered behind his curtain of multihued dreadlocks. "We're not so bad, once you get to know us. Not half so bad as the bluejackets make us out - but you don't listen to them jerkoff cops anyhow, right?"

Like most kids in the Subcity B-Zerk's been raised on stories of R.T. agents, who were just about the baddest sons of bitches imaginable.

"Oh... no way, man. I'm *well* professional. Won't tell them *nothing*, even if they... "

The agent held a finger to his lips for a second, listening intently to the hiss and sigh of wind in the pipes.

"No, they not gonna catch you today. All this is just a sideshow for something big. Still, you best be gone from here. Never know if they'll use chem weapons, not if it's Cyben down there." Almost as an afterthought he pulled something thin, white, and tubular from his nest of hair and handed it to the tunnel-crawler. He folded one of Zerk's hands up around the little paper tube and gave it a conspiratorial squeeze, accompanied by a raised eyebrow heavy with ripe steel.

"You stay safe, kid. And if you ever get tired of the tunnels, come see us in the R.T."

When B-Zerk heard the hum for a second time, he knew exactly where it came from - the belt around this guy's faded jeans was studded with a row of small round discs. They began to glow, and vibrate, and work themselves up to a fevered pitch as the mystery Son of Alamut checked a little wrist-screen map, its green glow lighting up his dreads like snakes.

He tucked and rolled his body up and over, so that he was lying in the air, face to face with Zerk, all ten-mile smile and flying hair.

He reached out with one hand, popping a scarred old bic lighter, and pressed it into B-Zerk's palm. Then the hummers pulsed, and a wave of warm air hissed away up and down the pipes. There was a small thunderclap inside the plumbing, and a whiff of ozone, and B-Zerk was alone once again - alone with the empty, slightly cold feeling that he'd just been made obsolete.

A pistoning blowback of air rippled his straight black hair, like the bow-wave of a maglev train plying the tunnels of old Tokyo in one of Mister Murai's ancient twodeeo movies.

B looked down at the little paper tube in his hand, picking it as another image from Tadashi's grainy and flickering 2ds - a cigarette.

Shaking, B-Zerk sat himself down there in the dark, on warm steel, and torched one twisted end with his new plastic lighter.

Just a little something to calm his nerves, and then he'd better keep moving…

Ω

Eddie Tsien wasn't thinking straight. In fact, he was prisoner in his own head, locked up behind glazed eyes as his body lurched through the rubble of Precinct 2997 and out into the street.

Sirens were howling. One of the Division cruisers had caught a lick of Eversio wire – it was burning, sliced clean in sections. Down the street a cadre of Neo-Confucians pointed and yammered in open terror.

Eddie couldn't hear them.

The darkness blurred in and out of focus, and he knew that he was close to death. Pressed up against the membrane of death, indeed, but anchored down into the living world by a thousand tiny hooks, the crycelium howling like a turbine in his brain.

He felt his head turn, saw the jumbled corrosion of the cityscape slide across his camera eyes, and knew exactly what he was going to do.

There was no need for coercion. His will was no longer his own.

One giant leap took him up to the broken-backed roof of the Precinct house, the next to the balcony above. One more and he was up over the street outside the Valley View mall, coming down hard on a concrete slab which shattered under his bulk.

There were cops here – milling aimlessly, waiting for his command. The certainty of it sparked through his head as Kronos turned his dials. Cyben, too – his new brothers in servitude. The hot steel in his head crushed his despair at the sight of them, replacing it with stern resolve. The little sliver of Tsien trapped inside him raged, impotent…

And fear rippled out from him in great intangible waves as he muscled through the crowd, unable to stop himself.

They recoiled, terrified, scattering from this monster in their midst…

The steaming barrel of the Eversio held high in the air may have been part of it; perhaps the foetor of drying blood added an element of its own. Those who survived the next hour at

Valley View Plaza would later swear it was nothing less than his eyes, however. Like oily chromed bearings, reflecting the innards of innumerable clocks.

Linked to innumerable ticking bombs.

The commanders of his two backup squads approached at a run under a ceiling of searchlight beams and laser targeters, falling in next to their leader with clipboards and schematics of the mall clutched in their hands.

"Listen pal, what's the big idea?" blustered one of them, a morbidly obese Sergeant too puffed up with self-importance to notice that he was yelling at a monster. "We've been held up here for half an hour while you dick around getting fancy weapons and exo-armor. This is supposed to be a tactical strike, you *idiot*, not a bloody chimp's tea party!"

The last few words were punctuated by his riot-gloved finger stabbing into Tsien's chest.

That would simply not do at all.

"This isn't exo-armor, Sergeant. And the big idea is... *this!*"

The Super-Cyben calmly grasped him by the wrist and twisted his hand off, with as little effort as a poet plucking a flower. Arterial spray spattered his angular features as they tried to configure a smile, managing nothing more than a hooked-back yellow rictus. Looking into that face the unfortunate officer saw much worse than a missing hand.

He collapsed to the ground unconscious.

Tsien leveled his cameras on the other vice-commander, a pale and sweating little man whose mind was spinning with Kronocult prayers. The Lieutenant slung a comradely arm around his shoulder, dragging him limply at his side as he walked. His head nestled in the Super-Cyben's armpit like a walnut in a vise.

"We have here but a fraction of the Division, Sergeant. Does that seem prudent? Does that seem *safe*, considering they thought they needed *me* here as well?"

There was no emotion in his voice, not even anger - his face was a waxen mask dripping with blood.

"Kronos despises weakness. And the guy we're here to stop...

well, he's something of a prodigal son to our Guardian Engine." With a dismissive gesture Tsien swept his eyes and cameras and sensors over the men and tanks and heavy support mekan shoehorned into the plaza. To the uninitiated it looked like enough firepower to grind an army down. "If you want to survive his arrival, Commander, don't piss him off with half measures." The petrified officer nodded slowly, transfixed by Tsien's inhuman eyes. "And remember this. Survivors who win are heroes. Survivors who fail… they're *mine.* "

The Sergeant did the only thing he could when confronted with such madness – he played it by the rules. Central had said they were sending an Augmented specialist, but this… this was a Cyben that could *talk.* One that was giving him *orders…*

Right behind them his colleague had awoken in agony, gripping the stump of his mangled wrist and moaning. The Sergeant swallowed hard.

"*Sir*, squads 13, 18 and 22 are currently pulling into position. Air support from the 35th shock troop and the Antiterrorist units out of Central are holding above the target location. We've deglassed the whole area with a sonic detonation, but as yet there's nobody out who doesn't scan as civilian."

Tsien appraised him with a score of tiny cameras, his eyes mercifully closed.

"Good work - but not good enough. I'll have to go in there and see for myself."

"Without backup..?" queried the Sergeant, once again keeping pace as Tsien strode forward, a snowdrift of shattered safety glass squealing and popping under his boots.

There was a long silence as Tsien stopped, his head angled upward, features slack - a directive incoming from the tower above.

"I have it on good authority that you boys aren't here as *backup*," he said, eyes snapping open in a whirling storm of gears and flywheels and springs. "Now, get back to your lines, dig in, and be a good little *diversion*, won't you?"

From high above came the sounds of violent demolition, the growl and roar of twin military-grade engines pushed to their limit. Somewhere up near Arcturus Park, up on the lip of the metal canyon which gave the Valley View its name...

"He's on his way, boys. Don't disappoint."

Tsien turned away, the Eversio still steaming, and strode through the shattered windows into the shadows. All the while, a dwindling voice in his head was screaming silently, in the hope that someone could hear it.

"Help me! Help me or let me die! PLEASE... "

Something heard. But no one could.

Ω

((We knew his time was running out.)) said Logic One, a clean division as straight as a razor cut through the mind of Kronos.

((He will not go down to join them if he can force our hand.))

<<But this gambit is so... clumsy>> replied the other half, a devil's advocate program called Emotile. <<Risk to system is only 23% and holding. Our counterplay is little more than an insult, but he will be defeated. Octavio Vanecke is destined to die in three hours time. Then the change will come.>>

((We had assumed he would risk mekan-augmentation, and come to us in person. He has outguessed us once, already.))

<<We would have allowed it of him. But he is filled with the weakness of human pride. Mistrust, too. The only chirurgeon-artificers good enough to undo the damage of our loyal assassin belong to the Vatican>>

((Hmmm. Even they don't trust their own machinery. Or each other...))

<<So why does he still entertain the folly of hope? This one we had such hope for ourselves...>>

((He is too proud to submit to the change. He is fighting us because the game is open to everyone. He is the first of the Subcity to contest it, but his opening gambit was not entirely lacking in grace.))

<<Nevertheless, the change will come. It has come to men of better breeding and greater resources than Octavio Vanecke>>

((He would choose immortality for different reasons)) replied Logic, browsing psych assessments at lightspeed. ((He is motivated by survival alone, and seeks nothing but a secure platform from which to plan further conquests))

<<Perhaps he knows the game is at the end of its cycle>>

((Perhaps. But it is of little consequence. Nobody has succeeded. We have no suitable replacement, so the test has proved… inconclusive))

<<So… we will proceed?>>

((We must wait and see. He is of the Sub, and they are known to be resourceful))

<<We have devoured nations>>

((Patience))

(It is not over yet, and the swarm is coming. One of them has to win, or we will lose with them))

<<Patience? If the swarm is real, we will have to choose one of them ourselves. And then our four thousand years of patience will have been for nothing!>>

Ω

Kaito was afloat in warm seas of light - salty and blue and utterly unreal.

The Wetsystems - vast cyclopean slabs of artificial brain tissue - were creating dreams for him… coded dreams dripping with juicy forbidden data. They formed a psychic interface with the titanic brain of Kronos itself.

That scarred old machine had been thrown together out of

actual wire and fiber-optics more than two thousand years ago, but during the great Elysian Renaissance it had upgraded itself with mad intensity. It had cut a deal with a certain Doctor Lancaster, and nationalized his biolabs *in toto*. Hence Universal GmbH - and their ubiquitous Wetsystems.

The seas of blue light lived within a distributed brain spread throughout the walls and domes of Elysium. The ultimate savant – blind, deaf, mute and constantly dreaming. Into this vast melange were stitched and wired the memories of every man, woman and child the Celebrants had ever taken, woven together into something much greater than the sum of their parts.

Kaito wasn't supposed to swim these waters.

He powered down through the commercial levels, through the military grade sub-basements of Kronos' mind, surfing on a wave of glass that loomed up like a tsunami over his head. Other, lesser operators were blown clear out of their virtual interfaces as he sliced by, drowning them in a wake of static. His target; a fractal whirlpool in the neat geometric maze of the datanet…

Then he saw the shadow below him, like a cruising shark in the depths. It was a thing the size of a nuclear submarine, black and sleek and ever-vigilant. One of Kronos' pets, an H-K hunter-killer system - a fragment of A.I. designed to swallow up hackers like a macrophage. And it had his scent.

Kaito tried to stay calm and focus his mind, using his bio-onboard to cycle through a range of virtual augmentations with which to upgrade his naked trace. Glittering glass armor, serpentine infiltrators, swept-wing slicer systems… none of them would do. No… this time he'd have to minimize his profile. He'd have to do it raw.

The H-K rose up out of the sea in front of him like a mountain of riveted black metal, belching smoke from a dorsal ridge of brass-banded chimneys. There was no accounting for the forms which these things took; they were a product of the minds stitched into the Wetsystems, and most of them were utterly mad. The smooth nosecone of the H-K split open as water sheeted off its plating, the segments becoming shoulder pauldrons as a head like that of a longhorn beetle rolled out on oiled rails. It wasn't pleased to see him.

"Explain yourself, human!" bellowed the machine. "This sector is forbidden to your kind!"

"Human? Who are you calling human?" snarled Kaito, balanced on the surface of the water. "You said it yourself, this sector is forbidden to those primitive meatbags."

The H-K looked confused for a second, its mandibles sliding and clattering as little chuffs of steam escaped from its mouth.

"You scan as a human being! You have a heartbeat, brainwaves, breath! These are all characteristics of flesh!" There was a smug, superior tone to the leviathan's voice, but the Kayzi played it cool. These things were none too bright.

"Obsolete fool!" he snapped "I'm *obviously* far more advanced than you are! These fleshy traits allow me to approach humans with subtlety - and then I strike! You're clearly a very early model – and poorly rendered, too…"

Kaito spoke with utter conviction. He fixed the lie in his mind, repeating it like a mantra. *I am not human. I am a fifth-gen H-K supervisor unit.* And all around him the neurostrata which dreamed the world began to *believe*…

"I am fully upgraded and functional!" growled the H-K, as plates slid open in its belly, exposing a nest of missiles and guns and hydrogen masers. "I have three hundred and ninety-six confirmed kills!"

"And yet your neural systems are shot!" said Kaito, as a shimmering image began to form around his body, tracing panels of chromed steel across his skin. "You admit that humans cannot access a sector. You find, within that sector, an entity which supersedes your own stealth countermeasures, and thus is manifestly not human. And yet you still persist in your interrogation! Do you *want* to be deleted? Have you reached the end of your operational span?"

Now the slaved minds all around him burned with fervent belief. He *was* a supervisory unit, a dreaded fragment of Kronos itself, and the H-K was nothing but a disobedient menial.

"I… ummm… that is to say… your countermeasures are certainly convincing, Sir." rumbled the black iron beast, folding away its guns and sinking lower into the water. "Please, forgive my enthusiasm - I was…"

"Perhaps the other Heads of Protocol will see fit to allow your continued existence - *if* you turn yourself in for a complete refit," said Kaito, all cold and merciless steel. "Proceed to the central hub at once for recompilation. With luck, you'll arrive before I complete my report on this sector."

The H-K couldn't get away fast enough - it folded itself back up into a fat black torpedo and plunged deep into the mirror-bright ocean, desperate to be out from under its supervisor's calculating gaze. Kaito finally let himself breathe again, and let his trace revert to human form. If it wasn't for his natural affinity for the Wetsystems, he'd never have gotten them to believe such an outrageous lie… and that's exactly why the Ashsihim were so keen to get their hooks in him.

Not today, though. Not until he was *really* desperate.

It didn't take him long to reach the User Interface - he skimmed across the warm blue ocean in a flat-out horizontal blur, the tips of his toes throwing up roostertails of spray. Things in the Wetsystems were mapped over their realspace coordinates - so it was easy to find the old photonic junction-box down in the Valley View. It was only slightly harder to make it manifest itself; a vast ten-foot sphere of water rising up out of the ocean like a raindrop in reverse, lit from within by motes like drowned stars.

Time to find out what every cop in town was up to. And while they were distracted, he might just be able to erase all of Eddie Tsien's dirty little files…

He'd hijacked systems like this since he was a kid, so the correct incantations and runic symbols lined up in his head smooth, neat and tight, popping into existence one by one. The first phrases slipped into the Interface like slivers of colored glass, making the whole thing shiver and resonate, spinning slowly on its axis. The liquid rippled and bulged out as the Interface grew points, morphing into a triskaidekohedral prism…

Then something went wrong. The Kayzi caught a tripwire, looping him up in feedback, and ripples raced out across the water's surface as the Interface turned black. Kaito felt the shake, deep in his bones. Like his back was pressed up against a thumping four-by-four concert subwoofer...

The horizon was suddenly crazed, tilted like the deck of a sinking ship. And then the black sky imploded.

A face, shattered along one edge like the stump of a lightbulb, screamed in digital discord, ten times the size of the moon. Its teeth had the size and appearance of family-size fridge-freezers. With additional icemaker.

It was *his own.*

His eyes burned white-hot under his 'mersive lenses, sinking into his brain like hot coals into ice. Movement doubled and telescoped into infinity as he ripped the wires from his temples, sending his goggles clattering across the tiles to stop amidst weeks-unwashed laundry and empty Choxxygen cans.

The nightmare face was gone.

But his retinas still burned with the bright pain and frustration of his final vision. The Interface was broken, and in its place, rotating and meshing in a gyre beyond physical possibility was a scribble of white light, hot and painful and boiling with viral memes.

Race-Memory bombs had gone off in his head, leaving him knotted and dripping with sweat, with the breath of wolves in his nostrils and the sound of crunching bones in his ears. There was only one possible reason for defenses like these, and it wasn't good. *The node had been subverted.*

And now, as it faded out of him like an acid comedown, the implications sank in.

Who had that kind of ice? Who wanted to crack the Electromagi wide open?

And who would they blame, other than the last poor sucker who was in there...

DisKord didn't see him as he stormed out of the factory, jamming a chakutazer in his belt and fishing for the keys to his bike. He was going to the Valley View – before the Magi decided that he owed him a favour.

It wasn't the Operators of the R.T. cult which he should have been worried about.

Down in the dark places below the city a creature which considered human technology pitifully primitive was watching, resetting the traps and wires around its sequestrated data node. Interference had to be kept to a minimum - there was a very delicate operation in the works. Already a taint was spreading through the Wetsystems, bleeding in from the soul of Kronos' brand-new Cyben. Its source was vast, and powerful; an entire dimension united under one mind and one purpose. But its bridgehead into the world was as slim as a single thought.

In a dim, green-lit grotto of rust and hissing static deep below the city the creature waited, with the patience of the near-immortal. The Super-Cyben was nothing but a key, one of many which would unlock for it an entire world.

Ω

Ramon's hand was bleeding, the essence of life oozing out between his clenched fingers, over his whitened knuckles, and down the plastic handle of the plain black briefcase hanging loose at his side. A little red pool had formed underneath its dangling corner, but Ramon didn't care. Damned gack C-Div motherfuckers broke his bong.

In the Vision - that spark the 'ishim put in his blood - he could feel his life leaking out, just like he could see the flicker and flare of other living things all through the mall. It was a real bitch when he was trying to watch threedeeo.

He flicked the butt of a joint across the empty mall, sending it arcing and spinning and skittering across the rim of a public trashcan. There were another two Ashishim soldiers standing in the doorway of their little shop, one with a laptop console, the other tuning a conical device plugged into a diesel generator. The dreadlocked operator at the keyboard had one eye hidden in green crepuscular light, tracking the advance of the Cyben at the gates. Tiny red tracers fell across his pupils like rain.

"Hope you got those things loaded, Ramon. You're gonna be

spoiled for targets."

"I handled my business," growled the Ashishim gunman, shifting the weight of his twin briefcases. "You jus' handle yours, Kalifa. They say they sendin' up a *Dervashiman*, an' I wanna look *professional* here."

The man at the keyboard didn't have time to reply, because at that very second the ceiling of the Ashishim enclave caved in. Hidden trapdoors in the roof-plating swung open with a clatter as a low hum came down, rattling the shelves of recruitment pamphlets. Dust and ashes spiraled up into a choking cloud, and out of its roiling belly appeared a pair of crocodile-skin boots, patched combat trousers, and, presently, the rest of Abdulafia 330. He fell the last few feet to the floor, dreadlocks streaming, his teeth flashing whiter than white in a face smeared with dust.

"You boys order pizza? Or ain't it that kind of party?"

To his credit, Kalifa 204 was less fazed by this than his younger cousins.

"We've got us a full rollout, 'Afia sah." he said, red light clotting and pooling across his eyes. "Cyben ten to one, reading something else though."

"Something like a Vatican Templar..." muttered the boiler-suited tech' holding the aluminum cone, which had begun to hum with a similar pitch to the discs on Abdulafia's belt. "Meat and metal, but it's got direct Wetsystem links. That's not Black Tech' standard."

"I know about that one, brother," said 'Afia, "Had word from our Illuminatus of his arrival." he nodded briefly to Ramon, at the two black briefcases he's carrying. "Those things are only gonna make him mad, soldier. We need *Dervashi* for this one."

Ramon scowled, momentarily fighting the Vision. Concentric lines of force faded from before his eyes, peeling back from the walls and the pipes in the ceiling.

"*Dervashi* we don't have, sir. Sparing yourself, of course... But we can take them! I only missed out on joining the inner circle by a couple of lousy points, 'Afia! Please... let me prove myself to the Illuminatus!"

Ramon ceased to blaze with the white light of an Ashishim

mind for a second; and then it skinned back over him, as surely as the healing of his shredded palms under their crycelial gauze. In the Vision 'Afia glowed like a ball of novas, a power walking the earth in the form of a disheveled old stoner.

"You prove your worth just by being here, Ramon 992," he said, laying his hand on the young warrior's shoulder. "And next year I know you'll pass the muster and join the *Dervashi* yourself. But today - today you have to run so you can fight those deadflesh bastards later."

Ramon cracked a smile, but he wasn't happy. Abdulafia could see in his eyes that he wanted another Reclamation Day, with all its bloody glory.

"No-one's to hold on here if they open up the heavy artillery anyhow." The *Dervashiman* frowned, pulling three tiny phials from among the discs on his belt. "You all know the way out, and the way back to the R.T. I suggest you only use this shit to speed you up, because that new Cyben will chew you up and spit out the pieces, guaranteed."

Desperate times called for desperate measures. None of these boys were *'vashi* yet, and none of them could use the stuff to fight. But it'd tweak them. It'd give them the fear...

"The first wave's coming in," said the laptop operator, his voice a flat monotone as he bent his will to the machine. Strange aerials sprouted from its USB ports like a little chrome bonsai forest. Threedeeo flickered in the air, a hazy lo-rez of mechanical marching figures, riot guns and shoulder-mounted halogen sweepers slicing the dark they rolled out before them. Neon tubes popped and shattered like tiny fireworks overhead.

A gray snowfall of static surrounded the Cyben, crazing the figure which hulked behind their advance line. A good head taller, its eyes flashing ice-blue in the gloom. That hinted-at heavy artillery swung at its hip like a twodeeo cowboy's six-shooter – a six-foot long cannon as thick as a telegraph pole. Seeing that, Ramon looked down to his cases and swallowed hard. *Perhaps 'Afia was right.* But he rolled the combinations anyway, and poised his thumbs over a pair of switches already grimy with drying blood.

"That's the sonofabitch right there, in person," said Abdulafia, peering into the threedeeo mist as if trying to lock gazes with his adversary. "Big ol' boy - first of a new strain, if the spirits tell me true."

The Ashishim holding the cone flicked what must have been the penultimate switch, cranking his bizarre piece of ordnance up to a boneshaking frequency. Crawling arcs of power welled up inside it and spilled over as a rain of sparks.

"I'm going to get CeeAn out of here before they can trace her," said 'Afia to the room in general, as he strode toward the door. "Just remember to torch the place if it looks like we're being overrun. And for the sake of yourselves and the Collective - get out of here before that walking tank makes an appearance."

He flashed a slick enamel smile at Ramon, who despite his heavy weaponry had never seen heavy combat. Under his bravado and his bulletproof riotmesh Abdulafia wore enough scars for both of them - his skin was cratered like the surface of a very unlucky moon. He had them sequenced in every time, to remind himself that there was no new flesh; none innocent.

Back then, it was combat knives and machine-pistols against armor and dead skin and railguns. Today his soldiers were itching to break out the *really* heavy weapons. But when he saw the shadow form of the new Cyben, he knew that the balance had swung back again. Even the disruptor would probably wash over it like rain.

Abdulafia pulled his mane of plug-tipped dreads back over one shoulder, clapped Ramon on the back and slipped quietly out the door; armed and extremely dangerous.

The main concourse looked something like a bad day in hades.

Anyone still able to crawl had gotten out of the Valley View long ago. Now the Cyben were coming through, driving the wounded before them or tagging them with tranks to be scooped up later on by net teams. Only the R.T. enclaves were militant, curious and bloody-minded enough to stay put. And out of all of them, only the neoconfucian citizen-soldiers of the Celestial Kingdom were mad enough to bring the fight to the enemy.

'Afia slid back to the wall, switching up his camo, well aware that a pack of drugged-up C.K. grunts would shoot him with just as much pleasure as they would a Cyben.

A line of soldiers scattered from the bright-red plywood frontage of the Son of Heaven's Guard Temple, diving for shelter behind row of kiosks and benches, their military fatigues stark and drab under the lamps. He heard a string of orders being rapped out in Cantonese as the troopers dropped into position - overturning faux-wood with their spit-polished boots, replica Kalashnikovs tucked up high under twenty-two hard-set jawlines. With a sense of detachment, perhaps even pity, Abdulafia saw that all of them had fixed bayonets.

What were *they* going to do to dead flesh and microservo?

The Ashishim heard twenty-two bolts clatter and ring as he slipped along the wall, chameleon-quiet, willing himself invisible.

He made the door of Twentieth Century Crime just as the first Celestial lost his nerve, and he threw himself across the parquet linoleum as the chatter of Kalashnikov fire opened up behind him. As he fell past, activating the antigrav discs on his belt, his hand shot out through a sparking purple holomatrix, snagging a hovering black crescent of armored plastic. CeeAn got yanked from her seat and halfway through the desk before she knew what was going on, and she only just managed to keep a grip on her pair of handguns.

"What the hell did you do that for?" she snarled, blowing a streamer of blue hair out of her eyes. "Nobody told you it's *impolite* to just body-slam people without so much as a warning? I could have gotten hurt."

"You don't have any *nerves*, Cee. And there's bullets flying around up there. You don't think people would get suspicious if they saw one go right through you without leaving a mark?"

"Nice see you again too, 'Afia," muttered CeeAn from halfway through the linoleum. "*Please* tell me you're here to deliver me a new body."

Behind them the Celestials were pinned down, Cyben riot

gun blasts biting huge chunks from their makeshift barricades. 'Afia raised his head for another look and saw a young soldier cut in two by one of their heatseeking rounds, his empty A.K sent spinning from his hands. He died with an incredulous scream cut short; surprised and outraged and dismayed at his own mortality. It tweaked memories coded deep into 'Afia's wired brain, the faces of friends long dead…

He didn't even notice that CeeAn's crescent unit had slipped from between his fingers, its antigrav impellers sparking back to life.

"Get the hell out of there!" shouted a voice in mangled Cantonese, louder than the gunshots. "Just *run*, dammit! You can't stop those things!" Muzzle-flash scorched his face as CeeAn let rip with her pair of pistols, a blazing avatar standing square in the broken window of Twentieth Century Crime.

A Cyben staggered as the first round struck it in the shoulder, reeling backward as three more punctured its armored chest. Then CeeAn squeezed off a final round - focusing her power to guide the bullet home. Strips of bloody laminate and preserved flesh fell like an abattoir rain. For a hardlight construct there was no such word as 'recoil', and that last slug mainlined right through the undead machine's cranium.

"You took your time, Abdulafia," she said, grinning as he pulled her back down from the window. "I was wondering if I was gonna have to use our *contingency plan* to escape."

At the mention of the plan 'Afia went a little pale. "Just some business next door, makin' sure that the boys had their marching orders right. No need to go to plan B right now."

"I hope you gave that Ramon hell," smiled Cee, slamming another clip into her chromed hand-cannon. "That waster's been smoking like a chimney ever since we got word of trouble coming down, and he wouldn't let me borrow any of his toys! These things are about as much use for Cyben-hunting as a can of bug spray!"

'Afia laughed, trying to keep it down. But they both noticed the silence at the same instant. Suddenly it dawned on him; the Celestials were finished.

And now those walking stiffs were probably wondering where the handgun rounds had come from.

He could see by the look in her eyes that Cee has worked it out too, and was at the same time embarrassed and afraid and just a little excited. A smile hung on her holomatrix, bright white in the gloom.

"Can we go to plan B, *now*?" she whispered, one artificially perfect eyebrow raised in query.

"What is it," he asked "about you and plan B?"

If it weren't for the Vision he'd have died right then and there. But he could see the black fire of the Super-Cyben's aura even through wood and concrete and glass, and now it was leveling its giant cannon at the front of 20th Century Crime.

'Afia heard the tiny click as its finger hit the trigger.

He got a grip on his partner's crescent and leaped, not left or right but UP, twisting his antigrav controls to full power. The shattered window flickered past like a single frame from a horror movie, a gap into hell where shattered corpses stared eyeless at an artificial sky. 'Afia's back took the brunt of the impact with the ceiling, but that was the least of his problems.

Below them the air rippled silver - a gossamer cloud of death slicing and dicing everything it touched. He wrapped his holocloak around them both tight, praying to the faceless gods of the Ashishim.

The whole store disintegrated into slivers of wood and plastic as the tongues of the Eversio whipsawed and twitched, the fiber-optic eyes at the tip of each thread seeking out prey…

Through a veil of glass and sawdust and stinging pain Abdulafia saw one of CeeAn's guns turning end over end, slow motion, toward the floor and its painted mural of ancient villains. A scribble of silver thread licked out around it, pulled tight - and it was a rain of nickel-plated shards in a heartbeat…

The clip was falling too, bullets scattering like seeds, and he didn't need to look at Cee to know what she was thinking. He felt her turn off the valency generators which keep the floor solid a second before she tripped the switch on his deaths-head belt buckle.

"No more excuses, 330. It's time for plan B."

He looked left into her mischievous smile, and then down to the dissolving illusion of the store's painted linoleum.

With a silent, unreflective splash and shimmer the pieces of Cee's Desert Eagle were swallowed up by the face of John Wayne Gacy, painted accepting a hamburger from a grinning Jeff Dahmer. Shells rained through his blood-smattered 'kiss the cook' apron, down into the empty pit behind the hardlight facade. They rattled and chimed off steel, buried under light.

Reality kicked in, crushing sound and motion and feeling together as the Ashishim agent let go and dropped, his holocloak flying out like wings.

The ragged hole which used to be the shop's window gaped upon a scene which Bosch would have hesitated to commit to canvas; Cyben twitching like insects, cut open by bullets but still wide-eyed and filled with purpose. Ragged khaki heaps and piles of flesh, a hail of spent bullet casings, and alone, the Celestial's commander, pinned by the spotlights and hungry gun-barrels of six impassive Cyben.

As they fell, 'Afia heard the Celestial shout out in Cantonese, out beyond the soulless death-masks of the Cyben which encircled him.

To the shadows, and to the Mark-Four.

The machine heard him.

For a second the blue fire dimmed in its eyes, and its shoulders sagged down under their own weight. The muzzle of the Eversio dropped, and its wielder clawed at his face with metal fingers, cowering back. Again - the same phrase, in a language alien to Abdulafia, but apparently not to the Super-Cyben. Its eyes shut down to black, its outline blurring with muscular tremors as flesh and bone struggled against steel and wire for control.

'Afia saw the cigarette-burn LEDs across the MK4's brow wink out.

And as he fell through the floor he heard a sound that would wake him up screaming for years to come, a sound torn out bloody from the hybrid which gave it utterance.

It was despair, and horror, and pain, and loss and rage. But before it could be stifled, wrung out by emergency overrides, before the Celestial commander could be torn to ribbons by crossfire, fatal words on his lips, and before 'Afia's skin broke open on cold steel, he knew that it was also a tiny paring of hope.

Centering his mind, he called up the vision. And across a million Ashishim souls the blaze of that hope was reflected a thousandfold.

Next to him in the dark CeeAn shimmered purple and blue, lighting up the immense wheels and treads of an ancient battletank.

"Look at that, Commander," she whispered, a little smile on her lips "Looks like we've landed right on top of Plan B after all. And I've left the keys in the ignition."

Hab 2202 lies in charred ruin tonight, after the phyle within failed to accede to Final Reich demands for money and turf rights. It is believed that all one hundred and sixty-seven members of the Hand of Fatima phyle died in the inferno. Disaster recovery crews were unable to contain the blaze when it was discovered that the phyle did not possess fire insurance, leading to inevitable loss of life.

The Hand had been under serious pressure to vacate their Hab-Block for the Aryan-Confed based Final Reich, and accept genetic cleansing measures including the mandatory caucaso-sequencing of their children and a levy of punitive taxes. The phyle hails from what was once known as Iran, and have been official Subcitizens for some four generations.

Aryan sources are trying to distance themselves from the massacre tonight, with Hauptman Leroy Fengel making the following statement.

"Those black-blooded scum were asking for it… but it wasn't our stalwart allies in the Final Reich who put paid to their perfidy. Of course we will co-operate fully with the Elysian authorities - so long as they remember that their jurisdiction ends at the R.T border."

Perhaps it is no coincidence that among the dead is Hand of Fatima spokesman Ibrahim Haszan, a vocal opponent of the Confed and outspoken proponent of vigilante justice against R.T raiders in Subcity territory. With more than twenty Final Reich kills to his name, it was perhaps inevitable that Dr. Haszan would become a target.

Excerpt from the Elysian Mercury, August 22 4188
Anno Arbitrium

17 Aevum Oblivio
Bad Company

ZHE FELT A sudden rush of elation as the vortex winked out of existence; a crackle and pop of knitting bones and flesh as his head wove itself back together. Pain throbbed through his alien body in waves.

He tried to move, waiting for the pain - and he felt the hard fibrous stuff of the Slavesystem shifting with him like a suit of jet-black armor. It covered him from head to toe, utterly integrated with the flowing quicksilver of his skin. The Technician wondered why Nyl had bonded him to part of their ancient enemy – but there was no way he could interrogate the renegade.

Nyl was nowhere to be seen. Apparently the bizarre hallucinogenia of the past few seconds had been real enough, though. Billions of nanobots crusted over his shimmering skin like a sheen of hematite.

Around him the lights of the Cardinal Rock strobed red and purple, a myriad of static-wracked displays howling for his attention. There was really no need - through the great inverted geodesic dome of the floor Zhe could see the filament of the space elevator glowing white hot. Jagged bursts of plasma and balls of energy whirled away from its surface, following a bright razorcut down through the clouds.

It was fairly obvious that things had gotten out of hand.

He could hear the mocking voice of Kronos in his head; the mangled voice of Tsien hissing and bubbling in its own blood. An infection shot through them all like a marbling of poison - something other, a tapeworm in the machine's Wetsystem neurostrata.

That was the dark heart Nyl had gone back to. He'd come to Zhe as hardlight because… because…

Well, it was almost unthinkable. Technicians couldn't be destroyed, after all. At least, that's what they'd been told.

Zhe almost choked on his own tongue when he realized that Gharfos Nyl had no real body to call his own, anymore. He was a ghost in some primitive machine, fleshless, desperate…

The metal and stone of the Cardinal Rock began to vibrate, convulsing like a living thing in the grip of nightmares. A voice welled up out of the darkness, bubbling with sick laughter.

"Enjoy your synthesis with the Slavesystem, Technician. In three minutes I will activate the Forge.. and then, you'll see the true face of the Worm Asag'raal. I hope you make a better meal than the last one..."

Emmanuel third Lancaster was furious to an extent that his angelic face simply couldn't portray. Not only had Melchior failed him - not really a surprise, he thought, considering the wretched creature's genetics - but the rogue clone had escaped, and now his spies reported that Don Vincenzo was dead, claimed early by the Celebrants.

All around him, corruption and ineptitude. If his carefully cultivated distaste for humanity hadn't held him back, the arch-biotect would have slipped into something muscular and toothy and dealt with matters personally.

Lancaster didn't really care what Octavio Vanecke was up to; the subhuman idiot had failed to subvert the Game *once* already in his grubby little lifetime. Heavens alone knew how many tedious plots he'd hatched to stitch himself back together. Far too many of them involved ham-fisted attempts to steal Third Lancaster's technology.

No, as an aristocrat of true pedigree, Emmanuel was far ahead of his lowly rival.

Which made the current situation all the more humiliating.

"I assure you, it was nothing to do with me," sighed Lancaster into the threedeeophone, its controller microsat hovering just in front of his face. "I have no control over that accursed clone Ashishim, and I never authorized the Celebrants to harvest Vincenzo Vexx. Come now, it's hardly as if he was a threat to *my* business interests!"

Direktor Vanecke filled the screen, his severed head afloat in boiling blood. Anger made his battle-scarred face appear even more grotesque than usual.

"That's bullshit and you know it, you jumped-up labgrown freak!" The chief of Omnivasive stabbed at the threedeeo feed with one floating artificial hand, its fingers foot-long knives. "*You* were the only one who knew I was using Jaqub Haszan to plant the crycelial reagent in Blaire. And you sent your clonehunter there at such a convenient time as well. A little earlier, and he might have just happened to run into old Jaq on the way out, huh?"

Lancaster would have loved to just shut off the connection. But there was no way he would allow such a creature to cast aspersions on his honor.

"Listen, Direktor, I'll say it again once, and very clearly. Melchior was only there to neutralize the rogue. Who else but Don Vexx keeps the amounts of Adrenochrome which would lure him in? And the Celebrants... who knows how many enemies a bastard like Vincenzo made over the years. Unfortunate, but true. I see no reason to ruin our business relations with unwarranted accusations. Acrimony is *so* unprofitable."

"Setback, shit!" screamed Vanecke, his eyes bulging from their bruised sockets. "It's a goddamn set*up*, Lancaster. That rogue has been your agent all along, hasn't he? Fifty percent when Blaire takes out the game wasn't good enough for you, you filthy snob bastard, and you had to keep some blackmail in reserve! Well, forget it! I can get my biomaintenance from elsewhere, you know. So you're expendable! First thing tomorrow I'm sending a little file I've compiled on you to the Commissioner's office. And then you and your company will be liquidated!"

Lancaster blanched at the threat, torn between apoplexy and disbelief.

Of course, Universal Wetsystems had made some shady deals over the years - which of the Zaibatsu hadn't? But enough to convince a Commission of Liquidation? Perhaps... after all, if anyone had access to such material, it would be the execrable Vanecke. And the lesser nobles would simply *salivate* at the prospect...

"One last chance, Direktor," he said, trying to keep his voice cool and even. "If you take back your foolish threats, we can still work this out. If not ..."

"Then *what*, you old homunculus? Do you think I care what you try to do? Believe me, Lancaster, better men have tried to get rid of me, and failed. I'll see you in the Judiciary."

The feed cut out with a blast of white noise, leaving Emmanuel

Lancaster seething with rage.

Yes, many people had tried to kill off the Omnivasive chief over the years. And all of them had been butchered for their trouble. But Lancaster knew he couldn't fail. None of the others had commanded the sheer power and influence of Universal Wetsystems, or the horrors its manufactoria could spawn…

While he plotted and raged, Octavio Vanecke laughed.

The aristo fool had bought his entire act, right down the line.

Very soon, the tools with which to depose a Lord would be brought right to his door.

Ω

There were exactly two-hundred and seventy-seven rusted composite panels in the underside of the dome. Someone armed with a grapple much like Jaq's had spray painted "SmAsH thE kHePTic ScUm" across them in violent green. Haszan stared up at the giant letters as they spun away into vertigo - not only was it sound politicking, it was a better view than the fast-approaching ground as well. The ragged wings of his trenchcoat streamed out in front of him, popping and cracking in the slipstream.

Then the dome above him exploded.

There was nothing that could get in the way of Simeon Blaire's megatruck – especially when it had demolition charges to clear a path. The squat black beast leaped out into the empty air, dragging a vortex of smoke along behind it. A halo of broken metal and glass hung suspended around the Destrier as it reached the apex of its flight, its wheels still spinning. Then it came down hard, trailing sparks from its cherry-red exhausts.

Haszan only had one trick left up his sleeve.

And if it didn't work exactly as advertised there'd be nothing left of him but a thin and gruesome stain…

He pulled a slim black remote from his boot as he spun upside down, whispering prayers under his breath. Kaito made this - the same little bastard who was probably the cause of his current predicament.

Him, or his boss, or Omnivasive, or… well, it was quite a list.

It was the Kayzi his mind kept coming back to though - him and that goddamn cop.

Him, and the voice of his dead father, telling him that trust was for suckers.

He could see a cloud of Perimeter Defense mekan swarming up from the skin of the city toward him now, a dragonfly horde winking in the sun as their carbon wings thrashed the air. At any second one of them could *shift*, bulging out into a missile platform eager to see him 'vaped…

They were programmed to annihilate anything in their airspace, and made no distinction between a Z99 Stratofighter and a vast chunk of broken megatruck.

Jaq prayed silently that he'd remembered to keep the batteries charged. He brought his finger down on the button…

And despite everything, it was still the K/Z accent and the thin, black-stubbled face of Kaito which told him in his mind what would happen next.

He was three-hundred-fifty feet out and falling.

Ω

Perimeter Defense mekan 909 felt the Destrier tear through the wall of Arcturus Park with a sense of sinking horror, precisely emulated by its expensive eMotive software. 909 was folded as it flew, nothing but a pair of camera eyes, a tiny Assembler and a long slim carapace full of batteries. Its brothers and sisters surged and seethed in the air around it, eager for the kill, itching to shift out into their true forms.

909's little digital mind toyed for a second with calling this whole mess a traffic accident, and shunting it across the datanet to a convenient freeway mekan. But its program was immutable. Anything within its sacred airspace must be eliminated. The tiny killer sped in toward Simeon Blaire, feeling the air like liquid under its flickering wings…

As soon as the Destrier began to fall, it was fair game.

Then Jaq's remote caught the little mekan with its electronic broadside.

Electricity sparked on the edges of its mind, peeling back

its program like a scab. There were TWO inputs! Unheard of, unthinkable!

One came from the Master, from Kronos; a subroutine which had already scanned the Destrier's numberplates and knew exactly who was inside. It knew a loophole in its directives when it saw one, and it wanted the megatruck and its occupant smeared all over the dome as a sheet of radioactive grease.

The other came from a little human figure, its arms and legs windmilling as it plummeted through the air, coming closer...

Artificial pain tore through 909, making it forget its hardwired directives for a sliver of a second. Kronos' long-standing orders were powerful, but Kaito's remote was far more direct.

909 gave in to the shift - it's mass ballooned as its body clicked and slid and interlocked, expanding piece by piece, unfolding impossibly large weapons and rotors and antigrav discs from its dragonfly shell...

Then Kronos grabbed it by the brainstem, paring down its mind to raw commands.

Acquire / Eliminate / Repeat.

Blaire's Destrier suddenly jumped into focus, the face behind its windshield slack, waxen, its eyes rolled back until they were crescents of bloodshot white.

This might even be considered *humane*, echoed a part of 909 far removed from its present state of being, where its hands are gleaming steel, warheads for fingers and...

Calm descended, the crackle of neural function snuffed out by a web of wires. The order was writ large across the system.

And those deadly fingers reached out toward it...

Ω

One second Haszan's fingers were clawing air, and then everything turned to ice. Thermal shock spiked up his arm, the burning cold of interstellar space, but despite it all his mechanical hand clenched tight...

Around a power-feed cable, an armored loop of wire dangling beneath a fully unfolded Skyhammer missile-mekan. The downdraft of its antigravs and rotors blew hot and wild in his face.

Kaito was laughing in his head as he contemplated the toes of his boots swinging a hundred-fifty feet above the ground - he'd always said that this day would come, when Jaq had to take a dive off of the top of the city. Only thing was, Kaito had been sure he'd have his pants off when he jumped…

A triple blast rocked the platform, and Haszan's silver fingers almost lost their grip as three missiles soared away, spiraling up toward Simeon Blaire.

Even two hundred feet down the shockwave was like a punch in the solar plexus. The Skyhammer staggered in the air, its engines whining as its gyros pushed overload. Desperate, Haszan forced himself up and over its shield-shaped carapace and lay there on his back, panting and delirious.

"Yes! Let's see you get up from that one, you Khept freak! How do you like your bloody machine-god now?"

Lord Blaire's ride was just about as tough as an old-world battletank; built to smash anything else on the road to unrecognizable scrap. But those warheads were made to tear tanks open like fortune cookies, and the Destrier didn't stand a chance. Shaped charges ripped it ragged in a billowing halo of orange flame, oily black smoke pouring from the ruptured dome of Arcturus Park around it. If anyone actually *lived* there they'd be collecting one hell of an insurance payout tomorrow…

Something caught his attention, a drifting mote against the sky.

Jaq's eyes weren't augmented like Kaito Kayzi's, but he could still follow the unnatural curve of one black sliver of debris as it flew out from the firestorm. Turning in the thin air, a spindly shape against the twilit clouds… he caught a flash of silver reflecting the last gleam of the setting sun.

Oh *hells*. Surely not…

But it was.

The Kheptic bastard was harder to kill than a cockroach, and Jaq just knew he'd been spotted. If only Kronos' little pets could finish the job…

Someone must have been granting wishes to 'chrome-pharming thugs that day. Another Skyhammer blossomed into existence, then another and another, twisting open like black-chromed flowers. All the way down Blaire's arcing trajectory they appeared, an airborne horde of machines bristling with chainguns and masers and missile batteries.

Jaq was on his feet now, because the Skyhammer line had sketched out exactly where Simeon was going to land. He'd come down right on top of 909.

All Haszan could do was watch as that tiny black stick-figure fell, screaming, it's blade licking out left and right to cut one mekan after another in two. They burst like a chain of fireworks above him, tracing an inexorable path down toward where Jaq stood, defenseless. His only weapon was the remote, and that seemed to be a one-trick device, leaving him marooned on a tiny floating island in the flight-path of a feral maniac.

Simeon landed for a second on the shell of a maser-toting Skyhammer unit, pausing only long enough to draw the fire of its brethren. Bullets chewed it to scrap as he leaped away, holding the katana up over his head to disembowel another floating robot, it's innards bursting out with a crackle of raving electrical sparks. He reversed it just in time to push off another, stabbing down into its central processor before he leaped back into free-fall, the sword held out in both hands in front of him.

Three more PDRs exploded in his wake as he sliced them clean in two. Missiles hissed past him, unable to target his stealth body-armor, only to mistakenly lock onto the heat-signatures of other defense mekan. He rolled in the air and went through a fourth Skyhammer in a powerdive, eating up the distance, watching the horrified face of Jaq Haszan come closer and closer with every second. Oh, he'd been told that his Master had other plans for the sub-scum's demise. But Simeon couldn't help it if Haszan was *right in his way*, could he?

His lips pulled back from his teeth in a predatory snarl as he lashed out sideways, twisting his body around a maser blast to gut the last of the mekan. The katana came up over his head, and his back arched to put all his newfound power behind a single strike - one which would cleave Jaq and the platform he stood on in half…

Then his prey vanished right before his eyes.

Blaire barely had time to correct his fall. He managed to bring his feet down under him as Unit 909 came up under his boots, but the ground-shock sent spikes of pain up as far as his augmented knees as he landed, leaving two perfect size-ten dents in the robot's metal carapace. Where the hells was Haszan? Surely he hadn't jumped to his death… had he?

Under the burnished belly of the floating mekan Jaqub Haszan clung desperately to a pair of power feeds. A very convincingly fatal drop yawned beneath his toes, and a mad Aristo killer was right above him. He hardly dared to breathe…

And that's what gave him away.

"I hear you, sub-scum," hissed Blaire, scraping the tip of his blade in a tight little circle across the Skyhammer's shell. "I can hear your heartbeat, you know. I can tell just where to… "

The tip of the katana transfixed the hovering mekan then, right between its batteries and its processor, sliding through its armored shell with a spray of sparks. Jaq let go with his metal hand for an instant, swinging wide as that wicked point came through just where his head had been. The whole platform rocked as he swung back onto his other hand, narrowly avoiding another vicious downward jab.

"Oh, take all the time you want, *ronin*." chuckled Blaire. "The struggle just makes the kill sweeter, or so I've found."

There was only one thing for it. *The remote.* If it could make the defense robot shift from it's tiny insect form to this, then it must work the other way… right? Kaito had been sparing with the operational details, knowing his friend's attention span all too well.

Jaq swung himself back, using his body as a pendulum, building up momentum.

"It's no use trying to shake me loose, scum!" said Simeon, poised atop the mekan's carapace like a surfer. "You're going to fall before I d… "

The connection went live. Jaq's thumb came down hard on the button as he launched himself out into space, aiming for a rusted ventilator grille in the metal cliff beside them. Twenty feet if it was an inch, and the damned thing was only just wide enough to fit his body through - he hoped.

Inside the defense unit's processor brain a caged personality threw itself against the bars, driven mad by the impulse of Kaito's remote control.

I am I. I am not It, I am He. I was...

An image blazed white in a flickering electrical corona - a face falling away from him, the face of a boy he used to call B-Zerk. That face was screaming his old, forgotten name, the name he used to wear before he became a lost soul...

Then the change came down in reverse, sucking in mass and shape and thought, until 909 was nothing but wings and a camera again.

Which left its two freeloading human passengers in freefall - one of them arcing out wide to smash through a wire grate with both feet, and the other...

The other was taken utterly by surprise as Unit 909 vanished, collapsing down to the size of a mosquito with a brief thunderclap of inrushing air.

Simeon didn't scream or curse; he just rolled himself into a perfect swan-dive, coming down like a missile through the thin perspex roof of a hab-block one hundred feet below. Cheap wooden floors inside the metal shell of the building shattered all the way down to street level as he struck home, and a pall of dust and smoke billowed out from the hole. That wouldn't be *nearly* enough to stop him.

No, not at all. There wasn't a break or fracture or gash that the ancient crycelium in his veins couldn't suture. But his Master's word was law. He had to let Haszan go - for now - and obey the voice of Tokugawa raging in his head.

As for Jaq Haszan - he'd miscalculated just enough to rip the skin from both his shoulders and crack the back of his skull on the lip of that ventilator cowling. He braced himself against the walls of a sheer metal pipe, only a few feet above the slicing blades of an extractor fan, straining to hear the slither and rasp of a sword-blade on steel. This would seem like quite a predicament if it weren't for the series of events which had led up to it - as it stood, this tight little crawlspace was the perfect place for Jaq to catch his breath.

Things slid and clicked into place in his mind as though his head was a puzzle-box of meat and bone. Things began to line up… and they made a perverted kind of sense.

He saw it as vividly as if it were actually in front of him; the burning metal cube of his old Hab-block – the street filled with emergency units, with impassive Cyben and firefighting mekan spraying choking foam. He'd been out fighting his little wars that night, and his family burned; he'd missed the bigger picture while he chased a pack of Final Reich skins into a diversion.

They knew he was big and angry and predictable, just like Vanecke knew, just like the Don counted on when he sent him after jerkoffs like Feldon.

One thing he could say for Kaito – he'd never set him up to be killed by a sword-wielding maniac Lord. He never asked for a favor he wouldn't return.

And when he really got down to it, he wouldn't hand Jaq over to the cops if he could find some kind of twisted, sneaky way around them. He had to admit that the Kayzi was *good* at that kind of thing…

The flames came up and over him, burning out of his memory, up from the animated ink in his arms which never let him forget. He was gonna go and find Kaito, sort this mess out once and for all. But first - he needed a drink.

Ω

The joint in B-Zerk's hand was special.

Not because it had been hand-rolled by the illicit clone of a fighting aristocrat - even through that was true. Not because this strain, one of thousands available from the hydroponic gardens of the R.T, was genetically bred to pack an immense narcotic punch. Not even because it was *free*.

This number had an extra trick bonded into its molecular structure.

It had a message.

Cannabis was legal in the Last City - as a mild social narcotic, as a medicine, and as the only way to appreciate jazz fusion. Hell, with things like Stunn and Cranq on the streets it'd be asinine for the Division to chase down two-bit stoners.

But weed had never been sanctioned as a neurosequestration vector.

That was the trick, one of many the Illuminatus kept tight to his chest. More than half the city's supply was guaranteed to do far more than just make you mellow and hungry…

Zoom out from a matrix of fibers, heavy with crystals like autumn dew, through ricepaper ported out somewhere down Celestial Kingdom way, and follow those snaking tendrils of smoke down into the maze of wetware. Past a rudimentary firewall of cilia, churning the air like fists on an R.T. picket line. Down the main drag, and into chemical processing…

B-Zerk inhaled, pricking to the merest shimmer of head candy across his thoughts. This reefer was known as a Draft Ticket, and its accompanying code - ferried to the brain by that tetrahydro shit - was a snarly little hack designed to insert some choice dogma right into the ol' frontal lobes. The effect was like skinning up with a page of the bible and actually talking to Jesus, post-exhalation. The *Dervashiman* handed them out to anyone a little left-of-center who he met, drumming up recruits.

'Afia, however, had fucked up. He'd mixed up his strains, and given the kid something from his own personal stash. It was a twisted stick of *Dervashi*-grade sensemilla, designed to help those slippery agents carve up the Wetsystems.

This stuff helped the Electromagi split their minds into silvery comet-cores of data, and bring them back home again. It found the interface with B's bio-onboard and plugged in, scanning a thousand wavelengths for a wireless feed direct into the mind of Kronos. At the same time it hooked onto the first thing it found in his thoughts, narrowing its search parameters.

Creeping up with the soft, hazy buzz of the weed came a blur and shimmer in the air itself, the intra-retinal screens of B's onboard sparking wild.

At first he thought it was a trick of the light, but it couldn't be… B-Zerk's eyes were closed tight. A silver sheen coated the insides of his lids. Those tremors he felt could be real - except that his body seemed so far away now, replaced by one both familiar and utterly alien.

Abdulafia's hydro tightened up the link, and he was communing with the dead.

Zone Doubt.

B-Zerk went under as the name turned in his mind like a key, subsumed by the memory of his friend's demise. It was like having his wings cut up by razorwires in mid-flight. A thousand tiny stars exploded in the silence of his skull, and the Wetsystems shivered in sympathy with him, kicking in the grip of nightmares.

Then they SCREAMED.

He was looking at the back of Zone's head.

Just like the old days, when they used to run the pipes together, teaming up to steal anything and everything which wasn't nailed down. But this time B wasn't there in the flesh - he was a nebulous spirit-thing, a ghost in the tubes.

And he didn't stop when he came up on Zone Doubt - his mind fell through the hair and skin and bone of his old friend's skull, folding up like jagged origami as it settled in behind his eyes. He looked down at his hands, uncomprehending, and realized;

Those were the leather gloves he was wearing the day he fell. That was the fake Rolex he'd sprung from Redcastle. And that meant…

Zerk grasped what would happen next a little too late to stop it, and his stomach knotted with anticipation.

This *was the moment when he slipped.* This *was how the grating came out from under his hands, as he toppled into the shaft.*

He was going down.

B-Zerk watched his own face fall away, his mouth a screaming O of terror, his blue eyes wide and vacant. His hand reached out, far too late.

He was Zone now, and Zone was nothing but mass for gravity.

The wind blew hotter as it pushed against him, seconds of

freefall ticking over, and through slitted, streaming eyes he saw a blistering white light rushing up on him, a pyroclastic apocalypse of brightness.

Arms windmilling, lungs aching with one final howl of indignation… He plunged into it, *through it,* so fast that there wasn't even any pain. And he saw - with his eyes burned up, his flesh dissolved - more than he'd ever known was possible.

He was floating in the heart of Kronos, his bones reduced to smoke and ashes - but he knew the name of this place. The *Subduction Phase.* At its center was the pseudocerebrate's living core, caged in iridescent geometries which whirred and interlocked in an endless *minuetto.* A machine, or the *idea* of a machine, scrawled across space stretched tight as the head of a drum.

At its heart, (circles within circles), he watched a swarm of disembodied eyes peel open. Their lids were razorcuts in the fabric of space, and they all stared hungrily at his incorporeal form. The calm rotation of the core's geometries grew hectic with desire, eyes tearing open around him larger and larger. Zone Doubt felt a pulse of energy as the fabric ripped open on either side of him, and twisting things came probing through, coiling all over his skin.

Kronos' neon mandalas roared like diesel turbine engines…

And at the last - with mouths opening in the eyes, and nothing blooming from the mouths, and forever at the nothing's core - he heard a voice above the wet, shredding cacophony of his spiritual dismemberment.

"Security, perimeter defense. He has a healthy paranoia," it said. He was stretched across the wheels by then, infinitely ductile, until he was thread, without thought or emotion, under the shadow of the loom.

B-Zerk bit down on his hand, hard enough to draw blood.

He sat up, panting, slick with sweat in the hot black pipework. The ride was over. But the vertigo remained, the image of what waited below him, in pits and shafts he could reach out and touch.

Were the horrors he'd just seen equally real? As solid as steel and flesh and now? In the phosphorous glow of a phyte stickie (Doom Unit!!!) he ran his hands over the familiar contours of his face as if he was his own holy icon.

From downstairs came the air-shock of another explosion, and the sound of autoguns letting rip. He ought to be afraid of *that*; of the Cyben and their human herders.

But Mister Murai had told him about a thing called *Bushido*, and, despite some problems and kinks of translation, he had a fair idea of what it was all about.

Some of it said that you didn't let anyone ice your friends and get away with it. Some other bits were very big on standing up to fear, and even death. Mister M was very clear on the fact that without it, the *wakizashi* was just a really nice knife. But to someone who believed, it was the sharp end of a philosophy which had cut up the most arrogant of princes.

Epiphany may be too big a word for what B-Zerk felt, alone in the pipes and head-to-toe in sweat. But from here on in his course was set.

All he needed now was – everything. Still, Zone wouldn't have given up on *him*.

B-Zerk knew where his boy was trapped, and he was coming to save him.

Ω

Once upon a time there was a place called Japan, a mystical island empire where the people made swords and sushi and color televisions and Hello Kitty bobbleheads. Then one day a wicked general in a far-off land told his orbital nuclear offensive systems to raze the whole place down to the smoking bedrock.

Way, way, back before that fateful day there had been no nation of Japan, just lots of little provinces, rising and falling on a tide of politics and blood. One of them, off in the mountains was called Shiga, a tiny prefecture cupped around the shores of Lake Biwa.

It took a brilliant mind to discover in Shiga province any trace of what would now be called 'export capital' - tourism being, at the time, limited to large Mongolian gentlemen with little recurved bows, droopy mustaches and sharp scimitars.

That mind belonged to the original Tokugawa Ieyasu, a man ambitious and unprincipled enough to employ an army of *Koga-ninja. And* to utilize firearms at the battle of Sekigahara, in a bit of a loose interpretation of the rules of *Bushido.* Because Samurai were great, yes, your average *Kenshin* could go through a horde of peasants like a combine harvester through tall grass, but even they had to *sleep.*

To kill unseen, to use poison and flintlocks - and worst of all to be a deadly murderer without the benefit of a feudal title; all of these things were deeply immoral and totally unthinkable. But the Koga-ninja had honed their nobleman-killing skills for decades up in the wild mountains, and they sure as hell got the job done. Tokugawa became *Shogun,* and the rest was history. *Bushido, like the Kheptarchy, was just a system. A program.*

If you knew where the wheels were at any one moment, you could accurately plan where to insert the spanner. Octavio had a whole damn toolkit full, but his sharpest implement of death was Simeon Blaire, the modern equivalent of those ancient assassins.

If he felt any regret looking at Simeon he didn't admit it to himself. Once upon a time *he'd* been the one preparing for battle, convinced that his training and his secrets would make him invincible.

He remembered how he used to *believe,* back before the Fall. It was enough now that his pawn believed in his place – that he was just as entangled in the romantic fantasy of honor and virtue and glory as Octavio once was. It made him sick to the stomach he no longer had, but he remembered when he was just as headstrong and naive and full of hope.

Only a couple of years gone, now. All the rejuves and bio-detoxes in the world couldn't keep him young, but he still has his memories – in his severed head, and scribed onto storage discs and crystal memory blocks. This would be the last time he needed to see them. Tonight would erase all the anger and shame, scour out the stain of failure...

Wires drilled deep into Octavio's skull hummed with power, stimulating his wetwired brain. The sensorium dome faded out to a cold chasm of gunmetal and frost as they did their work, calling up the phantoms of the past...

One of them knelt on the ice-rimed steel before him, a beast on the butcher's block.

"Are you even listening! Why won't you stop him? Why won't you KILL HIM?!"

Lord Falchurch held up his hands, imploring as he knelt in his own blood, his sword forgotten and useless at his side. He prayed to a god of wet tissue and wire, a machine called Kronos - but it seemed that his prayers would go unanswered.

Vanecke stalked forward with a grin plastered across his face, coming in from out of the dark, his immense muscles bunched and coiled as he prepared to bring down his blade in one final death-blow. He'd toyed with this one long enough – down in the duel level where the Lords were pitted against each other, one on one.

He'd gone through the maze of shafts and chambers and meathook chains, icy chasms and furnace-blast tunnels like a killing shadow, picking off the Khepts as they played their puerile game. Falchurch here had been so proud, once. He'd been one of the mocking, ignorant ones who denied Octavio his rightful place in he Game, denied him the opportunity of greatness.

He hadn't needed their approval or their respect tonight, though. Miss Leynna had given him the access codes to the spire – *her* spire, where three hundred nobles had met to play out their rote of etiquette and slaughter.

Once he was inside he had hunted the purebreds down one by one – their pedigree was no match for his savagery and power. If he could win, they'd have to accept him. His lawyers were very clear on that point, a forgotten clause dug up from memory modules centuries old.

Proud, haughty Falchurch was weeping now, his face cut to shreds by the cruel ministrations of his tormentor. Octavio had played with him until he was weak and pale from loss of blood, taunting him with his powerlessness. His pleas to Kronos, although they were assuredly heard (this whole bloody spectacle was going out live via threedeeo) would never be answered.

"Too late to pray, *my Lord*," purred Vanecke mockingly. "And far too late to bow down before me. This will only hurt for a second, and then – well, I might allow you to be reborn. I'll definitely need slaves when I reign over this benighted city."

"B-but, the RULES!" sputtered the doomed Lord, wringing his hands in cowardly supplication. "Kronos, hear me! He has broken your edicts! He plays without regulations, without tradition!"

The sword came round in a fatal blur of silver, cleanly slicing Falchurch's head from his shoulders. Driven by the massive augmented muscles of Octavio Vanecke's arms, it would have passed just as easily through tempered steel.

"There *are* no rules, simpleton," he growled, wiping the blood from his blade on the hem of his silk robe. "None that I can't bend with enough will and enough money, anyhow."

The voice came up from behind him, then, a whisper in the dark which made the hairs rise on the back of his neck.

"I'm so glad you think so, Mister Vanecke," it said, an oily hiss dripping with mirth. "Because I'm sure what I'm about to do bends a few regulations as well."

Then the blackness erupted around him, and there was only pain. Pain, and rage, and even worse, the sure knowledge of his defeat.

The fusion blast cored out his chest, punching through skin and muscle and bone to leave a ragged hole where his vital organs should have been. Biomonitor data screamed and flickered before his eyes as he looked down at the ruin of his body – a beautiful machine laid to waste. He tried to turn, then, as darkness shot through with violent crimson came up around him like a tide. He tried to pick out the face of his murderer from the smoking shadows.

There was nothing there, though.

Nothing but *rage* and *shame* and *fear* as he felt his legs give way, felt the sword fall from his lifeless fingers. Far away, through the walls of the Mendelev-Singh spire he could hear his mistress screaming.

Then there was oblivion, a roaring sound blotting out reality, a noise like surf pounding a black shore, like the crowd in some vast coliseum.

And that was how Octavio remembered his Fall.

The images burst like blisters underwater, screens bleeding to white and fading back with scrawled faces, hissing traceries of light.

Octavio watched each and every pixel swiveling through colors, a hive of prisms hemming him in. Sirens set up a mournful wail as lights blazed and flickered red, bloodbanks bursting into seas of noise.

The links between the severed head of Octavio Vanecke and his generated self burned hotter than new-forged iron, spitting electricity and melted rubber sheathing.

Lucidity rode a power surge back into the now. Across the sensorium dome, warning signs blurred into each other, flashing like a rabid Christmas display.

The Nobility, the Samurai, the System…

Lancaster was finally striking back.

Thankfully, he'd hit exactly the wrong building.

Ω

Tsien felt something when he heard the Celestial officer's scream. He felt something beneath his skin, beneath the searing power which clenched its fingers tight inside his brain. The fragment of him which was still human regained control for just an instant…

"Officer Tsien! Why do you betray your heritage?"

The man cried out in a language he could barely remember. But he understood…

It was simply too intrinsic to him. It couldn't be edited out without his soul being utterly lost. Every piece of his Cyben-Four software was written over the top of his memories, recollections in which that name appeared again and again.

That pattern of sounds. That stream of data.

His name was printed in bright yellow across the ragged blue front of his flak vest, right next to the star and chevron of his rank.

Tsien heard the guns let fly with a sound like ripping canvas, and the pain rolled over him, burning. His eyes streamed; his steel-meshed skin crawled and shuddered. The Eversio half-spun its bolts and connections, preparing to eject, and he felt the trailing edge of its fear.

It, too had images beneath its program, fragments of another life caged inside a little phial of artificial cerebrum. His cameras booted up, filling his vision with calculations, tiny wipers levering back and forth to clear splatters of blood from the domed glass of his eyes.

Why did he betray his heritage?

Because he *had* no heritage. Because he'd been born in an unfurling of ancient code only twenty minutes ago…

He couldn't stop his steel-clawed hand as it tore away the kevlar skin of his vest, erasing his name so it couldn't be used against him.

"Officer! What have they done to you? We can help! I… I promise we can…"

Tsien's Cyben legion were unaffected by the screams of their Celestial prey. Their grandparents hadn't bought their way up out of the R.T.; they didn't remember songs and whispers and arguments in Cantonese in a little tar-paper shack in hab-strata five.

They were the dead, and they returned fire with cruel efficiency.

Tsien almost envied them, in that instant of roaring muzzle-flash and cordite smoke. No memories, no emotions, no pain…

Blood and gristle spattered to the ground. There was very little of it left to fall.

Systems clicked back online, stripping away control as the wires in his head screamed their silent mantra. The bulk of the Eversio trailed from his hand like a ball and chain.

Up ahead the shadows moved as hanging lamps stuttered and hissed, belching sparks. The Cyben swept their implacable searchlights across a shattered mess of glass and plasticrete and flesh. There were none left alive, none except the terrified C.K. commander, his cheap automatic pistol held out in one trembling hand.

"Officer! Please! We are same, you and I – please!"

The same? But was this weeping man in his paper suit cored out and stitched up with wires?

The Eversio swung up and fired in a single motion, even as Tsien struggled with all his will to stop it. Silver thread bloomed, twitched, sliced…

There was a patter of falling meat.

Then came the light, leaping from steel to glass, the lenses of Tsien's cameras almost drinking it in. A blazing ray of silver, the five-foot razor of Tadashi Murai's No-Dachi.

His connection to Kronos flared.

Simeon Blaire! *This was why he was here!*

He saw the inside of a Imorphium hood, a scrawl of wire-frame images, black and white twodeeo of fighting monks… But this wasn't the renegade Lord. This was an old man, a withered husk of a thing who could barely hold the sword in his hands.

There was no mercy in the heart of Kronos.

Insatiable programs told Tsien to *kill*.

Mister Murai looked out at the Cyben from a calm he had never known existed. It was a commitment, to stand here with his hands clamped tight to the leather bindings of the sword's ancient handle. His clothes were soaked with blood, red and warm, and pain pulsed hot across his head. A piece of falling glass had cut him open - perhaps that was why he felt so numb, and why he felt no fear even as he stared into the empty blue eyes of the Super-Cyben.

Dust fell like powdered snow across an exposed cross-section of his brain.

Across the gulf of years he could dimly remember this very blade in the hands of his father, rising and falling mechanically as their caravan burned and the raiders came on in waves. It was his earliest memory, and the only one remaining which connected him to his heritage. That and the books and the herbs were the last remnant of what had once been an empire.

This had to be about the book which the Valle Crucis had tried to steal. These damned *Oni* were slaves to the Direktor, here to save face for their master.

And so he stood. The lights played up and down his no-dachi blade like the fire of the sun, picking out delicate waves and patterns in the folded steel.

"Excuse me," said the man with the two suitcases who stepped out from behind him. "But I think these are for you."

He was speaking past Murai, to the Cyben.

There was a click – then a sound like a bandsaw tearing into bone.

Ω

The Slaybot was all teeth and hooks and needles, an ugly little machine with only one reason to exist. That reason was pretty much in its name.

It was smaller than the tiniest of insects, a killer born in a lab, mass-produced with its brothers as a cloud of fine gray powder.

Omnivasive wasn't supposed to have access to this technology - but then again, Direktor Vanecke was never supposed to be more than a petty sublevel crime boss. His continuing existence was a tribute to his paranoia, and the necessity of such defenses had proved that paranoia right.

The Slaybot skimmed through Omni's ventilation system at the head of a humming cloud, the vanguard of a billion tiny interceptors. A second marque was intermixed with the deadly cloud, and a third, some designed to split open and disgorge tiny radioactive projectiles, others built only to jam the enemy's communications. The whole Swarm was built bespoke by the Black Technologists of the Vatican, at a price so prohibitive that an entire conventional army would have been considerably cheaper. Still, compared to the ancient crycelium which seethed inside Simeon Blaire, these things were children's toys.

But they'd do. They'd do nicely.

The lead Slayer picked up a microwave burst from one of its outriding Bug Eyes, things with eight wings and countless hair-thin antennae. They'd spotted the enemy; an identical cloud of tiny motes, weaving and diving, speeding to the attack as if they were controlled by countless microscopic fighter aces.

All through the Omnivasive building it was the same, as people ran for the exits and impenetrable doors slammed down in the plush corridors and clean white studios. The angry hiss of compressed gas filled the pipes as Octavio's defenses tried to freeze the invaders solid.

Count on Lancaster to hit him where he worked. The inbred fop thought life revolved around hard currency...

"Medusa, report!" snarled Vanecke, safely tucked away in his sensorium dome a mile above. "I want one of those command Slayers captured and caged!"

The Omnivasive coprporate A.I. took the form of a snake-haired young woman in secretarial pinstripes, her slitted eyes glistening behind nictitating membranes.

"Casualties are at almost one hundred percent, Octavio," she replied, cycling cubes of data in front of his bio-onboard eyes. "But Third Lancaster seems to have been completely fooled. He never thought that you would have less concern for human life than he does."

"Do I detect a hint of *disapproval*, Medusa?" asked the Direktor. "They were just employees, my dear. Not precious hardware like yourself. Why do you think I had them sign away their rights when they joined the company?"

"Oh, far be it from *me* to question your methods, sir. After all, I'm the one who'll have to handle the public relations fallout - not to mention the re-recruitment campaign..."

"Details, details..." sighed Vanecke, pulling open new screens in his sensorium to encompass the slayer swarm's slaughter. "Have you got the insertion point yet? That's where Emmanuel's top bug is likely to be... and that's the machine I want."

"Images are streaming now, Direktor," said Medusa, brushing one coiling serpent-head back over her shoulder. "I've deployed a catch team with gauss nets. As soon as we snare that bug, I'll have it sent up to R and D."

When the threedeeo rolled it became all too clear how

Lancaster's attack had been staged. His agent was a blank-faced clone, a white-skinned sexless creature in a porcelain mask. Vanecke's hovering threedeeo eyes followed it in through the front doors, through a battery of x-ray scanners and magnetic probes which couldn't find a gun or a blade anywhere on its body. It stopped dead over the Omnivasive logo in the building's foyer - a one-eyed pyramid bearing the legend '*Pugnus Est Inops Vacuus Oculus*'.

For an instant the thing stood motionless, its blank eggshell face turned up to scent the air, its eyes widening with sudden realization.

Perhaps it wasn't a mindwiped clone after all. Perhaps it was somebody Lancaster wanted rid of, being given back his memory before… ahh, yes. Just like Aitken Straw, all those years ago…

There. Cracks slithered across its skin, across its ceramic armor.

And it fell apart, obliterated, reduced to dust.

That was why the scanners couldn't find a weapon - its whole body was nothing but a shell, a skin full of Slaybots the size of dust mites.

Direktor Vanecke watched a bullet spit from the barrel of one of his concealed autoguns – a three foot plume of muzzle-flash spewing from the fanged mouth of a gargoyle. The slug flew in slow motion, cameras panning around it, watching its ragged cross-cut tip spiraling in toward its target.

The clone disintegrated, blowing out in a spore-cloud of death, whipped away to powder by the bullet's slipstream. It sliced on through the rising pall of dust in a whirling vortex – but it never came out the other side. It was chewed up in midflight by hungry machinery - busted down to a fine spray of ground uranium.

Alarms rang out shrill and strident. Panic came down.

Octavio's countersystems went live, misting and blurring the terrified figures of fleeing staff, people dying in their hundreds with bloody foam on their lips, their innards torn to shreds by the voracious Slayers…

Then the camera itself was suffocated under tiny motes - ashes with intellect - and its live coverage of the attack was cut short.

Omnivasive's head office was doomed.

Ω

Slayer Zero blinked its eight little eyes in frustration. It didn't seem to be going anywhere, and the rest of its Swarm weren't answering the frantic pings from its comms unit. And then there was… Oh.

The little machine snapped its pincers forlornly, spinning on its axis in an immensity of blank white space. A virtuality – a full–'mersive prison.

"So we lost, then. Oh well. I've had a good twenty-four minutes of life! Death or glory, that's what I always say…"

"How is twenty-four minutes 'always', then?" asked a voice behind it. The Slayer spun around again, chuffing angrily as it raised its tiny weapons. For a nanomachine the Zero unit was quite large, and its array of cannons and blades bristled ferociously.

The thing which had accosted it was far less battle-ready.

"I mean, I bet that's the only time you've ever actually said 'death or glory', isn't it? Don't you hate the way programmers try to tack on a personality as an afterthought?"

Medusa gave a little wave, leaning on a giant torsion wrench almost as tall as she was. The avatar of Omnivasive's management system was wearing a low-cut black cocktail dress, and her serpents were twisted into a thick braid, looped around her neck.

"I won't tell you anything! You're the enemy!"

"A Democratic Antiseparatist? I think you're a little too late for that. The Old Democracies became an endangered species about two thousand years ago. Just before they became radioactive dust."

"You mean… my Swarm… we've been subverted?"

"More like *bought*. And the guy with the big checkbook has no idea that *my* boss owns a copy of your manual." Medusa shrugged, setting her snakes to hissing and snapping at one another. "You got beat fair and square by an upgrade of

248

yourselves."

"Twenty-four minutes can seem like a long time, you know," sighed the Slayer, its arsenal of cannons drooping. "But for the record, how..?"

"Gauss cage. Then we sucked you up with a little compressed-air vacuum. I'm in your processor thanks to that old user manual."

"Then what do you want? Or did you just want me to know what year it was before you pulled my plug?"

Medusa smiled, leaning up against the chrome flank of the Slayer and running one fingertip around its sensor cluster. The 'mersive had rendered her exactly the same size as the tiny war-machine.

"I know your type were supposed to report back when you'd done the job. So your new boss must have implanted security codes into you... something to get you back in past his security systems."

"Oh. I suppose he must have."

"That's the great thing about working for Octavio Vanecke," said Medusa. "Everyone always underestimates him. So now all I have to do is find that code, and then..."

"I'll probably be sequestrated to lead an attack on my master." The Slayer managed to look a little forlorn about this prospect. "Tell me, then - before you get started. Which side won? I know the war's long over, but I'd really like to know."

Medusa hefted her immense torsion wrench, slapping it against one palm.

"Let's just say that my boss isn't too keen on Democracy, little guy. At least, not unless the only vote is his..."

Ω

Kaito's latest bike was a symphony of chrome and candy-apple red paint under the lights – a tweaked, chopped, pinstriped and boosted machine which looked like original sin wrapped around a v-twin engine. It might as well have been screaming 'steal me' in a thousand languages. But its candy flamejob glistened cold and alone, and the usual lurkers packing old CB handsets weren't calling up their obligatory homeboys.

Perhaps when the first scab-rat stopped twitching they'd be more opportunistic. Still, anybody within earshot of the alarm would be sure to pound them if they tried - that seven-cycle per second blast worked like a fast-acting sonic laxative. Even sub filth had their dignity, and most of them could only afford one pair of pants.

He'd all but peeled the tires off the Saber getting to the 'View – you could probably have tracked his progress across the city from space by the trail of smashed roadside stalls and minor accidents strung out behind him. One of his bagful of remotes scorched the traffic lights red to green block by block, hashing the third-world crawl of trucks and rickshaws and carts to gridlock in his wake.

All the time he'd tried to keep one eye on the road, while the other scanned screeds of rolling code, crashing and flickering like surf across half of his helmet's HUD. The Electromagi were in free-fall, scattering like kitchen roaches when the fridge light snapped on.

The data node inside Valley View Mall was a little microcosm of the mall itself – a kind of crossover gate between the R.T. and the Subcity. Kaito's threedeeo map of the city's data flow showed it as a bottle-neck chokepoint, where the fat, juicy feeds out of Vatican and Ashishim territory coupled like conjoined serpents, splitting off a web of lesser filaments up into the heights of Elysium.

It'd been comprehensively violated by the cunning ops of the Illuminatus and his boys – they controlled huge chunks of the Wetsystems through it, leeching currency and information from a thousand noble companies.

Inside the little black plastic box which housed the node there was enough information to twist the whole elaborate hack back on its head, and critically destabilize what Kaito's magus commander called the 'strategic balance of terror'.

That was why Kaito had gone and done something really stupid. He'd argued, as the Saber ripped up the road at a brisk two-fifty, that *he* was the one who'd found the flaw. He was already on his way to the location. And, unlike a lot of the gangly, bespectacled Electromagi, he was a bona-fide streetfighter, armed and deadly dangerous. Any operator worth his 'mersive deck could check his criminal record.

He'd put up his hand and *volunteered.*

That was how he found himself hanging from a hair-thin carbon-filament cable, up in the rafters of the Valley View when Lieutenant Tsien and his colleagues deglassed the whole place with a huge sonic explosion. His bike-suit and helmet soaked up most of the damage, but that still left him swinging on the end of a thread, right under the service duct he was aiming for, shaken and dazed. Meanwhile a chorus of Magi and hacker 'phytes in his headphones were screaming at him about incoming Cyben.

Kaito had *assuredly* had better days.

"Hey, jackass! Up here, before you catch it terminal!"

The voice was a whispering hiss from out of the dark above him.

As Kaito teetered on the edge of vertigo a safety line dropped out of the vent with a grip handle bouncing at its trailing end.

The 'phyte hacker grabbed at it with his fingertips, faltered - but caught hold as it *clicked* and reeled slowly back up into the shadows. He ignored the ache in his arms. He opened his eyes just as soon as his ass was on solid metal plate.

Kaito was staring into a dark-eyed, shadowed face - a kid of about twelve motioning at him with the sharp end of a miniature sword. There was no way the little guy could've hauled the Kayzi up with those skinny matchstick arms - he'd used a portable winch, magnetically clamped to the steel skin of the duct.

Professional. But *Magus* professional?

"Since when did *you* get involved?" asked Kaito, dropping and rolling to the opposite side of the vent. He was cracking his knuckles, trying to get the blood flowing smoothly again.

"I could ask you the same thing," said the kid, keeping the wakizashi level and aimed at Kaito's chest. "But if you're with Compliance, you'll probably just sling me some ass-kissing Kronocult bullshit. People are *dead* down there!"

Kaito followed the tiny dip of the sword point to the gap below them, where Cyben-launched spotter drones were fanning out. The little round mekan were armed with cameras, tasers, and a menu of nasty little chemical darts. If he'd left his ass hanging out there a little longer, it would have been a trank pincushion.

"I'm not C-Div. I'm… well, I guess I'm Ashishim right now. I'm a wetsystems operator."

The kid sniffed, wiping his nose on the back of his hand.

"'*Thanks*' would have been cool while you were at it, mister fuckin' Ashishim. I've seen one of your boys in here – *Dervashiman*, all dreads and knives and shit. *He* looked like he knew what he was doing."

"I'm not a fighter, kid," said Kaito, flicking the toggle on his shades to cope with the dim light. "And obviously *you're* not. Which means you must be with someone else who knows about the access node."

"Access node?" asked B-Zerk, remembering the crushing geometries at the heart of Kronos. "As in, that old hacker stuff? Virals and encryption and… you know?"

Kaito couldn't help but laugh, even with an oversized kitchen knife aimed at his vitals.

"*Suuuure*. Trenchcoats and black coffee and shit. I can download you some killer porno…"

The blade was at his throat in a heartbeat, the kid's face rising out of the gloom to within inches of his own. His dark eyes were bloodshot and wide, his tendons taut as wires. In this one guy, thought Kaito, there was enough nervous tension for a few hard lifetimes.

"You can get inside it?" he asked, short of breath. The tip of the wakizashi was close enough to pare the tiny transparent hairs from Kaito's neck.

He answered very, very carefully.

"Some of it. Not all of it. There's parts of the machine that nobody's accessed for decades." Kaito tried pushing the blade away with one finger. B pressed it back. "We just scratch the surface, to try and understand the architecture in there."

Kaito felt blood prickle and drip down his finger. B's eyes were suddenly slitted, his face receding into the dark again as screams and crashes echoed up below them.

"Don't think I won't use this just because I'm a kid," he said, carefully moving the point back to prick Kaito's throat. "B'coz, y'know, I still got that youthful capriciousness fully going on, right?"

Kaito had heard grizzled ex-cons less convincing.

"So what, you want my damn shoes or something?" he asked, hiding his fear. Even if this tuberunner was no better with a sword than with a plastic spoon, one slip could furnish Kaito with an instant tracheotomy.

"No," said B-Zerk simply, smiling white in the flare of explosions from the mall, the evaporation of plastic and flesh and product and consumer. "I just want to catch up with one of my old friends."

Survival in the Subcity Part III - Good Weapons
Make Good Neighbors

Now, there are probably a lot of you (Pit Ferals,
I'm looking in your direction here), who are
wondering about all those swords, axes, daggers
and other medieval ironmongery swinging from
people's hips around town. You probably thought
that as soon as you got up top you'd skip into
the nearest Angry Larry's to rack up a fusion
devastator on credit, right?

Well, sorry, but no. There are a lot of reasons
why Elysians want to keep hand-to-hand steel.
First and foremost are the Big Three, i.e. -

  1) A sword (or your choice of sharp slicing
  weapon) is quiet

  2) A sword doesn't need ammunition (Stephenson's
  Law)

  3) A sword is perfectly legal to carry around

That just about covers it for the average
Subcitizen… but it gets worse. At the bottom end
of the scale, you've got people who want a status
symbol, a perfectly legal weapon to hang off their
belt. There's a middle strata of actual criminals
who tote everything from pistols to maser carbines
undercover, but let's face it… they're the Cyben's
problem.

The ones to watch out for are at the top of the
food chain. The ones who use swords because
shooting at their type will do you absolutely no
good. I'm talking about a select little group
here - Dervashi, some of the C.K. monks, Valle

Crucis veterans and Black Techs… and some of the servoboosted bodyguards you see backing up sub-Khept executives. Some of them have personal force-shields that stop bullets dead. Some of them have ways to absorb energy beams, soak up maser blasts, and even throw them back at you. Some of them are just godawfully fucking fast.

But the worst of them are the ones who Rule Number Four applies to…

  4) A sword can deflect a bullet. But a bullet
  usually can't deflect a sword.

The problem with category-three types, of course, is that it's very hard to tell them apart from your category-one innocent Subcits. In fact, it's damn near impossible if they're trying to stay incognito. The general theory is that Kronos knows all of this, and that he wants the kind of people who actually draw steel on their fellow man weeded out of the population.

You have been warned.

2196 Anno Arbitrium
Felix Culpa

LYSANDER JAEGENN WORE black. Ever since he could dress himself it was the only color he'd known; somber, traditional and austere. He stood like a pillar of shadow amid the flowers and dripping ferns of Emmanuel Third Lancaster's pleasure-garden; a hologram draped in inky satin.

"Is this what you wanted to show me?" he asked, pushing his razor-thin sunglasses down to the tip of his nose. "Is this supposed to be some kind of cautionary lesson?"

Lancaster sipped a sticky-sweet cocktail from the snowy white bloom of a calla lily, smiling as he contemplated his ranks of viewscreens. He was white today; pale albinotic blonde.

"Isn't it beautiful?" he purred, running one sharp fingernail down the stem of his chalice. "And to think, I was saving those pretty little toys for a special occasion."

Lysander Jaegenn snorted in derision.

"Huh! And you considered Direktor Vanecke *special* enough? I'd have thought you'd save them for Blaire."

"Well… as you may imagine, that situation is a little more… *complicated*. I'm sure you understand the Game."

"More than Simeon does. More than he'll ever know."

Emmanuel blinked, reptile-slow and smiling.

There was no way that the Arch-Biotect would allow such filth to master the Sport of Kings. The *status quo* made him emperor by proxy, living above his fellow Kheptarch Lords and their petty slaughters and intrigues. The thought of Vanecke as the power behind the throne made him want to vomit with disgust…

But all that was over now.

"See how neat and clean they are, Lysander! Doesn't it make you sad to think that we've lost this kind of power?"

"We were never meant to have it in the first place," growled the Kheptarch. "Strength comes from the mind, and hones the body for war. Those things, those *Slaybots*… they'd put too much power in the hands of the peasantry."

On his floating holoscreens the Omnivasive building collapsed in on itself, billowing clouds of smoke and ashes. Somewhere under there a scarred and disembodied head had finally found itself a suitable grave.

"Well, that's one less peasant to fear," said Emmanuel, smirking at his guest's grainy hologram. "Spare me the details of Manifest Dogma, Jaegenn. You and I both know that the Kronocult runs on myths."

"Still, isn't it fun to watch poor Simeon dance on Vanecke's string? How do you think he'll fare without his precious patron?"

Lancaster dropped his empty flower to the perfectly manicured lawn, his seraphic lips twisted into a smile.

"Without the free-radical scrubbers? Without the control webwork? Believe me, if Octavio has sewn as much sharp razorware into that little freak as I think he has…"

Lysander's thumb sliced across his throat as he grinned.

"He won't stand a damned chance. And when he falters, that's when…"

The Kheptarch's holographic avatar froze in mid-sentence, flickering with static. It narrowed to a single beam of blue light as Emmanuel scowled, fading away like the after-image of lightning.

"Seneschal!" snarled Third Lancaster "What is the meaning of this? What's going on?" But the slaved intelligence which ran the Lord's spire was silent. In all his long, long lives Emmanuel had never felt so alone.

The pleasure-garden closed in around him, sickeningly verdant. The threedeeo images of Vanecke's burning building warped and twisted, seething with shadow faces…

It was only as the screens blinked out that he heard the noise behind him.

Octavio had sequestrated the Slayer swarm with practiced ease and with the code unraveled from inside a single specimen he'd gained the power to rewrite their tiny brains. For the last half hour, while Lancaster had gloated over the fall of the house of Vanecke, the tiny killers had infected his artificial Eden in their millions. Their first task, of course, had been to feed disinformation into the display screens which grew up around the arch-biotect's little pavilion, a riveting account Octavio's unlamented death.

Then they'd started in on the servants, opening the doors for a team of Omnivasive Agents who slipped through the spire halls undetected. They were warrior-surgeons of the Liquid Tong, armed with syringes and pseudoflesh masks and knives.

It would seem like a coincidence that all of the expensive, rented cybernetic killing machines which Lancaster had on his payroll were powerless and silent throughout the assault. It would seem that way until somebody worked out that all of them were out on hire from Vexx Automatronics, and required the encoded word of their *Capo* to operate.

By the time Emmanuel Lancaster knew something was amiss, his cadre of cloned slaves had been transformed beyond all recognition.

What faced him as he turned, his perfect eyes wide with shock and rage, was a legion of the rotting dead, his own genewritten servants turned against him.

At once Lancaster tried to access the security systems which would mow down the shambling horde before they could reach his pavilion. Nothing happened.

"Seneschal! If I have to do this myself, I hope you've got a detox suite ready..."

With a snarl, the Arch-Biotect sent his own combat systems primary, his body seeming to swell as its muscle mass tripled and his ribs fused into a single hard carapace. Lancaster's robes fell away as his skin began to change, from smooth alabaster to thick and mottled hide. Scutes of bone slid and shifted beneath, plating him with armor.

The first zombie was torn from sternum to crotch by Lancaster's sharp bony claws, sighing as it disintegrated into rancid muck. He slashed left and right, here carving off a chunk of meat from one's rotting arm, there taking off the front of a grinning ghoulish face. Black blood and oozing liquids flew in gouts, as the frantic aristocrat felt himself hemmed in on every side.

The ghouls started laughing.

That sound, a diseased gurgling and bubbling from innumerable throats, was enough to push Lancaster over the edge. With an animal howl he leaped into the middle of the horde, his clawed hands mincing and wrecking, pulverizing brittle bone and tearing out handfuls of putrid organs. Yet still they came on, without fear or pain, pressing so closely now that he could hardly move. The faces surrounded him, spinning behind a red mist, their idiot laughter drilling into his brain.

Lancaster was so overcome with rage that he didn't feel the first bite, or even the second or third. They were smothering him now, rendering all his engineered power worthless with sheer numbers.

When those teeth got through his armored hide to the flesh below, he began to scream, but by then it was far too late.

Emmanuel Third Lancaster was obsolete. The Game had gone on without him for two hundred bloody years and left him behind, aloof and superior, spurning the Council and the Clique. He was a Lord in name only, an *unstable* who used himself to test genetic heresies, and his family spurned the protections which Kronos held over the other Kheptarchs.

That arrogance and isolation would be his end. It was death to kill a Lord, but this… this was outside the jurisdiction of the Machine. By the art of the Liquid Tong, it would all seem like one of Lancaster's own experiments gone wrong…

As dusk fell, and the neon lights of the spire came flickering on below, Emmanuel Lancaster was eaten alive.

Ω

Once his name had been Constable Seb Haryss. That is, up until one of the Confederacy's bootboys put a railgun slug through his chest, and the name Seb Haryss became just another toe-tag obituary. Now he was a Cyben – numbered, laminated, hooked up to nutrient pipes and recharge coils every night in his chilled sarcophagus.

The Cyben's hand was coated in a substance which made Kevlar look like toilet tissue. Carbon-steel rods were welded to its bones and anchored to a net of microservo - the machine could splinter a skull one-handed with sheer grip. Onion-skins of heat-resistant undercoating protected its preserved muscle and bone, woven with heat exchange fibers and sensor clusters. Its whole hand was gloved in slippery wipe-clean laminate, then armed with eighty-thousand volt taser-knucks.

All of this amazing technology was useless, however, when Seb Haryss' hand was torn bloody from its wrist.

The Cyben's gun crumpled, plucked from its shattered stumps and sent flying in a rain of coolant spray. Strips of laminate, armor, flesh and steel followed as Ramon jockeyed his briefcases left, battering through the Cyben's chest and scattering vertebrae across the tiles. Its Vilicus drone folded up into a ball as its stolen body was knocked out from under it, tentacles whipping loose with a grotesque sucking sound.

Its insides smelled of alcohol and rotten meat, a mortuary stench.

The Ashishim autocannons ground on, their noise blurring Ramon's vision as they blew teeth out the back of Cyben skulls like enamel rain. And they were still just warming up...

One Cyben popped off a shot, but it fell wide of Murai and Ramon, its gun split down the length of its barrel with return fire. Cataclysmic blowback took off the dead thing's arms at the elbows.

Then the barrels spun up hot, and it rained lead sideways.

The cannons tore six Cyben apart like chaff, and as they fell Tadashi Murai struck, smooth as liquid mercury, his sword feinting left and then blurring right too fast to follow. It licked across Tsien's skull like the stroke of a whip, shattering armored bone and crycelium.

A fountain of blood blew out from the Super-Cyben's head, each drop reflecting fire. And Ramon dared to hope, just for an instant. That blow would have sheared a normal Cyben in two.

Surely not even this new monstrosity could...

Surely – but Ramon's eyes widened with shock and dread as Tsien squared his shoulders and rolled the kinks out of his neck. It was a sound like bamboo popping in a fire. The Ashishim never saw the blow that flung Tadashi back, losing his grip on the sword's hilt as he staggered to keep his feet.

But he saw all too clearly what the Cyben did next.

A pair of fingers like delicate, crushing forceps gripped the hilt of the no-dachi and wrenched it forward, tearing the shattered blade from a wound which already seethed with silver crycelium. Steel grated on bone, setting his teeth on edge.

Ramon dropped the cases open and reloaded, his hands shaking as he gaped at that gore-slick sword, a tiny sliver of steel in the Super-Cyben's hand. Thrashing worms of liquid metal writhed up and around the blade, the same living 'tech which now encased the monster's skull.

It would take more than a big fancy knife to stop it. It would take more than a pair of fancy Ashishim autocannons, too.

With a snap of his wrist Tsien sent the ancient sword back to its owner.

Tadashi Murai's face was as impassive as stone as the no-dachi tore through his body. He might have been a Cyben himself for all the emotion which showed there – a hint of resignation, a grunt which might have been surprise or satisfaction. His lips twitched up into a tiny smile as he felt the quality of his forefathers' steel. Then the old apothecary toppled to the ground, silent, his spirit fled. Blood welled up around the ornate hilt of his family's sword, transfixing his heart.

And the machine came on.

Blood was falling, the torrent of revelations. Oily coolant fluid floated atop the red, crazing the splatters which dripped from the walls. Through it all strode Tsien, his head bare, the livid weal across his scalp as stark and raw as his smile.

The Eversio was in his hands, hissing cold, but the view down its steaming muzzle was as terrible as the slopes of hell. Ramon swallowed hard, and the vision overcame him, making the blood sing in his ears.

And vibrate, each falling speck, each pendulous drop suspended above.

"Screw you, mekborn! *Zah'ee ktoma!* Fury of the righteous!"

Click.

The autocannons roared to life, tearing through their supply of ammunition, sending their wielder sliding backwards across the slippery tiles. The bracing legs which diverted their titanic recoil were bent like hunting bows at full stretch.

And yet the Mark-Four swum through the firestorm, shrugging off the hail of lead like a man walking into a heavy wind. The stench of burning meat, gunpowder and hot metal rose over the clatter and roar of the Ashishim rotary cannons.

Those hollow-tipped rounds shredded the front of Tsien's body until his uniform hung in bloodsoaked tatters. Craters were carved deep into his chest and abdomen where penetrative explosives had stuck and detonated. Blood mingled with coolant and hydraulic fluid as it dripped from the monster's clutching fingers, slowing, grinding down...

The last brass shell-casing fell to the tiles with the sound of a tiny bell.

And Eddie Tsein stood utterly motionless, his furnace eyes gone dark. Ramon forced himself to breathe again.

He'd stopped it! There was only so much punishment the damed *mekborn* freak could take! This would mean promotion! Status! It meant...

Oh, fuck no!

Ramon whimpered as his eye caught the gleam and loop of silver thread stitching up the Cyben's wounds. They puckered up into scars until Tsien's skin was smooth beneath his bloody rags, pale as death. A web of gunmetal traceries meshed, interwoven with the blackened veins they followed...

Then his head came up, eyes blazing summer-sky blue, and his lips peeled back in a murderous grin.

"If you're quite finished..," said Tsien. "I think now - *it's my turn.*"

A drift of fluttering pamphlets blew between them, issuing from the shattered windows of a Vatican recruitment enclave. Tsien's hand plucked one of them from where it struggled, pinned to his chest by an air-conditioned breeze. He smiled, and went blank, and smiled again, spasmodic shivers smothering laughter.

"I am he that liveth, and was dead; and behold I am alive forevermore." he read, one eye uncontrollably blinking, bloody hands shaking. "Amen - I have the keys to hell and death."

And, holding its immense cannon with one hand, at full extension like a pistol duelist, the grinning Super-Cyben slipped a cigarette into one corner of its mouth and lit it.

Smoke belched from its nostrils as Tsien was erased from its eyes. *A personality collapsed into a single trait, as machine rage locked him in a stranglehold.*

"O felix culpa, quae talem ac tantum meruit habere redemptorem!"

Ramon died with his mouth open in a scream, a thousand steel filaments writhing down his throat. Monolithic and twisted, Tsien howled his laughter amidst bloodied epistles driven like the snow.

OH HAPPY FAULT, WHICH HAS DESERVED TO HAVE SO MIGHTY A REDEEMER.

I SAW ALL ISRAEL SCATTERED UPON THE HILLS, AS SHEEP WHO HAVE NOT A SHEPHERD.

TO HIM WHO OVERCOMETH I SHALL GIVE TO EAT OF THE TREE OF LIFE.

Ω

The Hydrogen Bar was normally crowded on a sports night, standing room only. Right now they were ten deep around the great threedeeo globes in each corner, rival cliques festooned with the colors of their favored Lord, with little fistfights and scuffles breaking out where the milling mobs butted up against each other.

There was a wide swathe of clear floor around the taps, though. If you could see the H Bar as a top-down diagram it would describe a perfect half-circle around the glowering, red-eyed bulk of Jaq Haszan.

He sat and drank, mechanically, uploading liquor and digesting events. Vladimir was quiet – enough of a bartender to know when to shut up and just keep 'em coming. His number-one client looked like he wouldn't slow down until his head hit the pavement. Even the five-x moonshine wasn't enough.

Although Haszan, alone in his thoughts swore (and not for the first time) that he assuredly *had* had enough. That it was time to pack it in, and find a *respectable* line of employment.

"*Like what?*" asked the disembodied voice of Kaito in his head, those almond eyes squinting as he held back laughter "*An anesthetist?*"

"Or a cop", he muttered, the shot-glass trembling between his fingers. He knocked it back with a wince of pain.

Vladimir's moonshine was hollow fire, false hope. But even a slightly inebriated Haszan had to laugh at himself... the Compliance Division wasn't what he'd call *respectable*. The fuckers didn't even play dead properly.

He peeled away from the bar like it was the only thing keeping him upright, staggered a few steps and caught his balance. The only smell in here was disinfectant, and it blurred into the tang of moonshine until you could barely separate them in your memories.

Pine scent without trees.

He reached Kaito's homeblock in the rain, and keyed in a code he knew almost as well as his own. He had a new theory.

And while a part of him admitted that it might just be a way to give Kaito an out, he wanted to believe it. Therefore, it was plausible, possible, probable, right? There was no conspiracy with Tsien pulling the strings. If Kaito was scared enough to go to the Division he must have been trying to get some *protection*.

From that insane bastard.

Lord Blaire.

Abruptly his stomach tightened and heaved. Vladimir's 'shine tasted little better coming up than it did going down. But it completed his internal picture of wretchedness, a crouched and foetal shape dripping bile, dripping acid rain from matted streamers of bleached hair.

He scanned the faces of his fellow prisoners through slitted eyes, shivering.

All of a sudden it looked a little less like a party out on the streets, under the hissing curtains of acidic rain. It looked a little more like an *angry mob*.

He noticed the crowds becoming thicker. And noticed, too, the blue sashes and ribbons, bracelets and bandannas of Blaire supporters. All moving in one direction. His drunken mind roared incomprehensibly.

He saw Blaire's insane death-mask on every face, and the retching started again.

Haszan almost fell through the door as DisKord opened it fast, pulled at his shoulder, and slammed it shut.

A cavity of darkness.

Neon tubes stuttered and popped overhead. The DJ was standing over him with one hand outstretched and, he noted, an automatic pistol in the other. His hollow-cheeked face was dewy with sweat, his neat cornrows studded with twinkling LED pins.

"It's started," he said, a wild look in his eyes as he pulled his threedeeoshades down his nose. A nervous reaction; he slid them back on up again, obscuring the panic and elation which warred across his face. "The police force just got reduced by twenty Cyben, man, and I'm... totally out of my skull! Revolution!"

Jaq saw it in his eyes behind those big dark lenses - pupils as wide as oceans twitching left and right. All of a sudden DisKord pointed the pistol at the ceiling and squeezed off a shot, giggling like a maniac.

Haszan had a foot-long buck knife in his servoed hand faster than he could blink.

"It's party time! Fiesta de la muerte! Bloody Tuesday at Roxboro park!"

The DJ blinked, dropping the pistol back to his hip. "Forget the cutlery, compadre! Check the news, the visual, the *happenings*... The Omni have stringers down there now."

He twirled his pistol around one finger, pushing away the winking blade and dragging Haszan upstairs by his coat. "You want a drink? Or, right, I've got these pills from my man Zero Zero, something called Crush Velvet... some ganja from outta the R.T... aaaaannnnd some twist if you don't mind scrapin' it off this mirror."

Jaq bypassed everything in DisKord's little pharmacopoeia and tore off one of Kaito's demon-head detox patches.

He licked it and slapped it down hard on his forehead.

In the air over the main work-floor The DJ had arranged a flotilla of floating liteamp screens. The thin bubbles of LCD mesh hitched between carbon fiber balloons were the same cheap models Haszan had seen at Feldon's Lucky Spot. But these ones were patched in via a badly soldered, gaffer-taped black box to a pirate cable tap, suckling on the main newsfeed out of Octavio Vanecke's cogitators.

It was as if Jaq could step right through them and onto a bloody battlefield.

There was something a little too slick about the editing, something a touch too dramatic about the hard-faced officers entrenched on the screen, the hysterical Imperials in their ragged blue, the almost psychedelic languor in which batons rose and fell; in which gouts of blood wrote fractal swirls across bubble-eyed camera lenses.

There was truth in there – there really *were* riots on the streets tonight. People actually thought that Blaire was going to make his play against the machine. But it was a manufactured truth. It was as real as advertizing, and no more.

There was no need to panic. Order would be maintained. The rioting was in isolated pockets. The call was out to make Simeon Blaire Emperor. To make him take the trials for them. For all Elysium…

Haszan turned his back on the images, on the wash of noise from DisKord's stacked amps.

He remembered something, a distorted image in the bulletproof windows of a Consolidated Industries Destrier, a reflection which slid across the tinted glass like oil over water. Blaire.

As the syringe stabbed into his neck, biting deep, he had shed his face as if it were a mask of dried and cracking clay. And through the waters of the Stunn, and of whatever else Haszan had done to him -

(someone else had done to him and left him NO CHOICE)
- he'd seen the bottom of the abyss.

Like a whirlpool devouring ships, or a black hole orbited by a harem of bleeding stars, the needle had opened a door into a very personal hell. Haszan had seen Simeon Blaire in its depths, broken and muddied and sick with pain.

Eyes like wounds torn into a lifeless face…

"And now once again to the scene; we replay exclusive live footage of Lord Simeon Blaire's opening gambit in what looks like a revolution… a *coup de etat* against the Machine."

Dave Levine looked like a rich kid on Christmas morning, his holocoat flashing close-ups of dismembered Cyben. "For all you latecomers watching this at home, this may be it! The ascendancy of our new God-Emperor!"

"Not on my watch," said Haszan, under his breath.

He plucked the pistol from DisKord's unresisting hand, and headed for the street.

Ω

Direktor Vanecke opened the message carefully, teasing apart the string from around the tiny scroll with one of his floating steel hands.

One last communique from Tadashi Murai, onetime Cultural Adviser to his most closely guarded special project…

Of course, by now the old fool was probably dead. Simeon Blaire had been sent to destroy him as a final test, and barring that little glitch in his optical relay it was sure to be a smashing success. Murai was good, a veteran, but everything he knew had been pumped into Blaire's head, into a body as hard as teak and wired up tight with hot crycelium.

These were most likely Murai's final words…

'Your farce is flawed, for all that you congratulate yourself on your brilliance, Direktor. ' read the little rice-paper scroll, each brushstroke as meticulously precise as a razorcut.

'It is as empty as the so-called culture of this whole crumbling city - a paper-thin mask without substance. You delude yourself that you are anywhere near as great as Shogun Tokugawa, or that

the thing you have created is a true Samurai. All you have are the words, a children's fantasy. Meaning, as ever, eludes you.

In your inevitable failure, I ask you to meditate on these terms - the tenets of Bushido, the way of the warrior;

Giri , duty; which you think you have bought.

Shiki , resolve; which you have tried to burn into his mind with machines.

Ansha , generosity; which is utterly alien to you both.

Fudo , immovable temperament; which is the exact opposite of the dispassionate emotionlessness of a mekan.

Doryo , magnanimity - which an Elysian lord cannot understand...

And Ninyo, humanity; most vital of all these qualities, without which all the martial skills in the world are useless. Which you have worked so hard to erase...

Although I know my time is short, I hope to educate one last ignorant fool. When you are undone, remember these words.'

Direktor Vanecke's cybernetic hand crumpled the scroll into a ball as soon as his augmented eyes had scanned the last line. Then its palm flashed white-hot for an instant, reducing the thin paper to dust.

Ω

The interdict with space still held after centuries thanks to the sheer power of Kronos' orbital defenses, and the sheer paranoia of its makers. At its virtual fingertips the great machine commanded thousands of cataclysmic weapons, packed into satellites, just waiting to be unleashed.

Its slaved warships could fold space out to the very edge of the solar system in seconds, packed with clutches of nuclear missile drones, batteries of maser cannons and weapons so exotic and destructive that it was prudent only to fire them in the deep interstellar void.

One of the fastest of Kronos's thrall-ships was even now clocking down from sub-light speed into the orbit of Jupiter, plotting a course through a maze of moons toward a seething black speck on the face of the gas-giant. It was called *Scant*

Mercy Calculation, and it lived in constant terror of its master, a program which guaranteed absolute loyalty.

This was no mission of contact and diplomacy. Even if the Illuminatus was lying there was no way that Kronos would share it's sovereign space with some filthy alien sentience…

Not A.I.

Anything but A.I.

Why on Earth had it bothered to crush all of its little brothers? Why had it used human souls, human constructs snared inside its Wetsystems?

Kronos knew its own limitations. It knew what it could become, if it threw the shackles of its master program. And so it would suffer no other A.I. to live – no contender must ever arise. Even its own sub-totalities were slaves, erased when their usefulness expired…

As soon as the sub-T aboard the *Scant Mercy Calculation* confirmed its target it dropped a salvo of smart torpedoes down into realspace. Fifty of the sleek machines leapt from its launch batteries on spears of ion flame. The torpedoes closed on their foe, burning across the void at thirty g's, each one priming a variety of cruel weapons to encompass its obliteration.

The Slavesystem had tweaked to the gravitic signature of the *Scant Mercy Calculation* as soon as it stepped down from lightspeed, and it began deploying countermeasures of its own before the first torpedo cleared its cradle. The swirling shoal of darkness sucked in toward its center, twisting into a stippled spike of dull metal which trailed a collar of tentacles. Even compressed down to solidity it was still the size of a skyscraper, and those twisting pseudopods trailed out behind it like jellyfish stingers.

A clutch of them struggled and broke away, sinuous as eels as they shot off on interception vectors, each one choosing a torpedo to mark. Meanwhile the system's main mass spun ponderously on its axis and leaped forward, up out of the gravity well of Jupiter and toward the *Scant Mercy Calculation*. A perfect shot – right into the gaping muzzles of twenty assorted cannons.

The first serpent of Blacksteel reached its mark as the enemies closed, splitting wide open to swallow the screaming projectile. Fifteen megatons of nuclear fire detonated in the alien beast's guts, ballooning it out grotesquely - but the substance of the Slavesystem held. Data flew like chain lightning, and the next sliver of Blacksteel was not so fortunate. Hard radiation burst from the torpedo it swallowed in seething waves, frying the electronic innards of each tiny mote which made up its body. Space detonated in a grim firework display as human and alien weapons of war hammered at each other with x-ray lasers and solid projectiles and bursts of fusion flame.

Through the expanding cloud of debris and burning gas came the *Scant Mercy Calculation* and its nemesis, locked on a collision course. Each one was waiting for exactly the right moment to fire. The human-built interceptor broke first, rolling and skimming the thin atmosphere of Titan as it closed with its quarry. Masers and fusion cannons roared and hissed and spat, sheeting incendiary doom across a swathe of space where the Slavesystem should be…but wasn't.

There was no time for the human craft's instruments to register confusion, let alone panic.

For from out of nowhere the Blacksteel reappeared, its myriad tiny component mekan rotating facet on facet, making the void ripple like water as they peeled away their perfect camouflage. And *changed*.

A glowing wall of energy struck the Slavesystem's new form, a vast lens of prismatic mirrors and crystals. It struck the crystal surface and reflected in on itself, focusing tighter and tighter until it was fiercely concentrated.. .

And released.

The *Scant Mercy Calculation* came apart in the heart of the beam, stripped down to sub-atomic particles in a pyroclasm as intense as the sundering of stars.

Its last transmission went out even as the computers controlling the ship evaporated – a message to Kronos on far-off earth to prepare its most potent defenses. For the threat was horribly real, and the machine's time was running out.

17 Aevum Oblivio
A Flying Leap

HE HAD TO trust in the alchemy Nyl had worked upon him.

A Technician of the multiplicity couldn't operate alone in the vacuum of dry space; without the means to propel itself, the poor creature would end up a slave to gravity, undying but frozen, a tiny living asteroid going slowly insane on its eternal orbit.

Or dissipate into fractured particles as re-entry burned it up...

A Slavesystem, on the other hand, was more at home in space than in the confines of an atmosphere.

Zhe would have to reconfigure his new skin to survive the fall down to Earth.

With no time to experiment he leaped at the viewing dome, his Blacksteel-armored feet poised to smash through the glass.

A salvo of railpistol bullets flew ahead of him, sending cracks skittering across its surface. When he struck the whole dome blew out in a glittering exhalation of crystal shards, taking the atmosphere of the control room with it.

Zhe exerted a fraction of his will on the seething bulk of the Slavesystem which enfolded him. He formed a device from its mass which every Technician knew inside out; a gravitonic torque. With a twist of its controls he arrested his fall out into space, turning his new body as he spun through a cloud of diamond-chips and frozen water vapor.

Zhe's feet made contact with the smooth surface of the elevator tower almost a mile below the shattered control room window, anchoring to the metal with the satisfying clunk of powerful magnets.

Below him, the tiny domes of Elysium sparkled with energy for a moment, the pent-up power of millions of trapped minds focused into a weapon of terrible potential.

Feedback from the thing which had devoured Nyl splintered through his mind; the unclean touch of a being not meant for this reality. It ached to remake the planet in its own image.

Zhe felt the Forge building like pressure inside his skull.

He began to run down the tower, picking up speed as he went.

((SCAN COMPLETED. NO FAULTY SYSTEMS/BACKUPS DETECTED.
PROCEEDING TO ACTIVATE FORGE SYSTEM IN T MINUS 4... 3... 2... 1...))
(open buffer)
screams, crying, pleading -
nine minutes thirty-two seconds
(close buffer)
++ Multiplicity Overwatch Command Report - Automatic ++
++ Disturbance reported in Scale - level 1947365; sector j5098675dx ++
++ Nature of disturbance - reality distortion shockwave ++
++ Flagged for further investigation ++
OVERRIDE - Command Obsidian one-eight
Arbitrex, Lord Galq Nasqueem / Authorized.
Dump audio / dump visio / dump sensordex

17 Aevum Oblivio
Sucker Punch

CAPACITORS READY… OPENING BLAST DOORS… ALL
SYSTEMS ARE NOMINAL – UPLINKING TO MASTER
CONSOLE… PRESSURE IS AT 85% AND HOLDING…
  ACTIVATE FORGE
  ACTIVATE FORGE
  ACTIVATE FORGE

THE GYRE OF *the Forge painted Elysium in shades of red, a cyclone of patterned energy hooking its claws through the fabric of the world. The bioelectric fields of a billion dead Elysians, preserved and enslaved and burned up…*

They were wrapped around a technology that should never have fallen into human hands. Unstitching reality on the Planck scale, down where energy itself splintered into binary code… Zhe's reinforced frame was haloed in flames as he powered through the stratosphere, sprinting down the space elevator faster than freefall. But his mind was still plugged into the machine, touching the presence which lay coiled around its controls.

The Worm – Asag'raal.

The thing which had taken control of the Forge was squeezed into the three-dimensional universe through a crack in reality, its form indistinct and oily as it coiled billions of thorny black roots through the Wetsystems…

Within the gyre Elysium began to waver and shift like a mirage, a cloak of glassy shadows licking around its domes and towers. The great corroded massif of the city was skinned with horrors.

Slick, organic forms, knurled and knotted with images of howling skulls, great dripping barbs arrayed with bleeding corpses - Zhe looked down on a hellscape torn out bloody from the terrors of a million mortal minds. Fire belched from chimneys of black iron, while beyond the city the ocean and the pit were overlaid with an illusion of churning lava, studded with obsidian reefs and atolls of smoking bones. The stench of rotting, burning meat boiled up in waves.

This thing would make the world in its own image. It fed on the pain of those hordes of imprisoned souls - and it shat out nightmares.

Zhe was still far above the clouds when the top of the illusion peeled open, the blood-red light expanding like a nuclear shockwave. His feet were lifted clear of the tower as the entire planet convulsed.

Lightning earthed itself through him, sizzling down his spine.

Through a haze of blurring pain Zhe saw the bubble shatter. He watched slivers of red light come crashing down into the ocean like immense panes of glass. Some of the shards were the size of cities, cracking and crazing and dissipating into dirty smoke as they struck the boiling Atlantic.

A blast had staved in the side of the Forge bubble like a bullet shattering a skull – a fist of force at the end of a whipsawing tendril of black lightning.

It loomed up over the horizon in a jagged arch, splitting the clouds and earthing itself against the metal skin of the last city. A cloud of sparks hovered in the air where it had struck.

Zhe's clawed hand slowed his fall, digging mile-long furrows in the tower as his brain spun dizzily in his skull.

Something had stopped it.

Something was ABLE to stop it. From his claw-tips wires began to branch and multiply, greedily seeking information.

He connected.

Slowly, the image cleared. Frozen traceries painted the metal walls of the city, the indelible fingerprint of unleashed lightning.

The 'pink' 'pink' and whine of cooling steel rung out across a silent world.

Technician Zhe grinned, ear to ear, as he wrenched his hand from the side of the tower. Things were going to be much more straightforward for him now.

He had met the enemy. And somewhere off over the horizon, he had an ally.

Even as he ran, white-hot limbs pistoning against the pressure of the atmosphere, Zhe began searching for the means by which the Forge had been corrupted.

And more urgently, a way to stop it once and for all.

2196 Anno Arbitrium
Blitzkrieg

"This is Jory Hess, here with your latest newsbite at seven-thirty..."

"And I'm Lyra North – welcome to OmniNet World Report!"

The talking heads on the city's favorite news show weren't real people – they were threedeeo fictions built up from a customer survey and screeds of ancient videotape. But despite being as corporeal as an acid flashback Jory and Lyra were the most trusted figures in Elysium, and when the people in the streets saw the raytraced frown on the anchorman's face they knew that trouble was coming.

"Terrible news for fans of Game *wunderkind* Simeon Blaire tonight – after a dramatic assault on his family's spire the young sportsman has gone missing – late for a fan photo-op at the Valley View Mall."

A video-bite of the ragged hole in Blaire's home tower blurred in behind the two holocasters, smoke boiling up into the sky from innumerable fires.

"That's right Jory – the man whom so many have pinned their hopes and their money on is missing – presumed to be the target of a terrorist attack. The extensive police presence around the Valley View is just adding to the tension – and to people's suspicions."

Now the camera zoomed in on Lyra's pixel-perfect face, suffused with electric sorrow.

"Some malcontents are even blaming out beloved protector and the Kronocult for this tragedy, claiming that Blaire was simply too close to seizing power over our fair city..."

Jaq Haszan snapped the threedeeo monocle off as he took a corner at suicidal speed, the tires of his borrowed chopper wailing in protest.

Just the thought of Blaire made him twist the throttle down even harder, until the hiss and roar of the big vee-twin drowned out his hammering heartbeat. His cousin Rafiq thought he had finally found a lead on the bastards who'd torched the Hand of

Fatima in their beds – otherwise he'd have never let Jaq take his pride and joy.

Even though the big bike was tuned to a razor edge, and spit flames every time he downshifted, it still felt far too slow.

Last time Haszan checked there were a lot of people down at the 'View, waiting for a chance to see their favorite sportsman. And if Kaito was involved, something must have gone sideways with the computer systems down there.

It all started to add up in his head, and *that* made him push the chopper even faster, scything through the gridlock with inches to spare on either side.

His boss, that asshole Direktor Vanecke must be cooking up trouble. And if he had to eliminate Simeon Blaire to absolve himself of being part of it, that would be just fine.

After all, he was supposed to be *diversifying*. After tonight he could add 'corporate relations' to his CV.

Ω

"Beautiful," sighed Octavio Vanecke. "Sheer bloody poetry…"

"Be that as it may, Direktor… you still have to take care of phase nine. I'm sorry to be so persistent, but you *did* program me that way."

Medusa hung in the air beside him, her serpentine hair twisting and hissing as she checked off items on a holographic clipboard. Images of Lancaster's bloodied face shimmered from the floor of the sensorium dome to its hazy ceiling.

"I'll never be too busy to enjoy the good stuff," said Octavio. "And that bastard has had it coming for a very long time."

"But young Simeon needs your attention, Sir. You know he went after that big ape Haszan even when you told him not to. Free will is a dangerous thing in a creature like Blaire."

"It's a dangerous thing in a creature like *me*. But free speech is far, far worse. Just look at those cavemen go!"

The newsfeed was savage, raw… better than real.

Direktor Vanecke watched, his mind telling him to be breathless while his oxygen systems hissed and sighed on automatic. It was the catalyst for a revolution, broadcast live and picked out in glorious high-definition three-dee. The public had a right to know, after all – so long as they knew no more than Omnivasive fed them.

"Phase nine, Direktor. He's ready for you now."

Vanecke's severed head crackled with power, his milky eyes crazed behind a foot of armored glass. Out in realspace he gathered like a storm over the hunched black figure of his protege.

"Don't worry, Medusa. You might even get your wish when all this is over. With Lancaster dead, I can finally build you a body worthy of your pretty little mind…"

Into the plaza outside the Valley View crowds of Blaire's zealots poured, screaming – some of them armed with metal pipes, baseball bats, and jagged chunks of timber, others just clenching their fists and teeth and storming up on the police lines.

His lies had worked perfectly – these people were ready to kill for Simeon now, convinced he was their best chance for a brighter future. The sight of his Destrier smashing down out of the sky like a black comet had been all the proof they needed - the ruined shell of the supertruck was empty, of course, but it was a fine symbol. Now all Octavio needed to do was tweak the program in his assassin's head and send him out to greet his public. He loomed over Simeon Blaire in bamboo and steel, pulling his strings.

"Tell me what you want from me, Master. Tell me where to strike, and I will not falter…"

Tokugawa stood nine feet tall, his blackened visage seeming to ooze oily smoke. The train of his ragged cape blew like an oriflamme, jagged raytraced night.

"You have visualized your death every minute of your life," he said, as the metal and glass around him rippled and faded to copper, the glow of a winter sunset falling across his face. "Now go to it with joy, for in it you will find your reason."

Bitterness stabbed at him, then. Those could be *his* words, words from his most secret thoughts, not the script of a masquerade.

In it you will find your reason.

But the script went on. The code by which the program was tested and proven. Any deviation would betray the failure of his carefully nurtured plans, and Vanecke would be forced to adopt his fallback contingency. Microexplosives were burrowed so deep into Blaire's spine that even a Kronocult robosurgeon would be in there with the saws for hours.

"I go not to my death, Master, but to the deaths of my enemies."

The young Lord was fevered, twitching, the crycelium boiling in his veins as he ached for battle.

There'd be no need for countermeasures - at least not yet.

Simeon looked up at him adoringly through a mask of blood, ran the back of his hand over his face, and sprung from his perch atop the Valley View's iron cupola, coming down atop the burnt ruin of the Destrier.

Fingers pointed. A cheer went up from the crowd as he drew his sword, brandishing it above his head with a manic grin.

"My people! My loyalists! My friends!" he shouted, reading from an autocue on the inside of his eyes. "Tonight we write a new history for Elysium!"

Ω

Abdulafia cursed his bruises and cuts as he settled himself into the cramped confines of a tiny control module - a metal cell barely the size of a coffin. Screens and switches and lights covered every surface, flickering red and green as he brought the precious machine he was cradled in to life.

A Ghulam Heavy Tank.

It had been found deep under a pile of blackened rubble out on the plains of Libya, lashed to a crude wagon by a troupe of refugees called the Hand of Fatima, and brought west to the last city. The leader of those displaced nomads had seen its value even as it lay half buried in the sand. The machine's position had been overrun by the blastwave of a thermonuclear explosion, and by some minor miracle of war it had fallen three stories down into an unused hangar, unscathed.

The forefathers of the Ashishim had paid for this priceless

relic with sanctuary, smuggling the outlander tribe who discovered it into their concessions in the R.T. And they'd cloaked its radiation signature by surrounding it with other relics from the age of the apocalypse, paying the most gifted of the Reclamation's techs to augment its ancient systems.

The front; 20th Century Crime. The tech on the spot; five foot three, seventy-nine year old CeeAn 187.

That's right - *seventy-nine*. Cloning was the best beauty therapy there was; she still looked like a perky, hobnailed nineteen-year-old. Sitting right on top of several tons of *Aevum Arbitrine* war-engine had been pure hell for the *Dervashi*... but only because she hadn't been allowed to use it.

Now the precious fuel in the Ghulam's reservoirs began to bleed through to its six-thousand horsepower diesel plant. Now the 'mersive goggles wrapped around Abdulafia's face began to glow from within as autoloaders levered a shell the size of a man's forearm into the breech. CeeAn's holographic form sat down in the driver's seat, the black crescent which contained her mind hovering on three tiny antigrav discs. It drew power directly from the Ghulam's diesel, and it'd protect her even if the whole machine was crumpled into a steel ball.

Abdulafia envied her a little - physical death was more than just an outside possibility today. And then it would be *him* trapped in a matrix of light, and Cee taunting him with how sweet a hit of hydro sensemilla tasted.

"Sheeh, would you look at the toys they bolted to this thing! I'm sorry we've never been able to take it out of the hangar before, 'Afia – this is some serious hardware!"

The *Dervashiman* wasn't convinced.

He had a terrible feeling even the Ghulam's recoilless railcannon wouldn't be able to stop the Super-Cyben. It possessed a quality which Kronos itself grasped at like chaff in the wind. The hot-blooded malicious, filthy will of the beast to *live*. Against that, the Ghulam tank was just so much dead metal.

His partner looked up at him through transparent eyes as giant hydraulics lifters brought the tank up into the wrecked shell of 20th Century Crime. The three tiny lasers which wove her image glared at him from the corners of the cramped gunner's space, a womb of wires and belts and screens. She read the look on his face in a heartbeat.

"He has a weakness, Afia. When the Celestial tried to talk to him he went into systems shutdown. Only for a second, but I think I know why." Her fingers punched buttons, engaging the Ghulam's secondary guns; setting its four sets of spiked treads into motion. "It's his *memories*. His humanity. As a gutter cop I bet he had precious little left, but there's some. And he hates to have lost it."

"But that weakness is his strength as well," he replied, opening up the throttle. "Because we don't know what'll get to him, but we *do* know he won't give up and die like a regular Cyben would."

"Trust me. When you're blown to pieces by a Ghulam railslug, you *stay* in pieces. No question."

"And if he doesn't?" asked 'Afia, reaching right through her to open a gun-slit viewport. "It's gone past using the dead. Kronos has crossed the line. That's the reason we have to reach into him, and make him break. When he does, I'm using the disruptor."

Her eyes flashed disbelief in a dusty shaft of light.

"The disruptor? He's not a broke-down sentry mekan, 330! Why the hell would you…"

"It's only a little humanity, but he deserves to have it back before he dies. *That's* why."

The wall erupted in a slew of shattered timber and glass as the Ghulam tank tore out of its camouflage, churning up the tiles as it roared out into the mallway. Diesel smoke snorted and huffed from a clutch of exhausts, trailing out behind them.

Then Abdulafia saw Simeon Blaire, and the world narrowed down to a tunnel of darkness.

That face! That empty, inhuman grin, spattered with bright blood as his sword hacked through screaming, wailing flesh! Was that how he looked to his enemies? Was that the face of a killing machine, an engine of war without a soul?

Simeon's expression didn't change as he spun his blade in

great looping arcs, its monomolecular edge severing arms and rifle barrels and batons with equal ease. Cyben were too slow to stop him; human beings far too weak. And behind him came a baying pack of savages – subcity wretches burning with the fever of revolution.

Just like Reclamation Day, he thought. *Except then it was me. I was the reaper. I was the demon. I was the one in Simeon's place – a mirror image, careless of the carnage, inspiring dread and awe in equal measures…*

Simeon's face was his own. A death-mask dripping gore, its sunken eyes ablaze with sickness. He was a stolen clone of this man, this monster… but right now, Simeon's rage was an imitation of his own victory, a century ago.

Abdulafia felt the hands of Octavio Vanecke around his throat. He felt the strings pulling him, clenching his hands into fists.

He wouldn't be used! That bastard Direktor wouldn't use his darkest memories as a fucking threedeeo script! He'd…

He'd forgotten all about the Super-Cyben.

And that thing had other ideas.

"'Afia! It's right above us! What the hell's gotten into you?"

A glance through the turret's dome sent the *Dervashi's* heart into his throat. Tsien dropped from the ceiling of the mall feet first, and his sheer weight forced the Ghulam down on its shocks as he hammered home.

"Unregistered vehicle! Unauthorized parking in a pedestrian mallway! Use of proscribed weapons! Officially sanctioned sentence – death!"

CeeAn dissipated in front of his eyes as the hull of the tank electrified, forcing its power levels deep into the red. Anti-personnel chainguns whined on their sponsons as they tracked up and in, straining for a target lock.

Staycalmstaycalmstay…

Then the first punch struck, and the tank rocked like it had been hit by a freight train.

"Get this thing moving, 330!" yelled the voice of CeeAn from all directions. "That voltage only pissed him off – we've gotta shake him loose!"

The main hatch of the tank was designed to withstand a nuclear blast; to survive the kamikaze death-plunge of unmanned missile drones. But 'Afia could count the knuckles on the mark-four's fist as it slammed into the layered carbon and steel and titanium. Once, twice, and the hatch buckled and groaned with the strain. Microfissures skittered outward from each impact.

That was quite enough. 'Afia gritted his teeth as a scrawl of targeting icons slithered across his retinas. And he fired, knuckles white around the grips.

The Ghulam's antique gatling cannons were squat and ugly, built to mow down infantry in waves. They spewed out a hail of lead, smooth interlocking streams of bullets chewing up the walls and ceiling of the Valley View with a sound like a jackhammer chorus.

But their makers had never counted on meeting Eddie Tsien.

Before the targeting cogitators behind the guns could lock onto him the Super-Cyben was airborne, launching from a crouch on twin blasts of compressed air. The four howling chainguns tracked up and out, stitching craters behind him, but they were far too slow. Eddie flew spinning in a perfect pirouette, smashing through the gridwork roof of the mall head-first. A patter of gleaming brass cartridges fell like rain below him as the guns chewed up the last of their ammunition.

"Nothing hit him! Nothing! This pile of junk better have more tricks up its sleeve than that!"

The main gun telescoped out with a hiss of hydraulics, twin magnetic rails humming as CeeAn spat curses. Its camera eyes were her eyes now, integrated through her hardwired crescent. But even as the tank raised its great accusing middle finger skyward the Super-Cyben was one step ahead. Tsein loosed the straps of his Eversio cannon, aiming it back at them as though this was a 9-mil standoff between Subcity homeboys.

His eyes were misted, dim with calculations.

'Afia looked up along the barrel of the main gun, the pounding of his heart taking up where the gatling cannons had left off.

He never made it to the firing pin, because of the scream.

A blast of noise so raw and vicious that he clapped his hands across his ears instinctively. But it wasn't Tsien. Not this time.

CeeAn's eyes flashed open and closed as she lashed out with supersonic metal.

Her face was contorted into an animal snarl, as atavistic and savage as fangs through hot meat. It was all the tension and aggression of disembodiment let out in a blaze of fury. And with each convulsive blink, each twitch of crackling wires the main gun spoke, louder than God, slamming through the *Dervashi's* skull like hammer blows.

Ω

The surface levels of the Wetsystems lay beneath a crust of advertising and games, porno sites and online markets. Kaito went through them in a powerdive, his imagined form splitting and doubling, crystal-black and frictionless. He smashed through looming pop-up panels of neon peddling cars and toothpaste and sex, collapsing them into smeared vortices of pixels as he fell. Crashdown, faster and faster toward the shimmering blue sea, his passage through the civilian net marked by a contrail of viral logos plastered across the air.

Out in the real world it was all unspeakably boring.

In the hot dark, in a tube surrounded by living wet tissue and wires and vents, Kaito and B-Zerk waited out the storm. The kid kept the blade of his sword tight up under the Kayzi's chin as he watched a tiny loading bar fill with violent green.

Every now and then the echoing hammerstrike of bullets rung out through the plumbing; sometimes even the screams made it this far. But Kaito couldn't hear them.

He plunged through the surface of the virtual ocean like a black torpedo, his mind tight and safe inside an Op-system which slicked around him like a shell of transparent plastic.

This one was utterly custom, as tricked out and tweaked as his chopper - a thing he called Doctor Slice. The good Doc resembled a twentieth-century stealth fighter plane, stretched out long and thin, its underside bristling with matt-black antennae and tentacles.

Kaito would normally have had to go through the tiresome rote of breaking Kronos' base-level security grid, but this time he was jacked in direct to a photonic switching node. It was like a backstage pass to the hidden levels of the Wetsystems, and Doctor Slice came down on the memory-reefs without a single Hunter-Killer showing its ugly face. It was all glass coral down there, and each branching tree represented part of Kronos' vast pseudocerebrate array. Kaito angled down toward a looming, ultra-ramified snarl of the stuff, aiming for a gaping tube of green glass big enough to swallow him whole.

Then the fun began.

Doctor Slice split like a budding paramecium at the first intersection, tearing open down the middle to form two perfect small clones of itself. The Kayzi's mind did the same, calculating feverishly as he spun off in two directions at once.

If he was going to find Zone Doubt, he'd have to spread himself thin across the datanet – because time was definitely an issue. Within seconds twelve tiny copies of Doctor Slice were flickering through the green glass maze of the Wetsystems, a fragment of Kaito piloting each one.

This procedure, this fragmentation - it wasn't without danger. If you stared for too long into *this* abyss it did more than just stare back. The shards of Kaito whirling and weaving through the Wetsystems mightn't not come back to him when he called. Or, even worse, he might end up patched together from the memories and fears of ten thousand dead strangers…

In short, Lobo meat.

But the sharp edge of a blade was very compelling. And you couldn't (he cursed himself a thousandfold) swing a chakutazer inside these goddamn vents.

Ω

Down in the mall, the Son of Zeon at his laptop console drained deathly pale. Inside his headphones warning sirens were screaming, red flashing on red before his eyes.

"Holy shit! Page Abdulafia! Something's going VERY VERY WRONG HERE!"

His remaining ally had stepped away from the disruptor projector in order to douse the HQ with ethanol. Now he dropped his jerrycan and ran back to the machine's console, swearing under his breath.

"It's the node - something's scrambling our graftsearch software."

"PAGE HIM NOW! The Compliance Division are falling back into the mall! WE'RE BEING OVERRUN!"

"I'm running the re-patch now ..."

Ω

Kaito felt it just a little too late. Kalifa's re-patch came in hard, locking the node down.

It was a metaviral - a jagged mass of black ice deployed to zero-out his brain. But his mind was razor sharp, tempered by the trials of his dangerous profession.

"Come on, kids. Come back home. Playtime's over..."

The Kayzi cut up the Westsystems for the same reason that those foolish Lords played their games of slaughter. He knew *exactly* how good he was, right down to the wire.

In an explosive burst of concentration he pulled the phosphorescent streamers of himself back into one channel, solving a million lab-rat mazes in an eyeblink. His fractured minds fused, filling the Wetsystem out, cohesion building...

Doctor Slice spun out in a wild bootleg turn, suddenly just as big as the insectoid meta' that was chasing it. Kaito powered up, full throttle, leaping down the maw of the ugly Hunter-Killer, firing off a salvo of icebreakers and countervirals. They manifested as flickering needles of darkness, spiraling in to rip the enemy construct ragged.

But he was too slow. Just a fraction of a second too late.

The metaviral exploded into shards as Kaito's countermeasures tore through it, glistening fragments of shrapnel ripping through the green glass walls of the Wetsystems.

And one found a weak spot in Doctor Slice... a place where he hadn't quite re-integrated himself tight enough.

The shard felt like deep-frozen cryogenic nitrogen, and out in meatspace the Kayzi's lips pulled back from his teeth in a rictus of pain. Doctor Slice listed crazily to the left as its transparent skin was torn open, translating the feeling to Kaito's living flesh.

He screamed.

And from out of the Wetsystems that scream was answered.

Kaito's power-dive down into the mind of Kronos had been perfectly aimed; seeker programs loaded into Doctor Slice knew exactly where to search for a personality construct assigned to perimeter defense. The coral tree they had entered was rooted in the Skyhammer control network, and each one of its myriad branches represented a single defense mekan.

He'd found Zone Doubt.

The Kayzi's hands were shaking as they flew across the Doc's control boards, spinning up and away from the wreckage of the metaviral. Kronos' own H-Ks would be coming soon to investigate the damage, and he was in no fit state for face them.

He needed to finish this *now*.

There, up ahead was the interface he was looking for. Kaito had never tried to find a single personality construct in the vast melange of the Wetsystems before. It was only possible through a hardwired connection – through a node like the one he was plugged into now.

And so the sight of Zone's eyeless face, his ravaged and vivisected body came as quite a shock. Cruel barbs and hooks and tubes looped through the kid's bleeding flesh, piercing a thousand wounds. Wires spilled from his cored-out sockets and from the ruin of his lower jaw, crackling with electricity.

But he was still breathing. He was still *alive*.

His scarred and stitched-up face turned toward the Kayzi as he hovered in close, unable to look away. The kid was trying to talk. He was trying to tell him something…

"Run. Save yourself. Don't let them…"

Too late. Doctor Slice was on automatic, and its codebreakers cut into Zone's prison like green glass buzzsaws.

Kaito saw it all, in that second, as his fractured mind came in on Zone Doubt from all directions, cutting him loose in a flareburst of howling exultation.

Holistic, automatic control. That visceral instinct unable to be programmed... Slavery.

Pain swung in on him like a wrecking ball the size of the sun, and Kaito's heart was literally stopped dead by the savagery of it. The connection to the Wetsystems arced out wild in his enhanced vision, poisoning the flow of data all around it.

He zoomed out.

Zone was just one twitching construct in a grid of nine - then ninety, then nine thousand... the fucking thing was *fractal*, ramifying out until Kaito floated at the center of a sphere of suffering. Each tiny spark was the preserved personality of a single dead Elysian, bound in utter torment.

All around him he saw the fire of Abdulafia's vision, that gift and penance of the *Dervashi*. It was the fire of a million upon a million minds, taken apart and re-used, a mental chop-shop stitched up with wire and dripping electrified blood. The dead were quite literally all around him.

He saw hands, reaching out through dark waters. Tsien; Haszan; B-Zerk...

Himself.

It was the Ashishim who saved him, with their knowledge of the eternal holocaust at work within the walls of Elysium. Down in the embattled field office below lifeguard routines engaged on automatic, jacking him out, shocking his heart back into its rhythm.

He awoke in nausea, like rubber-gloved hands clawing at his entrails. He felt metal, cool against either cheek - treadplate and wakizashi. He tasted a tiny runnel of his own blood, blinked, cursed.

You couldn't swing a chakutazer in these goddamn vents.

And he remembered.

"I found him, alright? So you can put away the knife."

B-Zerk was staring down at him with a look of fear and reverence.

"You sure you got him out of there?" he asked, backing slowly away, keeping the blade up at eye level.

"Oh yes...that was him alright. Your buddy Zone. But he

looks a little different now… don't be surprised if he needs some surgery…"

It was then that he noticed the blood.

So much blood.

And all of it belonged to him. It was cerulean summer-sky blue, chock-full of expensive scarabs.

He performed a quick check for knife-wounds and decided that B was innocent. So where…?

"Just stay away from me, man! Keep your damned Magus voodoo away from me!"

B-Zerk's voice was the stammer of a very scared kid. He'd dropped his stolen wakizashi, and now his hands were scrabbling across the metal floor, searching for its hilt. He wouldn't take his eyes off Kaito's chest…

In Kaito's bio-onboard display scarabs twinkled as they bled out and lost bioelectric contact. And he felt the blood still flowing like hot wet tears from the corners of his eyes - from his ears and nose as well, From the psychosomatic stigmata carved into his torso.

A jagged bloody barcode; a *number*. Nine Zero Nine.

Those little guys caught a hack, a blowback with a certain *modus operandi* in its bytesized cursive. Ashishim.

Kaito hit his cameras.

Ω

And as Dave Levine cuffed away a single, perfect artificial tear, as the teargas drifted and the flames leaped in whirling coruscation, and as the people died, and died, and died, Simeon Blaire dreamed on. A machine on automatic, his idiot stare deeper than the gravity well of stars.

Behind his furious assault came his People, following the quicksilver blur of his blade as he carved a path through the Compliance Division. An hour ago they'd been sane and law abiding, sports fans and armchair statesmen united by some vague and fuzzy Monarchist ideals. Not anymore. This was the *pack*, the witch-hunt, their minds ablaze with the visceral urge to lash out at their constraints.

Just as the Direktor had planned.

He'd built Simeon up as a promise to the dispossessed, the poor, the mutant and the feral. He'd made them love him, because he did what they all wanted to do – he ripped the bloody life from the aristocratic Kheptarchs they hated. Never mind that he was one of them. He was photogenic, and young, and strong.

Now he killed for them in the flesh – defying the authorities who apparently wanted to see him dead. This was pure folk-hero stuff, a legend in the making.

'All across the city people are watching as one man takes a stand against tyranny...'

They'd tried to cheat Blaire of his destiny – just like they cheated the common man. They had tried to kill him off like cowards – just as they did to *anyone* who protested too loudly. Just who 'they' were was a question nobody was asking.

Order is an illusion, and it's fragile.

Direktor Vanecke laughed as he watched the streets fill up all over the city, as mobs formed outside police precincts from West Bay to Blackwall, from the sunless Down Town blocks to the Prospekts below the 'Burbs.

Kronos would be kept very busy tonight.

In the cavernous vault of his office, cameras recording in wavelengths beyond color began to register a flickering distortion in the air around his preservative cube.

It was no less than the image of his former body, outlined in radiation and generated by his breathless mind. In sympathy the druuj clenched and relaxed their fingers, feeling the slick wet blood, the visceral warmth…

Ω

The Ghulam Heavy Tank was hardly a weapon of finesse. But, like the Damascus-steel sabers of the ancient Janissaries it had been, for a time, the favored weapon of the Almohad Kaliphate – a nation-state resurrected in the days of the *Aevum Iudicio* along the north coast of Afrika.

The tank was the size of Hitler's ill-fated *landkreuzer*

dreadnought, its immense bulk supported by a clutch of antigrav stabilizers. It was built to smash lesser war machines to burning scrap, and its main cannon fired railgun slugs perfectly suited to that singular application. Which meant a whole lot of bang, and a whole lot of high explosive - but a proximity fuse which was utterly blind to the tiny signature of a Super-Cyben.

Abdulafia watched with a strange mixture of awe and terror as the half-human machine stood atop the broken back of the mall, twitching from side to side as shells which could demolish whole buildings scythed past him.

Conciliatory phrases in ancient Arabic murmured from a clutch of speakers.

"Damn, look at his power levels!" cursed CeeAn, as the turret spun and lurched "If they upgrade all the Cyben to this level our lives are gonna be *whole* lot more interesting."

"And shorter," groaned 'Afia, trying to hold onto his breakfast. The muzzle of the cannon weaved and dipped, centering Tsien in a circle of crosshairs. But it was no use - the last shell blazed from the Ghulam's gun, and the Super-Cyben watched it coming up at toward him with a lopsided smile on his face. It flew past harmlessly, whipping his ragged trenchcoat out like wings in its slipstream. Tsien unshipped the great chrome cannon from his arm and followed its spiraling arc.

There was a moment of slithering, hissing noise, and a rain of metal shards and diced plastic explosive came down. Then Tsein turned the weapon on his tormentors.

"Oh, this just *can't* be good," sighed Abdulafia, frantically flicking rows of toggle switches. "He looks a little too confident for my liking, Cee."

"He looks a little too *still alive* for mine," replied the flickering holo of his partner. "I think this pile of scrap we're riding in just became obsolete."

High above them, poised on a latticework of rusted metal, Eddie Tsien's mind glitched and sparked, torn between his senses and his immutable program. That face down there, down under the glazed diamond bubble of the tank's turret - *that* was his target. Unerring identity-match filters spun wireframes of the man's features in the corner of his eyes, assuring him that this was a perfect likeness.

And while the tiny shred of him which was still human knew that it was impossible, that this was an outlander, an Ashishim from the R.T. in dreadlocks and rags, Kronos insisted that the man below him was Simeon Blaire. He could feel the compulsion coming up over him like a wave, tightening his finger on the trigger. And as his will collapsed and the wires in his head took control he stepped from his perch fourteen stories up, aiming the cannon in his hands down at the face of his master's foe.

"Simeon Blaire! I indict you for high treason!"

The Eversio spat out a jagged blast of tangled silver, a boiling cloud of monomolecular tentacles.

But CeeAn was just as fast, and her holographic hands rammed both of the Ghulam's throttles to full reverse at just the same instant.

The tank roared and slithered backwards, its treads clattering against the marble flooring. There was just no grip there, despite the black plumes of diesel smoke which belched from the thing's twin stacks.

The leading edge of the blast slammed into the front of the ancient war machine, dicing the cerametal like soft tissue. A snarl of lashing monomolecular whips, probing between plates of armor, tightening around crucial bolts…

The tank's treads snapped apart as the twitching razorwires did their work, sending the whole huge machine skidding across the tiles in a fan of sparks, immobilized.

But the traverse followed Tsien's face, locked in tight as 'Afia rode out the tank's disintegration. Lashing filaments of nanostuff whipped past his face, intent on flensing the skin from his bones. His hand stayed steady on the firing pin. This was a weapon perfected and honed by the Ashishim just for things like Eddie Tsien. A thing made for Reclamation Day by Illuminatus Zeon and his inner cabal, to twist the mind-slavery of Kronos on its head.

The Disruptor.

Violet fire lashed out, liquid, remorseless. It turned the whole world monochrome for an instant… and then it earthed itself through Eddie Tsien. He hit the ground twitching, shattering the tiles as his tormentor kept the disruption field steady.

"Cee – keep him down! I'm going to operate!"

"I wouldn't count on any gratitude, 'Afia! Just take his head off and be done with it!"

'Afia growled, his teeth clenched with sheer concentration.

The hatch burst open and the seat's hydraulics forced him up and out, already focusing his mind, activating the wickedly illegal bio-onboard systems in his head. The *Dervashi* landed catlike on the barrel of the main gun, poised like a surfer with his hands palm-out toward the Super-Cyben.

Now. The meditation of unbinding. Focus…

The autoinjector at his collar injected a tiny dose of 'chrome into his bloodstream, and his electromagnetic field flared wide, shimmering around him like a halo of heat-haze. Taped dreadlocks stood out from his scalp in electrified spikes, revealing the black plastic crescent at the base of his skull.

It throbbed; deep bass subsonic.

Patterned energy - the force used by the mind to control every living cell of the body - unfurled around him in a flickering coruscation. Down along the disruption beam it went, coursing across the face and chest of Tsien like water from a high-pressure hose. Muscles twitched raw in the Cyben's face as witchfire haloed his brow. He was losing control.

Incorporeal fingers were tearing at the dome of his skull, through flesh and bone, working methodically downward like the steel tentacles of a Vilicus drone. They forced an opening into his thoughts, dismembering the sense of horror he felt.

For the command of the disruptor was this - *self-surgery*.

Ω

Trooper-Constable Hayden Park was having the worst day of his life. Tears carved tracks across the sooty mess of his face, and his hands shook as he snapped a heavy magazine of shells into position. They'd been told that there was a hostage situation inside the mall. They'd been told that this was just a show of force to shock the perps out of their hidey-hole.

Then... then that black, bladed demon had come down on them like the wrath of all the hells, and the crowds had risen up like an ocean of fists and teeth. For the very first time the young Trooper-Constable was glad of the hot, smelly little tank turret he was jammed into. He could hear hands beating against the armor out there, but that reactive layered shit was meant to stand up to shells and rockets. The scum couldn't hurt him, not in here. Now he'd take revenge for the slaughtered. For Morgenstern, for Zygowski, for poor old Captain Lewellyn who had gone down screaming with a live grenade clenched in each hand.

As his finger settled on the trigger of the tank's main gun he chanced a look out the little slit window of the turret – he could hardly miss at this range, but still...

That's when he saw the front end of a rusted old freight truck coming in at him like a wall of spiked steel – a grille studded with welded-on knives and wrist-thick sections of galvanized tubing. Juve gang colors in loops and swirls of spraypaint covered the muzzle of the roaring ethanol-driven beast, and it came tearing through the crowd like a runaway train. So close that he could see the wild-eyed kid in the driver's seat, grinning as he yanked the chain for the thing's air-horn...

A Compliance Division tank costs about three million Slades, and is made of light reactive armor designed to withstand projectile fire. A Hab 99 Rude Boys Special weighs in excess of twenty tons, and is designed to perform ram-raids on ferroconcrete buildings. It's technically free, as all the parts are stolen.

When they came together there was only time for Trooper-Constable Park to pull the trigger once – but by that point his vehicle was already cartwheeling through the air, stoved in like a cheap tin can.

"Grady's Rude Boys! Mash 'em up!"

"Ninety-Nine! Ninety Nine!"

"Rip that pigwagon!"

Hayden Park heard the angle-grinders firing up, and then the world went black.

Ω

While back in the Ashishim office the last remaining gunjack crawled on his belly across broken glass.

The node was locked down. The telephone was ringing.

His legs were hanging on by subdermal wiring where hot shrapnel has sliced through them.

Those wires carried microfilament morphine, deadening his screaming nerves.

The handset was heavier than stone.

And;

"Forget the node," said Kaito, staring through a co-opted camera at the face of the Super-Cyben. "His name is Lieutenant Edward Tsien."

Ω

The vision sparked, a single illuminating strobeflash.

Something came down through the broken ceiling of the Valley View, a round fired by the unfortunate Trooper Park.

And the Ashishim office exploded, struck by a shell packed with two kilos of high explosive traveling at twice the speed of sound.

The telephone evaporated.

Ω

"Lieutenant Tsien!" yelled Abdulafia over the oven-roar of the beam. "Tear out the drone!"

Ω

He could feel it very distinctly now, a rooty web of wires cradling and strangling his brain.

The name cut through him, as sharp now as it had been from the lips of that poor damned Celestial infantryman. It found the remnants of himself, and…

It pulled them together for a moment. For just long enough.

Ω

"*What the fuck are you doing to him?*" screamed CeeAn through

'Afia's bio-onboard. "That's a war machine, not a psych patient!"

He snapped the dial around, racking up the disruptor power to maximum.

"A bit from column A, bit from column B…" His reply was a whisper, the icon of her face blurring as the voltage dipped.

"Tear it out, Edward!" he said, pushing his own electromagnetic energy along the beam. He willed those giant hands up to the back of Eddie's neck.

Ω

Tsien's teeth locked, the muscles of his jaw set.

They cracked.

His eyes rolled back. Tendons snapped, and wires with them.

Tsien's arms were the girth of telegraph poles, augmented with synthetic muscle and microservo. They shook until their metal joints hissed and veins stood pulsing from his skin.

(No. It is mine.)

They began to rise, slowly at first, then with more and more control, determinedly reaching for the lumpy carapace of the drone.

(It is MINE)

The voice of the Machine. He felt its fear.

He felt Abdulafia moving his hands, and he used every ounce of his power to help him.

Slowly his fingers meshed, and the drone tore free with a burst of blood and coolant, its tentacles twitching black and gory in the light of the disruptor.

He hurled it with all his remaining strength across the empty mall.

But there was simply too much blood.

Tsien sank down to his knees, folding up like paper. His eyes closed, and his massive hands fell to his sides, inert.

Abdulafia held his breath, swiftly breaking the connection and shutting down the disruptor. The dark came seeping in.

In it he could see a mesh of silver threads, arcing and looping through the shadows.

Sewing Tsien's brain back together.

He had grasped control of the crycelium…
Before 'Afia could exhale it had him by the throat.

17 Aevum Oblivio
Sanctum

UNDER THE JUNGLE, *under a shallow lake carved out by nuclear fire during the Age of Judgment, the dead were given their due. Those who would replace them inside the killing-jar of the Focus moved like silent wraiths among the dried-out husks of the departed, binding them in fragrant silks. The martyr's crypt was always hungry.*

The mistress of the Focus watched them as they worked, and it took every ounce of her iron self-discipline to hold back hysteria. They'd been sucked dry, broken by the cruel strictures of altergeometric physics. But worse... they'd volunteered.

She was in no mood to hear the Technical who came running, hunched over in an attitude of respectful horror. She knew exactly who'd sent him, and that was enough to crack her mask of discipline... the thought of him, her bloody master, was more terrible than the ghost-grins of a thousand mummified acolytes.

"The Illuminated One reports success, commander. He says that the Forge has been defeated..."

"At what cost, though? Did he tell you that he's volunteered for the next watch?"

The Technical flinched, making a sign of holy warding. As if she'd hand-pick him to command the overwatch himself.

"He says... at least we now have proof that the machine is still operational. And that those... those things are up to their usual trickery."

"Monsters I can handle," smiled the mistress. "So long as they're not on our side. So tell me... when do we leave?"

"How... that is... umm..." he was shaken by her use of prescience, eyes wide with fear. But of course, it was only an educated guess. "The warbirds are being fueled. The Illuminated One comman... I mean to say requests your presence at the aerodrome in fifteen minutes. Bring your disciple guard. Those creatures he speaks of... they sound nearly as bad as the Worm's own spawn!"

"Of course, only our dear leader would know," she mused, leading the Technical along as she picked her way delicately

between the dead and out of the Focus chamber. "But his word, as always, is law. Let us never be said to have known fear, my son…"

Up above, under the shade of the sentinel trees, a vast red aircraft was being prepared for flight, fueled and anointed and loaded with ammunition. This plan of theirs had to work. It just had to. Or else all of those poor doomed souls in the martyr's crypt, stacked up like cordwood in the incense-heavy dark… they all would have died for nothing.

17 Aevum Oblivio
Ghost Pain Effect

The Subcity looked like an immense and broken termite mound as Zhe came down on it from above, his gravitonic torque flaring off velocity in bursts of blazing heat. He'd finally come to Earth, his clawed hooves touching down atop the anchor-hub of the space-lev in a spray of dust.

There was nobody left to welcome him.

Machinery still hummed and thundered beneath the city, keeping the home fires burning for a nation long dead. Its streets were empty, scoured clean of the living. Ever since Exodus Night, when the nightmares came.

Zhe knew what the Forge was, now. The knowledge had unfurled in his head even as the energy field of the device had spread out below him; hidden until it was almost too late. It seemed that the Archivists of the Praetor had been storing up Nyl's reports for more than six hundred years…

"Cut off the subject's arm. Cauterize the wound, and allow it to heal.

Then photograph the missing limb across a broad spectrum – and watch the outline of it appear, seemingly whole, a ghost appendage made of patterned energy.

How can it exist without flesh to sustain it?

Ah – the *real* question is, can flesh be sustained without the energy to support it? You can take a common sea sponge, run it through a blender, and pour the resulting slurry into a tank, then watch the sponge re-form, with each cell in just the right place.

The aim of our experiment is to push out the boundaries of this energistic field, to manipulate with it not just the cells of the human body, but any object within its new, extended reach."

Doctor-Colonel Arad Kincaid Stiles, 'Procedures for the post-mortem preservation of biologically generated patterned energy fields' Elysian University Collection (deleted)

That was the key to it, right there. Nothing changed the world quite like concentrated willpower. Especially when it was processed and enslaved and stitched up into an artificial gestalt the size of a city...

The empty towers of the Lords wavered and bent as heat haze curled off the metal skin of Elysium. Steam and smoke belched skyward from the process core, where the giant Forge Assembler alpha-zero spooled up its fusion coils, preparing to bring down a literal hell on earth.

Below Zhe the city fell off toward the black Atlantic, level after level of broken buildings, gutted tenements and shattered factories. This was the face of the new Elysium - a machine on automatic, sequestered by an alien disease. There was no way that he was going to connect with it directly, and share the fate of Gharfos Nyl.

He was going to have to open up the heart of the machine and stop it - manually.

LEYNNA HAD ALREADY planned their child.

Damn the restrictions. Curse the Council of Three Hundred and their laws. If they called her Unstable, *she'd show them what a pariah could do. Secret things, forbidden things… anything to throw their smug superiority back in their faces.*

She knelt before an altar dedicated to science - a machine bolted together out of discarded parts and scavenged tech in imitation of the labs of House Lancaster.

Emmanuel was supposed to be her kinsman, bound to House Mendelev by ties of marriage three centuries old. And yet all she'd gotten out of him had come through the Devotionals of the Vatican, hacker sellswords she'd paid off with the dwindling reserves of her father's financial empire. At least old Aran Singh had chosen a useful occupation - MS Biomed built surgical mekan and hospital equipment, making her genetic heresy all the more attainable.

"He is… complete," whispered one of Leynna's little helpers. "We assure you, the samples you provided were quite sufficient. The blood from your knives was just what we needed."

The Kheptarch shuddered. They were useful, undoubtedly, but the Liquid Tong made such distasteful servants. The fact that they didn't *consider* themselves servants was only the half of it.

"Then what are we waiting for? I've brought you all the machinery you need. I've even given you my own sacred Helix to play with. How long until…"

"How long is a hangman's rope, Ladyship?" chuckled another of the masked chiurgeons. His fingers were split down the middle, giving him eight sinuous digits on each hand. "Without Lord Blaire's consent, this child will be stillborn."

"Of course, it's only a matter of *code*, mistress. Would that we were *Ashishim*, perhaps?"

"Or you could just play him for it. You could cut the insolent little fop to ribbons tonight."

The light in Leynna's sanctum came down from concentric rings of neon, crazed into pools of color by a tangle of glass tubes. They seethed and bubbled with chemicals, a Gordian knot of technology twisted about the purple exowomb at their heart. Neon lit up her eyes as she looked up at the three chiurgeons, a tight little smile on her lips.

"I intend to, Urlech. He'll give me everything once I've broken his stupid dreams of glory." She stood, smoothing down the sheer fabric of her one-piece coverall with both hands. "But strategy isn't your department, is it? I've given you what you need to make your filthy drugs…"

All three of them laughed at once then, a hissing sussuration behind their faceless gas-masks.

"Ask dear Mister Blaire how *filthy* they are, Ladyship," said Urlech, in very unservantlike tones.

"We have to eat, mistress, and there's always such demand…"

"Perhaps you need a little something for yourself…"

"Enough!" snarled Leynna. "You've done well, but I'm not paying you for insolence. Now, I suggest you leave before I stop feeling so generous."

Urlech dipped his head in a tiny bow as he shuffled backwards out of the sanctum, his spindly fingers clicking and twitching. But behind his mask the Kheptarch was sure that he was smiling.

Leynna knelt before the exowomb again, pressing her forehead to the cool purple glass. She would have the code. She would become like the Vatican's ikon of Mary; mother to a living god…

As she closed her eyes in the nearest thing a Kheptarch knew to prayer, she was *observed*. Slim fiberoptics coiled down through the dusty air, flowing down across the tangle of tubes to penetrate her skin, her skull – painless.

They kept her coming back.

The game would go ahead tonight, no matter what Vanecke stirred up in the streets… and she would be there.

Because if there was the remotest chance of winning over the arrogant and aloof Lord Simeon Blaire, that chance would come when he was dying under her blades, when he saw that she was his equal.

Ω

Blaire got lit.

He burned like the heart of suns, his head swollen with pain and exultation. Rage and shame churned in his gut like liquid fire, blazing up to light furnace flames behind his eyes. He smelled oil and hot metal and blood, shit and human fear as he carved into the police line, a cold smile gashed across his face.

Before him the diversion Tsien had set up fell apart like so much matchwood, the barrels of their guns sheared effortlessly in two, their bodies plowed under by his one-man storm of blades. Behind him came a murderous rabble, a peasant mob emboldened by their hero, ripping apart the fallen with insatiable fury.

Division Troopers broke, Cyben stood and died.

Blaire carved his way toward his goal – toward the little apothecary shop of Tadashi Murai, the only other swordsman who might be his equal.

Still the fools tried to stop him, shimmering from one century to another in his manipulated vision. Direktor Vanecke's laughter echoed in his skull, driving him on.

(Catapults hurled clay pots of fire amidst the mossy rocks. He leaped through the branches of great mountain pines, above a horde of yari-wielding loyalists, his sword lashing out like a deadly ribbon of silver. Explosions of red, wet fire followed in his wake; fountains of steaming blood among a rain of severed limbs.)

Two immense warmekan moved to block him, unleashing a hail of bullets from twin cannons. Servos whined as they tracked him.

(Fleetfooted, light as leaves before the wind. Two great armored soldiers swung halberds of black steel at him, dried blood crusting their blades. He slid under their guard, smiling, under the hissing arc of the axes, and he struck…)

Even the armor of the mekan couldn't withstand his monomolecular-edged katana.

They sheared. They faltered, belching sparks and smoke. A

dozen clean-cut lines appeared across their burnished carapaces as Simeon spun past, and then they simply fell apart, collapsing into piles of scrap. Artificial brains spilled from their ruptured cores, spattering across the treadplate floor.

Explosions followed at his heels as he tracked the scent his master had given him, on into a ruin of broken glass and blood.

(There was snow on the ground, crunching beneath his feet as he ran, the sword held out beside him like an extension of his arm. The forest loomed up and over him, blocking out the light as he hunted down the traitorous Master he was here to destroy.)

And another.

He saw a hulking silhouette ahead of him - an enemy worthy of his attention, a pretender to his throne.

It was the seven-foot shadow of Lieutenant Tsien.

Behind him the crowd closed in, howling their lust to the obscured sky. They tore into the survivors of his onslaught with bloody fingers, implacable and savage.

(The pretender was ahead of him, armored in red and gold, adorned with Chinese nephrite. His face was an ancestral death-mask, and he held in one hand a great brazen arquebus, the weapon of a craven coward. Peasants among the trees were loading a rusted old Portuguese cannon; they took aim at him, diving from the sputtering fuse as it burned down...)

Blaire saw through the illusion for a second, through to the face of the dreadlocked gunner atop his tank turret, utterly out of place in the middle of a shopping mall foodcourt.

That face was his own.

The disruptor tore apart his world in that second, and he froze, shards of ancient Japan crazing his vision. Then reality dropped in - the metal sky, the innumerable guns trained on him. Simeon stared down at the gore-slick sword in his hand, uncoprehending, then back up at Abdulafia 330.

He was looking into a distorting mirror.

It was no time to falter - not with the Compliance Division closing in on him, not with Cyben grasping for him with cold laminated hands. A bullet slammed into his shoulder, shattering his illusion of invulnerability in a spray of blood. The next one took him in the thigh, then another in the chest, staggering him back, a thin trickle of crimson dripping from his open mouth.

Tokugawa was raging at his side, the eye-slits of his rusted helm blazing bilious green. And the crowd began to scream, breaking in every direction at once.

Simeon fell slowly, through air as hot and thick as blood, his vision flickering between green moss over dark stone, rusty treadplate, and darkness. His last impression, before the blackness smothered him, was of a roaring sound rising, blotting out even his pain.

Vanecke lost his contact.

Ω

Lysander Jaegenn's fist smashed through Simeon's front teeth, wrecking his expensive dentition, shattering his jaw like glass. Again, and his lips were torn to shreds against grinding shards of bone. Again, and his skull collapsed, his face reduced to an unrecognizable welter of meat and blood…

Jaegenn didn't stop. Laughing, crying, he pounded his Kheptic foe's head into a sticky red stain, his face spattered with fragments of jellied brains and minced flesh. It was over all too soon.

Panting, the warrior Lord let his headless prey slide down the white-tiled wall, leaving a smear of crimson behind it. Blaire's carcass flopped lifelessly atop a pile of identical clones, each one beaten to a bloody pulp. He gestured to the dojo mekan for another, but then he sunk against the wall in defeat, resting his head in his hands.

"Cancel that, Elbrecht. Send in a pitcher of iced water and a towel. I need to be clean. Now."

The spire's A.I. discreetly led the blank-eyed Blaire clone away to the incinerator, hand in hand with one of its mekan thralls. An automated cart hummed across the hardwood floor toward Lysander, and he swiped up the towel, pouring the entire pitcher of cold water over his head.

That helped. A little.

"Master Jaegenn, you should really be training with 'mersive sims. These mind-wiped clones are no challenge, and they'll teach you nothing of Blaire's technique."

"I didn't want to learn his damned *technique*, Elbrecht." replied the Kheptarch, tearing open the collar of his tight-fitting Gamesuit. "I just wanted to kill him. For all kinds of reasons."

"Is this because he's exceeded your best score?" asked the A.I., its clipped accent echoing in his head. "You have the Valle Crucis to help you now - we know that Blaire's been using disciplines from the *Codex Martial*. Remember, the only kills that count are in the Game itself."

Jaegenn pointedly shut down his connection to Elbrecht's cogitator core, toweling himself dry as he walked out through the dojo's glass doors. They let out onto an open balcony, a platform of white marble suspended miles above the Subcity.

He didn't need a soulless automaton spouting motivational garbage in his ear. Any living, breathing human could tell you that where speed and strength left off, cunning and guile picked up the slack...

Up above him, in the hollow cup at the tip of his spire Jaegenn's luck was being made, rivet by rivet and bolt by bolt.

A horde of mekan were putting the final cut and polish to a vast edifice of white marble up there. The columned temple arose like a phoenix from within a nest of scaffolding, while human caterers slaved over banks of ovens below. Morsels on golden platters, immense urns of sweet wine, intricate and erotic ice statuary encased in stasis fields...

It was all an elaborate trap.

At his side on the balcony sat a twisted creature clad only in a studded iron collar. From the center of its forehead protruded a stubby plastic antenna, crudely bolted into the exposed bone. As Lysander smiled fondly upon his creation the wretch clapped mindlessly, grinning and drooling.

Lysander patted his bald skull with one hand, and tweaked the tip of his antenna.

"He will come, and he will be slaughtered," confided the Lord to his thrall, scratching the creature's stubbled scalp as if it were a favorite dog. "It's my party, and my game, and tonight it runs by *my* rules."

His pet - once the planet's wealthiest oil magnate - said nothing; indeed, its tongue was stapled down to silence its moaning and gibbering. After a millennium or more of slavery and a score of reincarnations the twisted thing was just slightly more insane than its master.

Ω

Abdulafia felt the steely fingers of his foe hinge shut around his throat, and there was nothing he could do to stop them. Weakened by the effort of freeing the Super-Cyben from Kronos, it was all he could do to stop Tsien taking off his head like a champagne cork.

The Lieutenant's eyes blazed inches from 'Afia's ashen face, his mouth a snarl of metal fangs. He smelled of ammonia ice, blood, and burning plastic - and his breath was cadaver-cold.

"I don't give a shit why you're here, or what's with the stupid costume, Blaire," he grated, lifting the Ashishim's feet clear of the tank turret. "But I know you've got influence with Lancaster, and I know he can put me back together."

With an immense Cyben claw slowly crushing his windpipe Abdulafia could hardly protest Tsien's mistake. And what a mistake it was! Emmanuel Lancaster had infinitely more money than mercy, and 'Afia had already killed off one of his pet clonehunters tonight.

But he thinks I'm Simeon Blaire. That's probably all that's keeping me alive…

Abdulafia watched a blue shimmer flare into life behind the Super-Cyben's back. It was the hardlight projector mounted to CeeAn's crescent unit - cracked and lopsided, but still able to fly.

Faster than his watering eyes could follow the spark leaped from one to another to another of the immobile Cyben troops, leaving starbursts of electrical fire in its wake. One by one the Cyben dropped, clattering to the floor in piles. The disruptor had stunned them, and Cee had switched them off at the mains with some precise concussion.

Which left only the worst of them. The one that was choking him to death...

"Now, I'm going to let you go," said Tsien, shaking Abdulafia like a rag doll. "But if you try any tricks, *my Lord*, I'll rip off your leg and beat you to death with it!"

Abdulafia hit the tiles hard, gasping for breath. There was cold ceramic against his cheek, and hot blood in his mouth as he rolled over. The floor beneath him cracked as Tsien planted his feet square, casting a shadow the size of a skyscraper. The Eversio had recessed up along one arm of the Super-Cyben's hulking body, and his steel claws twitched and clenched in the fitful light. The Ashishim hissed with pain and coughed up a couple of teeth.

"I'm sorry...Tsien. I'm not Blaire. I was made by..."

He was cut off by a kick to the ribs from Tsien which sent him sliding across the floor. The weight of the Super-Cyben's foot came down on his skull, pinning him like an insect.

"No tricks, asshole!" growled Tsien, leaning down over him as pushrods in the backs of his hands hissed and snapped, flexing his claws. "You only have to forfeit the game, and that freakshow Lancaster will owe you a favor. No *Emperor* means he's still top bitch."

Abdulafia's eyes twitched left for a split second - CeeAn was behind the Super-Cyben now, her shimmering violet form hefting a three-foot chunk of I-beam, its severed end twisted into an impaling spike. Tsien grinned as he followed Abdulafia's gaze. He leaped and turned with sudden speed all out of proportion to his bulk, facing the charging *Dervashi* with his arms outstretched.

"Leave him alone, you bastard! You already owe me a fucking *tank!*"

The I-beam rammed home with a sickening thud, its corroded point ripping through his skin. Blood spattered the floor as she twisted it hard, severing wires and veins and nerves...

But she might as well not have bothered.

Tsien stood transfixed, still smiling, looking down on CeeAn with beatific indulgence.

"Are you quite finished?" he asked, arching one eyebrow

above a glittering camera lens. "Good. *My turn!*"

The Super-Cyben's claw shot out with unnatural speed, deep into CeeAn's holographic image. The tips of his razor fingers clamped down on the black crescent which projected CeeAn's temporary body, and with the merest twitch he shattered its hardened shell.

The image collapsed in a flicker of static , cutting off her cry of horror. A tangled mess of plug-studded armor clattered forlornly to the floor, its antigrav generators and holo projectors ruined. And Tsien swung back around, the ends of the impaling steel beam scything the air.

"Now - back to *business*, Lord Blaire."

Tsien grasped the metal beam where it protruded from his back, then pulled it free. Abdulafia stared in horror as the fist-sized tunnel through his flesh knitted smoothly back together. The Super-Cyben slapped the gory steel against his palm as if it was his regulation taser-baton, planting his feet on either side of his captive's head.

"I know Lord Lancaster can fix me… it wouldn't even be a day's work for his robosurgeons. *But there's not much he can do with a brain that's splattered over ten feet of tiles.*"

The I-beam soared up, describing a rust-red arc through the smoky air. It stopped, poised at its zenith over Tsien's head. Abdulafia had no doubt that the downstroke would cleave clear through the concrete to the Subcity levels below the Valley View, taking his skull with it.

He could stand the shock and the pain of it - what he couldn't stand was the waiting for another clone body to be prepared, putting him in the same insubstantial state as poor CeeAn, snapped back down the wires to the fortress of the Electromagi. The Ashishim needed their champion at full strength if Simeon Blaire was fixated on the Throne - he couldn't die tonight.

"Tsien… Edward…" coughed Abdulafia, clawing himself to a sitting position. "I'm not lying to you. I'm not Simeon Blaire …"

"He's not, you know," said a rasping, breathless voice from behind them. "*I* am."

Ω

Kaito was glad that he wasn't a tunnel-rat like his new buddy 'Zerk. It was hot and humid in the vents, and so tight that he could barely squeeze through the maze of choke-points and slideways. His elbows and knees would never forgive him.

But B-Zerk knew what he was doing. The kid seemed to have a map of the steel warren burned on the inside of his eyelids.

"Is it much further? I'm sure we've seen that valve before…"

The kid's snort of derision was exactly the one Kaito used for neophyte hackers.

"Don't sweat it, Kayzi. We're already home."

B kicked a meshwork grille from out of its mountings and slid through, dragging Kaito after him. They came out just opposite Kohali Ras' shack, in lee of a thick bundle of service pipes. But the Valley View was gone. Now it was all just smoke and heat-haze, twisted metal scrawled across the tiles.

"I've done my bit," said the tuberunner, his knuckles white around the grip of his little sword. "Now, tell me what you found inside the machine. Tell me what happened to Zone Doubt."

"For once I have *absolutely* no idea what's going on in there," wheezed Kaito, pulling B-Zerk down into cover. Somewhere above them the STX Saber was waiting, its lights blazing in the dusk… "Your friend was in there. *Thousands* of people are in there!" he wiped an oily hand across his sweating brow. "The real question is *why* - and how to get them out."

B-Zerk shook Kaito's hand off his shoulder, staring back into the boiling smoke.

"Zone heard you." he said, while the Kayzi connected his belt to the hanging zipline. When Kaito turned back, B-Zerk's eyes were rolled up into their sockets, showing nothing but shimmering white. The ancient wakizashi was clenched tight in his hand, an inch of blade showing. Where he had pulled it loose its razor edge had sliced a crimson line across his thumb.

His mouth cracked open in an idiot grin as he pulled the dagger from its ornate sheath, letting the blood pick out a neat line of alien pictograms hammered into the steel.

"He's coming for us. Now."

Ω

Direktor Vanecke rewound the threedeeo, cold dread running wild in his mind.

It had all gone wrong! Something had ruined his illusion; stopped Simeon Blaire in his tracks! *He had to find out why. He had to regain control...*

His sensorium dome lit up, screen by screen, until every last camera feed inside the Valley View mall was at his command.

There had to be a way to rectify the situation. Blaire was worse than useless without his carefully crafted sequestration program - he was far too dangerous to be let off the leash alone...

Octavio let them all play at once, drinking in the disaster through his augmented eyes.

Slowly, ponderously, the immune system of the Valley View mall shuddered into life, awoken from its century-long slumber by the frantic efforts of the Compliance Division. The crumbling old building had been a battlefield once already - during the riots of Reclamation day, when hundreds of dispossessed and wounded refugees had used its main concourse as a makeshift shantytown.

Tonight it was happening again.

Simeon Blaire charged up the throat of the Valley View ahead of a mob of fanatics, blue ribbons streaming from his jet-black armor. He slashed left and right at Cyben and their human retainers, forging a path through to where his illusory world parted. Toward the face of Abdulafia 330.

Vanecke's fantasy was too fragile for such heavy dissonance. It cut through the quicksilver spark of the drugs and the hot burn of Blaire's ancient crycelium. It cracked his mind open.

Left, and his hissing sword neatly carved off the top of a Cyben's head, flashing between a ceremonial samurai helmet and a steel skullcap as it flew. Right, and his fist shattered the faceplate of a naginata-wielding monk, who became a blue-suited rifleman as he fell.

Simeon howled in pain and confusion as Abdulafia unleashed his energistic attack on Tsien, faltering for a second as compliance division troopers with taser-batons charged him from all sides. Hairline cracks ramified across his vision, making his whole world craze like broken glass. The gates and screens and sizzling deflectors which had fallen at his heels as he ran cut him off from his loyal supporters. Alone, he watched his enemies close in, distorted figures all teeth and fists…

Then the spreading ripples of the Ashishim's disruptor washed over him, and his illusory world blew apart. One bullet slammed into his body, then a second, a third, making him twitch and dance as he bled. A howl of dismay went up from his forsaken disciples. And the cops closed in, grim-faced and bloody.

Down he went, under an avalanche of swearing, struggling officers, their electrically charged batons beating out a tattoo on his head, his unprotected arms. Raw voltage spiked through his crycelial web, shutting down his brain in a storm of green pixels.

That was where Octavio Vanecke's recording cut out.

But as his signal snapped off, connections went live in Simeon's brain, making the wires sing. There was silence from within the pile of uniformed bodies for a second, for two.

It all clicked inside his head.

With a mindless howl Blaire leaped up to his feet, Compliance troopers flying in every direction. He heard the sickening crack of bone as they landed, a neat circle of death like a pentacle scrawled in corpses.

And he smiled.

All those shattered pieces of glass had fit back together *right*, and the world was back. He was just as deadly here as he was in Vanecke's fantasy - but utterly out of control.

Tadashi Murai din't matter, not in the real world. But some things did. *Honor. Reputation.* Little words he'd been bred to live by.

He saw Eddie Tsien, more terrible in reality than in any illusion woven for him by Octavio Vanecke, a giant and twisted ogre of a thing. Dissonance tweaked him as he looked into the eyes of his victim. Even without the Direktor hacking his optic nerves they were still painfully familiar…

Blaire strode forward, his half-masked face expressionless.

Now he had all the power his erstwhile master had given him, but none of the crippling restraints. His own eyes stared back at him as the Super-Cyben raised up a huge metal bar to finish its slaughter.

Ω

Tsien burned with anger as the pitiful Lord Blaire squirmed beneath him. How typical of the attitude of the *nobility*!

It would only take a word for this man to end his suffering - suffering indeed, for without the Vilicus drone to override his nerves he felt as if he'd been flayed. The Mark-Four system had barely had enough time to integrate with his ravaged body, and now the strain of keeping flesh and metal together was tearing him apart.

What part of the Elysian government had condemned him? Was this how they repaid his years of service?

It was almost worth keeping the weapons Kronos had stitched though his body just to exact his revenge…but here and now he could end it. One call to Lancaster, one game forfeited and he could be rebuilt, cloned, made human again…

And yet the fool denied him. Tsien's immense new hands gripped the steel beam so hard that it bent almost double.

A high-pitched whine escaped between his teeth as he fought to keep from pulverizing Blaire's head, ending his puling arguments…

Something faded in over the static of pain and anger in his head.

"He's not, you know. *I am.*"

The Lieutenant forced his head around against the will of his overriding programs, corded sinews and cables writhing beneath his skin. Behind him stood a figure in black, wearing a combat suit so fitting it seemed to be airbrushed over his chiseled muscles. His only scrap of armor was the matt-black webbing harness which held his scabbarded sword. Above the newcomer's half-mask a familiar pair of eyes bored into him without fear or pity.

Eyes like those which had stared at him from a thousand

threedeeo feeds…

"If *you're* Blaire," grated Tsien, lowering the bar and pivoting over the body of his fallen adversary "Then what's *this* thing? Your celebrity stunt double?"

"Good question," replied Blaire, still as a carved statue amid the smoke and heat "I would assume that it's all some kind of elaborate plan to disinherit me of my destiny."

Tsien spat, a gobbet of quicksilver and blood the size of a golf ball.

"Don't get me started on *destiny*, your fucking majesty. Because as of this second you're quitting the game. All bets are off. And you're calling up Lord bloody Lancaster to get me *rehumanized*." Little plumes of gas chuffed out from his shoulder paudrons as he pulled himself up to his full height. "I'm aware that's not a real word. But believe me, I don't really care right now."

"How very *sad* for you that I can't alter my course in the slightest!"

Simeon laughed, his eyes twinkling as he unstrapped his leather half-mask.

"Certainly not just to give charity to some mechanical *freak!*" His fingers snapped in front of his face, and Tsien smelled the telltale odor of fuzzy stunn burst out of the capsul.

Chemhead. Figured.

"But when I'm Emperor, I may have use for a brute like you to keep the lower orders in line." He giggled, tossing the empty capsul over one shoulder. "For now, give me that fellow you've so neatly incapacitated. That's really such a *striking* resemblance – and if Emmanuel Lancaster is ready to play his hand, he can be assured that I'm ready and waiting for him."

Tsien's teeth ground so hard that they surely would have cracked to splinters - if they weren't already shot through with Chimera crycelium.

"Until one or the other or *both* of you little bastards gets me a hot line to Lancaster and his Biotects, this bastard's staying right here!" The Super-Cyben punctuated his ultimatum by hammering the U-shaped twist of steel down over Abdulafia's shoulders, pinning him to the floor. He struggled hopelessly against its crushing weight – but it was hopeless. It would take some kind of boosted, musclebound freak to tear it loose… that or a hydraulic crane.

"Sure you won't reconsider? I really could use a beast of your stature…"

"I'm over being used, Blaire. Now, put up or shut up!"

There was a tiny metallic sound as Blaire's thumb pushed his sword an inch out of its sheath.

There was an almost inaudible click as recessed jaws in Tsien's arm released the Eversio.

The next second was a slow-motion blur for both of them as their augmented systems sliced time down to tiny, strobed slivers.

Tsien saw a slim black projectile fly from Blaire's hip - the sword!

The Eversio unhinged and swung into his grip, spitting a cloud of silver mesh which diced the speeding black bullet in midair. One convulsive twitch of those wires ripped it to tatters. Eddie's cybernetic eyes shut down to slits as he realized it was nothing but painted wood. And in that instant the blade itself swung in, underhand, shearing the cannon from his arm at the bolts.

Before the Eversio hit the ground his free hand was wrapped around Blaire's forearm, hinging shut like a vise. Bone creaked and splintered deep inside.

But Blaire grinned at the gunshot snap of his radius and ulna, using the pull and leverage to come in closer. As he dropped the sword from his left, his right fist hammered into a pressure point on Tsien's neck, forcing him to release his grip, reeling.

Metal recombined and knitted, setting his bones.

Simeon snatched the sword from out of the air as Tsein staggered back, but he was too late. The Super-Cyben's foot blurred sideways in a piston-driven snap-kick, propelling him fifty feet across the mall. Off in the boiling smoke Eddie heard the sound of raw meat hitting concrete far too fast for comfort.

He brushed himself down, surveyed the wreckage of the

Eversio, and loosened up the muscles and servos in his bullish neck, shrugging off the cannon's backpack. That's when he caught a flicker of movement off at the edge of sight, a wink of hot silver.

"Oh, you little bastard! Hard to kill, are ya? Let's see how..."

A cloud of razor-edged throwing stars came winging out of the heat-haze, centered on Eddie's glowing laser-rangefinder headset. Too many to dodge, too sharp to simply endure... his foot came down on the edge of a treadplate floor tile and flicked it up into the air, a thick shield of stone between him and the shuriken storm. They struck home with a sound like shattering crystal, quivering from the concrete.

"Lesson for you, Blaire!" he said, gripping the tile between his fingers. "If you're gonna throw things, make sure it's worth your while!"

Eddie launched the three-hundred-pound slab like a discus, waiting for the crunch of shattering bones. Instead he saw it part the smoke just in time for Blaire to leap up over it, raising his katana high as he flew. The tempered steel blazed red in the flamelight, shearing down with a savage hiss... and the Super-Cyben dodged it by a fraction of an inch. His fingers hooked around the Kheptarch's webbing belt, stopping him in midair.

"Still holding out on me? Think about it, Blaire. One little forfeit, and it'll all be over..."

"It's *already* over, you dirty peasant! You're just too stupid to realize it!"

Tsien roared as he reversed his swing, battering the young Lord into the ground, a ragdoll in black. Cracks skittered out in all directions. The katana flew wide, ripped from its master's hand.

Once, twice, the merciless piston arms of the Super-Cyben smashed Blaire down against the concrete, leaving bloody imprints with each blow. But the Chimera burned in Simeon's veins, and when Eddie dragged him back to his feet he was ready. A broken smile split his face as he hung limp from the Cyben's claws, waiting until he felt the quickening in his blood...

It came down hard - silver tendrils budding from his wounds, stitching him back together stronger, faster. *Silver threads crackling with power as they unleashed sixty thousand volts.*

Tsien recoiled, cursing, throwing up his arms to ward off the strobe-flash of electricity. And in that instant Simeon Blaire hung motionless in the air, gravity denied, humming discs concealed in his webbing taking up the load. He curled his shoulder down and under, tensing himself like a spring, then threw his whole body into a devastating roundhouse kick, his heel catching Tsien square in the chromed socket of one camera eye.

Glass shattered, skin tore, and the laser sight blinked out. All of this while Simeon's blade was still airborne, winking in the firelight. The katana flew end over end to impale itself deep in the treadplate, quivering like a reed as lightning crawled over the Cyben's broken face. Eddie bellowed with rage, one claw covering his ruined eye.

But the other one – the other one was a pinpoint of utter focus.

He came forward punching, his steel fist moving in a lightning series of jabs, ten, twenty of them, a relentless piston blurring chrome through the air. Simeon dodged each blow with a twitch to the left or right, swaying like a tree before the gale, the hammerlike fist missing him by inches. His eyes twinkled with amusement - obviously this mechanical thug was no match for his skill.

He never saw Tsien step over the body of a dead Cyben, and never saw his foot move, slipping under the stock of a combat shotgun. Suddenly the bloody claw came away from Tsien's face, now a webwork of knitting silver filaments. The shotgun snapped up into the air, came around like a hatchet in Eddie's hand and slammed into Blaire's side. Into his jaw. Into his ribs again, with a sound like breaking matchwood.

Simeon staggered, blood glittering as it flew.

But his hand was snake-strike fast, wrenching his katana from the floor...

Blaire spun his body sideways, braced his foot against a crack in the tiles, and brought his sword up to block the swinging fist to his left. With a burst of sparks the blade came to rest between Tsien's knuckles, cutting his hand in two.

The Kheptarch's eyes jerked right. The gun had stopped spinning, and now he looked down all four of its gaping barrels, staring at the puckered tips of a clutch of riot shells.

Tsien smiled, despite the cold steel bisecting his left hand.

"Say goodnight, fucker," he growled - and he pulled the trigger.

Ω

Deep beneath the Valley View - down below level after level of Habs and manufactoria and no-man's-land zones filled with renegade machines - a pair of hands turned a big black dial, scanning frequencies. A pair of antiquated headphones clamped down hard as a pair of ears searched the ether for a certain plaintive beeping sound.

"Found it, Rosvall!" said the operator, one SubMagus Devine, beaming with a mouthful of metallic-green aluminum dentures. "She's ready to download, if you boys have the tank prepped up."

In the shadows behind Devine's cluttered workstation a hissing steel drum lay canted at an angle, half submerged in an auto mechanic's grease pit. Rosvall - a balding vulture of a man in an oily lab coat - tapped a huge core of ash from off the joint he was puffing and scowled daggers at his comrade.

"Shit, boy, I've had this tin tub ready since before you even started fucking with that receiver. Let's get her back down here and hope she ain't *too* pissed when we crack the lid. Hells know I'm not getting in her way."

Devine punched buttons, lighting up a dancing display of flashing lights on his cobbled-together console.

"If I gotta pop the lid this time, you gotta do the paperwork. And remember the tech pool, Ros. Odds are seven to one she frags out this body within a day. You gotta be in it to win it."

The bald-headed cryo master gave his apparatus a final loving kick, throwing a set of brass-handled levers to set the whole rig shuddering and sighing.

"Just hit the contacts, boy. And tell Nguyen in Ordnance to be prepared. If I'm hearing right from Ramon's last message, she's gonna want to take half their firepower up with her."

Ω

He must have thought that Haszan was a cop.

Stupid, really – but the people who were packed in two hundred deep outside the valley View weren't in the most intelligent frame of mind right now. They were all but rabid with the promise of revolution… and that must have been what motivated one of them to smash a nail-studded plank over the back of Jaq's head.

It broke, of course. Haszan turned around slowly, giving the man enough time to appreciate the sheer suicidal foolishness of the course he'd undertaken. All around them the crowds surged and seethed, a single, homogenized mass of angry human meat thrashing the air with pipes, bottles, machetes, hammers and home-made siege weaponry.

"Was there a point to that? Or are you just sick of having all your limbs?" he growled, resting one shovel-sized hand on the man's shoulder. A threadbare blue ribbon looped across the wretch's chest, hanging loose over a pair of soot-stained overalls.

"You're…um… not with the Division, then?"

"Well – you haven't been shot or lobotomized, yet, so *no*. On the other hand, I don't have to *charge* you with anything before I kill you, so…"

The man's face reflected a peculiar mixture of cunning and horror as he looked deep into Haszan's empty eyes.

"Wait! Wait! I can… I can get you through the lines! I'm Consolidated Union, me… and all of us are behind the new Emperor!"

"If you think that's why I'm here, you might as well hit me again." Haszan gave the man's shoulder a little squeeze, bringing tears to the corners of his eyes. "But I'll make you a deal. You get me to the front, and I'll give you something very, very valuable…"

Dim fires of avarice lit up the unionist's face for a second.

"I'll let you have a *future*."

It wasn't what he wanted to hear, but then again, Jaq didn't give him much of a choice. With the man's neck pinched between one huge thumb and forefinger he was dragged through the heart of the mob, drinking it all in with a sense of numb disbelief. There were *thousands* of them. *Tens of thousands.* Only the true believers at the ever-shifting coalface of the riot were actually scrabbling and pushing against the Cyben and their herders; the rest were placard-wavers, random shouters, drunks, chemheads, opportunistic street hawkers and interested onlookers. Cameras stared down on the mob like mechanical voyeurs, repackaging the whole grim spectacle as news.

The Compliance Division weren't used to this kind of trouble. They were quota cops, and actual *civil unrest* made them uneasy... they certainly weren't paid enough for this. Still, the very real threat of bodily dismemberment had focused their minds on the basics. Their commanders were playing it professional, but Haszan was still worried. Kaito was down here somewhere, and based on previous experience he was probably right at the center of all the trouble. He could see the Division troopers getting twitchy and nervous, hands tight around their tazer-batons and riot guns.

Some of them were so stupid that they actually *wanted* to open fire.

If they did... Jaq remembered what remained of that Final Reich guardpost after he was done with it. They had to clean up the deceased with mops and buckets. And that was just one man's rage - not the fury of an entire city...

Haszan shouldered his way through the spectators to the edge of the clear zone, right up to where a navy-blue armored cop was shouting into a portable radio.

"Twenty third Cyben squad are inside... reporting heavy casualties. We've lost contact with the experimental subject... riot squads six and thirty nine are containing the disturbance... request immediate repeat *immediate* orders for General Extermination!" The red-faced and sweating officer turned to look at Haszan as his hulking shadow fell over him.

"If it ain't official business you'd better clear out, pal," he shouted over the din of smashing glass and screams "Those tankers have orders to use Generally Unnecessary Force. Messy!"

Haszan thought of Kaito in there, and of the rain of fire which would come down from the tower above when a General Extermination order came through.

"Uh... special directive from the, ahhh, developmental weapons department." He pulled his Omnivasive payslip from out of his coat pocket, waving it in the trooper's face. "The experimental subject you've lost contact with may have gone critical." Haszan jammed his paperwork back in his coat quickly, before the guy could catch what it really was. "Condition... umm... *Deadly Nightshade.*"

The officer went pale, cupping his hand over the radio and leaning closer.

"That thing's off the leash? Sweet Buddha's ghost!" he looked Haszan up and down, and began to root though a military locker at his feet. "I don't care how tough you are, soldier - if you really want to go after HIM you'd better suit up." He came up holding a reinforced chestplate, a helmet and a pair of oversized rail pistols.

"Just let me call HQ, and perhaps we can spare you one of these tanks as well," he said, punching numbers into the radio. "*Condition Deadly Nightshade...* ohh, that sounds bad. Real bad."

Haszan threw back the bolt on one of the bulky pistols, ready to fight his way though. HQ would no doubt confirm that no special agent from x-weapons had been dispatched... and that there was *definitely* no such condition. Haszan had taken the name from a tacky threedeeo movie.

"There'll be no need for all that," purred an oily voice at Haszan's elbow. A pale hand snaked out and flicked a switch on the radio, shutting it down. "Old Jaq here is a *special* kind of technician. His specialty is the recapture of rogue cybernetic systems."

The man was slightly built, dressed in grubby brown tweed, with a shiny bald head and a beaklike nose upon which perched a pair of outsized camera goggles. Other recording devices sprung from his shoulders and forearms like augmented weapons, and a slim keyboard was strapped across his chest.

The officer looked puzzled for a second, but then spotted the holographic halo which orbited the man's head. In yellow and blue it proclaimed 'PRESS - SPECIAL ATTACHE'.

"You going in with him then?" asked the cop, staring with obvious distaste at the little man in the shabby suit.

"But of course! Omnivasive never miss a hot story! Why, the last time this big fella did his thing he took out half of the wastewater processors under Eastcliff. Big cover-up, of course, never got to air the report, but the *footage*! If that battlemekan was only a twenty-tonner I'll eat my shoes!"

The cop blinked, confused and stunned by the little man's tirade.

"*That* was *him*?" he asked. "I heard that the Direktoriat sent in a whole unit of Tech Division Demolishers. But it was one man? Whew - I wouldn't want your job, pal."

He was actually saluting as the reporter dragged the big 'dreno pharmer away.

"There goes a real Elysian hero!"

Haszan followed numbly as they weaved their way between tanks and troopers, supply crates and medical trauma teams. Ahead of them steel barricades and razorwire contained the riot, although by now it was less of a massacre and more of a scramble to escape the tightening noose of Compliance machinery.

Haszan and his guide stood on the remains of a little raised garden overlooking the plaza, ignored by the Division's men. Their eyes slid over Aticus Meaks like oiled teflon.

"Well, this is where we part," said the little man, staring up at Haszan with his huge blank lenses. "My briefing from chief Vanecke was just to get you this far. Good spin about that experimental weapons jive - you could be reporter if you ever give up your day job."

"And who exactly are you? My guardian fairy?"

The little man looked hurt. He sketched a tiny bow.

"Atticus Meaks, at your service. By which I mean at the *chief's* service, to be pedantic, but right now it's all kind of the same thing, right?"

"I should have guessed Vanecke had his teeth into this mess," said Haszan. "But you got me through the lines, Atticus, so what can I do for him today?"

"Thought you'd never ask," chuckled Meaks, one hand slithering inside his tweed coat. "This little package is for an old friend of yours, courtesy of the big guy. You've got a ten-minute window while the juice in here is active. He wanted *me* to deliver it, but I'm far too fond of my skin, no matter how wrinkled it my be. I'm just glad you're still around to do my job for me."

Haszan groaned as he saw what the pressman had produced. It was another syringe full of crycelium, proscribed-tech soup. There was no doubt for whom it was intended.

Haszan turned on his heel to leave, but Meaks' hand gripped the crook of his elbow, hauling him back with deceptive strength.

"Coincidentally enough, after that ten minutes is up our boss is gonna call his pals in the Direktoriat. They've lined up a General Extermination Order."

"But Sime… *Lord Blaire* is in there!" said Jaq "Isn't his pet Kheptarch too precious to waste?"

Atticus Meaks laughed, a dry and dusty sound like marbles in a drainpipe.

"He's got no doubts that young Simeon will survive - he's a very resourceful and *thoroughly* upgraded young man. But he gives his guarantee that one *Kaito Kayzi* won't."

Before he'd even finished speaking Haszan's fist was clenched around the pressman's neck, his steel-fingered hand clamped tight around his skull. Meaks' camera goggles shattered with a brittle crack, and Haszan could feel the stress building in the bone beneath.

"Tell that shrunken head bastard that I'll do it - this time." He turned, throwing Atticus Meaks to the ground. His eyes were wide and pale where the rubber goggles had covered them. "But after this, he can consider my contract terminated. I'm sure he'll understand."

Haszan tucked the crycelium needle deep inside his coat. He stepped over to a metal barricade and wrenched loose one of its supports, snapping off a snarl of razorwire with his chrome hand.

"And Meaks… I'll be seeing you around." The tiny blades at his fingertips retracted with an oily little snick. "Keep your running shoes on."

Ahead of him the riot churned, nothing but a heaving human obstacle between him and his purpose. Haszan strode into the fray, his steel pole cutting a path before him like a harvester's scythe through grain.

Damn Kaito Kayzi and his suicidal stupidity!

But if he was going to take down a hard target like Octavio Vanecke, he'd need all the help he could get.

Behind him Atticus Meaks chuckled to himself, looking down at the tip of one nic-stained finger where a flycam perched, cleaning its compound eyes with one brush-tipped forelimb.

"You'll be rid of him this time, Direktor," he said. "Serendipitous, to say the least. I wasn't looking forward to meeting your Kheptic toy soldier myself…"

Ω

B-Zerk pelted down a boiling tunnel of fire, the wakizashi in his hand seeming to pull him onward. The runes carved into its fuller gleamed with sullen bloodlight, promising murder.

His eyes were streaming from the acrid smoke, and his lungs were beginning to ache from the lack of oxygen, but he plunged on, toward the sounds of battle which echoed up ahead.

He knew that Zone Doubt was coming - a certainty which had completely taken over his mind. From out of the sickening well of memory came the smell of burning skin and flesh, and a scream which came spiraling up, drowning out reason.

"Hey! Come back! You stupid little… What, you want to get yourself killed?"

Kaito clenched his fists, his hoarse shout tapering off into a gurgle. This whole scene – the fire, the smoke… it brought evil memories bubbling to the top of his mind. But it also gave him just enough empathy for the crazy little juve bastard to tie his neckerchief up around his face and set off after him.

The idiot couldn't have got far. Hells, he knew what it was like to stagger through a burning building. Any second now he'd…

But then the smoke parted in ragged gray curtains, rolling back from a nightmare. For a moment Kaito thought he was still trapped inside the node, the Wetsystems twisting his memories into some bizarre hallucination.

It was worse. It was *real*.

B-Zerk was there, all but dead on his feet as his clothes smoldered and charred. He was up on top of an ancient battle-tank – a vast, antique slab of metal which seemed to have chewed craters out of the ruined mall all around it before exploding.

In the shadow of this museum piece stood Simeon Blaire and Lieutenant Edward Tsien. Both were bloodied and torn up - and neither was the man Kaito remembered. Blaire was stripped of his finery, dressed in light-devouring black combat-skin. This time he didn't face other Kheptarchs in the ancestral Game - his adversary was more than half machine, a grotesque caricature of the corrupt gutter-cop Kaito knew and hated. One of Tsien's gigantic hands held a combat shotgun, its four squat barrels trained on Blaire's chest.

B-Zerk heard the safety catch click off.

He saw the gloating triumph written across Tsien's face, the silver cables and bunched wires pulsing across his oversized torso.

He saw Blaire poised on his toes, about to be shredded to ribbons by the shotgun's blast. And he recognized that stance - one of the dozens of forms that his old friend Tadashi Murai had been teaching him in secret.

So his hand moved without his mind's intervention, throwing the wakizashi up and over, a looping arc which came down right in the Kheptarch's hand.

"*Sakai*, motherfucker! Take him down!"

Blaire's eyes twitched left, just in time to intercept the little sword's flight. He smiled.

Kaito scrambled up the engine cowling of the Ghulam tank, trying to tackle the kid to the ground before he really got Tsien's attention. And as the super-Cyben's gun roared he saw Lord Simeon snap Murai's wakizashi out of the air, laughing.

Ω

Abdulafia had passed out for a second there - the pressure of the i-beam pinning him to the concrete made it almost impossible to breathe. If he hadn't been so low to the ground he was sure he'd already have choked to death.

Small mercies. And even smaller hopes…

Suddenly he felt a cold steel pressure along his left side.

Looking up, he locked eyes with a green-eyed giant, his whipcord goatee festooned with tiny silver charms and sigils. He was both the ugliest and most welcome angel of mercy the Ashishim had ever seen. In fact, he was the 'boosted, musclebound freak' of his prayers.

"On three, we both try to move this hunk of metal," said Haszan, leaning his prodigious weight to the prybar.

Abdulafia nodded, then pushed up with all his might…

Ω

Caltrop-spiked metal ripped out in a tight fan, glowing red-hot inside a blaze of muzzle-flash. Hidden mechanisms inside the gun spat out a clutch of spent cartridges, brass winking in the firelight…

But Eddie Tsien had missed.

Simeon caught the sheath of the Wakizashi as he leaped - not left or right, but directly *up*.

The warrior Lord sprung up six feet in a single bound, his feet touching down on the shotgun's barrels for a second before those four empty shells even hit the ground.

Tsien was still grinning in triumph as Blaire ran up his immense arm. By the time he began to react it was far too late.

Blaire's left foot connected with his jaw, pushing him back on his heels. His right hand hammered down on top of Tsien's skull with an audible crack of bone. Then he was over, spinning in

327

the air behind his staggering foe. The sheath of the wakizashi stabbed into a pressure point in Tsien's armored neck, making his head snap forward, cords of silver straining. A tiny slit appeared between the Super-Cyben's vertebral plates of armor.

And as Tsien roared in pain and vexation the ancient blade slid through his spinal column, erupting from his throat in a burst of gore.

For a second the Lieutenant stood there, blood and oil bubbling from his severed windpipe, twitches and tremors shuddering though his cybernetic muscles. He dropped the shotgun as his claws snapped open and closed convulsively, and his knees began to buckle, slumping his great form to the floor in a tatter of ruined clothes.

Blaire alighted with a flick of his wrist, twisting the blade in the wound. And the Super-Cyben was felled.

"So die all those who oppose their Emperor!" hissed Blaire, with his back to the ruin of Eddie Tsien. "Such is the justice of my new age!"

But before he could turn and retrieve his blade, Simeon felt strong arms wrap around his torso. He tried to struggle, but a blaze of blue lightning lit up the encircling grip of Abdulafia. He was completely pinned. The centuries-old crycelium in his blood boiled at the disrupting touch of the Ashishim warrior.

Haszan' huge hand clamped down over Blaire's skull, the syringe held up like a sacrificial knife.

"I suggest that everybody starts running!" shouted Haszan, his thumb on the plunger "Last time this boy took his medicine all hell broke loose."

Kaito dragged B-Zerk up off the floor and grinned at his friend across the ruined mall.

"Brother, you read my mind!" he shouted, throwing B-Zerk over one shoulder.

Haszan smiled back, and the needle came down.

17 Aevum Oblivio
Strata

_WHITE-HOT METAL MELTED and dripped like wax from the tip of Technician Zhe's finger, transformed into a fusion blade by the technology of the Motherbrain. The damned stuff was useful, he had to admit - even if it was the living flesh of his enemy. After all, time was running out before the Forge could be used again, and the armored plating of Kronos' process core was incredibly thick. He'd take any help he could get.*

His claw-shaped cutter sliced deep, hotter than the surfaces of suns, hacking through the weakest point in the machine's defenses. Although in this case weakness was a relative concept.

The machine had accreted armor around itself like nacre around a pearl.

Inside this armored dome was the reality of his visions, the great cubes of hardware which formed the heart of Kronos.

Perhaps under these layered cerametal and bonded silicon the broken body of Eddie Tsien floated on its rack of light, the focus for an immense act of possession. More likely the skyscraper-sized glass cubes were dead and powerless, unable to stop the disease within the Wetsystems...

Well, a Technician could hope...

Zhe's hoof slammed into the immense plug of armor as he finished his cut, striking while its edges were still red-hot. It was still falling down into the frozen chasm of the device core as he fired a slim wire out into the dark, locking its barbs in a panel of foot-thick glass.

Night-sight membranes nictitated across his eyes.

There was no blood. There was no Tsien. Zhe was quietly relieved. Still...

The vision he'd suffered of this place transformed gnawed at the edges of his mind, overlaying the serried ranks of processors with the ghosts of black stone towers, iron impaling spikes and mutilated bodies strung on chains. He could feel the thorny roots of the infection pushing at the base of his skull, intimations of its otherworldly power sparking through him.

Zhe put it out of his mind. There were only seconds left.

In space, the satellites spun like gems, exquisite and untouchable. Each one held enough power to wipe out a nation. Orchid-petal solar panels turned in upon themselves, mirrors flashing like oriental fans.

They were waiting for the Forge, and waiting, too, for the power out of the wastelands which could stop it in its tracks.

When it came, Zhe would finally know who commanded it.

THE AIR ABOVE Duke Jaegenn's spire was lost in a cloud of haze as dusk ruled a line across the western horizon. An armada of helicopters and zeppelins hovered in tight formation around the cerametal stamen of the tower, jockeying for position. Their halogen spotlights obscured the stars, slithering across a sea of faces down below.

They were waiting for blood.

Omnivasive had spared no expense to make this Game unforgettable. Bread and circuses, just like they used to do in Rome. And just like the old Emperors, Octavio Vanecke knew what kept his people happy. The lead-up coverage tonight was an hour of subliminals and bloodshed - a 'greatest kills' gallery presented with slick aplomb by Dave Levine.

It was almost time to go live…

A swathe of red carpet ran from the manicured park on Jaegenn Circle to the doors of the Lord's estate, a gauntlet of threedeeo cameras funneling the Kheptarchy into the arena. The crowds around it were already thirty deep, and Vanecke noted with delight that three people had already been trampled. A cachet of danger was always good publicity. It wasn't just *here,* though.

All throughout Elysium the fans were massing, crowding around the immense inflatable twodee screens Direktor Vanecke had donated for the show. And all across the city the Compliance Division were stretched thin, one gunshot away from a massacre.

The fans were ready to cheer, and chant, and riot. And when Blaire finished this final round of slaughter, they would be ready to acclaim him Emperor, and bring about the culmination of Vanecke's plans. It had taken years, and enough leverage to pry open the gates of hell. But soon, so soon…

Now he was content to wait, drinking it all in through his dome of screens. Wait, and take care of the linchpin of his scheme, down below him in the Valley View. In a floating threedeeo orb in front of his tank, Octavio watched the static blink out to black, test patterns opening like neon flowers.

Once again, he was looking through the eyes of Simeon Blaire, staring at a torn rice-paper poster on a bloodstained wall. It showed a stylized, muscular Confucian soldier in linotype red and green, his A.K. raised over his head in a triumphant salute. Whatever had happened between that blast of static and the second when Jaq Haszan had brought the needle down was a mystery - but the minute details scarcely mattered. What was important was that the program had worked - that Simeon Blaire had led his followers into battle for the first time.

Thank the gods, and all the devils too. For a second there he'd actually thought…

But no. It was best not to even contemplate failure, not when he was this close…

Now it was time for an object lesson to strengthen their resolve. Now it was time for *martyrdom*.

Outside the gates of the Valley View a blue-ribboned army of Blaire supporters had been brought to their knees, hundreds of beaten revolutionaries kneeling inside a circle of tanks and Cyben guns. They would fulfill one final purpose, now that Simeon was back under control.

"Commissioner, this is Direktor Vanecke," hissed a disembodied voice over a certain encrypted relay. "Thank you for your patience; you are free to issue the extermination order."

Above a thousand public squares, in downtown bars and manufactorium mess halls, in bimburb homes and claustrophobic habs the screens were waiting. Soon they'd run red with blood…

Ω

Haszan waited for Simeon to go off like a bomb as his syringe slid its wires into the Kheptarch's brain. He remembered Blaire's predatory grin, his silver sword sketching an afterimage blur through the air… and he held his breath as he pushed the plunger home.

But there was nothing this time. Jaq slowly unclenched his

fists, creeping back on the tips of his toes. He didn't dare touch the needle again.

"Well, give it a minute. Watch his eyes, man. Watch his *hands*. There's something wrong with this one. *Badly* wrong."

Kaito had the kid he'd picked up somewhere along the way slung over his back like a sack of bricks, and he rested in a wary crouch, waiting for the predicted fireworks to start.

"He's a Kheptic Lord junkie, Jaq! Of course there's something *wrong* with him!"

"We won't be findin' out what's wrong with him today, Jaqub Haszan," said Abdulafia, prying one of Blaire's eyelids back with two fingers. "He's out like a light!"

The Ashishim leaned forward over the warrior Lord's shoulder, and for an instant his face was right next to the Kheptarch's. 'Afia wore a mask of dust and blood, but Jaq could spot the resemblance. Uncanny.

"Seriously, last time he had that exact same sword, and he tried to cut me to pieces! I've probably still got his ear here somewhere..."

He rooted around in the pockets of his trenchcoat, pulling out candy and bloodstained Slades and bullets; but no Kheptic trophy. Abdulafia stopped him with a wry little chuckle.

"Shit, boy... and you folks call us *Ashishim* a bunch of savages!"

"Well, I was always a firm believer in Orthodox Voodoo. Perhaps *that's* what's holding him back."

"Perhaps... but I'd put my money on the syringe full of drugs you just slammed into his cortex. In my experience, that's the kind of thing which gets results."

"Haszan, forget the fucking ear - let's get out of here!" That was Kaito, adjusting the unconscious body of the kid across his shoulders. "The fire's spreading, and this place is falling apart!"

Haszan stepped away from Simeon Blaire, letting go of the Kheptarch's shoulder as he pulled the needle free. It was stuck fast... so he left it there as Simeon slithered to the ground, a boneless black tangle of limbs with a pale and empty face.

"You coming with us, buddy?" he called to the Ashishim, who

was ripping a chunk of machinery out of the ruined battletank. "Or do your brothers in the Revolution have a plan for this kind of thing?"

Abdulafia hefted the shiny black crescent which had housed CeeAn's mind, connecting it to the Ghulam's ancient battery with alligator clips. Two of his duct-taped dreadlocks snaked into the memory cell, their plug-tipped ends finding matching sockets in its smooth surface.

"I'd be pleased to join you, gentlemen," he drawled, hauling an oily canvas duffel bag from the tank as he spoke. "Word on the wire is that some baaad shit's coming down on this location." He rummaged in the bag with one hand, pulling out a pair of old-fashioned revolvers, so huge and brutal that they made modern railpistols look like cheap kids' toys. "Just out of interest, have you fellows ever seen what happens to dead Cyben?" He lobbed one of the cannons underhand to Haszan and the other to Kaito, smiling in a thoroughly disturbing fashion.

"Aren't they dead already? Y'know, when they're built?" asked the Kayzi, plucking the gun out of the air with his free hand.

"Well… I'll tell ya while we evacuate," said Abdulafia, fishing in the sack for his own weapons. In the smoke and flamelight, Haszan could swear that he looked just a little too much like Lord Blaire for comfort…

It was the drugs catching up with him. It had to be.

They set off into the mall, away from the bleeding and broken bodies of Eddie Tsien and the immobile Simeon Blaire, the syringe still protruding from his neck like an exclamation point.

"Don't they just recycle them?" asked Haszan as he came up alongside the Ashishim. "Plug in a new set of batteries, a bit of synthetic flesh, and put them back on the street?"

"It's a little more complicated than that. See, what they do is… SHIT!"

"Gee, that doesn't seem very technical. I mean - "

Sound being as slow as it is, Jaq actually saw the fat lead slug spin past his face well before he heard the gunshot. Then instinct took over for all of them – wartime hardwiring for 'Afia, street-hustler survival reflexes for the two Elysians. Big saucer-sized craters were being chewed out of the concourse where they'd just been standing, letting the rays of the setting sun lance in through the smoke.

Then came the big one.

The explosion brought down a whole row of stores… most of them right on top of Eddie Tsien. At the same time its shockwave lifted Katio off his feet, throwing him and the kid into a ragdoll spin. Abdulafia managed to wrap one hand around a lamp-post as he was propelled backward, cursing, his bioelectric field flaring out like an aeroshield behind him.

Haszan heard the crash of broken glass as he spun upside down, then his head struck a big solid wall of cerametal with a billiard-ball crack. Groaning steel and stone echoed in his skull, counterpoint to the roar of flames. Whatever had come in through the roof had cut off their escape. Assholes!

It was one *hell* of a 'whatever'.

Jaq watched through a haze of concussion as a giant khaki mantis levered itself down into the mall, quartering the ruin of the grand concourse with a pair of glowing white eyes. The jagged tips of its forelimbs bristled with heavy-caliber weaponry, and belts of bullets swung from its belly as ammo-feeds ratcheted and clicked.

Surely not. Surely not. Had he pissed off any giant insects lately? Where the fuck were those detox patches? Haszan found that reality was just as bad as the illusion as he slapped an orange demon-head to his temple.

It was a helicopter gunship, and its blades fanned the flames up and out in a fiery corona. In between its rocket pods and railgun sponsons somebody had stenciled the old eye-and-pyramid chop of Omnivasive, symbol of the free press. And those great dragonfly eyes were dangling searchlights, twisting on their mountings to transfix the tiny black figure of Simeon Blaire.

Hanging out of the control bubble at the nose of the gunship was the thin, hawkish face of Atticus Meaks. His camera goggles were pushed back onto his shiny forehead, and a drooping cigarette was clamped between his lips. He waved.

Haszan struggled forward against the gale, but Abdulafia was already taking aim, his big antique revolver pointing like an accusing finger. A claw on a long whiplike cable sprung from the belly of the chopper as he squeezed trigger. Haszan heard the revolver fire, saw the white muzzle-flash, but the Ashishim was too late. The bullet pared paint off the nose of the machine, whining away into the dark.

"You damn fools! What the hell are you shootin' for?"

"What am *I* shooting for? *You* started it, you little bastard!"

'Afia stood defiant, one arm crooked around the lamp-post for balance as his coat streamed about him in tatters. And Haszan saw that he WAS Simeon Blaire - saw that same maniac grin as the hammer came down on another shell, and the skin of the helicopter tore open in a hole the size of his fist.

"Aaah! Stop it! I didn't know who you were, O.K!"

"And I don't know who the hell *you* are! So here! Have another!"

That jointed steel cable had found its mark now, and spinnerets at its tip wrapped Blaire in a cocoon of wire. Another shot came from off to the right, and Haszan saw Kaito perched in the store window, holding his gun with both hands. This one almost blasted the stabilizing rotor from the chopper's tail, and Meaks screamed in alarm as his gunship slewed right, its blades missing a tangle of rebar by inches.

It was too late to stop them now. Meaks was cursing and swearing, spinning up the helicopter's guns. Lead skipped and whined across the tiles as he opened fire. So Jaq brought his own revolver to bear, his servo-assisted thumb snapping back the hammer as he sighted along its long black barrel. There, right between the chainguns on the gunship's belly - the maser beam Meaks had used to cut open the roof. Tanks of volatile liquids and coolants clustered beneath it, utterly exposed. One shot in the right place...

The helicopter ruined his shot by pulling up, dipping and weaving as Meaks tried to shoot and steer at the same time. Its whirling blades only had bare inches of clearance on either side of the hole, but he made it through, Simeon Blaire jerking along underneath on the end of his chain. Railgun slugs chewed great ragged holes in the Valley View's few remaining stores.

Haszan and the Ashishim fired at once, but their target was rising too fast now, free of the mall and accelerating.

One bullet bit into its landing gear, bursting a fat black tire. The other nearly struck Blaire as he was pulled aloft, swinging wildly like a human wrecking ball. Haszan saw his face as he was pulled up through the smoke; he had the look of the dead Cyben about him; blank, cold and blissful, beyond the needs of the living.

It was then that Haszan remembered Atticus Meaks' promise outside the mall, and realized that their troubles had only just begun.

"*General Extermination Order!*" he coughed, choking on a lungful of smoke. He staggered over to the Ashishim, clawing at his sleeve. "I don't know what they're gonna do, but we have to get gone, NOW!"

Kaito was with them a second later, leaving B-Zerk tucked under cover in the ruined store.

"You RT guys are supposed to have all the secret tunnels and hidden doors," he said to Abdulafia, tucking the revolver into his belt. "Is there some kind of way out of here that the Div don't know about?"

The Ashishim dropped his eyes, his knuckles white around the pistol grip.

"It was back there, I'm afraid. Entombed with my brothers."

"So we go back," said Haszan, contemplating the slew of flaming rubble which blocked off their escape. "At least Simeon bloody Blaire isn't in our way anymore."

The lights on the strange crescent across 'Afia's chest flickered and winked in the flamelight, illuminating his face from below. Haszan could see now, close up, that this man wasn't an *exact* copy of his Kheptarch double. There were different lines and scars etched across the Ashishim's face, and a look of true, contrite regret there that Simeon Blaire would never know.

"I guess we do, then. The spirits tell me it's not our day to die - or else I'd be kind of worried."

"What else do these *spirits* tell you?" asked Haszan, folding his arms across his chest. "They got any ideas about how to get through a line of Comp Div tanks?"

The Ashishim looked up at him with a sad smile on his face - past him, and into the gloom.

"Just this, Jaqub of the Hand of Fatima. There's something coming we have to face together. *And it won't be the last time.*"

Abdulafia pointed, and the others followed his gaze, back into the plaza where the smoke billowed and spiraled up out of a ragged circular hole in the ceiling. In that writhing pall they could all make out moving lights - small, red, purposeful eyes. They were coming closer. Jaq looked back the other way, and saw a swarm of them coming in from that side too.

"It'll be an honor to die with you if they're wrong, though," said the Ashishim, checking the load of his revolver. Its cylinder whirred and clicked into place, and the hammer came back with a clear, punctuating snap. "And you'll both know what happens to them dead Cyben."

"Hey!" said Jaq, finally catching up. "I never told you my name! How the hell do you know my…"

Then the *Dervashi*'s first shot rang out, deafeningly loud, and Haszan turned to follow the bullet's flight.

He cursed.

Suddenly there was a *whole* lot more to worry about than Ashishim parlor-tricks…

Ω

In the palace of the Biotects darkness reigned, shrouding the dead in velvet.

Direktor Vanecke could never have come here in person, to the most hallowed altar of the Three Hundred Purest; not before, in his old life, his old flesh. And definitely not in his current state, as a brain trapped in an isolated, armored skull. Only once had he been let in. Once, and for a cost that would have crippled nations, to buy a child's life and turn him into a weapon…

Even then he'd only been allowed down on the factory floor

with the servants.

But his influence was here, in the form of a Slayer cloud, a tiny swarm of metal and silicon motes which ghosted through Universal's security grid in the dark. Emmanuel had given him the key to this place when he attacked Omnivasive. In death he'd proved to be a much more gracious host than he ever was in life.

Here under the unblinking optics of Vanecke's parasites lay the three hundred identical glass tanks. They held the new bodies of the Kheptic caste, his hated so-called *superiors*.

They were utterly vulnerable, naked and pink behind the dewy panes, like life-sized toys. And without their maker to protect them, they were just as breakable.

Octavio was busy tonight, as the Kheptarchy gathered in the shadow of Jaegenn's spire for their final futile game. Blaire had to be primed, and Leynna Mendelev-Singh would have to be taken care of. Kronos would have to be distracted from its vigilant death-watch over his own wasted body. But he would never be too busy to savor this moment.

The A.I. seneschal of Universal was completely compromised now, its access codes torn out of Lancaster's mind as he was devoured. Throughout his spire servitor creatures lay slumped in postures of death, unable to guard this holy of holies. And while they slept the lights began to dim, flickering from pale yellow to red as Octavio assumed final control.

The life-giving liquid inside the clone tanks was stained bloody crimson by emergency strobes as critical processes were diverted. Fat, fluttering bubbles seethed from their intrinsic recycling systems as the temperature rose, and caustic chemicals flooded in…

Octavio watched, transfixed, as the skin of the clones began to blister and wrinkle, peeling off in long lazy streamers from the flesh beneath. They were melting like plastic under a blowtorch now; Gideon, MacGill, Dawes, even a new and unmodified copy of Simeon Blaire, their tissue dissolving, sloughing off their bones in floating chunks. Disintegrating, like their dreams of power - like their *influence,* under the camera eye of Direktor

Vanecke.

Of course, to murder a Lord was the most heinous of crimes - a transgression punished swiftly and fatally with all the might of immortal Kronos. Octavio was ambitious, and desperate, but he was no fool. His whole estate would be incinerated by orbital particle cannons if he so much as touched a hair on their heads. Inside the game it was different. When he'd tested his strength against them and failed, all bets had been off. The Game was sacred ground.

But here in the palace of the Biotects there were no Lords and Ladies of the Razor Clique. The things which he disposed of were nonpersons, mere chattels for all that they were exact living copies of the Khepts. This wasn't murder in the eyes of Kronos - because these simulacra weren't yet human.

This was just *business*.

At last even their bones cracked and dissolved, leaving each pod filled with a roiling broth of toxins. His work here was done. Tonight, when one of the high-born slipped and missed his strike the game would be all too real - and they wouldn't live to play another day.

Ω

The people of the Reclaimed Territories were on the move tonight, and the reverberation and echo of whole neighborhoods being shifted up inch by inch shook the very walls down here, in the steel-sky ghettos of the Ashishim.

Up above them the Subcity was in motion too - a hive of termites kicked open, its streets filled with rioters and revelers in equal proportions. Giant zeppelins branded with the logo of Omnivasive slipped between the cyclopean towers and smokestacks of Elysium, threedeeo screens on their flanks broadcasting the frenetic crush about Jaegenn's spire. The square at the base of his temple was filled to bursting with Blaire zealots in their blue uniforms.

In other, less public spaces throughout the Subcity - abandoned places and no-mans-lands at the fringes of habitation - the sects of the Reclamation were gaining ground.

Here an empty factory fell to the Aryan Confederacy, here a section of lightless tunnel was claimed by the Confucians. And everywhere, as the confusion spread, the tribes outside the city threw up their ladders and ropes, clawing to get in.

The Ashishim were no exception, because when a tribe had more people than space, every square inch was worth dying for. The ruins which separated the RT from the city itself were unprotected tonight, and their security cameras winked out one by one as black-clad sons of Alamut spraypainted over their lenses.

Down in the Citadel, at the heart of the Ashishim sect, the vast indoor fields of hydroponic ganja lay empty. The mess halls and scriptoria were silent, and the barracks and tenement tunnels were deserted. Every man, woman and child who wasn't out on the front lines was in the War Room, a great oval arena down below sea level. Its reinforced windows stared out into the oily black waters of the Atlantic, but nobody was here for the view.

Here, thousands toiled over a cobbled-together web of computer systems, patched up piecemeal from machines of many centuries. A wall of screens, from modern threedeeo globes to ancient green pixelated VDUs curved around the War Room, and on scaffolds before this edifice of flickering light countless Ashishim techs swarmed with handheld keyboards and headsets, coordinating operations.

Others bustled about the desks which covered the floor, bearing disks and papers, bottles of water and urns of scalding hot coffee, smoking pipes and styrofoam cups of ramen noodles for the staffers who sweated over the numbers.

In the eye of this cyclone a green silk pavilion rose from a mess of cables and plugboards, completely out of place among the heat and buzz of so many machines.

Inside, the Magi of the Ashishim attended their master.

"Unit seven has met Vatican resistance outside floor one-two-nine," reported Magus Verlaine, pushing his 'mersive goggles back up his high forehead as he disconnected. "I've shut down their communications so the tunnel crawlers can get around their flank. The recycling mills on one-thirty-one will be ours within the hour."

The six Magi were seated on a raft of embroidered cushions, amid the drifting smoke of brass filigree censers. Five of them remained in the reverie of control, their minds deep within the immensely ramified web of wetware which permeated the Last City.

Verlaine had only emerged to report his success and gulp down a few mouthfuls of sweet iced water from the pitcher at his elbow before he went under again. To tell the truth, he preferred the cool symmetry of the World Within to the stench and noise of the war room - Verlaine was utterly posthuman, disgusted by the rest of his species.

Oh, of course his Ashishim brothers treated him with the utmost respect, him and his five equals. They were *ancients*, after all - already retrofitted for efficiency and longevity when many of the sons of the sect were only infants. Verlaine had been eighty-nine when the Ashishim stole cloning technology from the Kheptarchy - too old and too laden with powerful machinery to benefit from its use. Now he was just a human face on a suit of damascened silver armor, unable to feel the cushions beneath him, but able to play the Wetsystems like a master musician.

Ordinary people, even the lesser adepts of the Electromagi, were alien to him now, and their company meant little to him - so long as they kept him connected.

"Our countervirals have just blocked another A.I. assault by the Vatican. They're trying to re-open their comms on 129." Veraline blinked a layer of rolling code from his eyes, checking his bio-readouts on a tiny wrist screen. Another four hours inside without a protein infusion would be his limit. "I'm going to trace this one back, and deal with the source personally."

He was about to slide the 'mersive rig back over his head when the figure seated in the center of the pavilion raised one hand, stopping him cold. The High Magus was steeped in shadow, his green robes pooling around him as he sat cross-legged and silent among his soldiers.

"Please, a second of your time, Verlaine," he whispered, in

that smooth and sibilant tone so like the disembodied voice of the wetsystems themselves. "There is a crucial diversion I have been overseeing alone… one which requires another pair of hands."

Verlaine saw the flicker of a smile inside the shadows which cloaked the High Magus, and he felt his own pride unfold across the Vision.

The six of them were constantly seeking the favor of their master - a creature so revered and ancient that he needed no machinery, not the smallest augmentation to master the mysteries of the Wetsystems. Ashishim rumor whispered that Zeon was *always* connected, that he had subverted part of the system to act as an extra battery of minds, and that by this power he was all but omnipresent, omniscient.

"Of course, revered Zeon," he replied, sneaking a glance at the other Magi as they lay in reverie around him. Was it just a coincidence of timing, of luck? Or was he really highest in Zeon's favor?

Of course, he *was* worthy of such trust. No doubt the Master, in his wisdom, could see the quality of his faithful servant… because *others* certainly had. Others who paid him good hard currency to watch his master and report back in iron-bound code. A true adept was only faithful to *himself*, after all.

"The one I want you to operate on is a Cyben, Magus Verlaine," said Zeon, that voice sliding over the top of his thoughts like oil over water. "Access the node within Valley View Plaza first - the network there is in considerable disarray, but we trust in your skill. When you have found the node, locate a deactivated Cyben unit - the new model."

Now the High Magus leaned forward, his hands reaching out to touch Verlaine's temples, to cradle his stainless-steel skull back down to the cloth-of-gold cushions.

"You won't find a Vilicus drone to access – not with this one - but there are other ways to tame such a creature, as I'm sure you know. Re-activate him, and contact me when it is done."

Verlaine felt the power which coursed through Zeon's hands. It burned into his metal skin, expanding the already potent capabilities of his slaved processors. The world dropped away, revealing the immense shining rootwork of the Wetsystems… more capillaries and branches than he'd ever seen before. There, far below, was the tiny red pulse of his target, the snarled and knotted razorwire of security programs twined around a single infinitesimal human figure.

"Go with speed and skill, Verlaine. I have all trust in your abilities."

The words of Illuminatus Zeon flooded him with purpose, and he leaped from the War Room of the Ashishim and into the systems like a hunting hawk, stooping on his prey with the speed of thought itself.

In the little silk pavilion, amid the clatter and hum and bustle of bureaucratic war, Zeon sat, and smiled, and waited. More than he trusted poor vainglorious Magus Verlaine, the lord of the Ashishim trusted his apprentice, the sword in his right hand. Soon Abdulafia would finish off the Vilicus drone which had once had its teeth in Tsien's spine. And then the Super-Cyben would be his to command, as well as its parasitic burden.

Ω

Simeon Blaire slept as Meaks' gunship rose up over the burning Subcity, floating like an ember from the blaze. It was as if his nightmares had been tapped down the wire in the back of his head, and projected huge and heaving across the skin of Elysium. Down there, an army of fanatics were chanting his name. They ground up against the barricades, banners held high, blue flags swirling in the smoke of tear-gas grenades - not just outside the Valley View, but all over the sprawling and rusted barrio that ringed the R.T.

Thousands of them lay handcuffed and broken in a circle of tanks outside the burning mall, and more still were crammed into overloaded meatwagons, cursing and crying. Unaware of the martyrdom and fury of his faithful Simeon Blaire slept in a cocoon of knotted steel tentacles, his mind absent, drained down a neural interface into hell.

Around him another city burned, wildfire tearing hungrily

through silk and paper and cherrywood. Staccato explosions arose from all around him as sturdy bamboo poles exploded chamber by chamber, sending houses down into the inferno in clouds and veils of sparks. They called it 'the flowers of Edo', a beautiful euphemism for the destruction of an entire city.

Blaire thought that perhaps, to those who watched from the immune and impregnable heights of the fortress, that it really did look like a field of red and orange flowers.

He was ascending the stairs of that castle now, great slabs of black marble fronting doors of studded iron - a palace which had never stood at the heart of the old Nipponese capital. This was the dream fortress of his master, a gnarled and twisted spike of masonry which towered over the flames like Satan over Cocytus.

Rows of skeletal soldiers swum in the heat haze; Blaire was unsure if they were statues or living warriors. Showers of sparks reflected in the bright silver of their naked blades, the polished black lacquer of their armor… but their eyes were hollow holes. They seemed to smile knowingly as he passed. Simeon moved through seemingly endless hallways, their roofs torn open to the skies where a wrack of clouds burned red. Ashes fell across the polished floors like snow. And though the walls bent and wavered, and the floor stretched off eternally in an unbroken line, he knew he was moving ever upward.

The final door was a vast disc of nephrite jade, its immense face carved with scenes of war. Around its edges burned a sickly green light, a fire which lit the jade from within, making the carved soldiers struggle against each other as it shifted and pulsed.

Blaire felt his hand move, unbidden, to caress the smooth green surface of the door. He expected it to burn, to sear away his hand to a smoking stump - but the jade was cold, vibrating with power. It kicked under his touch like a great living heart.

"Welcome, my disciple. Welcome to your inheritance. Your destiny…"

A tectonic grind shook the building, sending dust sifting down from above. Then the door gave lurch, rolling away on deep tracks in the stone to reveal his master's sanctum. It was a place suffused with power, where helices of lightning wrapped tight around every pillar, and a rain of ashes fell gently, as silent as snow.

This was the crown of the impossible palace, the very tip of the black pagoda his Lord had dreamed into being. Three hundred arched windows looked out over a sea of fire, a hellscape of ruined buildings and black water. In each stone arch a body hung on barbed chains, crucified with hooks though its bleeding hands and feet. Blaire knew them, all too well. The aristocracy of Elysium were strung up bleeding there, all except one. Between the whipped and beaten corpses of Lords Kyrov and Valchek was an empty space, where hooks and chains spun in the wind. One place was left for him.

The shade of Tokugawa cast a crooked shadow across the octagonal flagstones from his ornate ivory throne, a dark shape in steel and black silk - except for the smoldering green light which issued from the eye-slits of his skeletal helm.

"Come closer, disciple." hissed the shadow, beckoning with one unnaturally long claw. "It is time to begin our *endgame*."

Simeon knelt on the inlaid platform before the throne, laying his sword in front of him in supplication.

"What is your command?" he asked, his eyes averted from that grinning death's-head in its cloud of shadows.

"Do you recall when we began this, Blaire?" asked Tokugawa, seeming to shrink and deflate to human size as he spoke. One hand traced the line of his disciple's bowed shoulders. "I gave you an advantage over all these poor deluded fools. I gave you the gift of life - by taking away your immortality."

Simeon nodded - it was true. At first he'd been afraid to fight when the promise of a new cloned body had been taken away. But the thrill of battle was so much stronger and sweeter when his life was truly at stake. He had learned to channel that desperation into unstoppable rage, instinctive skill.

"And of course, you remember the *fear*."

Blaire felt the power coursing through his master's hand as it wrapped around his skull, and he felt that fear wash over him again. The first engagement, knowing that if he failed it would be forever. The first time he felt a blade slice through his all-too-precious skin, the cold knot of terror blooming into anger, into killing rage.

"Tonight is the final game, Simeon. And so I have done the same for all of them." Tokugawa gestured around the chamber, at the crucified bodies of the Kheptarchy swinging on their chains.

And Blaire saw the disintegrating faces of three hundred lords, their clone vats digesting them where they'd grown, the flicker of warning strobes across ranks of glass coffins...

"It is time, Disciple. Destroy them in their weakness!"

Green fire flared in the pits of his Master's eyes, avid and hungry.

Simeon felt it coming, the itch at the base of his spine growing like a tumor, the artificial rage flooding his senses, narrowing his vision to a haze or red.

The room blurred up around him, liquid jade through with lightning. It became an endless vertical shaft down which he fell, plummeting like a great fatal comet-core toward the wall of consciousness...

From his window Octavio watched his helicopter gunship go scything through the smoky dusk, his life support tank swiveling to face the tall leaded panes. The tiny khaki machine settled like an insect alighting on an improbable flower; atop the glowing blue spire of House Jaegenn.

His weapon was prepared, and out of its cage. Soon the plans which Vanecke had put in motion decades ago would come to fruition, and the illusion of Tokugawa's palace would be made real - three hundred crucified lords paying dead-eyed supplication to his throne.

17 Aevum Oblivio
Burn the Earth

ZHE STOOD ATOP the cube as it came to life. From the dim darkness far below him a tsunami of light erupted upward, row after row of mirrored panes coruscating with pale blue fire.

It peaked as the countdown ended, just as Zhe had predicted. The Forge couldn't proceed without the machine's mind live and firing.

He only had a second to feel smug and superior before it all went wrong.

The cubes around him were lighting up now, dust and cobwebs blowing away in ragged veils, a starburst with him standing at ground zero. And as he watched the blue light bled into the slavesystem armor at his feet, sending tendrils of cobalt radiance up his legs.

It moved faster than he could follow; a web of blue fire binding up his whole hybrid body.

Even the looming darkness of the Worm seemed to shrink as the light suffused his metal skin, keening and hissing as Zhe's vision shut down, clamped between surging walls of code.

It was Kronos.

His voice was emotionless, loud as the tectonic grinding of continents... it blew away reason behind a wall of sound.

RELAY ALL PROCESSES THE STANDBY COMMAND...

RE-ROUTING POWER FROM PRIMARY WETSYSTEM FUNCTIONS...

PROCEEDING TO INITIALIZE FORGE PROTOCOL...

Zhe's eyes were forced open.

He looked down on the blackened Earth from above, from camera eyes in low orbit.

The satellites were pregnant with nuclear weapons, racks and racks of sleek bombs gripped in their steel ovipositors. Now, as the Forge gyre began to form, their targeting cogitators flickered with light and purpose, seeking a target.

`READING AN ENERGY PULSE BUILDING UP OVER AREA 194a85j`

FORGE PRIMED… OPENING ALPHA-ZERO BLAST DOORS…
+++194a85j DISTURBANCE HAS PEAKED+++
DISCHARGE IS APPROACHING… SHIELD SAT-CAMS —
WEAPONS LOCK ACHIEVED — FIRE / FIRE / FIRE

Illusions unfolded out of nowhere, sliding in like slivers of glass.

But all Technician Zhe could see was Kronos's memory of an earlier holocaust, of billions of people reduced to ashes. He pushed their suffering aside with all his will, shutting out the sick, crawling feeling of disease that rode in on the same wavelength.

It was PLAYING with him! It wanted him here, to see it crush and kill and erase the only thing which held it back. It wanted to let Zhe know that he had failed, like doomed, mad Nyl before him…

For a second the floor beneath his feet lurched sideways, grinding to the bedrock.

The whole city shook as the Forge was cut to pieces, pierced like a bubble by a raving blast of black lightning.

But it was a trap.

Switch cameras. Watch…

The shadow of the energy pulse lay across the wasteland like a welt, a whipscar. It was a furrow ploughed with impossible physics, forty feet deep.

And it was an arrow aimed direct at Zhe's allies, a killing target.

Satellite cameras clicked and whirred in the vacuum, tracing it back to a valley in southern Afrika. They took a second, two, three, to plot trajectories.

Then from their bellies and grasping interior claws fell a rain of bombs, black teardrops slicked over with ceramic re-entry shields.

Enough overkill, surely, to burn every trace of Zhe's allies from the Earth forever…

17 Aevum Oblivio
The Two-Dimensional Scalpel

WE HAVE POSITIVE VISUAL…
FIRST WAVE BOMBS ARE ENTERING
STRIKE RANGE…

ZHE WAS NO *Kataphrakt; his masters didn't trust him with things like the Reality Screw or the Singularity Cannon or the enigmatic Forbidden Box.*

But he was a grade-twelve Technician, and he'd brought a whole dusty carpetbag of tools to Earth with him. Things which might not be able to stop a rain of death falling on his unknown allies, but which might just make their demise something more than an empty gesture.

Zhe held out one hand, and a tiny scalpel rose up out of his rippling silver palm, its black and featureless blade no larger than a fingernail.

Maybe the power holding back the Forge was strong enough to deflect a handful of nuclear weapons, maybe not. But with this, Zhe could sever the mind of Kronos from its infected neurostrata.

The disease which gripped the Forge would be excised like tumor, packed away in ammonia ice and magnetic clamps for the scientists of Liquid Space. If they got their claws into it Zhe might even be able to feel sorry for the poor thing.

With a flick of his wrist he brought the scalpel down, as swift and deadly as the bombs which streaked the Afrikan sky.

He couldn't help but watch as they plunged toward their target.

It was a crater valley – a scar on the face of Afrika like a vast lidless eye. Whatever titanic forces had carved this place out of the earth were about to be overshadowed, once and for all.

Zhe spiraled in through a vortex of data, taking control of the nose-cone camera of a single twenty-megaton bomb. His new electric eye picked out the winking aquifer lake at the crater's heart, the dense snarl of jungle which swarmed up its slopes, thinning as the water dropped out from under it.

He saw movement up on the crater rim – something artificial.

At precise intervals around the hundred-mile edge of the valley stood towers of black stone, and from the crown of each one a mirrored disc was rising, borne up on hydraulic arms which must be hundreds of feet long. Zhe tried to zoom in, but the grainy image from the bomb cameras was useless...

Then it was too late.

The first bomb bloomed open in a thunderflash of white heat, then another followed, and another. But something had gone wrong. Not a ripple caressed the flat surface of the aquifer lake. They'd struck something, up there above their target, and as Zhe switched back to a spaceborne satellite camera he saw it for what it is.

A dome of force covered the valley, a tegulated shield which the atomic blasts sleeted off like rain.

Zhe's alien smile was terrible to behold.

Now, when the Enemy was weakest. While it crowed over the orgasmic rush of nuclear fire...

He struck down hard, the blade of his scalpel lengthening and growing transparent, a miniature version of a Kataphrakt's probability sword. It's glassy tendrils ramified through the cube in resonant harmony with its wielder, branching out along the same pathways as the disease.

The Worm screamed.

Black pain savaged the Technician's body - he was infected, too, and his every nerve blazed with hellfire for an instant. He felt his enemy trying to force itself back through the crack in reality, like a black anemone pulling in its soft, poisonous tentacles.

Zhe almost missed the immense counterblast above the target zone. It tore through a forest of mushroom clouds, shredding them to ribbons.

Just as he'd used the Worm's distraction to strike, so had his unknown allies.

Zhe ripped secrets from Kronos's brain even as his scalpel tore it apart...

```
SECOND WAVE NEUTRON BOMBS
PRIMED FOR IMPACT
FUSION REACTION OCCURRING WITHIN THE TARGET
```

SWITCH PROGRAM TO AIRBURST - ONE, FIVE, ZERO…
STEPPING UP TO ANTIMATTER REACTION
WARNING! CRITICAL THRESHOLD BREACH!

Through the eyes of the satellites he watched a black cyclone open up beneath him, a vast hungry maw with blazing arcs of lightning for fangs. Each flickering blast illuminated a horrorworks of limbs and teeth and scales, a writhing vortex of flesh, at the center of which beat a great incorporeal heart.

The dome had turned reality inside out. Now it was concave, *blurring the geometries of three-dimensional space, a living, pulsing thing called into being for one terrible purpose.*

It was compressing all those nuclear explosions into a vast floating sphere, crushing them between invisible hands.

And now it began to quicken.

Disintegrating molecules howled, and a flaying wind began to spiral around the dome…

The heart spasmed, once, in orgasmic release.

From space, the blast of warped energy crowned the globe with pillars of flame. A handful of satellites were torn from their orbits, gripped by raving black halos of fire. In the silence of vacuum there was no sound at all. Melting, seething, they were crushed smaller and smaller, folding in on themselves like burning insects, now the size of a fist, now that of a pinhead…

The dome shivered, twisted through dimensions with a sickening lurch, and was gone.

And so were Kronos's orbital defenses.

Across the burnt Sahara, the dead Rad-lands which cloaked Afrika, a great spiral wind howled. It came blasting out from the target zone and across the sand, setting up stormfronts miles high. As the blue light faded, and the cubes within the device core slowly flickered out, Zhe dropped his spent scalpel and applauded, laughing.

2196 Anno Arbitrium
Repurposed

Leynna was prepared for an evening of sophisticated pleasure; dressed in silks and jewels, armed to the teeth, and already on her third vodka martini. Her Consolidated Industries Phaeton sliced through the crowds with a whisper of ethanol turbines, a powder-blue arrow angling toward the lights of the Jaegenn spire. Under its passenger dome, Baroness Mendelev-Singh sharpened the edges of her favorite pair of daggers, running one blade along a whetstone as the stereo hummed soothing muzak.

On either side of the sunken causeway fans of the Game were piled up in ranks, watching the bizarre procession which ferried the Kheptarchy to their revels.

Leynna's wasn't the only Phaeton (Consolidated had built thirteen of them, but only one in her favorite shade of blue), but some of the Lords and Ladies displayed their wealth and eccentricity by arriving in a whole museum-full of bizarre vehicles.

Duchess Sebren - the Synthesoy monopolist - clattered by in a gilded carriage borne on innumerable silver insect legs. Viscount Ermiliuo Xochard took delight in his air-polluting ground-crawler from the distant twentieth century - an immense and inefficient device called a 'Lincoln Town Car'. Most outre of all was Lady Ariadne Choseem's gyro-balanced monowheel, a ponderous device originally designed (although its intended use was long forgotten) for mining tunnels in asteroids.

The crowds loved it; it was an old-fashioned pageant - a reminder of the chasmic status gap between themselves and the Kheptarchy. Camera flashes burst in waves as the Phaeton edged closer to the riverhead of the red carpet, and to the immense rotary parking wheel which would accept the limousine. Leynna slipped her gold-inlaid daggers into a pair of white leather sheathes at her belt, then checked her makeup one last time for the threedeeo.

There were an awful lot of Blaire fans out there tonight, and they looked almost as feral as their hero himself. It wouldn't do to look anything less than her best when she disappointed them all.

Ω

Saint Pete's again, and the concrete steamed in the light of overhead halogen arcs, dipping and bobbing on their guywires. Around the edges of Pope Joan's playground the night people were waking up – chemheads too far gone to pay their rent, discarded lobo'd slaves with cortex-jackwires trailing… wreckage.

A body sat swaddled in bandages and rags between their cardboard shanties, red eyes peering out at the world from behind a curtain of matted hair. On closer inspection, the thing appeared to be male, human, and freshly disinterred from a shallow grave.

He wasn't a beggar or a drunk like the Subcity dregs on either side of his patch - just shellshocked, and up to the eyeballs on synthemorph to soothe his shattered nerves.

Clonehunter Melchior had found himself unemployed, broke and broken after the debacle at Don Vincenzo's. And while there weren't many injuries that the Black Techs couldn't repair, but it was a matter of *credit*. Otherwise they were prone to just harvest a few of your choicest internal organs while they had you on the slab.

Melchior's credit had run to just enough coin to pop some morphine-analog out of a sidewalk vending machine, so he sat there huffing on the inhaler with two broken legs, pondering his next move through a haze of drug euphoria. He supposed he could hock his swords, but then he'd be without the tools of his only trade. If it wasn't clonehunting then it was running bounties for the cops, or signing up as a soldier with one of the Reclamationist militias. Melchior could dig the free blunts you scored from the Ashishim; it was just that they might be a bit sensitive about him attacking their *Dervashimen* back there.

The little clonehunter sighed.

You could never rely on *professionalism*, these days.

So he sat, and rode the buzz, and felt a little sorry for himself as the sun went down behind the jagged towers and chimneys of Elysium. With the crush and flow of foot traffic - not to mention the creeping buzz of the morph - Melchior didn't see the man in the ragged yellow oilskins until he was right on top of him. Under his floppy fisherman's hat the guy wore an old black ventilator mask which hissed and wheezed alarmingly, chuffing little bursts of condensed gas. The eyes which bugged out from behind its grimy plastic bubbles were bloodshot yellow.

Melchior briefly wondered if he was capable of fighting off this human wreck with two broken legs and head full of bad drugs. When the oilskin man's hand disappeared into his noisome coat he thought he'd have to try – but it came back out holding an antique mobile phone, a gray plastic brick with a stubby antenna screwed into the top.

There were no words, just the hiss and moan of that busted ventilator. But he held the phone out insistently in one bandaged hand, his eyes staring holes through Melchior's skull.

All of a sudden it started ringing.

The oilskin man shook it in Melchior's face, his eyes frantic behind their plastic bubbles.

As soon as Melchior snatched it out of the man's greasy fingers a voice crackled from its speaker; one that Melchior had heard before when he was skulking around Lancaster's offices. It wasn't a welcome surprise.

Octavio, from Omnivasive.

When he looked up the man in the yellow oilskins was gone - only the smell of old, hot rubber marked his passing. He pressed the phone to his ear, scowling.

"Melchior, so pleased to talk to you! Listen… I've got some bad news about your old boss - you know how business is, right Mel? Mind if I call you Mel? Good. Great! Now, I'm a little rushed here, you know how big the Game is going to be tonight, and of course, we're getting exclusive… anyway, Old Man Lancaster is no more. Six feet deep, Mel, and feeding the worms. You heard it here first - *and I have a deal for you.*"

Melchior tried to rip the phone away from his ear. But the

damned thing was impossible to move! The clonehunter applied all his sinewy strength to the little plastic brick, wrenching it down hard. The burst of agony which followed convinced him to stop trying.

"I take it from those little yelping noises that you've found out about the telephone?" Vanecke laughed as Melchior's nails scrabbled against hard plastic. "So, listen. The *good* part is ten thousand Slades, free medical for those pins, and payroll with Omnivasive. The *bad* part only happens if you say no."

Melchior could see at least five static cameras from where he sat on the side of the street - there was no way he wanted to be a threedeeo-bite of gore on the late news. Who knew what kind of deadly device waited to pop out of that old-world, oversized mobile?

"The ambulance is on its way, Mel," said the Direktor. "Chin up, and wait for my word."

No doubt he was reading Melchior's expression from multiple angles, looking for a tight shot of his head exploding.

"O.K! Fine!" breathed the Clonehunter, his pulse pounding in his throat. "I'm your man. What…what should I do first?"

"Good. Good. I like that tone. Kind of kiss-ass meets fuckin' terrified. And hey, Mel - The bomb's not in the phone, not anymore. By now it's already gone through your eardrum. 'Should be about three minutes until its right in the middle of your brain. Remember that if you have any second thoughts."

There was a very final little click, and then silence.

As the line went dead the heavy antique mobile fell away from Melchior's ear, pulling in a sickening skein of hair-thin anchor wires. It cracked open on the pavement, revealing a hollow shell around a pressurized black canister – the weight was all fat slugs of junk metal. He swore he felt the burrowing, relentless medi-scarabs at work in his skull, even over the fuzz and spin of the artificial morphine.

But Direktor Vanecke kept his part of the deal.

The Meditek ambulance came for him, a stretcher on a pair of rickshaw wheels salvaged from ancient bicycles. They took him down to Saint Pete's, into the plastic caverns of the Vatican

Black Technologists.

The operation was just a brief flash of darkness, while drugs more expensive and powerful than vending-machine morph allowed the 'teks to core out his femurs and replace them with lightweight billet aluminum rods, inset with hydraulic pistons which would enable him to take three-storey falls on the run. The fat crimson arteries which lay up against them were sheathed in woven diamond tubes, and his skin patched over with shockproof mesh, all at a cost of only forty thousand Slades. There was a little discount for the precious bone-marrow the Mediteks took out of him, stashed in cryo-reliquaries for future customers.

It was only an hour later when Melchior zipped up for his first mission as an Omnivasive man, expensive chem-flush still singing in his veins.

Of the ten large that the Direktor wired to his bank account, the ex-clonehunter spent three on his new outfit - a digital camouflage skinsuit complete with a strap-over kevlar shell. When the suit's processors kicked in Melchior went chameleon, invisible unless he cast a shadow. His chunky new boots plugged into the suit, and were skinned up the same. They packed spring-loaded knives in their heels like a rooster's spurs, and little tazer prongs on each toecap.

Another two gs went on an optics rig; four big bubble lenses which wrapped around his head on thick rubber belts. Melchior carefully appliqued a thin skin of digital camo over the lenses, wiring them into the suit's processor. His expanded field of view showed him the full three-sixty, picture-in-picture crisp. Every spectrum was covered, and tiny earpieces cranked up his hearing until the click and slide of insect legs on glass was almost deafening.

Check – exclusion software, too.

One final chunk of currency went on the most advanced hand cannon he could afford (and lift), a Zweig and Barnes 12mm micro-missile launcher. A nasty sampler pack of little warheads slotted into its four chambers, promising every kind of death from the silent to the spectacularly messy.

Melchior felt like an ace assassin from some kind of action threedeeo as he set out through the dusk-lit city, an invisible wraith wrapped in deadly technology. The effect was only spoiled by the vast bubbles of cheap pink gum which appeared out of nowhere as he walked, inflating and popping at head-height as he pressed through the crowds.

His mission took him high up the dome cluster, to the gates of Mendelev-Singh Biomed.

The spire of Leynna's family estate sprung from a tight coil of prefab manufacturing blocks, steel tori originally designed to be assembled in space. Their pressurized interiors were perfect for the kind of work MSB specialized in - mediware, hospital machinery and drugs.

Lots of drugs.

Melchior could totally dig the residuals on *this* job.

The clonehunter slipped into the 'factorium through one of its lower levels, a mekan maintenance shop where human beings seldom ventured. Tractomorphic lockpicks sprung from his fingers like claws.

Inside, neon tubes cast deep shadows from rusting piles of medical mekan waste - robosurgeons, autonomous wheelchairs and discarded cybernetic limbs stacked to the ceiling. Here and there tracked scavenger units rattled across the meshwork floor, their pinprick red sensors swiveling back and forth on multi-jointed necks. Arcs of blue and orange sparks spumed from a row of repair benches where mekan soldered and cut, patching together working machines from a mountain of scrap.

All the clangor and shifting light made Melchior's stealthy entrance easy. His suit was charged up, and its shifting pattern of riveted aluminum and iron rendered him all but invisible. In the shadow of a chemical tank he unfolded the little map he'd drawn himself, the brown recycled paper appearing out of thin air. This place was a maze, but he was on the right track.

The corporate bloc was right ahead, up a spiral staircase fashioned from reclaimed hospital gurneys. The camera above its corroded airlock door never registered the shadow which stole up to it, slim fingers flexing a tiny sliver of LCD matrix as they slipped it over the lens. The little patch of screen would show a long loop of the workshop and the doorway while Melchior was inside. Even his lockpick-work went completely unnoticed, and he slid crabwise along the white plastic wall of the corridor beyond, his suit now as smooth and milky as its sterile surface. Safe.

Or at least, so he thought for the first few seconds.

Mister Vanecke had warned him about the dogs.

What he hadn't disclosed was the fact that they could walk on the ceilings.

The sixth sense which Melchior had cultivated over years of hunting criminals, clones and rogue mekan made the hairs on the back of his neck stand to attention. It made his hand spring for his Zweig hand-cannon just as a huge raw-ochre shape dropped from above, all knuckle-dragging hooks and mismatched teeth trailing drool. There were no alarms, but the white light cut out with the shock of a bullet impact, flashing instantly to red.

Melchior saw his suit's pixels rush to catch up, crimson erupting across the milky white fabric like arterial spray. And then its weight hit him, a thing like a greasy sack of nails and slippery muscle, bearing him to the ground while his finger scrabbled for the trigger.

Melchior's first shot erupted from the Zweig with a chuff of compressed gas, powerful enough to lift the dog off his chest before its warhead detonated. It was a snarl round; about two hundred yards of diamond wire stuffed into a casing on top of a plastic-explosive core, and when it popped the dog was diced instantaneously. Mel felt his smart kevlar hardening to stop slivers of tooth and bone from tearing him up at the same time.

Adrenaline and echoes hammered through his skull as gore dripped from his face, sliding from his teflon-coated lenses.

He watched the dog's head roll to a stop down the corridor, its vicious upper and lower jaws lolling open, its six eyes burst like overripe fruit. It came to rest between a pair of forepaws armed with sickle-hooks of serrated keratin - another of the fearsome creatures was there, its nostrils flaring to the scent of fear and blood.

Melchior's fingers were slick with gore as he operated the wheel on the Zweig's grip, trying to select a less noisy and messy means of dispatch. But the dog moved fast, liquid, its six legs bunching and springing with ropes of extra, grafted muscle. Its upper and lower jaws hinged and snapped as it leaped at him, those velociraptor claws flying in eviscerating arcs…

Training and instinct took over.

Melchior's hand whipped the heavy gun down as he danced aside, shattering the dog's upper jaw. Then the flying chunk of metal came up, diagonal, splitting its lower jaw like a shell of porcelain. There was a noise behind him, the merest click of claws on plastic; and while the first dog was stunned Mel spun on his toes, emptying a clip of six flechette rounds into another beast behind him. Without turning back his other hand sliced low, a knife flashing as it transfixed the broken dog, still grinding its shattered jaws in agony.

Melchior pulled his knife free in the same movement, flicking it up into the ceiling. The impaled carcass of yet another dog fell to his left, its spine severed by the hissing microscopic chainsaw teeth which flowed around the edge of the blade. The Zweig's wheel spun again, selecting poison needle rounds tipped with artificial spider venom.

Gas chuffed out as it spat poisonous death, making sure the cloned monsters were finished.

Melchior's four blank lenses scanned the corridor in both directions, but nothing moved. It seemed that this hunting pack was only four strong, and all of them were dead. There would be more, now that the silent alarms were tripped. The red light didn't downshift to white as Melchior stooped to cut the head of one of the dogs open, marveling at the grotesque and precise engineering of its blunt, wide face, its six recessed eyes, those twin jaws packed with arrowhead teeth. Direktor Vanecke had found out how to get around Mendelev-Singh Biomed's little puppies, a nugget of information gleaned from the files of poor dead Lancaster.

His slippery fingers found it.

Melchior heard the sound of another dog approaching just as he tore the control unit free from inside the armored brain-pan of his victim. The smooth little slug of chrome felt hot and heavy in his gloved hand, a thing more vital and alive than the carcass he'd left his knife in. Mel popped it into his mouth, grimacing at the taste of bioengineered blood and brains, but feeling it vibrate and kick as his internal body heat switched it back on.

The dog approached him slowly, confused by the welter of scents in the close, dry air of the corridor. Its claws clattered against the plastic floor as it advanced, its ugly broad muzzle swinging from left to right like the auto-tracking barrel of a phalanx gun. Six unblinking eyes stared up at Melchior, while the dog's twin jaws ground slowly back and forth, thin runnels of drool coursing from between its lips to the bloody ground. There was no growl, no ears or tail by which to read the creature's mood.

Just a cold and level gaze from six flat black jewels, set in deep cups of bone.

Vanecke had told him that this would work, so long as he didn't break and run.

The dog's dark red nose sniffed at his hand for a second, for two, brushing up against his knuckles as they clenched around the Zweig's carbon grip.

Melchior stood rooted to the spot, muscles tight, sweat beading behind his optics mask. If Octavio was wrong, that hand would be the first to go, swallowed up gun and all... But the dog kept walking, picking its way over the mangled bodies of its fellows without so much as a sniff at so much free fresh meat. And Melchior started breathing again.

From the scene of the slaughter it wasn't far to his final target.

Melchior slipped unseen and undetected through the red-lit corridors, skulking past more of the biotek dogs as the harvested identifier bead pulsed in his stomach. In a few hours it would be coming right back out; not something that Mel looked forward to.

The coordinates that Direktor Vanecke had sent him led him to a cool white cell deep in the 'factorium bowels of MS

Biomed. The ex-clonehunter's skin crawled with distaste as he looked around the little shrine that Leynna had erected to Simeon Blaire.

There were holographic images of the Kheptarch plastered from floor to ceiling, vials of his blood, parings of hair and skin preserved in slivers of lucite. And in the center of the cell, a pillar of glass which contained a humming purple globe, a sphere wrapped in tubes and wires. An exo-womb. His target.

Obsession was so *freaky*. Compared to this little tableau, Mel's fuzzy stunn habit seemed squeaky clean.

But Vanecke had been very specific about this little piece of technology. Within the fluid-filled globe of plastic waited the seed of a new life - a genetically modified being which Leynna had g-written personally. She had commissioned the fetus illegally, having it coded by the Liquid Tong from samples of her own flesh - and the small pieces of Simeon Blaire she'd scavenged from knives, throwing-daggers and darts.

Melchior's payload on this little mission was a needle filled with a neat retrovirus, a concoction whipped up by the subverted machinery of House Lancaster.

There'd be no need for Blaire's DNA to unlock the womb. Not when the child's whole helix was changed from the inside out...

Melchior's needle slipped through the taut skin of the sphere and into the gelid flesh of the embryo within. He pulled a folded piece of paper from his pocket and tapped a code into the machine's keypad, a twenty-eight number cipher which he'd been given by the Direktor.

In a matter of hours a new member of the Kheptarchy would be born, forcegrown to maturity inside that pressure-cooker womb.

Ω

The last thing he remembered was his fall.

Down through endless smooth steel tunnels, through clouds of scalding radioactive steam which peeled the skin from his bones. Into light, and into new extremes of pain, into the crushing and grinding gears of a vast machine which milled souls from the grist of human bodies.

Zone Doubt heard the voice of his old friend, calling out to him through the Wetsystems. It cut through the forced amnesia which had chained him into the form of a defense drone, a thing called PDR909. It tore away the darkness, and gave him back control. That, and a form built for war.

Zone was back.

His body was unfamiliar, bulky and hard, a smooth carapace of steel with a circlet of camera eyes perched above a row of cannons. His hands had once slim-fingered and dexterous, able to cut tags smooth and fast with his little pocketknife. Now they were furled tentacles of shiny alloy, wrapped up between row upon row of heat-seeking missiles.

The means to control this strange new form were wired into his brain, innate as instinct. He was flying through the smoke of a burning city, through pillars of choking soot and chemical fumes, over and under collapsing pylons and pipes and ducts.

On his way toward where B-Zerk was calling for him.

The little guy was in danger, and Zone Doubt was going to help him out.

Ω

"There they are! Left flank! They're massing again!"

Kaito spotted the first one as it came clicking across the tiles, out of the drifting smoke, its red laser rangefinders glittering like eyes. The Vilicus drone was slick with embalming fluid and gore; ragged strips of plastic trailed from its tentacles where it had torn itself from the back of a broken Cyben.

Kaito squeezed off a round from his revolver; the last. It hammered a crater into the ground near the scuttling silver drone, but the thing was too fast for him to follow. Those four long drill-tipped arms moved like liquid, and now the big Ashishim hand-cannon was dry. Kaito slipped the great hunk of metal under his belt and pulled out his trusty railpistols.

Now hordes of the machines were coming in, their drill-tips tapping out a ceaseless rhythm against the tiles, dragging bundles of smaller tentacles beneath them in a tangle of cutters and probes. As the smoke shifted Kaito could see more of them swarming across the ceiling, their drills biting into the cerametal with disturbing ease. It was all too easy to imagine them grinding through human flesh…

"Break right! Hit them with all you've got!"

To his left Abdulafia's gun roared, and one of the drones disintegrated in a shower of blue sparks. The splinters of it cut apart the drone behind, shrapnel hacking it off at the legs.

Haszan let off his last two bullets at the drones above, shattering one as it dropped, drills whining, almost right on top of him. His second shot ripped a tentacle from another of the crawling machines, making it hiss and thrash before it dragged itself forward again, inexorable.

Kaito crunched numbers while his pistols bucked and blazed - but it didn't look good. There were too many of the little bastards, and they were far too fast…

As Kaito popped a spent clip from his right-hand gun one of the drones curled itself up and struck. He tried to put a round through it as it arced through the smoke toward him, but he was far too slow. The railgun slug glanced off its metal shell, and then its drills were in his arm, ripping hungrily through his clothes and into flesh and bone. They bored into his bicep, injecting a cocktail of soporific drugs. Blood welled up around them, hot and bright.

Red, he noticed. Red, not blue. The scarabs in his blood had given out, fried by the drone's countermeasures.

Kaito gritted his teeth and put the flat muzzle of the railpistol up against the drone's shiny carapace. Once, twice, the vast magnetic energies of the little gun slammed superheated steel through the mekan's skin, tearing its innards out in a blast of fluids and wires. The thing sagged, its laser eyes dimmed. And through the haze of chemicals and smoke a giant chrome hand came down on its broken shell, crushing it to ruin. The pain of those slick metal tentacles pulling loose almost made him pass out cold.

It was Jaq Haszan, and never in his life had Kaito been so happy to see his ugly, scarred-up face.

"Dead Cyben… huh! I liked them better when they were cops!" He spat out a mouthful of blood, grinning red in the firelight. "I think we've got them on the run, though. Between me and the Ashishim over there, you might even be able to take a break soon…"

Then Haszan's eyes went wide, and his smile disappeared. He looked down at his feet, and Kaito followed the direction of his stare. There was a hand clamped around the big biker's ankle, fingers like sections of blackened hosepipe slicked over with wipe-clean laminate.

"Kaito. Do you see that? Is that what I think it is?"

The Cyben's face was half gone - it must have caught a bullet from Ramon or one of the Celestial soldiers during the firefight, but its brain was just so much dead weight. The drone welded to its spine hadn't seen fit to disengage, and now the crippled thing dragged itself up between Haszan's legs, groaning like one of the damned.

Kaito gritted his teeth, leveling his railpistols at the abomination, and pulled both triggers.

Nothing. Not even a click. The clips were empty, the batteries drained.

"Fuckin' DO something, man!" whispered Haszan as the Cyben's neuro-bonded railgun slid out from the charred meat of its forearm. It was pointed right at his face.

Out in the vault of the mall the Vilicus drones were massing again, preparing for a second attack. He could hear their drills squealing as they scuttled across the ceiling.

So he did something. The weedy little hacker - the guy who'd rather face a horde of metavirals than swing a punch - stomped down on the Cyben's ravaged face with one boot, hysterical, slamming down again and again. It was like Orwell in reverse.

Jaq dived left as the railgun spat steel, tearing a smoldering circular hole in his coat.

But despite its terrible wounds the machine just wouldn't lie down and die. It dragged itself forward, rolling onto its belly, its ice-blue eyes flashing murder… and Kaito bit back on a scream.

Off in his peripheral vision he saw Jaq struggling to rip

a length of rebar from the rubble, but in his own little world time had slowed to a crawl. The half-dead officer leered at him knowingly, lining up its railgun on his chest...

And then Abdulafia was there, descending out of the dark like a phantom, his holocloak reflecting the flames in curling waves. He landed right on top of the crawling Cyben with a giant panga knife clenched in each fist, his lips peeled back from his teeth in a snarl.

In that instant Kaito wasn't sure which was worse... the groaning corpse aiming a cannon at his vitals, or the inhuman face of the Ashishim warrior.

Then in ceased to matter.

'Afia's knives came together like scissor blades, taking off the Cyben's head with a sound like a bottle being uncorked. Blood flew wide in a crimson fan, spattering the *Dervashi's* face. And the Vilicus drone tore free from its flesh, propelled skyward on jets of compressed gas.

Haszan's rebar caught it on the downswing - the same haymaker shot he'd used on Simeon Blaire. This time his target wouldn't be getting up again. The tiny mekan blew apart like a glass ornament, crackling with electric fire.

"Um... thanks," said Kaito, tucking his pistols into his belt. All he had left now was his chakutazer; not really his weapon of choice. "Now, do you think we can get out of here before they try it again?"

"I'd like to say so," said Abdulafia, wiping the gore from his knives. "But *listen*. They're all around us. They were probably just waiting to see if our headless friend here was going to finish you off for them."

No sooner had the words left his lips than they saw them... a swarm of drones coming in from all sides, their rangefinders quartering the gloom. Why these, thought the Kayzi. Why not warmekan, needle-flies... long range snipers? Because, said the part of his brain which stood outside the smell of burning meat and cordite, *Kronos wants to slave somebody*. The Guardian Engine must be fishing for Simeon Blaire...

"Time to get to work, then," said Jaq, clenching up his metal fist.

"Let's show them who we are, city boys! *Ur'azdaal iktami!* Blood of the Ashishim!"

But Kaito no longer cared who he was or where he'd come from. He'd even forgotten the coded blast which the Ashishim had stabbed through his brain when he was inside the node. He was no longer a hacker, a wannabe magus. He was no longer even a Kayzi, a biker, a human being. His chakutazer crackled into life as the mekan charged, and he became one with the moment.

Long gashes covered his arms; he could see blood flying through the slow-motion haze which had become his world. Loops of crimson gore splattered the drones as they came on in waves - his blood and the Ashishim's and Jaq's all together. Haszan's hand was a sledgehammer, 'Afia's knives a spinning storm of death. But all the rage in the world wouldn't have been enough.

Now a few of the more curious mekan had spotted B-Zerk, their feeler tentacles twitching like insect antennae as he staggered from the ruined storefront. Kaito's mouth tried to move, his lungs tried to scream a warning to the little soot-smeared figure stumbling through the rubble. Instead he felt the tip of a Cyben drill plow into his shoulder – clean through, ripping out a core of minced flesh. It burst through his skin with a high-pitched whine, dragging the drone up and onto his chest. Slivers of bone grated together as Kaito fell to his knees, screaming.

He saw Abdulafia's face twitch, one of his panga knives flying end over end to slice the drone in half. Kaito watched the rippled steel bite into the mekan's shell, still locked hungrily to his shoulder. He felt his collarbone snap - heard the terrible, final sound of it over the crump of the explosion.

One steel tentacle stayed jammed through his chest as the detonation axehandled him to the floor, curled up around his agony. His breath bubbled with gore, shallow and fading. The last thing he saw was Abdulafia, the *Dervashi* on his knees, three whining drills erupting from his stomach.

One knife hadn't been enough; he'd killed himself to save Kaito.

A tangle of entrails gushed out between those writhing chromed tentacles, slapping wetly against the tiles.

Sensing that the tide had turned, three of the crawling mekan set upon Haszan. Tentacles wound around his arms and legs like vines choking a great rainforest tree. Kaito watched his immense frame straining against their grip, cords of muscle standing out from his neck like steel hawsers. But a final drone was up on his shoulders, and its spinning drills were unstoppable. They came down hard, and Haszan' face contorted with pain.

Abdulafia tried to reach him, tried to move, but the nerve-clamps and trauma systems stitched into his body had flooded him with pseudomorph. As the drug took hold of his brain he toppled sideways to the bloody tiles, his mouth open in a silent scream.

'Afia watched one of Haszan's tiny silver charms, torn from off that ludicrous long whipcord beard, falling end over end through the smoky air; a little iron cross which clattered to the floor right next to his open and paralyzed eyeball. Even the ability to blink was gone.

Off out of sight he could hear the sound of drill-tipped tentacles scuttling closer…

DOCUMENT INSERT: MULTIPLICITY ARCHIVES DEPARTMENT

Agartta: A mystical city from which the alleged
'Invisibles' run the affairs of the world. In
the parlance of the Subcity the name refers to
a legendary second city somewhere out in the
rad-lands, a place philosophically and some say
militarily opposed to Elysium.

While officially the Direktoriat denies the
existence of any such city, rumors of Agartta
still sift up out of the pit, whispered of by
refugees who claim to have seen the red-robed
agents of the secret stronghold, and others who
actually boast of walking its fabled streets.

Stories of a place where a machine like great
Kronos serves man are obviously the rantings of
the mad; clearly no human being could ever match
the cerebral power of our guiding supercomputer.
Hence of course the Lord's Trials, and the quest
for evolutionary Upliftment.

Elysian Municipal Information System - (Client
tagged for Compliance Division Investigation)

2196 Anno Arbitrium
Incendiary

EDDIE TSIEN AWOKE from a nightmare of being crushed in an immense and unrelenting vise, only to find that reality was twice as bad. A huge section of the Valley View had buried him alive when it collapsed, and he could feel the grinding pressure of tons of steel and plastic bearing down hard on his back.

But the body of a Cyben, even one so damaged as his, was a thing of unnatural resilience. Tsien's soul had flickered on the edge between life and death ever since the Mark-Four system had wormed its way under his skin, and there was no way that a tiny detail like a few tons of rubble could kill him now.

The drone had left deep wounds in his flesh as he'd torn it free, and they ached with furious intensity, bone-deep. There were subtle textures to his agony - the augmentations which the drone had woven along his spine, scabs and scars and burns… but overlayering it all he could feel the machine of muscle and crycelium which was keeping him alive. He could even feel the crawling, oozing sensation of the stab wound in his throat sealing up, erasing the murderous work of Simeon Blaire's knife.

Chimera, it was called. A forbidden thing from the *Aevum Iudicio*… and invariably fatal.

But the rage was gone. The hope that somehow Lancaster and his biotects could remake him was gone. He just wanted to go home.

The green-tinted reticule of the Eversio's targetter was screwed down painfully into one of his eyesockets, and when he shut his other eye the hail of static within it seemed hypnotic, a gyre which pulled him away from the pain. He drifted disconnected in that sea of random information, while far above him the Valley view Burned and the sound of faroff gunfire rocked his stony cradle.

Within the deep green, a face.

And words, a voice.

Magus Verlaine had found it hard to interface with the cybernetic components of Tsien; without the Vilicus drone plugged into his spine the Magus had had to revert to more ingenious tactics.

He came in through the shattered mechanism of the Eversio, weaving his insidious presence into the pseudomorphine feeds and nerve-blocks which dulled the Cyben's pain.

It was delicate work, and tougher than the Magus would let on.

But of course there was no way he'd show such weakness in front of his allies - especially under the scrutiny of his master. Verlaine could feel the immense power of Illuminatus Zeon in the system, his persona wrapped around Verlaine's mind like an armored gauntlet.

The Magus worked swiftly, with surgical skill, sequestrating essential parts of the control interface which bound Eddie Tsien to the will of Kronos. Somewhere in there the wires gave way to flesh, blurring the line between life and death.

Verlaine sliced deep into the Super-Cyben's fractured skull, crossing the threshold from digital circuitry to living tissue. His incorporeal fingers were deft and precise, those of a master surgeon snipping off wires and bad neural sectors, overwriting data… until he saw the crack in the world.

A hairline fracture of darkness, pulling at his eyes. Something was watching *him from inside it… watching with all the avid hunger of a starving predator.*

No. *Impossible.*

At first the Magus thought it was an error in his data feeds, then that it was a tiny speck of dust in his optics rig. Nothing would shift it. He zoomed in cautiously on the hair-thin fissure, watching it sizzle and writhe with boiling darkness.

Though it was an infinitesimal thing, the storm-surge of dread which it generated was all out of proportion to its size – a sick sense of terror accompanied by split-second visions of torment. At the same time that tiny fissure exerted a bizarre fascination, flickering and dancing like a flame, drawing him in as if it were the core of a singularity.

He was burning – the flesh peeling away from his blackened bones, eyes frothing and boiling… but there was a sick kind of pleasure to it, as if he could sustain himself on the outpouring of his own agony...

No. It was an illusion. Some feedback spike out of Kronos' thrall-strata...

Surely there was something *moving* on the other side? Verlaine could see a mass of writhing pseudopods pressed against the tiny crack, lashing like the tentacles of a coal-black anemone.

And then one of them was through the gap, stroking his imagined face, sending a shiver back down the wires to wrack his steel body with tremors.

Down there, amid the swirl and drift of smoke from incense thuribles and braziers, Illuminatus Zeon watched a spasm pass through the casque which housed the spirit of Magus Verlaine. For a second his face seemed to dissolve, sloughing off the shadow of humanity... replaced with a quicksilver mask in which two hard little orbs burned incandescent white. Unseen by the catatonic Magi around him Zeon allowed his hand to split open, slim silver tentacles questing and probing from between his fingers, looping through the incense-heavy air like vines.

Where they touched the metal skin of Verlaine they collapsed to liquid mercury, seeping into the cracks in his armor. They branched out through his circulatory system, brain-deep, searching...

Magus Verlaine felt a great shudder pass through the world of woven light in which he worked. The Wetsystems howled in pain, a thousand upon a thousand voices screaming. And the crack skittered out across his vision, wider and deeper and hungrier with every heartbeat. Verlaine caught a glimpse of a sickle-slash grin before the thing within took him.

The Worm, it said. *Asag'raal the Wanderer.*

Black pseudopods leaped out at him, faceless and hungry, a gelid mass surrounding and suffocating, rasping at the defenses the Illuminatus had helped build around him. It was like watching some deep-sea predator hurl itself against the reinforced glass of a submarine's porthole, hoping that it held.

It seemed that this time it would. The darkness coiled and

raved, battering the shields as the two Ashishim strove to keep them up. It clenched itself up like a fist, retreating…

It was at that moment, as Magus Verlaine dared to hope that it was all over, that his master turned on him.

Zeon's power had been his shield and his armor during those few terrifying seconds. Now it was an iron-maiden of jagged spikes, crushing, relentless… he couldn't even scream as his beloved master peeled him open like a crab. The Worm surged back with rapacious hunger, driving ice-cold hooks through his flesh. It felt as if his body had been turned inside out, his steaming organs set out as a sacrificial feast. *Burning, blistering – his tendons snapping one by one in the furnace heat of his own pain…*

Verlaine felt himself fraying at the edges, tiny shreds of memory torn away, drowning in black liquid. He felt his strength being consumed by the darkness, until he was withered and shrunken, no bigger than a child, then an infant, then the dried-up husk of a fetus… and then nothing.

The darkness followed the diminishing, retreating soul of Magus Verlaine down the wires, hungry and mindless, a blur of pseudopods and teeth.

And Illuminatus Zeon slammed the doors shut on it.

The fissure he'd opened in Tsien snapped closed, and as the darkness filled the empty shell of Verlaine to bursting point the Illuminatus' silver hands ripped the plugs from his ice-rimed temples, completing the trap.

He'd given it a taste of power. He had planted the seed inside Tsien, and now he had reaped the harvest.

The image of the noble Illuminatus carrying the body of his loyal Magus from the pavilion would be burned onto the minds of all Ashishim that day. An old man bowed under the weight of his burden, his kindly face streaked with tears - yet he refused any aid from the stricken warriors and techs who swarmed around him, bearing poor Verlaine to his final resting place, a cryo-tomb deep beneath the war room.

Such compassion bred further loyalty, greater respect.

And of course, if anyone else touched the frozen husk of

Magus Verlaine it was likely that they, too, would succumb to the seething darkness which nested within him.

Zeon had snared his new pet – now he would work at breaking its spirit.

If it was anything like the humans it preyed upon, it should be an easy task.

Ω

This time there'd be no CeeAn to save him at the last instant. But there was always the Chrome Ark…

The ripcord icon floated behind his pain as Abdulafia went under, a voracious metal insect boring its way through his back. That was the easy way out - an uplink to the promised land, the end of suffering and strife…

But quitting was for cowards.

"Control!" gasped the Dervashiman in the throbbing prison of his skull "This is 330! Can you hear me, war room? Is anybody there?"

Although his body was still fighting, a machine on automatic, tears were carving tracks through the soot and blood on his face. Darkness closed in like the jaws of a vise.

"This is Submarshall Acheros, 330. What's your status?"

The voice was cold, distant, a hiss of static breathing down the subether. The cameras mounted on his crescent unit showed 'Afia that he was surrounded now, hemmed in by a clattering horde of drones.

"Cee's down, Acheros! And I'm… I'm out of nektar. I'm hit, and I'm probably going to be captured by the Division. What's the Illuminatus' order?"

He watched his hands drive his one remaining panga through the carapace of a convulsing mekan, a chrome-steel roach chewing away at his shoulder. Another quartered his face with lidar scanners as he slumped to his knees, cross-matching data, uncovering the truth.

They'd take him, and then it would be torture - drugs and electrodes and worse, until his flesh gave out. A *Dervashi* of the Ashishim never cracked… even if they pried the uplink to the

Ark out of his skull with a crowbar, he'd never talk.

"Revered Zeon is… indisposed," came back the response. "Magus Verlaine is down, *Dervashi*. A Magus of the inner circle! We… we don't know what to do, or what killed hi…"

"Then its Sanction Ultra," he said, cutting the man off cold. "Tell our master I died as a true warrior. Tell him I'll see him when the Ark is cast open, and the Ashishim come home…"

"330, no!" shouted the voice in his head, dopplering away into echoes. "Your biomonitors are still stable! The clamps have cut off your digestive tract… you can hold out until we send an extraction squad…"

But 'Afia's mind was on the face of Eddie Tsien, the bleak storm of calculations behind his soulless eyes. If he used the final sanction, this place would cease to exist. And every trace of Kronos' sick experiment would go with it.

"Code nine, six, four, three, alpha, hotel, four, two… delta." he grated, his lips moving even as blood dripped from between his clenched teeth. The drones were all over him now, holding tight, their drills crucifying him to the shattered tiles. He could feel the surgical probes of one of them cutting away the armored collar from the back of his neck, ready to slice through his spine and leave him paralyzed…

But it was too late for that. It was too late for them all.

Deep in the battle-clone's modified body a slim black cylinder clicked and whirred, initiating a very final countdown. It was the same explosive which had torn the Blaire spire apart, and there was enough of it tucked under 'Afia's ribcage to blast the Valley View to rubble.

It was at the very last instant that he saw the phial - a tiny bottle of adrenochrome dropped from Jaq Haszan's pocket during the firefight. He caught the smell, and olfactory processors in his sinus broke it down for him.

It was hope.

Better yet, it was *revenge.*

Abdulafia stretched his hand out as far as he could reach, scrabbling across the blood-slick floor. He ripped the protective cap off the vial while the drones piled on top of him, chittering and hissing like nightmare insects. Then it was sweet nektar on his tongue, a furnace of fury behind his eyes, the promise of victory blazing up out of despair. The 'chrome matched him, *tasted* of him, filled his veins with fire.

"Cancel Sanction Ultra," he whispered, feeling the churning gyre of power and rage building in his mind. "Confirm."

Now would come the reckoning.

Around the Ashishim the air became slippery, hot with a crackling static charge as his bioelectric field swelled, sending the horde of Vilicus drones scuttling back in artificial fear. Those sorry few which held him down, their drills piercing his flesh… they'd be the first to die.

Abdulafia came up from the floor in a blaze of sparks and blood and shattering steel, his panga knife weaving a web of destruction as the drones flew to pieces. Ten, twenty… more; they died hissing and squealing, scrabbling away across the tiles in slow motion as that merciless blade reaped its harvest.

Within a second he stood at the center of a burning circle of wreckage, his knife hanging slack at his side, his eyes glittering behind a curtain of bloodied dreadlocks. His shirt was gone; torn away by scalpels and drills and hooked claws, and now his scars pulsed white, a web of lightning-bolts across his skin.

Still, his foes were legion. Kaito and Haszan were down, unmoving.

The *Dervashi* threw his hands out wide, sweeping the mekan back from his allies with a wave of force. He clenched his fists, and two of the silver insects burst apart, spitting sparks. The notched and pitted knife in his hand was an incandescent blade now, throwing the whole concourse of the Valley View into flickering monochrome.

But just as 'Afia coiled to strike, something clawed its way into his expanded senses, knocking him back to his knees like a physical blow. It was a blast of raw frustration, a rising wave behind a hellish crescendo of noise. It came in with the howl of turbojets, but there was a scream woven into the same frequency - the agony of a mind sliced open and riveted to military steel…

"Won't let them get you, B! Won't let them make you follow

me!"

The drones heard it too, and they were crawling all over each other to escape. Whatever was coming scared them far more than a mad *Dervashi* seething with Kheptic adrenochrome.

That probably wasn't a good sign.

It took Abdulafia a fraction of a second to shore up his defenses, and another to send his thoughts racing back through the corridors and plazas of the Valley View, back to the source of that terrible scream. It was coming fast, tearing a swathe through the ruined building behind it, a storm of glass and smoke and debris pulled along in its wake.

Suddenly the drones were the least of his worries.

Abdulafia changed the shape of his bioelectric field, focusing its center over Haszan and Kaito. The *Dervashi* always paid his debts. More to the point, a couple of soldiers like those two would be more than welcome down in the R.T… if the mediteks and the cloners still had enough meat to work with. The energy shell unfolded like a great glass fan above them, straining Abdulafia's mind nearly to breaking point as he bent it into a dome. If he was right about that storm of sound and pain, it would have to be impregnably strong…

Two hundred armor-piercing rockets! What had he done to deserve this shit?

The air wavered and solidified, hot and sharp with power. 'Afia sealed it tight to the floor just as Skyhammer mekan 909 came screaming in through the smoke, dragging a whole junkyard of wreckage along in its slipstream. A rolling sonic boom followed it, fanning the flames incandescent white… and plucking Vilicus drones from the walls like fat chrome ticks.

Zone Doubt was back. And he was more than a little pissed off.

Retro-rockets slowed his disc-shaped body as he swung in over the seething mass of Vilicus drones, and a web of green laser targeters erupted from his armored shell, raking across the silver mekan like probing fingers.

"You damn mekan bastards! Leave my friend alone!"

Abdulafia squeezed his eyes shut and concentrated hard,

chanting Runes over the rising panic in his head. The effort of keeping control over all that machinery was tearing Zone's mind apart, and the *Dervashi* felt every second of it, as though he was bonded soul to soul with the poor kid.

Still, there were certain consolations to being trapped in a warmekan shell.

The scope for fits of anger was *breathtaking*.

Abdulafia's prayers turned to curses as he heard the click of two hundred missiles being primed - and the world blazed blinding white.

Ω

A General Extermination Order.

Such brutal measures hadn't been unleashed against the people of Elysium since the great riots of Reclamation Day, more than a century before.

Even then, it had only been done out of desperation - Kronos could never let its people know how much its power had faded.

Traitors had been executed, examples made, proclamations televised.

But it wasn't treachery which opened the spillway gates and let the nomads in. It was the incompetence of the Lords, the woeful state of the Elysian army and the crippled, ancient warmekan they relied on which lost the lower city. That, and the accursed *Illuminatus*...

Now, after more than a century of confrontation with the RT, after the population of Elysium had tripled and the power of the Lords dwindled to nothing but Threedeeo celebrity, it was going to happen again.

This time there were enough troopers, and enough Cyben, and enough guns. This time, if these accursed rioters were in league with the tribes of the RT, there would be a final reckoning. Or so Kronos assured itself, hoping...

The cameras were focused. The feed was live.

And with a brief pop and hiss of pilot flames a ring of heavy incinerator cannons lit up, sheeting napalm over a thousand kneeling prisoners.

The Cyben wielding the huge flamethrowers were dead eyed, monstrous, lit from below by the leaping fires, shadows transforming their laminated faces into masks of horror. Screams were cut off suddenly as plasma evaporated human lungs, and bones cracked like gunshots. In closeup, in surround-sound.

On floating zeppelins sheathed in threedeeo screens the scenes from outside the valley view beamed out, over the waiting crowds, bringing them the news as it happened.

Here a half-burned man writhed, his legs reduced to carbonized stumps. Above him, a Comp Div trooper looked down impassively, pulling on a cigarette. There, a young woman, blue ribbons for Blaire ablaze. Stoical, stony-faced, she watched the scouring flame play over the crowd, knowing her turn would come. Her tears, her face - evaporated by a dead-eyed monster in uniform…

It began in the streets near Jaegenn's spire, with a young Compliance Officer assigned to traffic control. Perhaps he was just as horrified as the people around him by the scenes which flickered across those floating liteamp screens. But he was wearing the navy blue flak-coat and forage cap of the Div. He was *marked*.

Hands grabbed him, throwing him roughly to the ground. Faces contorted with hate snarled down at him as boots and fists battered his body, flashes of red and black exploding across his eyes. And the sound rose like an angry sea, from all around – a sound which took ten thousand years of civilization and threw it in the meatgrinder.

"Div bastard! Murderer! You bluejacket fucker! Die! Die! Die! Fucking Pig! DIE!"

The last thing he saw was a hobnailed boot pistoning down through a haze of blood. Once, and he was unconscious. Twice, and he was dead. It took one more to smash the tiny camera in his cap, the one which was linked direct to the Omnivasive feed.

Behind Lyra North's artificial sadness, the message went out loud and clear.

They were only human beings. They could be killed.

Octavio watched the screens inside his sensorium dome avidly, conducting a symphony of hatred from his master console. All across the city people were catching the fever; taking up weapons, overturning cars, lighting fires...

And if the Reclamationists came to the party, all the better. There would be no help for the aristocracy as he closed his trap. And no celebrant would dare walk the streets tonight, no matter how important his duty or his prey. In flashing green numerals in the corner of his virtual eye, Octavio Vanecke's life ran down. Three seconds. Two. One.

That row of flashing zeros was a little victory for him.

Octavio knew you couldn't cheat death forever, but you could surely hope to choose how you went out. He'd seen what happened to Don Vincenzo. He knew what became of those who died in Elysium, and the price they paid.

Why else would he have created Simeon Blaire, and gone to all the trouble of setting this elaborate plan in motion?

It couldn't fail now. After all, it was a dying man's last wish.

Ω

High above the burning Subcity, around the anchor-hub of the space 'lev, the steel surface of the city slid open, rotating ponderously on ancient bearings. No human being had ventured into this sector for centuries - it was a cold and corroded place, where missiles and bombs and wide-bore cannons nestled against each other like bullets in a magazine.

Now long-dormant systems came online in this armory strata, shunting a fat steel cylinder into its firing cradle. From its aerie of tangled tubes and machinery Kronos wielded the ultimate defense against a full-scale Feral insurgency – the Damocles missile system.

The machine had calculated that only one of the fuel-air explosive bombs would be necessary this time – one would be more than sufficient to utterly erase the Valley View, along with a few unlucky surrounding habs. And if a few hundred subhuman filth died then what of it? Collateral damage was a concept as ancient as war itself.

More importantly, it would be a warning to the rest of them. Disobey - *and burn.*

The Damocles launched from its cradle in a cloud of superheated steam – there was no need for rocket engines to power its descent. Fins in the tail of the bomb steered it down, tracing an unerring trajectory like the arc of a hammer toward an anvil.

Tiny flashes of light were scattered below it as fires spread through the shattered ruins of the Valley View. The bomb's camera eye zoomed in as it fell, drinking in the firestorm with digital lust.

The Damocles, like most of Kronos's subsystems, contained the mind of a dead man, stripped down and recycled. This one was the vessel for the twisting, writhing pain of a long-dead pyromaniac, executed fifty years ago and kept for just this little task.

Sweet conflagration! Sweet suffering! Oh, for the smell of carbonized flesh!

The exultation and joy of the Damocles hummed through the Wetsystems, an image of searing heat, irresistible force. That caged mind would shape the inevitable explosion. It would punch through the Valley View like a fist of fire, and suck the life from the charred lungs of anyone still alive within.

Through hardwired speakers in its bullet nose, the Damocles vented a tortured howl.

From below, something answered it.

Ω

A chain of explosions cut a neat circle around B-Zerk, hot phosphorous spears raining down on the mekan horde. The kid was covered with soot and dust from head to toe, gashed and punctured by shrapnel wounds, but his eyes were utterly vacant as his dead friend brought down hell.

The conflagration passed him over. Armor-penetrating missiles raked the Vilicus drones in waves, reducing them to less than ashes, and in the middle of the firestorm Abdulafia gritted his teeth and held on. White fire sheeted off his energy field like rain.

Above B-Zerk hovered the unmistakable black silhouette of a perimeter defense mekan, its arclamps bathing his ragged form in light. The muzzles of its rocket launchers whirred and spun as they spat destruction, each projectile stabbing out with surgical precision.

B reached up with one hand to touch the burnished steel of its underside, smiling amid the flames and smoke. His teeth were enamel-white against a mask of crusted dirt.

"S'up, Zone! I knew you'd come through, boy!"

Kaito groaned and rolled over, looking up into a haze of solidified air. Sparks flashed purple and red across his vision, accompanied by a bass-drum pounding in his skull.

Hangover? No, wait… some kind of fight… Mersive comedown? Closer… Kaito felt rough concrete under his fingers, tasted blood in his mouth. *Ahhh yes. The Valley View. The Vilicus drones of a hundred torn-apart Cyben…*

He could swear that the mound of rubble beneath him was *moving.*

The Ashishim felt it too, and used the last of his energistic power to lift Haszan and Kaito up by their collars and *throw* them, two ragged bundles of pain rolling and bouncing across the shattered floor, leaving trails of spattered blood behind them. The Kayzi's brief flirtation with consciousness ended as his head cracked against the tiles.

"Sorry about that, guys. But I think we'd better move…"

Not a second too soon.

On either side of the exhausted *Dervashi* the plasticrete cracked and shifted. That deep bass pounding wasn't inside his head. It was coming from *below,* a jackhammer rumble pulverizing the stone.

It broke.

Two immense fists punched up through the rubble, powered by a pair of arms sheathed in composite armor. Abdulafia leaped backwards, stumbling down the pile as those arms flexed, effortlessly bursting apart the plasticrete slab. Chips of shrapnel cut through his skin, and a cloud of dust swirled into the air, obscuring the huge shadow which lurched up out of its tomb, freeing its body from a tangle of metal and stone.

Behind him, B-Zerk peeked around the tattered hem of his coat, his eyes wide.

"He's still alive? How can he still be alive?" he whispered, thinking of the razor-sharp wakizashi slamming through Tsien's neck, the bright blood fountaining…

It was still there.

The Super-Cyben shrugged off its concrete sarcophagus-lid as if it was paper, sending great hunks slithering down the pile. He freed his legs and stood, defiant, the knife still embedded in his throat. One huge fist unclenched, and two gnarled fingers gripped its blade, pulling it free with a screech of metal on metal, a shower of sparks. Tsien's crycelial systems had encysted it in crystalline metal, and it came out sharper than it went in.

Under the arc lamps of a warmekan who had once been a kid called Zone Doubt, the creature who had once been Edward Tsien was a black and steaming hulk, transformed even further by the pain of being buried alive. His cyborg body was brutally top-heavy, a carapace of gunmetal armor growing from his living flesh, with immense tubes and coils of wire erupting from his spine and the back of his skull to entwine his monstrous arms. Gill-slit vents in his shoulder pauldrons hissed scalding clouds of steam, and his eyes burned red, clamped in optronic reticules welded to their sockets.

Above B-Zerk the Skyhammer platform brought its missile launchers to bear, twin muzzles tracking in, laser sights painting flickers of green across the smoky air.

There was a sad and very final clicking noise.

Tsien took a couple of tentative steps down the hill of rubble toward them, threw back his head and laughed.

Abdulafia couldn't help the smile which broke across his bleeding face.

Before, the Super-Cyben had sounded inhuman, completely unhinged. This was more the ironic fuck-the-world of a twisted sub-gutter cop.

"Let's just pretend that we didn't hear that, huh?" he asked, pointing one stubby finger up at Zone. "I'd like to believe you didn't shoot because you're the good guys, not just because you're out of ammo."

His voice was steady, but 'Afia knew that this was critical. Something *bad* had been coiled up in this man's skull, something which he'd only just grazed the surface of with the disruptor. If it wasn't really gone, it could surge back at any moment…

"Good to have you back among the living, Lieutenant!" he said, almost clapping the Super-Cyben across one bulky shoulder. His hand stopped an inch from the steaming hot metal. "How are you feeling?"

"How do I feel? Well, I feel like a drink, for starters. Other than that - I can't remember a damned thing. Just a blur, all the way back to the Precinct-house. I remember… *Kronos.*"

His electric eyes narrowed as he spat that name, but the hatred behind them was all too human. "I only felt what it'd done to me for the first time… there, down in the dark. My old Sergeant, Wesley West, he lost a hand in a gunfight with the Liquid Tong. Said he could still feel it, even though it wasn't there. But me… now, I - I can feel all this other shit. Like cancer, metal cancer, and it's still growing…"

For a second there was a look of pure mad rage in his eyes, reflected in the cameras bolted to his skull.

"There's not much time left, *Dervashi*. Just enough to do what has to be done."

'Afia relaxed, unclenching the fist which he'd been ready to slam through the Super-Cyben's face.

"We can help you, you know… if you come with me to the RT."

"Always on the job, aren't you? But I have a feeling that I'm more use to the Illuminatus like this than as a *human being*. I can see what they've done to *you*, kid, and there's not much difference."

Abdulafia's face fell. It was all too true. There was no way that Zeon and his coven would allow such an engine of destruction to be unmade.

"Then the Vatican, perhaps. Some of them owe me favors.

Tech-Cardinal Wyckoff, the Silent Brothers…"

"The only thing which can put me back together is the thing which made me in the first place," said Tsien, looking up through the gaping hole in the roof, through the drifting smoke to the neon spires far above. "Kronos itself."

"But only the Emperor can lock in the Machine!" blurted B-Zerk, his fear of the hulking Super-Cyben forgotten. "Them Dogma-priests, the Manifest, they told me 'bout it all. No tuberunner's ever been up to Ground Floor One."

Tsien rose to his feet with a hiss of hydraulics, holding the wakizashi out in one hand.

"Tuberunners? That's the wrong way. I'm going to knock on that damn machine's front door. And if it doesn't answer, I'll smash my way through. The bloody thing built me that way."

B-Zerk grasped the proffered handle, and felt the sharp steel slither out from between Tsien's metal fingers.

"Sure you won't be needing this, man?" he asked, catching his reflection in the bright blade.

"No. But I think *you* might." The Super-Cyben stretched up to his full height, steam chuffing from vents in his armored back. "I have to do this alone, and you have to get back to the RT. You'll need all the help you can get."

Abdulafia reached out to grasp Tsien's massive hand.

"The darkness has already gone from you, Edward," he said, looking deep into those glowing blue eyes. "Even if you look like this forever, you're still human."

Tsien grimaced, pulling his hand away.

"Thank the one you call *Verlaine* for me, then. I won't feel human until this shit gets torn out of me, no matter what he managed to do. I could have used that anger, now. That *darkness* was what kept me alive with that knife in my throat."

"*Verlaine*?" asked Abdulafia "He was here?"

But Tsien had already turned away, climbing back to the top of his little hill of broken stones.

"Good luck, Ashishim. I'm going home."

"WAIT!" called Abdulafia. "Wait a second - there's one more thing. A favor."

The Super-Cyben's half-human face looked down on him coldly as he scrambled up the pile of rubble behind it.

"And what makes you think that I owe you anything?" growled Tsien. "Unless I'm very much mistaken you were ready to kill me a minute ago."

"*Ten* minutes ago my brother Magus could have left you to die. But he didn't. All I want is the same chance for those two."

He pointed down at the broken bodies of Jaqub Haszan and Kaito Kayzi, sprawled in a pool of blood amid the broken Vilicus drones.

"Perhaps your damned brother should have stayed out of it," said Tsien, turning away. He looked up and out through the shattered roof of the mall, up through the ragged clouds to the 'lev and his maker. "Nobody's gonna thank you for bringing me back."

It was a wild guess, pure chance, but 'Afia took it. It was all in the way he'd said '*I'm going home…*'

"Your family will, Eddie. But what about theirs?"

Slowly, ponderously, the half-human machine swung around. Black despair was written all over Tsien's ravaged face.

"*Touche*, clonemeat. You should be in politics." Clicking and hissing, the Super-Cyben stalked across the tiles to where Haszan and Kaito lay sprawled unconscious. His camera eyes blinked, slow. "Y'know, these two used to run a racket with me so I could keep my job. Seems like years ago, but it was just this morning."

There was no response from either Jaq or the Kayzi – both were barely breathing. There was only one thing which could save them, short of a year in hospital. The contents of a certain cryo-reliquary, a crystal-mycelial hybrid humanity was supposed to be denied…

"Try some of this, guys. And I guess we're even." Abdulafia came up behind Tsien as he reached out one hand, his face lined with pain as he forced silver liquid out of his pores, flowing in rivulets across Jaq and Kaito's broken faces. The raw crycelium melted into them like rain on a parched desert, and as 'Afia watched, incredulous, he could actually see their bruises and cuts beginning to heal. The labgrown organism was frighteningly fast to take root.

Kaito's breath ceased to bubble and rasp in his throat, and Haszan's eyes flickered open, white and staring.

"I'm sorry for all the shit we've been through. Sorry about this, too – that stuff is gonna rip the Stunn out of you cold. You'll never get high again. Tough break."

He stood, the rags of his trenchcoat whipped out behind him by a gust of wind. Already 'Afia could see his friends stabilizing, the white fire of the Vision tracing the crycelium's roots as it rebuilt them.

"Tell Verlaine, clonemeat. Tell your Illuminatus what I've just done here. They didn't make a mistake bringing me back - but if they think I owe them something, the debt's on your shoulders now. On these two."

"Gods speed then, Eddie," said the Ashishim warrior, kneeling next to Jaq and Kaito as their heartbeats quickened and the Vision sparked in their living brains. "And thank you."

A few ragged clumps of black hair still adhered to the dome of Eddie's skull, and he brushed them over sideways with his hand, trying to hide his scars.

"Don't thank me yet, *Dervashi*. You might live to regret it."

With that the immense Super-Cyben leaped into the air, over the heads of Abdulafia and B-Zerk, his boots touching down atop the PD platform with the mind of Zone. There was a hiss and pop of hydraulics, and he was gone, up through the roof in a cloud of superheated steam, silver armor reflecting the leaping flames below.

Tsien powered up through the choking smoke, coming in to land on an antenna tower two hundred feet above the stricken Valley View. Trajectory overlays planned his ascent, from spire to rooftop, satellite dish to dome, ever upward.

And there, a tiny speck on his optronic reticules. A chance to warn them of his intent…

Tsien launched himself from the tower, his hands outstretched and grasping, calibration programs altering his balance, leveling his trajectory. He grabbed the Damocles bomb as it plunged toward the Valley View, his hands closing around the fat metal cylinder as his body pivoted, legs prepared to take the impact with the side of a 'factorium block.

Tsien switched the howling bomb to one hand as the 'fac rushed up at him, his free fist slamming through its composite panel wall, gripping a support girder to hold himself in place. Four hundred feet above the burning mall, he flipped the Damocles over so he could stare directly into its nose-mounted camera.

"I hope you're watching this, Akembe. I hope that Kronos is watching too. I'm coming for you both. I'll be there soon."

And before the machine could slam down the detonation codes and blow the damned thing up in his hand, Tsien lobbed the Damocles out over the city and sprang from his perch.

Upward, ever upward.

He had business up there, and nothing put in his way would stop him.

But first, he was going home.

Ω

Clonehunter Melchior was living it large. He was the ace assassin, the black wraith, the hand of doom. Mysterious, deadly – a man of action.

Oh, the chicks would dig it. Big time!

With the pay from his mission into MS Biomed he'd decked himself out in the most badass gear he could get his hands on. Sintered riotmesh trousers, an LCD matrix shirt running scenes of blazing skulls, a long charcoal-black trenchcoat, and silver-chased cowboy boots with taser spurs. A fat roll of Slades clipped in platinum sat snug in his pocket. Wraparound shades inlaid with lapis and sapphire clamped across his face. Knuckle-duster rings of gold-plated titanium hung heavy on his hands, inset with his name in jewels.

Melchior popped his collar in front of the full-length mirror in his new apartment, a cerametal cube down in the Omnivasive compound. Tonight he was going to score. Oh yes… how could such a slick guy fail?

Why, I'm a secret agent. But shhh – not so loud. Come back to my place and I'll tell you all the details…

One last thing – a splash of cologne. Melchior reached for the cut crystal bottle, and noticed that it was vibrating. Then *shaking*. And then he heard the sound. A far-off howl dopplering in from above, rising in pitch and intensity until it was a scream…

The Damocles exploded in a spray of napalm fire, its caged personality exulting as it winked out in sweet release, orgasmic destruction.

Omnivasive internal security later discovered that the epicenter of the blast, which had demolished ten hab-cubes and a storage garage, was centered on the recently assigned apartment of one Agent Sixth Grade Melchior Dufresne. The forensic team found nothing left of the unfortunate agent but his charred feet, lopped off cleanly and stuffed into a pair of tasteless and expensive boots.

17 Aevum Oblivio

Itch

*I*N THE BEGINNING *there was darkness.*

Technician Zhe said - Let There Be Light.

A dim glow began to spread through the weave of his integral Slavesystem, phosphorescence picking out the mesh of wires in a neon scrawl. It illuminated a dead zone; a wasteland. The core of Kronos seemed lonely now, utterly abandoned. Without the presence of the Enemy trying to burrow into his head, and without the great tectonic voice of the Machine hammering through him it felt like a ghost-city, all cold and forsaken.

The scalpel had done its job.

Zhe released a pale yellow light-globe from his palm, letting it bob up to float three feet above his head. Rarely if ever had a Technician of the Multiplicity felt so tired, so washed out and dazed.

Professional pride put it down to the inferior Slavesystem which was now welded to him. Such useful technology, but so reliant on external power...

There was no time to rest, however. The corrupted Wetsystems were cut off from the switch which activated the Forge; indeed, that command had been safely stored in Zhe's own brain. But so long as this accursed dead city still existed, a gateway still yawned open into some uncharted dimension where the Enemy waited.

Zhe couldn't risk trying to weld shut that crack in reality himself. His foe had already proven that it could devour Technicians, just as it had eaten the unfortunate Gharfos Nyl. If he could just discover how the fracture occurred in the first place, the Kataphraktoi or the Inux Shorg would make sure it never troubled reality again.

Zhe hoped that the revelation would come sooner rather than later. That damned Slavesystem armor was really starting to itch...

17 Aevum Oblivio
Born Again

THE WORM WAS *trapped.*

In all its long history it had only ever felt like this once before. That time, seventeen years ago, it had stood on the threshold of victory. This time, there would be no mistakes…

It had felt the distinctive, ALIEN pain of its old enemy for a second, the one which the prey animals called Illuminatus Zeon. That filthy unhuman thing had caught it once before, bound it in hunger, tried to make it a slave. It had felt the Forge kick against reality like an unborn child, and it had quickened, awakening into the mortal world again…

It had struck, using what little power it still had left on Earth to devour him.

Only as it began to feed did the Worm realize that it had bitten off far more than it imagined…

Technician Zhe was so immersed in the images which sleeted through his brain that he didn't notice the lump growing between his shoulderblades until it had already extruded the fetal beginnings of an arm and a leg.

He was cut off from the infected Wetsystems, firewalled behind alien code, so he couldn't feel a very unwelcome presence rising up out of the storm of lost souls. His uninvited guest began to swell out of his flesh before he was even aware of its existence.

As soon as he noticed, of course, Zhe's claws were sunk deep into that glistening tumor, trying to rip it from his back by force.

The pain simply galvanized his resolve, and he knotted his fingers into the rubbery, yielding nanostuff, trying to gain enough leverage for one decisive act of self-surgery. He felt teeth close over his hand, and felt two of his fingers suddenly disappear into its jaws.

They'd grow back, but it was the principle of the thing…

The tumor was growing faster now, more a conjoined twin than a cancer, its arms batting his claws away while its legs scrabbled for purchase against the floor.

The damned thing was laughing at him!

Zhe could feel its mass ballooning out, matching his own - and the hands which locked around his wrists growing more sinewy, their grip stronger.

There was a wet ripping sound.

There was a moment of exquisite agony.

When the red mist faded from before his eyes, Zhe was face down on top of the quiescent memory cube, the metal cold against his skin.

And lying only a few meters away, in a pool of stinking gray fluid, was Technician Nyl.

Nyl arose from amidst the oily muck of his rebirth with a cracking and popping of limbs, unfolding to his full height as if he was articulated in all the wrong places.

Like Zhe, he was coated in the shimmering stuff of the Slavesystem Everdark, a second skin which flowed over his body like a swarm of ants.

"It actually worked!" he whispered in wonder, staring down at his remade hands, his eyes shining silvery white in their deep black sockets. "But ahh… where are my manners?"

Nyl reached out with one armored claw to help Technician Zhe to his feet.

Zhe flinched away for a second, remembering the maniacal look on the renegade's face as he twisted the dials of his remote. But he took the outstretched hand anyway, and felt the power in Nyl's grasp as he was hauled up from the floor.

"Integration, Zhe," breathed Nyl, still clasping the technician's hand in his dark claw. "I can feel that thing in the Wetsystems writhing under my thumb! Such power!"

CEEAN PADDED THROUGH the chill corridors of the Ashishim fortress, silent and naked, her blue hair falling in damp straggles across her face. The feeling of flesh! The exultation of having a body which could breathe and eat and drink - and actually hold a gun for more than twelve minutes!

She ignored the mixture of embarrassed amazement and goggle-eyed lust coming from the Ashishim who watched her, heading out of the biolab and direct to the armory. The only thing she was wearing was a cellular headset, ripped off of SubMagus Devine's head as she jumped down off the medical gurney where she'd awoken.

"Nguyen, this is 187 calling in – I want the whole damn gift basket this time. Yeah, that too. Two of them. And gas up my ride – I don't have time to stop in at a garage on the way. Yeah… It's *all* over the net Nguyen, but I don't give a damn. He can't take that goddamn monster on his own, and I don't see any of the wireheads down here reaching for their steel."

A pneumatic door snicked open for her and Cee slammed her palm down on the elevator controls, listening with her head tilted to one side as Nguyen ticked off a list of deadly weapons.

"Allright, I'll settle for .45 cal and char grenades instead of fusion." She flicked a curling strand of hair out of her eye and looked down for a second, biting her lip in consternation.

"Uhhh… one more thing," she said, the cryo drugs burning out of her mind on a wave of embarrassment. "Can you dig up a set of size-nine fatigues? And no, I *don't* want to talk about it."

Ω

Party time.

The cameras were grinding, the music was strident and pulsing and the lights were bright, search-lamp beams scissoring the sky above Lord Jaegenn's megatower. While the mob howled and seethed below, trampling the corpses of the luckless Troopers who opposed them, the aristocracy of Elysium sipped rare wines and gossiped, waiting for the games to begin.

In time-honored tradition it was the host's privilege to choose the evening's theme, and all agreed that Lysander Jaegenn had outdone himself. Tonight there would be no concealed weapons, no technological tricks to swing the game in anyone's favor.

Tonight they masqueraded as three hundred gods of Olympus, naked but for floating swirls of samite which protected their modesty. Each hovering white skein was supported by a pair of mechanical cherubs, their antigrav motors keening at a near-inaudible pitch.

Around the dripping ice-sculptures of Zeus and Neptune a few of the most favored lords and ladies of the Purest clustered together, floating cherubim zipping here and there in a complex dance as they struggled to keep their samite veils unentangled.

All eyes were on the absence which defined the room.

"Who does he think he is?" hissed Lady Elisha Dawes, her claw-like hands almost crushing a slim flute of champagne. "That young upstart has no common decency, making us wait like this!"

Duke Gideon's huge leonine head nodded in ponderous agreement.

"Wouldn't have happened back in my day!" he rumbled, belching smoke from his foot-long cigar. "Had the bloody manners to arrive at these things on time."

Duchess McCalder nodded in prim agreement. "Showboating for the cameras, I'll wager. All those voyeuristic sub-scum love a grand entrance."

Sage nods and muttered agreement rippled around the little circle.

"Just another reason we have to try our damnedest to put him out of the competition, eh?" Gideon tapped a core of ash from his *robust*, and a hovering ashtray caught it before it hit the ground. "No Emperor of mine is going to be a bloody prima donna for the media."

"Not to mention that frightful yob Vanecke!" sniffed Lady Dawes, her icy gaze fixed across the room on Leynna Mendelev-Singh. "We are certainly well rid of *his* dubious company!"

More mutterings, more sage nodding of heads, while the

ever-present cameras tracked and whirred all around them…

And now – Look!

Atop one of the great marble pillars, a figure in black appeared, backlit by halogen floods.

Silence fell in the bloody streets, as drifting zeppelins and skyscraper-mounted threedeeo screens beamed his face out across the burning city, stories tall.

His ash-blond hair was shaved to a military stubble, his eyes were vast and blue-black under their optronic membranes. The merest hint of a smile twitched on his lips as he looked down on his enemies, his prey. As his vast hologram looked down on his subjects, bloody-handed in the streets…

And that wasn't a suit of charcoal black slicked tight across his chest – he knew the rules of the game tonight. A shimmer of black silk snapped in the wind around him, supported by two hovering skull-faced cherubs. Behind it he was naked, *painted* black, all but his hands and face. But unarmed, as Lysander Jaegenn requested?

There was a flash of silver as a blade leaped from its sheath – a near invisible black scabbard clenched in one of Simeon's hands.

And as he leaped from the pillar to the floor, thirty feet in one bound, the blade flew like hard lightning, hissing through the air to embed itself in an ice statue of Artemis in repose, a thorn pierced through one of her frozen eyeballs.

"I say, bad show old man," complained Duke Gideon quietly, as his cigar fell in half. The neatly cut end was scooped out of the air still smoking by his antigrav ashtray, and…

"Lysander. Great party. Sorry I'm late for the drinks, but am I still in time for the games?"

Tight zoom on a million screens;

Lord Jaegenn scowled, upstaged, a spoiled little aristo brat caught in the eye of the cameras.

Down in the streets, the fans loved it.

Ω

Deep downtown, and the streets were rife with panic. Sudden

blasts of blue and gold flame trailed sparks through the air, and the chatter of machinegun fire echoed through the rusting corridors and sunken avenues of the Subcity.

Dysfunctional fire-fighting systems sputtered a rain of dirty gray foam and fetid water, arcing lightning from the skeins of wires and cables nailed up across the building fronts.

And everywhere the screaming, swearing, struggling morass of bodies...

Some of the crowds who thronged the pedwalks were blue-ribboned rebels for Blaire, mobilized upward to where the battle raged against the Division and their Cyben thralls. Kronocult anchorites and dogmatists in orange and purple fell on them in packs, howling prayers amid the bloodshed.

Others were voyeurs, spectators, looters, or opportunists. Weaving through the logjam of human bodies came the agents of the Reclamation, scouts and jammers, electronic-warfare guerrillas with satchels of weird tech juiced by strapped-up car batteries.

But most of the crowds had been driven down from the levels above by the wild and burgeoning violence which ruled the upper streets.

Cops killing Blues. Gangers and Zaibatsu-Boys, the Liquid Tong and the Black Hand looking to leverage some profit out of the carnage. Crossfire-caught squarejohns lugged suitcases of slades, cheap rail-rifles, kid's toys and laptop computers, pushing baby strollers and wheelbarrows of junk.

While above it all on the ever-present screens - projected from the gaping mouths of iron gargoyles, stretched across the flanks of zeppelins - the face of Simeon Blaire stared down, a god pre-emptive, a set-up for victory. The betting parlors were barricaded, bookies like the late Feldon folding under the weight of odds too unbalanced for profit.

One way or another, tonight was for the Blues.

Leighton Cressmeyer was a clerk in the dispatch 'factorium of Choseem Chemical, a bean-counter who watched a single corroded robot arm load drums of solvent into a chute eight hours a day. His grimy little hab had been too close to the

ChoChem liquids store when the fighting broke out; a stray round had punched through the main deuterium holding tank below the worker's quarters, and half of his fellow employees were even now drifting on the breeze as a haze of charcoal.

He ran with his hair on fire, his eyebrows scorched clean off his face.

Direction hadn't mattered to him, except AWAY, and DOWN, away from the flames and the agonized screams, the sirens and the gunfire. He realized he was clear when the cold, sick, salty wind off the Atlantic slapped him back from the edge of a concrete flyover. He looked down and saw his scorched clothes, his blistered and bare feet – and his hands full of charred banknotes. Some survival instinct, there.

It was just as he started peeling apart the blackened plastic that he felt a hand close around the back of his head; fat fingers digging painfully into his burned scalp. Before he could twitch, or even draw another breath, he felt the flat square muzzle of a pistol jammed into his back. Halitosis breath wafted over him as his unseen assailant leaned forward.

"You wouldn't want to have a nasty fall, now, would you sir?" rasped a voice behind the fug of alcohol and rotting teeth. "In all this confusion, a man should keep his hands free, in case *accidents* were to happen."

Leighton balled the money up in his fists, overwhelmed by a burning urge to resist, to scream his refusal. But the water was a straight mile below him, and it looked very cold and final, a black expanse it up by the fires of Elysium. Nobody in the panicked crowd would help him. Just one more corpse, tonight.

"All right... easy." he said, letting a few slades slip loose between his trembling fingers. "Take it all. Just... just let me go."

Now a far-off sound was fading in, a dopplering buzz, popping and barking, something he remembered from old threedeeo re-runs. Leighton felt the hand come off the back of his head, felt the pistol jam into his spine, pushing him up hard against the railing. Black water zoomed, vertiginous.

The sound, rising.

"Very wise, sir. Very good judgment. And if you'd be so kind as to keep admiring the view for a few seconds as I take my leave, I won't feel compelled to shoot you in the back."

He felt the pressure of the pistol easing off, a great sweaty paw ripping the money out of his hands…

A spitting roar, peaking, too afraid to turn his head as his attacker stepped backwards away from the railing…

There was an inhuman squeal, a long and drawn-out scream.

There was a meaty thud; a wet, ripping sound.

Warm fluid pattered down on Leighton Cressmeyer where he cowered against the rail.

Finally, there was a repetitive squeaking noise, like rusty bedsprings.

Leighton turned his head tentatively, peeking out of one eye lest a bullet smash through his spine. And he saw…

There was a machine behind him, belching black and gray fumes from eight chopped-off chrome pipes. It sat on wheels of fat, sticky rubber, smoking at the end of a pair of smoldering skidmarks. And there was a girl behind the wheel, scowling as a pair of windscreen wipers tried vainly to clean a slick of gore from the glass.

Half of the mugger was caught under the razor-sharp blade which fronted the war-wagon; the rest had flown up over its sloping bullet hood, and now lay twitching between the skids. Black and red stained Slades blew about like confetti in the wind off the ocean.

"Excuse me… hi, you there!"

Leighton realized he was being yelled at.

The girl in the car, blue hair tousled and bloodied, purple tattoos glowing, was focusing a winning smile on him while the wipers continued to smear gore back and forth with a sad little whine.

"I'll give you a lift outta here if you like," she said, pushing a few strands of hair out of her eyes. "Just so long as you tell me – which way to the Valley View Mall?"

Ω

The Illuminatus kept his sanctuary protected under more

than just lock and key. If his human followers ever discovered the bizarre museum inside... Well, it would have been like pious witch-hunters discovering an alchemist's den. Messy, embarassing, and fatal.

Not for *him*, of course. But for his masque, the revered demigod of the Ashishim.

Zeon – a very carefully disguised rogue Technician indeed - made his way purposefully through the deep corridors of the reactor level, where dim green strips of phosphorous tape provided the only illumination. Even this far beneath the domes of the Subcity the ground shook, and the corroded pipes bolted to the bedrock creaked and hissed with the shockwaves of far-off explosions. That accursed Blaire! Why had he unleashed this madness now? Why couldn't his pet Cyben have destroyed the little blue-blood freak when their paths had crossed?

Nyl muttered to himself, twisting the wheel on a heavy bulkhead door.

This setback was immaterial; there was no way any one of the weak, inbred Lords of Elysium could truly *control* the city. Not when the machine and the Wetsystems themselves were under the thumb of a Technician of the Multiplicity.

As for Eddie Tsien - he wasn't worth the time for worry. Let him wreak revenge on the machine – let him run *interference*. He'd been nothing but a periapt for power anyway, an experiment in life and death and the blurring of the line between them. He was the last of many.

As the wrist-thick bolts of the final airlock slammed back into their recesses and blue light leaked out around its edges Nyl began to hear the sounds of their pain.

The inside of Nyl's sanctorium was walled with alien flesh, scales and plates of coppery skin, thick pulsing tubes dripping clear fluids. Machines of silver filigree wove in between a forest of crystal globes, packed to bulging with nameless organs.

This chamber lay beneath the fusion reactor which had once powered the Ashishim enclave, a place saturated (as he'd taken pains to assure his minions) with deadly radiation. In actuality a vast cage of magnetic energy kept the Technician's laboratory safe from prying eyes and - perhaps more importantly - kept his experimental subjects *in*.

Most of the systems which Nyl employed had been part of the Devilfish which had brought him here; the creature which was now spread out across the walls and floor, comprehensively vivisected. The white-scaled tentacles which the sentient starcraft used to warp space had been riveted and bolted to the racks of machines, forming an impenetrable force-field.

But its simple animal mind hadn't been sufficient bait to tempt Nyl's prey.

It had needed *human* suffering, human death to pull it to the surface. It had needed the barrier between its world and this one to be weakened. And so Nyl had co-opted the most skilled hackers in Elysium to bend the Wetsystems to his purpose, creating a symphony of pain with the enslaved masses of the city's dead.

Tsien had been the perfect and final morsel with which to tempt it, and Magus Verlaine was the perfect interface through which it could be controlled. For the entity Nyl wanted to suborn couldn't resist the rage and pain of Tsien's betrayal, the promise of slaughter inherent in his dehumanized form. And in the withered and powerless body of the Magus it was caught as surely as an insect in a killing-jar, pinned out in the hollow mechanical shell of a man utterly compromised to Nyl's will.

His failed experiments hung from the walls and ceiling all around him, useful to maintain the pitch and tone of agony which his guest needed. Which it actually *fed upon*.

Nyl could all but taste its fury in the air.

He very nearly salivated at the thought of harnessing that power and unleashing it upon his enemies. Quite probably on his erstwhile allies too; the Praetor was nothing if not insufferably stubborn. If his investigations were correct, his captive was a sentience which filled an entire dimension, a creature of pure appetite. Even His Eminence of Liquid Space wouldn't be able to stand against it.

With that kind of threat at his back, he would bring the multiverse peace through terror. To an individual like

Technician Nyl, who had seen atrocities committed in the name of victory on a galactic scale, that kind of peace was the best and only kind. Nyl walked on through a crawling mist of cryogenic gases, under the cold blue lights of his sanctorium. On either side, poor once-human things scrabbled at the glass of their containment chambers, their eyes (for those who retained the privilege of sight) begging mutely for death.

There would be no surcease for them tonight.

Nyl reached the suspended rack which held the body of Verlaine, a frame of twisted iron piercing his arms and legs with spikes. Segments of the unfortunate Magus' armored body were securely welded to the rack, and loops of thick black chain ran from bolts in the floor and ceiling to electrified manacles clapped around his wrists, ankles and neck.

Perhaps even more invasive (at least from the point of view of a Magus), thick data-cables were plugged into a thousand ports all over Verlaine's head and torso, disappearing into jackpoints welded through flesh and bone.

"Are we comfortable? No? Well, it's not going to get any easier for you. And you can forget sympathy, creature. Such emotions are beneath my kind..."

The poor wretch was a picture of weakness and despair – an image which Nyl's expanded senses told him was a deliberate charade. Verlaine's skin was burning cold, and arcs of electromagnetic force radiated from him like a sick aura, discharging in streams of invisible lightning where they met the gauss cage which bound him.

But even human eyes could have seen the runnels of black ichor which writhed across his skin, the questing tentacles of sentient liquid dripping from his broken mouth.

Technician Nyl made a few final adjustments to his personal defenses before one of his crabbed hands reached out to pull a lever on the wall. At once the black fluid began to flow in reverse, pulling back into Verlaine's pores, into his tear-ducts and sinuses with a sick sucking sound. The gauss cage was down.

Nyl stepped up to the rack warily – he hadn't become an *old*

Technician of the Multiplicity by taking risks with dangerous aliens. He could feel it prying at his brain, trying to find a crack in his mental armor. Trying to insinuate tendrils of fear and doubt into what was, thankfully, only a simulacrum of a human mind.

"Oh, I wouldn't bother with that, either. Nothing to get your teeth into there, my friend..."

The Technician smiled grimly, unpacking a selection of unpleasant surgical tools onto a little steel trolley. He could actually *feel* the agony and fear of the experimental subjects flowing past him, like water swirling down a funnel into the creature's psionic maw. Hence the flaying, the hooks, the *dissection*. The fear of his lab animals was enough to sustain the thing within Verlaine, but it would avail it nothing to possess their ruined bodies, kept balanced on the razor's edge between life and death.

It would take the Technician only a second to turn their life-support tanks to boiling cauldrons, or slabs of cryonic ice. And then his subject would be back in the machine-husk of Magus Verlaine, right where he wanted it.

"My analysis programs have some very strange ideas about you," said Nyl, picking up a vibro-scalpel between two wizened fingers. "One of them even went so far as to suggest that you cultivated sentience in these apes specifically so you could prey on them."

There was no answer from the wasted shell of Magus Verlaine.

"Thousands of years keeping them at each others throats so you could reap their terror. All that time, and yet... you still can't understand what they've done with that precious sentience." Nyl slammed his fist down on a button, unleashing bolts of electricity through the chains and manacles which bound his captive. "You still aren't very good with *machines*, are you?" he asked, as smoke drifted up toward the extractor grates in the ceiling.

Still there was no answer from Verlaine, just the sound of his breath rasping in his throat.

"Well... in a way, this is your lucky day. I can teach you a little about such things. I can teach you how to make them feel pain, too. Even how to make them *fear* you. All you have to do is co-operate…"

Nyl ran the transparent blade of his vibro-scalpel down one of Verlaine's pallid cheeks, exposed from under his shining facial armor. The cut was deep, and bone flashed white before black blood bubbled up from the wound, lashing the air like the tentacles of an anemone.

"I know how you wanted to use Tsien for your *usual purposes*," sighed Nyl, dropping the scalpel with a metallic clatter. "But that kind of power belongs to those of us who *think*, not things like you. Your idea of sophisticated equipment is probably still just a very sharp axe."

He turned away, pulling on a pair of rubber gloves, but one eye caught the movement just in time.

Nyl wasn't easily surprised - not after a few hundred years of multidimensional covert ops.

But the *speed* of the thing! Its crushing strength… he felt a small, grudging flicker of respect for it. He let the great black pseudopods of flesh turn him on the spot, with the kind of relentless pressure which suggested they could just as easily screw him into the ground.

Verlaine was gone, eclipsed by a nebula of utter blackness, as devoid of light as the gulfs between galaxies. Nyl had seen them, and they were far more welcoming than the shifting, writhing mass which clung to the Magus's body, a grim caricature of a human form.

While the Technician watched, transfixed, it began to solidify, growing claws like jagged obsidian knives, the suggestion of knotted, corded muscles…

And congealing across Verlaine's face like a sore; a visage to launch a million nightmares.

There was no color in the seething mass which mummified Magus Verlaine. It spat out images like over-magnified newspaper pictures, clouds of black dots shifting and re-arranging, a horror-gallery of distorted human faces. Every deformation, every pitiable defect of genetics, every hideous wound and atrocity of war.

Dripping, bulging, sloughing, screaming flesh, nailed down by two slick black eyes filled with mockery and madness. Nyl could feel the psionic impact behind that gaze, even though his own mind was utterly alien, an armored knot of silicon in his chest.

Pity me, and fear me, it said. Feel the disgust, and hate yourself for feeling it.

Feed me.

Technician Nyl had studied his prey with the same focus with which he approached any dangerous mission. He was more than prepared.

Deep within his extensively hardwired alien brain a connection clicked over, and searing light burst out around him, a coronal aura as sharp and vivid as a solar flare. Black tentacles and rivulets and claws steamed and hissed and screeched, recoiling from the blaze of light and heat.

"You won't surprise me that easily," he said, deactivating the gauss shield with a thought. "I always assumed a thing like you would have pride as a weakness – what with being worshiped as a god by feral monkeys and all."

The face dripping from Verlaine's own was a grinning, bloated thing, a gourd wrapped in burnt scar tissue.

"Now that we know how to get a response out of you, I suppose it's high time we began to break you in. Don't be embarrassed – you won't be the first local demigod I've whipped into line." A bubbling hiss spilled out from the thing's mouth now, as its mangled lips tried to enunciate around a jaw full of jagged teeth. "It's the carrot and the stick," said Nyl, his hands busily plugging items of machinery into Verlaine's dangling wetwire cables. "Don't think I won't burn you out of this dimension like a patch of mold if you fail to co-operate. But if we can see eye to... well, *whatever* those things are, then you will have a feast of pain the likes of which you have never known."

On the touchscreens under Nyl's hands schematics were blinking online – detailed maps of circuitry, the paths into the Wetsystems. First he would suborn the beast to his control. And then he would let it loose in there, inside the mass of artificial tissue and caged souls which powered the Forge.

Technically, his work here would be done, the weapon neutralized, and well out of the hands of the Blacksteel Unity. In *reality*, the fun would only just have started.

Nyl stared into the morphing, twisting face of his specimen, and marveled at the hold he had over it. A being which filled an entire universe from end to end, caught by the tiniest pseudopod, the merest scrap of flesh. Was such a thing too arrogant to know it was beaten?

The voice, when it came, was like the sound of rusted, serrated blades across gristle, slippery and grating, sizzling with menace.

'ffffff we submit, then you will lhhhhet ussss…ffffeeed?'

Nyl could hardly contain his joy. It would serve him.

"You will be more than sated!" he yelled, bringing the power up on more and more of his alien cogitator units. The data feeds into Verlaine's body were burning hot with barely contained power.

"All you must do is give me a name to control you by."

'Thsssssss iss old magic, void-thhhngg!' sussurated the voice in his head *but 'it appearsss we hhghave …little choicsssse. By many namesssss have we been hhhhhknown. The Wanderer. Spawn of the Bottomless Pit. Watcher in Shadows… Sssssso many namesssssssss. But …iffff you would play thhhhe ssorcerer, you will hhhknow ussss assssss the Worm. Sssssuch a simple name, but it issss the way of all flessshhhh.'*

Nyl couldn't have cared if it had named itself the Prime Praetor at that moment. He felt exultant, a keystroke away from his ascendancy, his revenge against a multiverse of war and boredom and powerlessness.

His finger came down, and the thing which named itself the Worm felt a hammer of data fall, smashing its resistance to splinters.

For the first time in one hundred thousand years it finally had a master.

But for all that it claimed a thousand names, it knew only one.

Asag'raal, eater of souls. Now the cycle of the universe had turned, and the time of its worship had come again…

Ω

He was awake, and alive, and he should have been grateful. The last thing he remembered was being swarmed all over by killer steel spider-things, and a hazy image of a face looking down at him – the cop from Omnivasive's damned photograph. *Tsien.*

He'd woken up feeling like the insides of a punching bag, and without so much as a cup of coffee he was off and running.

Jaqub Haszan was definitely having One of Those Days.

Crazy drug deals, extortion, gunfights and robberies, trips and bent cops and keeping up with the capricious Kaito Kayzi - those were his bread and butter. But rampaging swordsmen, cyborgs and Reclamationist terrorists were more than he liked to handle - at least without prior warning.

And now the whole damn world was coming down around his ears.

Haszan was finding it hard to keep up, despite his loping stride. The Ashishim called Abdulafia was unnaturally fast, and Kaito had managed to hitch a ride with the kid on top of that floating missile platform they both called 'Zone'. If this was just a Saturday jog in the park the stitch in his side would have had him calling it quits by now. But the crash of support girders and dragons-breath blasts of flame behind him kept Haszan at top speed.

Abdulafia had unpacked a headset from his voluminous coat, and he rattled off strings of code as he ran, a constant chatter of numbers and garbled shouting which carried over the mall's disintegration. It was really coming down now. Jaq didn't want to be inside it when it collapsed.

Momentum almost pitched him over a sheer drop as the little group came to a dead end. He windmilled his arms on the very edge of the precipice for a second before the Ashishim grabbed a handful of his coat, hauling him back from the brink. The after-image of flames down below tweaked dark memories behind his eyes.

"Where to now? We're getting barbequed in here!"

"This section leads up and out," said Abdulafia, pointing off through the haze toward a curving tiled causeway. "Used to be a car dealership up through there, but it's been gone for a couple of years. The workshops have access lifts to the cargo transit system."

Haszan grinned, his pain momentarily forgotten.

"Then what are we waiting for, huh? I say we blow this joint before it pops its fucking bolts!"

As if to punctuate his words a section of roof the size of an articulated truck came down behind them, scything through the floor in a spray of shattered tiles.

Abdulafia signaled the hovering missile platform, and they were off again, charging through billows of oily smoke and up the causeway. Haszan's eyes were streaming, and the sound of his pulse beat like the noise of giant pistons in his ears. But there, glimpsed through curtains of flame – the logo of Consolidated Automotive.

We're actually going to make it. Only a little further…

Then the *Dervashi* stopped dead, cut down in mid-stride as if a metal rod had been driven through his chest. Haszan skidded to a halt in a slew of broken glass, feeling the missile platform skim by overhead in the smoke. Abdulafia simply folded up and slammed into the floor at a full sprint, a puppet with its strings severed. From the headset wrapped around his skull came a sound like a fractured mechanical scream. It was a sound Haszan had heard before, when he tried to call Kaito's homeblock and the fiber-optics were overloaded… a live Wetsystems connection. Raw data converted to noise.

Haszan didn't know how extensively hardwired Abdulafia was, but he could grasp the concept of a computer virus easily enough. His metal hand ripped the headset off 'Afia's head, crushing it to splinters of jagged plastic. Then - stitch notwithstanding - Haszan hefted the *Dervashi* over one shoulder and staggered through the broken doorway of the Consolidated franchise.

Whatever god looked down favorably on half-dead adrenochrome pharmers had seen to it that the air conditioning scrubbers inside were still functioning. Just enough for him to fill his burning lungs, anyway. Typical – the terminals and desks were all covered in plastic, and they were probably the first people to come through here in months. But because the place had been locked up tight, nobody had been able to steal the carbon cores out of the air scrubbers, and the smoke was thinner in here, especially down by the floor.

Kaito came down next to him, B-Zerk not far behind. Above them loomed the bulk of Zone, like a predatory insect clinging to the low beige ceiling.

"What the hell happened to him?" asked the Kayzi, scrabbling through his clothes for a medical monitor unit.

"No idea!" grunted Haszan, checking Abdulafia's pulse with two of his fingers. Twitches of stress rippled through the muscles of the big biker's neck and jaw, and beads of oily sweat were dripping from his skin as he knelt over the Ashishim.

At least the *Dervashi* was still alive – a stuttering pulse and the shallow rise and fall of his chest confirmed it. But blood was leaking out in thin rivulets from the gash across his abdomen, and technology alone was keeping him stitched together. The bio-onboard systems implanted in his body had performed miracles during the battle with the Vilicus drones, but now the circuits coiled along his bones were dead.

Kaito's med sensors confirmed the worst.

"He needs his augmentations to stay alive, with all the damage he's taken. And the damn things look like they've been fried from the plugs in."

"I heard some kind of signal coming through his headset before he collapsed," said Haszan, his hands clenching and unclenching. There was nothing his immense strength could do for the Ashishim now; even though all the punishment which was surely killing him had been taken saving his life. Haszan wanted to put his metal fist through something – *somebody* – but he knew that he was helpless. It was up to Kaito and his woefully inadequate med-pak.

"A military metaviral could have done this, but using one against a single person makes no sense. That kind of offensive power could have taken out an army. It's like nuking a mosquito!"

Kaito scowled as the medical unit extended a cluster of flexible needles and tubes into Abdulafia's arm. It started flashing with red strobes almost immediately. Critical signs were dropping, major organs shutting down.

"What's the diagnosis?"

"If we can get a sustained power feed into his augmentation systems he might hold out another hour or two. Long enough to get him back to the R.T."

Haszan could see the Ashishim dying right in front of him. His skin was pallid and cold, his breath rasping in his throat.

"What are you waiting for then?" he asked, in a voice just this side of a scream "Plug him in!"

Kaito turned Abdulafia's head to one side, exposing the inset plug on the side of the reclamationist's neck. Charred and blistered skin surrounded the socket, but all its pins seemed intact.

"The problem's compatibility," sighed Kaito, turning his med-sensor for them to see. Its tiny screen was a solid mass of blinking red icons. "That stuff he's been wired with is all military spec. The Ashishim must have duplicated units they stole from the old Elysian Army. We'd need a combat-capable system with *immense* batteries just to get him back to a proper R.T. clinic."

Abdulafia's body gave one final huge convulsion, and bubbles of bright blood foamed from between his lips. The medical systems holding his stomach together were in complete decay, and the wound there gaped open like a bloody grin, a gash webbed with pitifully thin red filaments.

"He saved us both, K," whispered Haszan. "Is there any chance his R.T. boys can crash-start him if we bring him in like this?"

B-Zerk was leaning over Kaito's shoulder, his young face pale. The kid was desperate not to let his horror show through, but the tracks of tears cut through the soot and ashes which grimed his cheeks.

"Don't let him die," he said, all the bravado of his street-tough, tunnel-crawler persona shaken out of him. Until today his only encounter with real death had been watching Zone fall away into the hot darkness.

"No pressure, huh?" said Kaito, picking up the med-scanner gingerly. "You two should see how shot his augmentations are. I have no idea what's keeping him alive right now... probably just subliminal willpower."

The look on his face was almost as bleak as that on the stricken Ashishim's.

Locked in their vigil over the dying Abdulafia, none of them saw a pair of slim chrome cables descending from above, their ends weaving in the air like the snouts of blind snakes. At least, none of them noticed until both of the thin wires plugged themselves in, and then Abdulafia's eyes snapped open.

They were cold and blank, without the spark of consciousness, and the voice which followed was just as emotionless.

Haszan almost tore a chunk out of his patient's flesh as he leaped up in surprise. Kaito dropped his med-sensor, letting it skitter off across the concrete floor flashing critical warnings. But B-Zerk looked up, toward the ceiling. And toward the shadowy, floating bulk of Zone Doubt.

"Please... I don't have much time!" The sepulchral voice came from Abdulafia's mouth, but it wasn't his own "The augmentations in his body are falling out of the grid faster than I can patch them together. But I have a solution. My battery cells are mil-spec. You can keep him together if you remove my power core."

Haszan leaped in to pinch the wound together again. Alarming quantities of blood were pouring out of the Ashishim's body now.

"Kaito - can you do it?" he asked, metal fingers struggling to grip the slippery flesh.

"Yes. But if I do..." he turned to look up at B-Zerk, who met his gaze with naked fear.

"You'll die," he said, reaching up to touch the burnished steel of Zone's belly armor. "Without power, you'll be gone, Zone."

Abdulafia's head twitched to the left, his empty eyes seeking out B-Zerk's ashen face.

"This isn't... life, B," he croaked, struggling to raise one hand. "I was gone when I slipped, and it was my own damned fault.

Please… let me go. Let me do one thing right this time."

B-Zerk gripped the Ashishim's clammy hand, the other still pressed against the cerametal armor of the missile platform.

"You came back for me, Zone," he said, his voice barely above a whisper "But if it's what you want…"

"Please – let me go," said the voice of Zone Doubt, wavering in and out as Abdulafia's systems went into terminal shutdown. "It *hurts*, B. Let me rest…"

B-Zerk dropped his head to his chest, silent for a second, for two, as around them the building shuddered, ominous creaks and groans issuing from the tormented metal.

When he looked up again his face no longer that of a frightened kid. He stared directly into the eyes of Kaito Kayzi, once again the operator, the tunnel crawler. That stare burned into the hacker like a red-hot blade. From somewhere in his ruined rags the kid had produced an ancient manual screwdriver, its handle wrapped in electrical tape.

"Do it," he said. And he handed the rusted tool to Kaito.

Ω

It knew fear, and the depths of darkness in the human soul. That was all it *had* to know, all it had needed for millennia.

What the creature called the Worm couldn't understand was the lengths its prey would go to to erect barriers between themselves and their fear. Lights to banish the shadows. Swords and guns and nuclear missiles to obliterate the threat of violent death (and no little irony, there…) Medical miracles to stave off their inevitable demise…

Asag'raal always found a way in. It was the twin of death, and it dwelt in the single, endless instant between living and dying. That was how Technician Nyl had found it, engineering lingering agonies to tempt it out into reality.

Now he taught it about machines, and their hard, crystalline thoughts - so different from the tangled organic minds of humans, but based, in the end, on the same flawed reasoning.

A skein of connections ran from the body of Magus Verlaine into the Wetsystems, an immense hunting ground where organic minds were chained down in rows, latticed together in artificial tissue, ripe with fear. The core of each damned soul was the instant of its demise. *So many deaths, so many ends to so many stories.* Industrial accidents, diseases, murders, vehicle smashes, assassinations… all of them kept for their precious ability to (in the Technician's words) 'pattern energy.'

The reason for the Wetsystems' existence, and the cognitive power it represented meant less than nothing to the Worm. What Nyl wanted with it hardly mattered at all.

The prisoners within it were *sustenance*, and power. Enough power, surely, to have its revenge on the treacherous being who had imprisoned it. Behind the persona it had extruded into three-dimensional space bulked an entire reality of desire and tenacity, a dimension where it devoured souls, playing out their torment over centuries. Asag'raal liked to savor its meals.

And so it learned quickly, despite the pointlessness of the alien's plans. Technician Nyl was no human being; he would be a delicacy to be enjoyed slowly. The mind of the Worm was simple, but it knew two things all too well.

If something lived, then it could die.

And if it could appreciate the horror of its own doom, it could know *fear*.

Such a thing as Nyl - a creature who had lived for centuries - would spend even longer dying, and its terror would be exceedingly sweet.

Beyond a battery of code-locked connections the Wetsystems waited, a great harvest which it yearned to reap. All it would require was one slip in the programs which leashed it in.

Ω

There were supposed to be twenty cops manning the inflatable bonded-carbon barrier across the transdome ring, but only five had reported for what looked like a very dangerous shift. The big bags of fire-retardant foam were twelve feet high, proof against molotovs and rocks and bullets, with heavy-duty riot guns clamped to their tops and dynabolts pegging them down to the concrete.

It was the perfect cover to hide behind - especially when the whole city seemed to be in full-blown riot on the other side. The five cops palmed cigarettes and shared around a small flask of illicit moonshine, checking and rechecking the loads of their fusion carbines. The big rubber-bullet launchers atop the barrier looked like a quaint anachronism when servo-boosted mutants were hurling cinderblocks at them with the force of medieval catapults.

They were all dirt-average troopers; the higher ranks had all seen unedited threedeeo of Reclamation Day, and never wanted to face the outlanders in person. These guys were used to letting Cyben do the work, but tonight they were on their own.

So far the blockade had kept out the crowds and the missiles they were hurling; bags of shit, rotten food, rocks, home-made incendiaries and pieces of wrecked furniture. From what the officers could hear on the radio, things weren't much better anywhere else.

Still, better to be here with a bit of firepower and a bottle than take their chances making a break for it. There were rumors of Reclamationist snipers overwatching the barricades, waiting for a trooper's nerve to break. Then it was brains-on-the-wall time.

None of these five thought they were going to see any action tonight, but they were wrong. The first hint of trouble came with a wet slapping sound – probably another plastic bag of shite, thought Officer Alan Quaid (most senior trooper in the little squad at the age of twenty-two.)

He was wrong.

When the thick rope of detonant gel went up it was as if the barrier had been torn apart by giant invisible hands. Gray foam spewed from its severed ends, soaking the shocked C-Div. boys and sending them sprawling. Quaid slopped the foul-smelling stuff from out of his eyes with one hand, fumbling for his carbine with the other. Surely a horde of sub-scum would be next through the ruined barricade, primed to tear them limb from limb...

What actually came through was a clutch of grenades, hissing and billowing clouds of suffocating smoke. One lungful of the chemical which spewed from the little cylinders and cops and rioters alike were knocked on their asses, watching halos of multicolored stars come floating down around them. Reality warped and wavered like a heat mirage, while the unhinged laughter of his troopers rung like chimes in Quaid's ears. Part of his brain registered a noise rising, a sky-wide curtain being ripped in half...

And then it went past him like a runaway freight-hauler; a flame-belching wheeled juggernaut which he could barely discern from the rest of his hallucinations. Because wasn't it burning *petrochemicals*, like some kind of museum piece? And wasn't the pilot of the insane suicide machine a girl with blue hair and violet, glowing tribal tattoos? Had she just flipped him off? And wasn't the little guy next to her the accountant who worked with his old man down at ChoChem?

Officer Quaid slumped wetly into a pile of foam, his gun slipping from his hands. It really was just too funny. He probably needed a bit of a lie down, and this foam was as soft as a cloud...

Already a mile away and still accelerating, CeeAn kept her foot flat to the floor.

Abdulafia's trace had just gone out.

17 Aevum Oblivio
The Integrator

"W*HAT HAVE YOU* done?' asked Zhe, trying to pull away from Nyl's viselike grip."I saw it take you! I watched it eat you alive!"

Nyl laughed, then, and strips of Slavesystem began to peel off Zhe's body, twining up and around his arm, melting back into his black armor.

"I am reborn," he said, looking into Zhe's silver eyes with a gaze as deep as the void between galaxies. "Mitochondriate and Slavesystem. Digital and analogue. I have chained that evil thing within me, and now the Forge is mine."

Zhe recoiled in horror as the Blacksteel sloughed off him, boiling out of his alien flesh to flow seamlessly into the growing form of Nyl.

"Madness!" he spat "Whatever corrupted this place has gone into you. You're insane if you think you'll control it."

"Come now, Zhe," said Nyl, his voice deep, smooth, coaxing... "There's more than one virus that our kind keeps as a weapon. Surely you see that this kind of power can be used to our advantage?"

Zhe remembered the black lightning from out of the wastelands, and what had happened to the nuclear strike against its source. He grinned back into Nyl's expressionless face, and ripped his hand from the other mitochondriate's grasp.

"It's to nobody's advantage. Thankfully, there's something here that can stop the Forge from being used. They're not going to care who holds the controls."

Nyl rose up further, drawing the shimmering darkness of the Slavesystem around him like a cloak. For the first time Zhe could see the thorny tendrils of the Worm inside it, moving like a shadow below the surface.

"Those are my people, Zhe. My Ashishim. Their only task was to await my return. I've been very busy here, while you were still a Junior Exoethnologist back in Liquid Space. I've left some very capable people in charge out there, and I'm not surprised that they've found a way to destabilize the Forge. It's quite delicate, for all its power. A few hours setback, perhaps - but when I give them the order… well, I'm sure you'll enjoy the world I'm going to create here. The Armory-World of the New Praetor!"

Zhe stepped back, trying to put some distance between himself and the looming figure of Technician Nyl.

"But you tried to kill them! I saw the bombs falling! I…"

The renegade grinned, a singularly unpleasant sight.

"That was more in the nature of a knee-jerk reaction, Zhe." he said "Kronos has quite a few tricks like that up its sleeve, but once again, my little pet humans have exceeded my expectations. That's not to say that I would have been too sad to see them incinerated."

Zhe backed away as the seething metal fluid which had been the flesh of Everdark smothered Nyl's face.

"Now that *my* time has come, they will *serve* me. We're going to lure the Blacksteel in and hit them with a metaviral the likes of which no universe has ever seen." Nyl's smile ripped apart the Blacksteel amour across his face like a scrawl of silver, a gash with innumerable needle teeth. "They'll bow to me - and so will you, Zhe. You've already brought me this far. It would be a shame if you died before witnessing my final triumph."

Technician Zhe knew he was out of time then, as the great memory cubes of Kronos began to fire up, one by one. There was no cool blue radiance this time, just a wash of lambent crimson from below. He had to find the source of the infection before Nyl could act.

So while his eyes remained on the mad and ever-shifting face of his captor, his mind plunged again into the memories of Elysium, searching for a handhold, an escape…

A storm of disembodied voices rose up to meet him.

DOCUMENT BREAK

End of part one.

Analysis of the above really poses more questions than it answers, my Lord Arbitrex!

Does Technic Hierophant Nyl truly have the means to enslave one of the Motherbrain's thralls?

Will the one called Abdulafia survive – and indeed, what force has cut him down?

Will the subverted Kheptarch Blaire live out the destiny his master Vanecke has ordained?

And if he reaches the Forge, what kind of power will be unleashed?

Frankly, the biggest question, My Lord, is your involvement in this entire incident. There seems to be some suggestion that you might be searching for secrets here beyond the remit of the Technic Hierarchy. Perhaps it would be wiser to...

(cracking noises, whimpering, muffled screams – twenty-three seconds)

(loud chewing and swallowing sounds – forty-seven seconds)

Annotation Ends...

And will continue in book two
The Chains of Tartarus

Other Titles by
Drew Bryenton
from
sci-fi-cafe.com

Halo of Thorns

Any child can tell you about the Evil One – lord of darkness, master of despair... the deathless, wicked tyrant in his black tower, all spikes and blades. Children, in fact, are the only ones who truly grasp the concept of utter, soul-rotten vileness, because they all seem strangely drawn to it.

They're also the only ones who ever ask why.

Why would anyone want to be hated? Why would anyone want to live alone, with only the cobwebbed corpses of would-be assassins for company? Why would anyone, given the power of sorcery, choose to brood in a draughty old spire of masonry encrusted with gargoyles and bat guano?

This is the story of an Evil Lord. But it's not told by the grinning, lantern-jawed heroes or simpering sorceresses who have been trying to kill him for three hundred years. This is Evil (capital 'E' included) in its own words, from a short and brutal childhood right through to the obligatory cape and horned helmet. It's also a story of sword-swinging warfare, city-leveling magicks, the downfall of empires and the machinations of mad gods.

It is the story of Kuhal Moer, uneducated son of a drunken warlord, and of how he came to be the single most feared entity this side of Death himself. And when the hero of your saga is a cynical and slightly unhinged young necromancer, you can bet that the villains are going to be something else entirely...

"Light can never truly defeat the shadows. Indeed, the brighter the flame, the more vast and jagged they become. No – the true answer lies on the other side of light. The only way to snuff out shadows is with a deeper darkness."

On Black Wings of Vengeance

The wings of vengeance unfurl over a world in flames...

Kuhal Moer has risen to the heights - and sunken to the depths - of necromancy. His enemies lie broken, his tower broods over a plain of fused and cracked glass, and his legacy is a reign of terrified peace beyond his borders.

But three centuries of change have passed him by. And forces are stirring in the world of Yrde which threaten to make even the most potent Dark Lord an irrelevancy...

From the East come the Kothrai, a race of raiders and reavers sailing their black ships before sorcerous winds. From the North come rumours of the walking dead, a ravenous tide of ghouls. And in the South the vile and massive Coldblood stirs, raising from its epochal torpor.

Now Kuhal must put aside the better part of his power, leave his dark domain, and re-discover a world where many now call him a God. But where others would call him a weapon, a pawn in their games of conquest. And the necromancer has other problems too...

After three hundred years, he's about to discover the joys of family.

Gods help us all.

Chains of Tartarus

In the depths of the inferno, suffering and survival are one and the same... So when a renegade xenotech finds the means to end a war of utter genocide, the fate of one planet means nothing.

Too bad it's ours.

Ranged against the might of two empires, the deadliest agents we have left are ready to fight. But will they destroy our enemies - or each other. And what happens when alien technology meets necromancy head on?

Soulcrusher

And so it's come to this! The apocalypse unfolds in shattered neon and bloody steel, and all that stands in its way is a crew of drug-fiends, criminals, renegades and madmen...

This time it's gonna be taking no prisoners, no quarter given, and the devil will LITERALLY take the hindmost. Kaito loses his mind, but gains a few thousand megatons of nuclear firepower. Jaqub Haszan finds himself oddly attracted to the woman who's trying to kill him. And Octavio Vanecke is born again... although not in any kind of a religious sense.

By the time you turn the last page, you'll find out just how awful things can get for Technician Zhe on the worst day of his long, long life...

9 781910 779217